…na Gregory is …demic …was previously …Wales …her husband.

…s also the author …eries, …Restoration L…

the author's website at www.susannagregory.co.uk

26/11/16

Also by Susanna Gregory

The Matthew Bartholomew Series

A PLAGUE ON BOTH YOUR HOUSES
AN UNHOLY ALLIANCE
A BONE OF CONTENTION
A DEADLY BREW
A WICKED DEED
A MASTERLY MURDER
AN ORDER FOR DEATH
A SUMMER OF DISCONTENT
A KILLER IN WINTER
THE HAND OF JUSTICE
THE MARK OF A MURDERER
THE TARNISHED CHALICE

The Thomas Chaloner Series

A CONSPIRACY OF VIOLENCE
BLOOD ON THE STRAND
THE BUTCHER OF SMITHFIELD

TO KILL OR CURE

Susanna Gregory

SPHERE

First published in Great Britain in 2007 by Sphere
This paperback edition published in 2008 by Sphere

A CIP catalogue record for this book
is available from the British Library.

ISBN 978-0-7515-3888-5

Typeset in New Baskerville by Palimpsest Book Production Limited,
Grangemouth, Stirlingshire
Printed and bound in Great Britain by
Clays Ltd, St Ives plc

Sphere
An imprint of
Little, Brown Book Group
100 Victoria Embankment
London EC4Y 0DY

An Hachette Livre UK Company
www.hachettelivre.co.uk

www.littlebrown.co.uk

For Barbara Sage

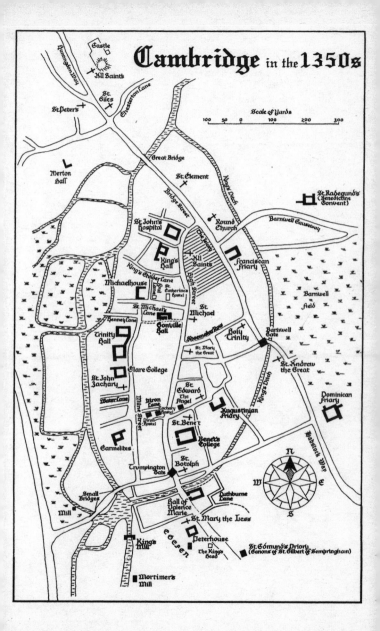

PROLOGUE

When Magister Richard Arderne first arrived in Cambridge, he thought it an unprepossessing place, and almost kept on driving. It was pretty enough from a distance, with a dozen church towers standing like jagged teeth on the skyline, and clusters of red-tiled and gold-thatched roofs huddled around each one. There were other fine buildings, too, ones that boasted ornate spires, sturdy gatehouses and forests of chimneys. Arderne supposed they belonged to the University, which had been established at the beginning of the previous century. From the Trumpington road, in the yellow blaze of an afternoon sun, with the hedgerows flecked white with blossom and the scent of spring in the air, the little Fen-edge settlement was picturesque.

However, when Arderne drove through the town gate, he saw Cambridge was not beautiful at all. It was a dirty, crowded place, full of bad smells, potholed lanes and dilapidated houses. The reek of the river and ditches, which provided residents with convenient sewers as well as drinking water, was overpowering, and he did not like to imagine what it would be like during the heat of summer. The churches he had admired from afar were crumbling and unkempt, and he suspected there was not a structure in the entire town that was not in need of some kind of maintenance or repair. The so-called High Street comprised a ribbon of manure and filth, trodden into a thick, soft carpet by the many hoofs, wheels and feet that passed along it, and recent rains had produced puddles that were deep and wide enough to have attracted ducks.

Arderne surveyed the scene thoughtfully as he directed his cart along the main road. The servants who sat behind him were asking whether they should start looking for a suitable inn. Arderne did not reply. Was Cambridge a place where he could settle? He was weary of travelling, of feeling the jolt of wheels beneath him. He longed to sleep in a bed, not under a hedge, and he yearned for the comforts of a proper home. He wanted patients, too – anyone glancing at the astrological configurations and medicinal herbs painted on the sides of his wagon would know that Arderne was a healer.

Like any *medicus*, the prerequisite for his success was a population that was either ailing or willing to pay for preventative cures. Arderne glanced at the people who walked past him, assessing them for limps, spots, coughs and rashes. There were scholars wearing the uniforms of their Colleges and hostels, with scrolls tucked under their arms and ink on their fingers. There were friars and monks from different Orders; some habits were threadbare, but more were made of good quality cloth. And there were finely clad merchants and foreign traders, smug, sleek and fat. Arderne smiled to himself. Not only were Cambridge folk afflicted with the usual gamut of ailments that would provide his daily bread, but there was money in the town, despite its shabby appearance. Now all he had to do was rid himself of the competition. No magician–healer wanted to work in a place where established physicians or surgeons were waiting to contradict everything he said.

He reined in and flashed one of his best smiles at a

pleasant-faced woman who happened to be passing, knowing instinctively that she would be willing to talk to him. Ever since he was a child, Arderne had been able to make people do what he wanted. Some said he was possessed by demons, and that his ability to impose his will on others was the Devil at work; others said he was an angel. Arderne knew neither was true; he was just a man who knew how to use his good looks and unusually arresting blue eyes as a means to getting his own way.

He beckoned the woman towards him. As expected, she approached without demur. He asked directions to the town's most comfortable inn, and was aware of her appreciative gaze following him as he drove away. Most women found him attractive, and he was used to adoring stares. Indeed, he expected them, and would have been disconcerted if Cambridge's females had been different from those in the many other towns he had graced with his presence.

The landlord of the Angel tavern on Bene't Street was named Hugh Candelby. He was not particularly amenable company, but Arderne soon won him round, and it was not long before they were enjoying a comradely jug of ale together. Arderne's pale eyes gleamed when Candelby described how the plague had taken most of the town's medical practitioners, leaving just four physicians and one surgeon. The physicians were all University men, and were saddled with heavy teaching loads on top of tending their patients. Arderne almost laughed aloud. It was perfect! Now all he needed was a house where he could set up his practice, preferably one that reflected his status as a man who had tended monarchs and high-ranking nobles, and a week or two to reconnoitre and rest his travel-weary bones.

And then, he determined, Cambridge would never be the same again.

* * *

3

Walter de Wenden was not a good man. As a priest, he had been appointed rector to several different parishes, but he never visited them. He did not care about the welfare of the people he was supposed to serve, and he did not care about his crumbling country churches. He hired vicars to perform the necessary rites, of course, but the plague had taken so many clergy that it was difficult to find decent replacements, especially for the pittance he was willing to pay. So, his flocks were in the hands of half-literate boys and dissolute rogues who would have been defrocked had the Death not created such a desperate shortage of ordained men. But, as long his parishes paid the tithes they owed him, Wenden seldom gave them a moment's thought.

He was not a man given to introspection, but he was reflecting on his life as he walked home from visiting his friend, Roger Honynge of Zachary Hostel. Hostels were buildings that contained a handful of students and a Principal who taught them, and were invariably poor. Honynge was better off than most – he could afford a fire when he wanted, and there was always food on the table – but even so, the flaking plaster and mildew-stained cushions made the fastidious Wenden shudder. *He* was a Fellow of Clare, a College that enjoyed the patronage of the wealthy Lady Elizabeth de Burgh, granddaughter of the first King Edward. *His* room was tastefully furnished, and *he* could afford the best meat, decent wines and dried fruit imported at great expense from France. He allowed himself a self-satisfied smile.

He thought about the evening he had just spent. Honynge and his students had been discussing Blood Relics, an issue so contentious that it was threatening to tear the Church in half, with Dominicans on one side and Franciscans on the other. Wenden was not particularly interested in the debate – he was not very interested in scholarship at all, if the truth be known, and was only allowed to keep his Clare Fellowship because he had promised to leave them all his money when he died. He had tried to change the subject – usually he and Honynge talked about mundane matters, such as the gambling sessions they both enjoyed on Friday nights or the slipping of standards among bakers since the plague – but Honynge was an excellent teacher and his students were bright lads; Wenden had become intrigued by the complex twists and turns of the various arguments, despite his natural antipathy to anything that involved serious thought.

Unfortunately, it meant he was later leaving Zachary Hostel than he had intended. It was already dark, and most people were asleep in their beds. He glanced around uneasily. He was not worried about being fined by beadles for being out after the curfew had sounded – it would be annoying to give them fourpence, but he was a wealthy man and would not miss it – but Cambridge was an uneasy town, and he did not want to be attacked by apprentices who would love to corner a lone scholar and teach him a lesson.

It was not far to Clare, so he lengthened his stride, aiming to be home as quickly as possible. He had just reached the overgrown tangle that was the churchyard of St John Zachary when a shadowy figure emerged from the bushes. It was a moonless night, so Wenden could not tell whether the cloaked shape was scholar or townsman, male or female. He was about to order the person out of his way when there was a blur of movement. He felt something enter his stomach, but there was no pain, just a cold, lurching sensation. He dropped to his knees, aware of something

5

protruding from his innards – an arrow or a crossbow bolt. He toppled forward slowly. The last thing he heard was the rustle of old leaves as his assailant melted back into the undergrowth.

CHAPTER 1

Easter Day (April) 1357

Michaelhouse was not the University at Cambridge's most wealthy College. It suffered from leaky roofs, faulty gutters, rising damp and peeling plaster. Worse yet, its Fellows and students were sometimes obliged to endure the occasional shortage of food when funds had to be diverted to more urgent causes – such as paying carpenters and masons to stop some part of the ramshackle collection of buildings from falling down about their ears.

Yet life was not all scanty rations and dilapidated accommodation. When Michaelhouse had been founded some thirty years before, one benefactor had predicted that its scholars might appreciate an occasional chance to forget their straitened circumstances. He had gifted them a house, and stipulated that a portion of the rent accruing from it was to be spent on special Easter foods and wines; in return, the scholars were to chant masses for his soul each morning in Lent.

The Michaelhouse men had kept their end of the bargain and, after the Easter Day offices had been sung, they hurried home to see what the bequest had brought them that year. Unexpected subsidence under the hall – which had proved expensive to rectify – meant the Master had been obliged to enforce the Lenten fasts more rigorously than usual, and everyone was eagerly awaiting the feast. Matthew Bartholomew, the College's Master of Medicine, had never seen his colleagues move so fast, and any semblance of scholarly dignity was lost as they raced through the gate in anticipation of their benefactor's generosity.

However, the meal was not quite ready. Agatha, the formidable laundress who had taken it upon herself to run the domestic side of the College, tartly informed the Master that the servants so seldom cooked such monstrous repasts, they had miscalculated the time it would take and there would be a short delay. Technically, Agatha should not even have been inside the College, let alone allowed to wield so much power – the University forbade relations between its scholars and women, on the grounds that such liaisons were likely to cause problems with the town. But Agatha had been employed there for more than two decades, and it would have taken a braver soul than anyone at Michaelhouse to oust her now.

Restlessly, the Fellows and their students milled about, waiting with ill-concealed impatience for her to finish. Delicious scents began to waft across the yard, almost obliterating the usual aroma of chicken droppings and stagnant water. To pass the time, Bartholomew looked around at the buildings that had been his home for the best part of thirteen years.

The heart of Michaelhouse was its hall, a handsome structure with oriel windows gracing its upper storey; the smaller, darker chambers on the ground floor were used as kitchens, pantries and storerooms. At right angles to the hall were the two ranges that comprised the scholars' accommodation. The northern wing boasted twelve small rooms, arranged around three staircases, while the newer, less-derelict southern wing had eleven rooms with two staircases between them. Opposite were the main gate, porters' lodge and stables. Combined, the buildings formed a square, set around a central yard, all protected by sturdy walls. Cambridge was an uneasy place at the best of times, and no academic foundation risked being burned to the ground by irate townsmen for the want of a few basic defences.

That morning the sun was shining, and it turned Michaelhouse's pale stone to a light honey-gold, topped by the red tiles of its roofs. Agatha had planted herbs in the scrubby grass outside the kitchens, and their early flowers added their own colour to the spring day. Hens scratched contentedly among them, jealously guarded by a scrawny cockerel. Also present was a peacock, which was owned by Walter the porter. Walter's surly temper was legendary, and Bartholomew suspected the only reason he had formed an attachment to the magnificent but deeply stupid bird was its unpopular habit of screaming in the night and waking everyone up.

Eventually, Bartholomew's book-bearer, Cynric, walked towards the bell, intending to chime it and announce the meal was ready. He could have saved himself the effort. The moment he reached for the rope, there was a concerted dash for the hall. Students jostled each other as they tore up the spiral staircase; Fellows and commoners – young hopefuls who helped with teaching, or 'retired' men too old to work – followed a little more sedately, although only a very little. It was not just the junior members who were hungry that morning.

The hall had been transformed since Bartholomew had seen it the night before. Its floor had been swept, and bowls of dried roses set on the windowsills to make it smell sweet. Its wooden tables had been polished, and the usual battered pewter had been replaced by elegantly glazed pots and the College silver. A fire flickered in the hearth and braziers glowed on the walls, lending the room a welcoming cosiness – the Easter benefaction included an allowance

9

for fires *and* lamps, which was a rare luxury for anyone. Some of the food was stacked near the hearth, being kept warm – or drying out, depending on whose opinion was asked – while the rest sat on platters behind the serving screen at the far end.

The Fellows trooped to the high table, which stood on a dais near the hearth, and the students and commoners took their places at the trestle tables and benches that had been placed at right angles to it. Michaelhouse was a medium-sized foundation. Its Master presided over seven Fellows, although two were currently away, and there were ten commoners and thirty students.

'A whole sheep!' crowed Brother Michael, rubbing his hands together in gluttonous anticipation. He was a Benedictine monk, and by far the fattest of the Fellows, despite shedding some weight the previous year. 'And I count at least two dozen fowl.'

'Oh, dear,' whispered Father Kenyngham, the oldest member of the gathering. He had been Michaelhouse's Master until four years before, when he had resigned to concentrate on his teaching and his prayers. He was a Gilbertine friar, whose gentle piety was admired throughout the University, and many believed he was a saint in the making. 'How are we supposed to eat all this?'

'I foresee no problem,' said Father William, a sour Franciscan famous for his bigoted opinions and dogmatic theology. He was as unpopular as Kenyngham was loved. 'In fact, I would say there is less here this year than there was last. Prices have soared since the Death, and a penny does not go far these days.'

'Do not harp on the plague *today*,' hissed Michael irritably. 'You will upset the students or, worse, encourage Matt to wax lyrical about it. Then his lurid descriptions will put us off our food.'

Bartholomew opened his mouth to object, but closed it sharply when his colleagues murmured their agreement. However, he thought Michael's accusation was still unfair. The plague had shocked him to the core, because all his medical training had proved useless, and he had lost far more patients than he had saved. As a consequence, the disease was a painful memory, and certainly not something to be aired over the dinner table.

'My point remains, though,' said William, who always liked the last word in any debate. He wiped his dirt-encrusted hands on his filthy grey habit – a garment so grimy that his students swore it could walk about on its own – and began to assess which of the many dishes he would tackle first. Some strategy was needed, because Michael was a faster eater than he, and he did not want to lose out for want of a little forethought. 'Everything costs more these days.'

The Master of Michaelhouse stood behind his wooden throne, watching the students shuffle into place in the body of the hall. Ralph de Langelee was a large, barrel-chested man with scant aptitude for scholarship and an appalling grasp of the philosophy he was supposed to teach. To the astonishment of all, he was proving to be a decent administrator, and his Fellows were pleasantly surprised to find themselves content with his rule. The students were happy, too, because, as something of a reprobate himself, Langelee tended to turn a blind eye to all but the most brazen infractions of the rules. His policy of toleration had generated an atmosphere of harmony and trust, and Bartholomew had never known his College more strife-free.

One of Langelee's wisest decisions had been to pass the financial management of his impecunious foundation to a lawyer called Wynewyk, who was the last of the Fellows present. Wynewyk was a small, fox-faced man, who loved manipulating the College accounts, and Michaelhouse would have been deeply in debt were it not for his ingenuity and attention to detail. That morning, he was basking in the compliments of his colleagues for purchasing such an impressive quantity of food with a comparatively small sum of money.

'Come on, come on,' muttered Michael, as Langelee waited for old Kenyngham to reach his allocated seat. 'I am starving.'

'Do not make yourself sick, Brother,' whispered Bartholomew. The monk was his closest friend, and he felt it his duty to dissuade him from deliberate overindulgence. The warning was not entirely altruistic, though: Bartholomew did not want to spend his afternoon mixing remedies to ease aching stomachs. 'The statutes do not stipulate that we should devour everything today. We are permitted to finish some of it tomorrow.'

'And the day after,' added Kenyngham.

Michael shot them an unpleasant look. 'I shall eat whatever I can fit in my belly. This is one of my favourite festivals, and I am weary of fasting and abstinence. Lent is over, thank God, and we can get back to the business of normal feeding.'

Before they could begin a debate on the matter, Langelee intoned the grace of the day in atrocious Latin that had all his Fellows and most of the students wincing in unison, then sat down and seized a knife. The servants, who had been waiting behind the screen, swung into action, and the feast was under way. Michael sighed his satisfaction, William girded himself up to ensure he did not get less than the portly monk, Langelee smiled benevolently at his flock, and Kenyngham, who was never very impressed with the Master's famously short prayers, began to mutter a much longer one of his own. Bartholomew looked around

12

at his colleagues, and thought how fortunate he was to live in a place surrounded by people he liked – or, at least, by people whose idiosyncrasies were familiar enough that he no longer found them aggravating.

Because it was a special occasion, Langelee announced that conversation was permitted. Normally, the Bible Scholar read aloud during meals – the Michaelhouse men were supposed to reflect and learn, even while eating. It was some time before anyone took the Master up on his offer, however, because Fellows, commoners and students alike were more interested in what was being put on their tables than in chatting to friends they saw all day anyway. Silence reigned, broken only by Agatha's imperious commands from behind the screen and the metallic click of knives on platters.

'Can we use the vernacular, Master?' called one man eventually, once he had satiated his immediate hunger and was of a mind to converse. Bartholomew was not surprised that the question had come from Rob Deynman, the College's least able student. Deynman would never pass the disputations that would allow him to become a physician, and should not have been accepted to study in the first place. Yet whenever Langelee tried to hint that Deynman might do better in another profession, the lad's rich father showered the College with money, which always ended with the son being admitted for one more term. Bartholomew was acutely uncomfortable with the situation, and did not see how it would ever be resolved – he would never agree to fixing a pass, because he refused to unleash such a dangerous menace on an unsuspecting public, but he doubted even the wealthy Deynman clan would agree to paying fees in perpetuity.

13

'It should be Latin,' objected William pedantically. 'Or French, I suppose.'

Langelee overrode him, on the grounds that he did not enjoy speaking Latin himself, and his French was not much better. 'English will make a pleasant change, and we do not want our dinner-table chat to be stilted. I am in the mood to be entertained.'

'I am glad you said that, Master,' said Michael. He beamed around at his colleagues. 'I anticipated the need for a little fun, so I invited the choir to sing for us.'

There was a universal groan. The monk worked hard with the motley ensemble that called itself the Michaelhouse Choir, but there was no turning a pig's ear into a silken purse. It was the largest such group in Cambridge, mostly because Michael provided free bread and ale after practices. Most of the town's poor were members, and he accepted them into his fold regardless of whether they possessed any musical talent.

'How could you, Brother?' asked Wynewyk reproachfully. 'They will wail so loudly that it will not matter what language we use – we will not hear anything our neighbour says anyway.'

'And we shall have to share the food,' added William resentfully.

'We will,' said Kenyngham, when Michael seemed to be having second thoughts; the monk was rarely magnanimous where his stomach was concerned. 'But it will be the only meal most of them will enjoy today, so I do not think we should begrudge it.'

Michael inclined his head, albeit reluctantly. 'Do not worry about the noise, Wynewyk. I have been training them to sing quietly.'

'Here they come,' warned Bartholomew, as the choristers marched into the hall, caps held in their right hands.

14

They were a ragged mob, mostly barefoot, and Deynman was not the only scholar to rest his hand on his purse as they trooped past him. In the lead was Isnard the bargeman, who hobbled on crutches because Bartholomew had been forced to amputate his leg after an accident two years before. He was a burly fellow with an unfortunate tendency to believe anything he was told, especially after he had been drinking, which was most nights.

'You can lead the music today, Isnard,' said Michael, barely glancing up from his repast. 'You are here earlier than I expected, and I am still eating.'

'*Me?*' asked the bargeman, stunned and flattered by the unexpected honour. 'Are you sure?'

'Quite sure,' replied Michael, reaching for more chicken.

'Right,' said Isnard gleefully, turning to his fellow musicians. 'Ready? One, two, three, go!'

And they were off. Unfortunately, he had not told them what to perform, as a consequence of which half began warbling one tune, while the remainder hollered another. Jubilantly, they seized the opportunity to out-sing each other in a bit of light-hearted rivalry. The result was not pleasant, but Michaelhouse was used to cacophonies where the choir was concerned, and most scholars thought it no different from the racket they made when they were all trilling the same piece.

'Did you hear about Robert Spaldynge?' yelled Bartholomew to Michael, to take the monk's mind off the fact that all his careful instructing had obviously been a waste of time. On the physician's other side, Kenyngham closed his eyes and began to pray again, perhaps for silence. 'He is accused of selling a house that did not belong to him. It was owned by his College – Clare.'

Michael nodded. He was the University's Senior Proctor, which meant he was responsible for maintaining law and

15

order among the disparate collection of Colleges and hostels that comprised the *studium generale* at Cambridge. He had an army of beadles to help him, and very little happened without his knowledge. 'He claims he had no choice – that he needed money to buy food. It might be true, because his students are an unusually impoverished group. Clare is furious about it, but not nearly as much as I am. Spaldynge's actions have put me in an impossible position.'

Bartholomew was struggling to hear him. The singers had finished their first offering, and had started an old favourite that, for some inexplicable reason, included a lot of rhythmically stamping feet. He was sure the monk had not taught them to do it. 'What do you mean?'

'I mean that his antics have come at a difficult time. The University is currently embroiled in a dispute about rents with the town's landlords – you should know this, Matt; I have talked of little else this past month – and I issued a writ ordering all scholars to keep hold of their property until it is resolved. If we lose the fight, we will need *every* College-owned building we can get our hands on, to house those scholars who will suddenly find them-selves with nowhere to live.'

The monk *had* held forth about a 'rent war' on several occasions, but Bartholomew had taken scant notice. The previous term had been frantically busy for him, because two Fellows on a sabbatical leave of absence meant a huge increase in his teaching load, and he had not had time to think about much else. 'Spaldynge's is only one house, Brother.'

Michael regarded him balefully. 'You clearly have *not* been listening to me, or you would not be making such an inane remark. The landlords are refusing to renew leases, and we have dozens of homeless scholars already – scholars *I* need

16

to house. Thus *every* building is important at the moment. Did you know the one Spaldynge sold was Borden Hostel? He was its Principal.'

'Borden?' asked Bartholomew, a little shocked. 'But that has been part of the University for decades. It is older than most Colleges.'

Michael's face was grim. 'Quite. Unfortunately, the landlords have interpreted its sale to mean that if stable old Borden can fall into their hands, then so can any other foundation. As I said, I am furious about it – Spaldynge has done the whole University a disservice.'

Bartholomew was puzzled. 'You say he sold his hostel to buy food, but where does he intend to eat it, if he has no home? He has solved one problem by creating another.'

'He is a Fellow of Clare, so he and his students have been given refuge there. He said he made the sale to underline the fact that most hostels are desperately poor, but we collegians do not care.'

Bartholomew looked at the mounds of food on Michael's trencher. 'Perhaps he has a point.'

'Perhaps he does, but it still does not give him the right to sell property that does not belong to him. Did I tell you that these greedy landlords are demanding that all rents be *trebled*? As the law stands, it is the University that determines what constitutes a fair rent – and that rate was set years ago. It means these treacherous landlords are questioning *the law itself*!'

'But the rate was set before the plague,' Bartholomew pointed out reasonably. 'And times have changed since then. Perhaps your "fair rent" is fair no longer.'

Michael did not hear him over the choir's caterwauling. He speared a piece of roasted pork with uncharacteristic savagery. 'If the landlords win this dispute, it could herald the end of the University, because only the very wealthy will be able to afford accommodation here. At the moment, nearly *all* our students live in town-owned buildings; only a fraction of them are lucky enough to occupy a scholar-owned College like ours.'

Bartholomew decided he had better change the subject before the monk became so weighed down with his concerns that it would spoil his enjoyment of the feast. He said the first thing that came into his head, before realising it was probably not much of an improvement. 'Clare seems to be causing you all manner of problems at the moment. How is your investigation into the death of that other Fellow of theirs – Wenden?'

'Solved, thank God. Wenden was deeply unpopular when he was alive, but he is even more so now he is dead.'

'How is that possible?'

'His colleagues endured his unpleasant foibles for nigh on thirty years, on the understanding that Clare would be his sole beneficiary when he died. However, when his will was read, it transpired that he had left everything to the Bishop of Lincoln instead.'

Bartholomew raised his eyebrows. 'He bequeathed his College nothing at all?'

'Not a penny. I might have accused his colleagues of killing him, but for the testimony of the friend he had been visiting that night. Wenden had forgotten his hat, and Honynge was chasing after him to give it back. Honynge saw a tinker lurking about, and heard a bow loosed moments later.'

'A tinker?' asked Bartholomew. 'Not the one we fished from the river a few days ago?'

'The very same. You ascertained that he fell in while he was drunk – an accident – and I found Wenden's purse hidden among his belongings. So, the case is closed.'

Michael turned his full attention to his food, and

18

Bartholomew winced when the choir attempted a popular dance tune, delivered in a ponderous bellow at half-speed. Meanwhile, Kenyngham opened his eyes at last, and began to fill his trencher with slivers of roasted goose.

'Our musicians are discordant today,' he said, in something of an understatement. 'Wait until they finish this song, then offer them some ale. That should shut them up.'

It was a good idea, and the physician supposed someone should have thought of it before they had started in the first place. He went to oblige, assisted by a commoner called Roger Carton. Carton was a short, plump, serious Franciscan, and had come to Michaelhouse to help Wynewyk teach the burgeoning numbers of law students – lawyers tended to make more money than men in other vocational professions, so law was currently the University's most popular subject. When Bartholomew and Carton approached the choir with jugs of ale, the clamour stopped mid-sentence, and the singers clustered eagerly around them. A blissful peace settled across the hall.

'Will you visit your Gilbertine colleagues later?' Bartholomew asked of Kenyngham, when he was back in his place. 'You usually spend at least part of Easter at their convent.'

'Not this time.' Kenyngham patted his hand, and Bartholomew noticed for the first time that the friar's skin had developed the soft, silky texture of the very elderly. 'I am too tired. Your students are laughing – what a pleasant sound!'

The source of the lads' amusement was a medical student named Falmeresham, who was intelligent but mischievous and unruly. Bartholomew doubted Kenyngham would be amused if he was let in on the joke, because it was almost certain to be lewd, malicious or both.

'Michael is pale,' said Kenyngham in a low voice. 'The rent war is worrying him more deeply than you appreciate, so you must help him resolve it.'

'Me?' asked Bartholomew, startled by the suggestion. 'It is the proctors' business, and none of mine. He has a deputy to manage that sort of thing for him.'

'Yes, but his current assistant is neither efficient nor perspicacious, and Michael will only win the dispute if he is helped by his friends. Good friends, not crocodiles.'

'Crocodiles?' echoed Bartholomew, bemused.

'Crocodiles,' repeated Kenyngham firmly. 'Timely men with teeth. And *you* must oppose false prophets. Like shooting stars, they dazzle while they are in flight, but they burn out and are soon forgotten. Crocodiles and shooting stars, Matthew. Crocodiles and shooting stars.'

Bartholomew had no idea what he was talking about, but Kenyngham had closed his eyes and his face was suffused with the beatific expression that indicated he was praying again. There was no point trying to question him when he was in conversation with God, and Bartholomew did not try. He turned to Michael, and was about to comment on the baked apples, when the choir resumed their programme. Fuelled by ale, they were rowdier than ever. Gradually, they veered away from the staid ballads Michael had taught them, and began to range into the uncharted territory of tavern ditties. The lyrics grew steadily more bawdy until even the liberal-minded Langelee was compelled to act. He stood to say grace, and Fellows and students hastened to follow his example. There was a collective scraping of benches and chairs, and then everyone was on his feet. Except one man.

'Give Kenyngham a poke, Bartholomew,' said Langelee. 'He seems to have fallen asleep again. It must be the wine.'

'Or the restful music,' added Wynewyk caustically.

The physician obliged, then caught the old man as he started to slide backwards off his seat. After a moment, he looked up. 'I cannot wake him this time,' he said softly. 'He is dead.'

Space was in short supply for University scholars, and only the very wealthy could afford the luxury of a room to themselves – and sometimes even then, no purse was heavy enough to overcome the need to cram several men into a single chamber. Bartholomew was uncommonly lucky in his living arrangements. He was obliged to share his room with only one student – and Falmeresham preferred to be with his friends than with his teacher, so was nearly always out. It meant the physician had a privacy that was almost unprecedented among his peers.

He occupied a pleasant ground-floor chamber with two small arched windows looking across the courtyard, and had a tiny cupboard-like room across the stairwell where he kept his remedies and medical equipment. The bedchamber was sparsely furnished: it contained a single bed, with a straw mattress for Falmeresham that was rolled up each morning and stored underneath it; a row of pegs and a chest for spare clothes; and a pair of writing desks.

Michael, meanwhile, shared his quarters with two Benedictines from his Mother House at Ely, but spent most of his daylight hours at the proctors' office in the University Church, commonly called St Mary the Great. It was generally acknowledged that he was by far the most powerful scholar in Cambridge, because Chancellor Tynkell was a spineless nonentity who let him do what he liked. The monk's friends often asked why he did not have himself elected as Chancellor, and claim the glory as well as the power, but Michael pointed out that the current arrangement allowed him to make all the important decisions, while Tynkell was there to take the blame if anything went wrong.

The sudden and unexpected death of Kenyngham had sent a ripple of shock through the College that affected everyone, from the most junior servant to the most senior Fellow, and the monk did not want to be with his Benedictine colleagues or haunt St Mary the Great that afternoon. Instead, he sat in Bartholomew's chamber, perching on a stool that creaked under his enormous weight.

'So Kenyngham just . . . died?' he asked, holding out his goblet for more 'medicinal' wine.

'People do,' replied Bartholomew. 'He was very old – well past seventy.'

'But how could he? He was at a feast, for God's sake! People do not die at feasts.'

As a physician, Bartholomew was used to being asked such questions by the bereaved, but that did not make them any easier to answer. 'He closed his eyes to pray, and I suppose he just slipped away. He loved Easter, and was happy today. It is not a bad way to go.'

'Are you sure it was natural? Perhaps he was poisoned.'

'You have been a proctor too long – you see mischief everywhere, even when there is none.'

Michael was thoughtful. 'I went to his room last night, and caught him swallowing some potion or other. When I asked what it was, he told me it was an antidote.'

'An antidote for what?' asked Bartholomew, mystified. He was Kenyngham's physician, and he had prescribed nothing except a balm for an aching back in months.

'He declined to say – he changed the subject when I tried to ask him about it. But supposing it was an antidote to poison, because he knew someone was going to do him harm?'

Bartholomew regarded him askance. 'You have a vivid

imagination, Brother! Besides, you do not take antidotes *before* you are poisoned – you take them after, once you know what you have been given. But there was nothing strange about his death. He was obviously feeling unwell, because he said he was too tired to visit the Gilbertine convent today, and you know how he liked their chapel. Besides, who would want to harm Kenyngham?'

'No one – but I cannot shake the feeling that a *person* is to blame for this. Kenyngham was a saint, and God would never have struck him down so suddenly.'

'Good men are just as prone to death as wicked ones.'

Michael stood. 'Come to his room with me – now. We shall find this antidote, and then you will see I am right to be suspicious.'

Bartholomew did not find it easy to open Kenyngham's door and step inside his quarters. The Gilbertine's familiar frayed cloak hung on the back of the door, and the pillow on the bed still held the hollow made by the old man's head. Bartholomew stood by the window and thought of the many hours he had spent there, enjoying Kenyngham's sweet-tempered, erudite company.

'I cannot find it,' said Michael after a while. He stood with his hands on his hips, perturbed.

'We should not be here,' said Bartholomew uncomfortably. 'It feels wrong. He gave you an evasive, ambiguous answer when you asked him what he was swallowing, which tells me he did not want you to know. Can we not respect his wish for privacy?'

Michael sighed. 'Very well – but just because I cannot find this antidote does not mean I imagined the whole incident. He really did take something, you know.'

Bartholomew nodded. 'I believe you, but it could have been anything – a mild purge, a secret supply of wine. It does not have to be sinister.'

'Right,' said Michael in a way that suggested he would make up his own mind about that.

Once back in Bartholomew's room they sat in silence for a long time. 'We shall have to elect someone to take his place – and soon,' said the monk eventually. 'Suttone and Clippesby will be away again next term, and we cannot manage with a third Fellow gone.'

Bartholomew found he did not like the notion of someone else taking Kenyngham's post. 'He is barely cold, Brother,' he said reproachfully.

'I know, but he would not want us to be sentimental about this – and nor would he approve of us neglecting our students' education by being tardy about appointing a replacement. Who will it be, do you think? Principal Honynge of Zachary Hostel is always sniffing around in search of a College post, so I suppose he will be calling tomorrow, to remind us of his academic prowess. Now *there* is someone who would harm Kenyngham. I have never liked him, and he strikes me as the kind of man who might resort to poison to further his own ends.'

'And how did he commit this crime?' asked Bartholomew, supposing distress was leading the monk to make wild and unfounded accusations. 'We all ate the same food.'

'Kenyngham's age made him frail, rendering him more susceptible to toxins than the rest of us.'

'You should watch where you express that sort of theory,' warned Bartholomew. 'Our students are upset, and a rumour that Kenyngham was deliberately harmed is likely to ignite a fire that does not need to be lit. Besides, Honynge is not a killer.'

'What about Tyrington of Piron Hostel as a culprit, then?' persisted Michael. 'He has been its Principal for three years now, and he told me only last week that he would rather be a collegian.'

'No one killed Kenyngham,' said Bartholomew firmly. 'And he would be appalled to hear you say so – of all the men in the University, he was the last who would want trouble on his behalf.'

'That is true, but I cannot stop thinking about this "antidote" . . .'

'Perhaps he used the wrong word. Some of what he said to me today made no sense, either – talk of crocodiles and shooting stars. You are reading too much into an idle remark, and we should discuss something else before you convince yourself that a crime *has* been committed and go off to investigate. Tell me about your rent war. I could not hear what you were saying once the choir was under way with its repertoire.'

Michael grimaced. 'It is growing ever more serious, and I am struggling to maintain the peace. The landlords' spokesman – Candelby – has recently purchased several new houses. He objects to the fact that the law insists they should be used as hostels for scholars.'

'He *owns* these buildings?' asked Bartholomew. Michael nodded. 'Then I can see his point. Why should he rent them to us for a pittance, when he could lease them to wealthy merchants for a good deal more?'

Michael regarded him icily. 'Not you, too! That is what *he* says, and he is encouraging the other landlords to think the same. The reason is that it is the *law*, Matt. Once a house has been rented to scholars, it must remain rented to scholars until the University no longer needs it.'

'It may be the law, but it is hardly fair.'

'What does fairness have to do with anything? The law has never made any pretence of being fair, and nor will it, I imagine. However, the real problem is that I find myself unable to enforce this particular statute. I could fine Candelby, but what would I do if he refuses to pay? Send

25

beadles to his house and take the money by force? Put him in prison? If I did either, the University would be in flames within an hour, and every scholar would be ready to fight. There would be a bloodbath, and I do not want that.'

'Does Candelby?'

'Yes – he is a greedy, selfish villain, who would willingly squander lives for personal gain. But *I* want the matter settled amicably. I have offered to negotiate a slightly higher rate – I cannot *triple* it, as he demands, because even I do not own that sort of authority – but he refuses to treat with me.'

'Then ask the Sheriff to intervene. He will force Candelby to talk to you, because he will not want a riot, either.'

'I wish I could, but he is away, summoned to Huntingdon on shire business.'

'Then can you send to the King for help? He set his seal to the University Statutes – the laws you are trying to enforce – and will not want them flouted.'

'That would see His Majesty descending on the town in a fury, fining anything that moves. We are unpopular enough as it is, and I do not want to exacerbate the situation by telling tales. Damn Candelby! Most people had never heard of him before he whipped his fellow landlords into a frenzy, but now his name is on everyone's lips.'

'Not mine, Brother. I know very little about him.'

'He is a taverner by trade. He runs the Angel Inn on Bene't Street and, much as I detest the man, he does sell excellent pies. Have you tried one?'

'If I had, then I would not tell you – the Senior Proctor! You would fine me.'

The University had decided years before that taverns were not for scholars. Not only did such establishments provide strong drink, which encouraged riotous behaviour, but they were frequented by townsmen. Inebriated students and drunken laymen were to be kept apart at all costs, and Michael's beadles patrolled the alehouses every night in search of anyone breaking the rules.

Michael smiled. 'I shall assume the answer is yes, then.'

'Just once – a month ago. Carton took me, because he said I was the only man in Cambridge who had not eaten one.'

Michael nodded. 'He was probably right. Candelby hired a Welsh cook at the beginning of Lent, and it is common knowledge that his wares are a vast improvement on anything else on offer in the town.'

'What are you going to do about him?' Bartholomew was concerned by the way his friend's face had become pale with worry. 'Candelby, I mean, not the cook.'

'What *can* I do? I do not want to be heavy handed and spoil University–town relations for ever. Yet I represent scholars, and cannot let burgesses ride roughshod over them. However, my first duty is to avert the riot I sense brewing, so I shall continue to be calm and reasonable – and hope Sheriff Tulyet comes home while we are all still in one piece. Lord, I miss him!'

'We do not want a riot,' agreed Bartholomew fervently. He was the University's Corpse Examiner, which meant he was obliged to inspect the body of any dead scholar – and he disliked seeing people killed by violence. He was about to add more when the door was flung open and Falmeresham burst in, the commoner Carton at his heels. Falmeresham and Carton had struck up a friendship that had surprised everyone, because their personalities meant they had little in common. Falmeresham was fun-loving and reckless; Carton was a sober, quiet friar who was some-thing of an enigma.

'There has been an accident,' declared Falmeresham. 'Master Lynton was riding down the road when he collided with a cart driven by Candelby. The messenger said there is blood everywhere.'

'Lord!' groaned Michael, putting his head in his hands. 'A spat between the landlords' spokesman and a high-ranking scholar. Now there will be trouble!'

'Do you mean Lynton the physician?' asked Bartholomew alarmed. 'My colleague from Peterhouse?'

Falmeresham nodded. 'I am glad I did not study with *him*. He is dogmatic and narrow-minded, and refuses to embrace new ideas.'

'That is unkind,' said Bartholomew reprovingly. Falmeresham was only a term away from graduating, but Bartholomew had still not cured him of his habit of speaking his mind. 'He does prefer traditional medicine, but he is a good man.'

Falmeresham snorted in a way that suggested he disagreed, but there was no time to argue.

Michael heaved himself upright. 'I suppose I should see what can be done to avert trouble.'

'You are right to be worried,' said Carton. 'The messenger also said the onlookers have taken sides, and your beadles are hard-pressed to keep them apart. You are both needed on Milne Street.'

Easter Sunday was a time of feasting and celebration, and even the town's poorest inhabitants marked the occasion by decking themselves out in their best clothes and strolling along the town's main thoroughfares. It was a time for visiting family and friends, for enjoying bright sunshine and street performers. Strictly speaking, entertainment was forbidden on such a holy day, but neither the University nor the town made any effort to enforce the rule, and the narrow lanes were full of singers, dancers, magicians, fire-eaters and jugglers. The streets echoed with rattling drums, trilling pipes and the babble of excited conversation.

It was not just townsmen who were making the best of a mild spring day and some free time. Students wearing the distinctive uniforms of their foundations were out in force. Normally, the presence of so many liveries would have resulted in brawls, as ancient grievances between Colleges and hostels were resurrected. This year, however, the scholars had laid aside their differences to concentrate on a common enemy: the town. The rent war was seen as an attempt to suppress their *studium generale*, and the more alarmist among them were braying that it was the greatest threat academia had yet faced. If the town won, they said, and rents were indeed trebled, other privileges would disappear, too – such as affordable ale, bread and fuel, the prices of which were also kept artificially low by the University Statutes. Michael did his best to control the rumours, but it was like trying to stem the flow of a river. The scholars believed they were under attack, and the uncompromising stance taken by the landlords was doing nothing to dispel the illusion.

The hostels were bearing the brunt of the dispute. Landlords declined to carry out essential repairs until their tenants agreed to the new terms, so students were forced to leave when conditions became intolerable. Alternatively, when leases expired, the owners refused to renew them, so scholars suddenly found themselves ousted from houses they had inhabited for years. Naturally, the University fined the landlords for their audacity, but the landlords were refusing to pay up – and the University was astonished to learn that it did not know how to make them.

'Look at the way those lads from King's Hall are glaring at the mason's apprentices,' panted Michael as he waddled along at Bartholomew's side. The fat monk was not built for moving at speed. 'They would dearly love to fight.'

Bartholomew nodded. 'And the students of Rudd's and Margaret's hostels, who have hated each other for years, have joined forces to menace those pot-boys from the Angel.'

'But they are still outnumbered,' said Michael. He heaved a sigh of relief when the scholars backed down and moved away. Immediately, the pot-boys broke into a chorus of jeers and catcalls, but the students showed admirable restraint, perhaps because the Senior Proctor was watching.

He and Bartholomew, with Falmeresham and Carton in tow, hurried along Milne Street, a major thoroughfare named after the mills that thumped and creaked at its southernmost end. First, they passed Ovyng Hostel with its rotting timbers and dirty plaster, then the back of Gonville Hall, a small but wealthy institution that specialised in training lawyers. Then came Trinity Hall and Clare, both with high walls protecting them from the ravages of resentful townsmen – and the ravages of rival foundations. Beyond Clare lay the little church of St John Zachary, and in the distance were the thatched roofs and gables of the Carmelite Friary.

Sandwiched between the University's property, mostly on the eastern side of the road, were the homes and shops of merchants. Elegant pargeting and glazed windows indicated that Cambridge was a thriving commercial centre, as well as a place of learning and education. Bartholomew's brother-in-law, Oswald Stanmore, owned one of the grandest, although he preferred to live outside the town, using his Milne Street premises as a place of business. However, when Cambridge was uneasy he liked to be on hand to protect his assets, and he was in residence that day. He and his wife Edith – Bartholomew's sister – were

30

in the yard, handing out Easter treats to their apprentices. They waved as their kinsman raced past.

The accident had occurred outside Clare's main gate, and had attracted a large crowd – scholars as well as the men who worked for the Milne Street traders. Michael's beadles moved among them, but it was clear they were struggling to keep the peace. Bartholomew saw one student push a jeweller hard enough to make him stumble, then dart away when the fellow whipped around to reciprocate. The student's cronies raised their hands to indicate they had not been responsible, but there was a jeering, gloating quality to the gesture that was designed to aggravate, not pacify.

'I am glad you are here, Brother,' said Beadle Meadowman, stepping forward to greet the man who paid his wages. 'But Doctor Bartholomew's services are no longer needed. Robin of Grantchester and the new healer are already here.'

'What new healer?' asked Bartholomew, startled.

It was Carton who replied. 'He means Richard Arderne, who arrived on the first day of Lent.'

'I am surprised you have not come across him, sir,' added Falmeresham helpfully. 'He did nothing for the first few weeks, then last Saturday he made his debut with some very public cures.'

'Matt was busy on Saturday, trying to rectify that unhappy business Deynman precipitated,' said Michael. 'He did not have time to wander around and watch other medical men at work.'

Falmeresham rolled his eyes. 'I had forgotten. Deynman misread the dosage on old Master Hanchach's medicine, and Doctor Bartholomew was obliged to spend hours making sure the poor man did not die as a result.'

Bartholomew winced. Deynman was becoming a major

31

liability, and he had been appalled to learn that the lad could not be trusted to follow even the most simple of instructions. It told him more than ever that Deynman should never be let loose on the general populace, and he lived in constant fear that the student would decide to abandon his training and go into practice without the qualification that was taking so long to acquire.

'Arderne has been saying some very rude things about Surgeon Robin,' said Carton, changing the subject when he saw the cloud pass across the physician's face. 'He says his methods are outmoded and dangerous, and that people would be wise to avoid him.'

'It is true,' said Falmeresham bluntly. 'Robin is a menace, and everyone knows it.'

Robin of Grantchester had been in Cambridge for as long as anyone could remember, and held a surgical monopoly. Unfortunately, he was not very good at his trade, and a large number of his patients died. Some perished while he was wielding his filthy instruments, while others expired later, of the fevers that were an inevitability after encounters with Robin. He was summoned only by the desperate or the uninformed, although he was said to be a master at trimming beards.

Luckily for his own patients, Bartholomew was not averse to practising surgery himself, despite it being forbidden to him on two counts. Firstly, it was against Canon Law, and, as a member of the University, he had taken minor religious orders, so was bound by its decrees. Secondly, physicians were supposed to remain aloof from the messy business of cutting and sewing. He had learned, however, that people were more likely to survive if he performed the procedures himself, rather than asking Robin to do them. Therefore, he was pleased to learn that another healer was available for him to call upon, because although he did not mind plying the skills he had learned during his unorthodox training, he disliked the recriminations that often followed from his fellow physicians.

He followed Michael through the press, and surveyed the scene in front of him. A horse stood with its head drooping disconsolately, surrounded by people who seemed more concerned with its welfare than that of its rider. He supposed he should not be surprised, given that the beast was obviously a valuable one. The rider lay on the ground, and the fact that someone had covered him with a cloak suggested he was beyond earthly help.

A cart was on its side nearby, and its passengers sat on the wreckage. Bartholomew recognised them both. One was Candelby and the other was a dumpy, middle-aged woman called Maud Bowyer. Maud's husband had died during the plague, leaving her one of the wealthiest widows in the county. It was common knowledge that Candelby had been paying her court for the past few months, and everyone was waiting to see whether she would succumb to his charms. Candelby cradled an injured arm, while Maud was bleeding from a splinter that had been driven deep into her shoulder. She was weeping, heartbroken sobs that did not sound like cries of pain. Bartholomew supposed it was shock.

In front of them, wielding a brightly coloured feather, was a tall, thin man who wore the red robes of a surgeon. He had long black hair, and a neat beard. His pale blue eyes were unusually – disconcertingly – bright, and he carried himself with an arrogant confidence.

'Do not let *him* near me,' cried Candelby, when he saw Bartholomew and Michael approach. He waved his un-injured hand at them, but it was not clear to which of them he referred. 'He might try to make an end of me while I am weak and defenceless.'

There was a growl from the onlookers. Some thought Candelby was right to be cautious, while others resented the slander directed against two of the University's senior scholars. Bartholomew saw some unfriendly shoving start to take place between a gaggle of Carmelite novices and half-a-dozen burly men who worked at the mills.

'They would not dare,' declared the red-robed man confidently. 'Not while *I* am here to protect you. *I* am Magister Richard Arderne, and *I* protect my patients with my life.'

'Actually, Candelby is *my* patient,' said another voice. 'So it is *my* right to protect him.'

A small, grimy fellow stepped from the crowd to hover at Arderne's side. It was a major tactical mistake for Robin of Grantchester to place himself near the new *medicus*, because comparisons were inevitable, and none of them worked to his advantage. Robin's gown was filthy, and his hands and face were not much better. His hair was oily and unkempt, and he bared his brown, rotten fangs in a grin that was decidedly shifty. The bag over his shoulder contained his tools, and some were so thick with old blood they were black. Robin was comparatively wealthy, because of the surgical monopoly he held, but he still looked like a vagrant.

'I do not want *you* touching me, Robin,' said Candelby, alarmed. He glanced at the sobbing woman at his side. 'Or Maud. Magister Arderne has offered to mend us, and we have accepted.'

'Fortunately, you paid the retainer I recommended last week,' said Arderne comfortably. 'I said at the time that you never know when you might need the services of a healer, and you were wise to part with the ten shillings that grants you unlimited access to my skills.'

'Ten shillings?' echoed Bartholomew, staggered by the colossal sum.

Arderne ignored him and addressed the onlookers. 'Does anyone else want to insure himself against future illness or accident? I sew wounds with no pain, and cure common ailments with minimal fuss. Of course, I am expensive, but quality costs.' He looked Robin up and down disparagingly, to indicate what he thought of the cheaper alternative.

'I will send an apprentice with the coins later,' said the town's leading mason. 'Accidents happen, as Candelby and Maud can attest, so it is sensible to be ready for them.'

'No!' breathed Robin, appalled. 'You are mine; you have been with me since the Death.'

'And you half-killed me the last time I was obliged to summon you,' said the mason baldly. 'But I saw Magister Arderne at work on Saturday, and I was deeply impressed.'

'If Candelby and Maud are in your care, then help them,' said Bartholomew to Arderne in a low voice. Touting for business while patients suffered was unprofessional in the extreme. 'She looks as if she might faint.'

'She will not,' declared Arderne with considerable confidence. 'I have shaken my magical feather at her, and a complete recovery is guaranteed.'

'I might swoon,' countered Maud in a voice that was hoarse from weeping. A woman, who appeared to be her maidservant, had hurried to her side and was comforting her. 'I do not feel well, and want to go home. Who will take me?'

'*I* shall,' said Arderne grandly, pushing Robin away when he started to step towards her. 'I have already sent a boy for my personal transport, and it will be here soon.'

She nodded gratefully, while Bartholomew thought a pain-dulling potion would have done her more good than the wave of a feather. Still, bloody wounds were the domain of surgeons, not physicians, and Bartholomew did not want to cause trouble by pressing a scholar's opinions on a man who had so clearly won the approval of the town.

'I cannot *bear* him,' muttered Robin, shooting Arderne a furious glare. 'His "personal transport", indeed! If he means his cart, then why does he not say so?'

While Michael tried to disperse the crowd, Bartholomew knelt next to the crumpled figure covered by the cloak. He could tell from the tufts of dandelion-clock hair poking above it that the victim was indeed his elderly colleague Master Lynton from the College of Peterhouse. Despite Bartholomew's frustration with Lynton's narrow-mindedness in medical matters – and Lynton's horror at what he called Bartholomew's love of heretical medicine – they had never been serious enemies, and had rubbed along well enough together. Bartholomew gazed at the kindly face with genuine sorrow, sharply reminded of his own distress for Kenyngham. He pulled more of the cloak away, wondering what had actually killed him. What he saw made his stomach lurch in shock.

Bartholomew was so intent on examining Lynton that he did not hear Arderne come to stand behind him. He leapt in alarm at the hissing voice so close to his shoulder, and hastily tugged the cloak to conceal his colleague's wounds. He did not want anyone else to see them, given the volatile mood of the people who milled around the scene of the accident.

'I understand Cambridge has four physicians, every one of them a charlatan,' Arderne was saying, his pale eyes burning curiously. Bartholomew stood quickly, not liking the way the man hovered over him. 'Which one are you?'

'Well, he is not Lynton,' sneered a red-faced taverner named Blankpayn. He owned a disreputable alehouse called the Lilypot, and was Candelby's most fervent supporter. 'Because Lynton is dead.'

Blankpayn was accompanied by three lads who worked in his tavern, plus several of his regular customers. The patrons were rough, greasy men with ponderous bellies, who looked as if they would do anything for a free drink. There was a pause as slow minds digested what Blankpayn had said, followed by hearty laughter as their companion's wit eventually hit home. Bartholomew stifled a sigh. He needed to talk to Michael about Lynton, and did not want to waste time bandying words with men who wanted to quarrel with him.

'He is Doctor Bartholomew, from Michaelhouse,' replied Falmeresham coldly. Carton was plucking at his friend's sleeve, trying to pull him away from the confrontation. Falmeresham freed himself impatiently. 'And he is no charlatan, so watch your tongue.'

There was a murmur of support from the Carmelites and a group of scholars from Clare. Bartholomew was alarmed to see the crowd had separated into two halves. He put his hand on Falmeresham's shoulder, silently ordering him to say no more.

'You are a surgeon?' asked Bartholomew politely. He pointed to Arderne's red robes, fighting the urge to walk away from the man and talk to Michael. It would be deemed rude, and he did not want to antagonise anyone.

'I am a *healer*,' replied Arderne loftily. 'No mere sawbones – and no urine-gazer, either. I am superior to both trades, because *my* remedies are efficacious and *I* know what I am doing.'

'A leech,' sneered Falmeresham. 'A common trickster.'

'Perhaps we can talk another time,' said Bartholomew hastily, before Arderne could react to the insult. 'But now, your patients need you, and I must carry Lynton to his College.'

'Here comes my personal transport,' said Arderne, turning as a cart clattered rather recklessly into the onlookers. It was painted with herbs, stars and signs of the zodiac, and looked more like something a magician would own than a *medicus*. He addressed its driver. 'Help my new patients, but be gentle. My cure is working, and rough treatment might see it all reversed again.'

'Damned liar!' spat Falmeresham. 'A cure either works or it does not.'

Arderne chose to ignore him, but a nondescript man, whom Bartholomew had seen working in the Angel when he had bought his pie – his name was Ocleye – was unwilling to let the matter pass. 'What can apprentice physicians know about the power of magic?' he demanded. 'Your teachers do not choose to initiate you into such mysteries, so you will always remain ignorant of them.'

'Lynton will not be teaching any mysteries now, magical or otherwise,' brayed Blankpayn. He had enjoyed his cronies laughing at his first witticism, and was eager to repeat the experience. After another pause, his friends cackled obligingly.

'Poor Lynton,' said Carton. He knelt, and Bartholomew thought he was going to pray. Instead he began to tidy the cloak that covered the body, straightening it with small, fussy movements that betrayed his unease at the hostility that was bubbling around them.

Michael had ordered his beadles to stand between the two factions, in the hope of preventing more violence. 'Who saw the accident?' he asked, looking around.

'Lynton came racing along Milne Street at a speed that was far from safe,' replied Blankpayn immediately. 'His death serves him right. He might have killed poor Candelby.'

'Perhaps he intended to,' said Arderne slyly.

Bartholomew glanced sharply at the healer. Arderne knew perfectly well that such a remark might stoke the flames of hatred. Of course, a brawl would almost certainly result in casualties, some of whom might require the services of a *medicus*. The physician struggled to mask his distaste for the fellow's unethical tactics.

'Did you actually *see* cart and horse collide, Blankpayn?' pressed Michael, choosing to overlook Arderne's comment. The monk was pale, and Bartholomew sensed his growing unease with the situation.

'I was close by,' hedged Blankpayn, indicating that he had not. 'And Candelby told me the whole incident was Lynton's fault.'

'I shall question Candelby myself – we do not condemn anyone on hearsay.' Michael raised his voice. 'Everyone should go home. There is nothing to see here.'

'Lies!' shouted Arderne, startling everyone with his sudden vehemence. 'How can you say there is nothing to see when *I* am at work? How *dare* you denigrate my performance!'

'Your *performance*?' Bartholomew was startled by the choice of words.

'My miraculous healing of Candelby and Maud. They would be dead by now, had it not been for my timely intervention. I healed them with my magic feather.'

Bartholomew declined to argue with him. He knew from experience that such characters were best ignored until they destroyed themselves with their outrageous boasts. He glanced at Lynton again, itching for the confrontation to be over, so he could talk to Michael.

'It is time Cambridge was blessed with a decent medical practitioner,' Arderne went on. 'The age of amateurs is over, and the people of this fine town will now benefit from the best that modern science can offer. I, Richard

Arderne, can cure leprosy, poxes, falling sicknesses and contagions. I can make barren women fertile, and draw teeth with no pain at all.'

'Can you turn lead into gold, too?' jeered Falmeresham. Bartholomew poked him in the back.

'I am working on it,' replied Arderne, unfazed. 'And when I succeed – which is only a matter of time – I shall share my good fortune with my loyal patients. But now I must take Maud home before she weeps herself into a fit. Good afternoon to you all.'

He was gone in a flurry of clattering hoofs and wheels, leaving the crowd somewhat bemused.

'You see?' murmured Robin, suddenly at Bartholomew's elbow. The physician jumped, on edge and uncomfortable. 'How can I compete with that sort of announcement? He will ruin me.'

'He will not,' replied Bartholomew. 'It is only a matter of time before one of his clients points out that he *was* in pain when a tooth was drawn, or that she is still barren. Then his reputation will—'

'But that might take weeks,' cried Robin. 'And he will destroy me in the meantime.'

Bartholomew did not know what to say, aware that Arderne's brash confidence would certainly appeal to more people than Robin's sly deference. He watched the unhappy surgeon slouch away.

'*I* shall not mourn Lynton,' declared Blankpayn. 'One fewer scholar is good news. I heard old master Kenyngham has gone to meet his maker, too, so it is definitely a good Easter for the town.'

Before Bartholomew could stop him, Falmeresham had launched himself at the taverner, who instinctively drew his dagger. Falmeresham saw it too late to swerve, and his mouth opened in shock as he ran on to the blade. He stumbled to his knees. Blankpayn dropped his knife and began to back away, his face white with horror at what he had done.

'No!' breathed Bartholomew. He started to run towards his stricken student, but did not get far. One of the patrons swung a punch that caught him squarely on the side of the jaw. He went down hard, and was forced to cover his head with his hands when there was a sudden, furious rush to join the ensuing affray. He tried to stand, but was knocked down again by someone crashing into him. He heard Michael bellowing, ordering everyone home. Then the bells of St John Zachary started to ring, warning scholars that trouble was afoot. More men started to pour into the street.

Bartholomew managed to struggle upright, looking around wildly around for his friends. He could not see Falmeresham, and hoped that Carton had dragged him to safety. Meanwhile, Michael was backed against the broken cart, fending off two masons, who were threatening him with daggers. Bartholomew retrieved the heavy childbirth forceps from the medicine bag he always wore looped across his shoulder, and struck one on the shoulder. The other spun around to fight him, but backed away when he saw a knife was no match for an expertly wielded surgical implement.

Michael gazed at the pushing, shoving mêlée with undisguised fury. He stalked to a trough that was used for watering horses, and in a massive show of strength – for all his lard, he was a physically powerful man – upended it. Green water shot across the street, drenching the legs of anyone close by. There were indignant howls as the skirmishers tried to duck out of the way.

'Enough!' roared the monk. His livid face made several scholars slink away before he started to issue fines. 'You should be ashamed of yourselves, brawling on Easter Day! Go home, all of you, and do not come out again until you are in a more peaceful frame of mind.'

Bartholomew was astonished when people began to do as they were told. There were some resentful grumbles, but it was not long before the horde had dissipated.

'Where is Falmeresham?' demanded Bartholomew of Carton, who was standing uncertainly nearby. 'I thought he was with you.'

'I thought he was with *you*,' countered the Franciscan alarmed. 'I saw you dash towards him, but I had no wish to fight Blankpayn and his henchmen, so I hung back.'

'He will have gone home,' said Michael, still glaring at the dispersing mob. 'He is not a fool, to loiter in a place where daggers were flailing.'

'He could not go anywhere – he was stabbed,' said Carton in a hushed, shocked whisper. He put his hand to his side, just above the hip bone. 'Here. I should have overcome my terror and tried to reach him.'

'Easy,' said Michael. There was blood on Carton's mouth, indicating he had not been entirely successful in avoiding the violence. 'We will find him.'

'Perhaps Blankpayn took him prisoner.' Carton declined to be comforted, and was working himself into an agony of worry. 'Perhaps he intends to hold Falmeresham hostage, to blackmail our University over these rents. He is Candelby's lickspittle, and will do anything for him.'

'Blankpayn does not have the wits to devise such a devious plan,' said Michael. 'Falmeresham will be home at Michaelhouse. Go, see if you can find him.'

The friar hurried away, anxiety stamped across his portly features, and Michael sighed. 'Lord save us! Will you fetch a bier for Lynton, Matt? We cannot leave him here, because our students may use his corpse as an excuse for another fracas – claim he was murdered or some such nonsense.'

'Actually, Brother,' said Bartholomew softly, 'he died because he was shot. He *was* murdered.'

CHAPTER 2

The conclave at Michaelhouse was a pleasant chamber adjoining the main hall. It was the undisputed domain of the Fellows, and they used it when they met to discuss College business or to relax in the evenings, leaving the hall free for students and commoners. It was an arrangement that suited everyone – the senior members had a place where they were safe from the demands of over-enthusiastic students, and the junior ones were left to their own devices for a few hours, as long as they were not too unruly. Fortunately, the students liked being trusted, and were invariably better behaved when they were alone than when anyone was monitoring them. The upshot was that Michaelhouse had a reputation for harmony among its scholars, and Langelee had been asked by several envious masters for the secret of his success.

However, there was none of the usual laughter and music in the conclave or the hall that Easter. Kenyngham's death created a pall of sadness that hung over everyone, and the College had never been so quiet. Langelee, who had been fretting over the fact that he would be three teachers short in the forthcoming term – with two away and one dead – asked his four remaining Fellows to join him in the conclave an hour before dawn the following day. They would hold an emergency meeting, during which a replacement for Kenyngham would be chosen. It was an unusual time for such a gathering, but Langelee was not a man to dither once his mind was made up.

Bartholomew was early, so he began to prepare the room while he waited for the others. He placed stools around the table, retrieved the College statutes and the Master's sceptre from the wall-cupboard, and found parchment and ink so Wynewyk could make a record of the proceedings.

'I did not sleep a wink,' said Michael, when he arrived a few moments later. He took his customary seat near the window. 'Neither did you. I heard you come home just moments ago.'

'I was out all night, looking for Falmeresham,' replied the physician tiredly. He had changed his wet, muddy clothes, but there had been no time to rest – not that he felt like sleeping anyway. Each time he closed his eyes, he could see the student falling to his knees, hand clasped to his bleeding side. 'I cannot imagine where he might have gone – or where someone may have taken him.'

'Does he have family in Cambridge? Or friends in another College?'

'His family live in Norfolk. And you always advise against fraternising with scholars from other foundations, lest it leads to quarrels, so his closest friends are here, in Michaelhouse.'

'How badly do you think he was injured? Perhaps he has collapsed somewhere.'

Bartholomew rubbed his eyes. 'Cynric and I have searched every garden, lane and churchyard between here and the place he was attacked – and knocked on the door of every house. If he had wandered off and lost consciousness somewhere, we would have found him.'

Michael was worried. 'Do you think Carton is right – that Blankpayn has done something to him? Blankpayn *is* Candelby's henchman, and Candelby will do anything to harm the University.'

'I tried to talk to Blankpayn, but he is mysteriously unavailable.'

'Not so mysteriously. *I* would not linger if *I* had stabbed someone. It looked like an accident, but that may not save his neck if Falmeresham is found . . . harmed. I hope it does not mean he *knows* he killed the lad, and is lying low until the fuss dies down.'

Bartholomew refused to contemplate such an eventuality. 'Blankpayn's friends say he has gone to visit his mother in Madingley. She summoned me once, for a fever, so I know he *has* a mother.'

Agitated, Michael paced, his thoughts switching to another matter he was obliged to investigate. 'After this meeting, I want you to examine Lynton's body. I need to know *exactly* how he died.'

'I have told you already – there is a crossbow quarrel embedded in his chest.'

'That does not correspond to eyewitnesses' accounts. The Carmelite novices – an unruly gaggle, but not one given to lying – say Lynton was riding down Milne Street when his mare began to buck. He tumbled off, and a hoof caught his head as he fell.'

'Then perhaps the horse was frightened by the sound of the bolt impaling its victim. There *is* a cut on Lynton's head, either from a flailing hoof or from him hitting the ground, so the Carmelites' account is not entirely incompatible with the evidence. However, the fatal injury was caused by the missile, not the nag.'

Michael sighed. 'If you say so. But who would want to kill Lynton? Other than you, that is.'

Bartholomew regarded him in astonishment. 'Why would I want to kill him?'

Michael smiled wanly. 'I am not accusing you. However, it may occur to others that Lynton challenged you to public debates on several occasions, because he thought your teaching was heretical. You must have found it a nuisance – I certainly would have done.'

'On the contrary, I enjoyed the discussions. That is what a university is for, Brother – to pit wits against intellectual equals. I learned a lot from sparring with Lynton.'

'I doubt *he* felt the same way. He was not very good at defending his preference for old-fashioned practices over your more efficacious new ones, and I suspect the reason *you* enjoyed these dialogues is because you always won.'

'Medicine was not the only subject we aired,' said Bartholomew, sure Michael was wrong. Lynton might have disagreed with his theories, but their many disputations had always been conducted without malice or anger. 'At our last public debate, we talked about Heytesbury's mean speed theorem – whether it is correct to assume that velocity is uniformly accelerated.'

'I bet that had your audience on the edge of their seats,' remarked Michael dryly.

Bartholomew nodded earnestly. 'It did, actually. In fact, I was surprised by how much attention it generated. We were scheduled to use Merton Hall, but so many scholars wanted to listen we had to move to St Mary the Great instead.'

'I remember. My beadles thought you and Lynton were up to no good, because they could not imagine why else so many men would be clamouring to hear a debate on such a subject.'

'Is that why they were all standing at the back? To avert trouble? I assumed they were there for the theoretical physics.'

Michael struggled not to laugh. 'We are getting away from the point – which is that Lynton held archaic beliefs, and that you were his intellectual superior. *Ergo*, you must prepare yourself for accusations. If he really was murdered, then his academic rivals are the obvious suspects.'

'Then perhaps we should keep the truth about his death quiet until we know who did it.' Bartholomew took the bloodstained missile from his medical bag, and studied it thoughtfully. 'No one else saw the wound, and I have the bolt here.'

Michael gaped in horror. 'You hauled it out in the middle of the street? After I had just quelled a riot, and when Lynton's colleagues were standing around him, bemoaning the tragedy of his death? My God, man! What were you thinking?'

'That it seemed the right thing to do,' said Bartholomew defensively. 'The Peterhouse Fellows were distraught, and I did not want one to see the bolt and claim Candelby had put it there. If that had happened, you would have had your riot for certain.'

'Why did you not tell me what you had done straight away?' demanded Michael, unappeased.

'Because I forgot in the race to find Falmeresham. There has been no time for chatting.'

Michael regarded him with round eyes. 'Well, please do not do it again. I have more than enough to concern me, without worrying about what my Corpse Examiner might be doing behind my back. Do you know how I spent much of last night? Trying to persuade Candelby that Lynton did not ride at him on purpose. It was a difficult case to argue, because I could tell from the wreckage that Lynton *was* the one at fault. His mare *did* career into the man's cart.'

'Perhaps he was already dead at that point.'

'You think he was shot first, and then the horse panicked? It did not happen the other way around – Lynton rode at Candelby and was shot as a consequence?'

48

'Medicine cannot tell you that, Brother. However, Lynton was gentle, and I do not see him using a horse as a weapon with which to batter people.'

Michael was thoughtful. 'The obvious suspect for Lynton's murder is Candelby.'

'Why? He did not emerge unscathed from the encounter.'

'Perhaps he did not anticipate the horse bucking in his direction. The rent war has turned him hostile to *all* scholars, and a wealthy one on a fine mare might well have inspired a murderous rage. However, crossbows are unwieldy objects – you do not whip one from under your cloak and slip a quick bolt into an enemy. It has to be wound first, and that would have attracted attention.'

Bartholomew showed him the missile. 'It is a very small arrow, so I suspect it did come from a weapon that was easily concealed. However, the murder was committed on a main road in broad daylight, so some degree of stealth was needed, or someone would have seen him.'

Michael inspected it thoughtfully. 'The Church of St John Zachary has a nice leafy churchyard – an ideal place to lurk with a bow.'

'Then Candelby is not your culprit, because he was in a cart with Maud Bowyer when the weapon was discharged.'

Michael was becoming frustrated. 'Who, then? One of Lynton's Peterhouse colleagues?'

'Peterhouse has its squabbles, but none are serious enough to warrant murder.'

'A patient, then? Perhaps he killed one by mistake.'

Bartholomew considered the suggestion. 'It is possible. There are so many illnesses that we cannot cure, and bereaved kin make for bitter enemies.'

'That healer – Arderne – claims *he* can cure anything. He waved his feather at a man Paxtone said would die, and the fellow was up and strolling along the High Street yesterday.'

Bartholomew frowned, but declined to say what he thought of cures that required the waving of feathers. 'There is a famous physician called John Arderne. He specialises in anal fistula – not a life-threatening condition, but an acutely uncomfortable one. Perhaps he and Richard Arderne are kin.'

'My beadles tell me that our Arderne has already provoked public spats with Rougham, and we saw him denigrate Robin ourselves, so he is clearly intent on locking horns with the town's *medici*. We cannot have a quarrel leading to a brawl, just because he wants a forum for advertising his skills, so stay away from him – no asking questions about his family, please.'

'Did he quarrel with Lynton, too?' asked Bartholomew.

'We will have to find out. Did I tell you that two men died during yesterday's fight? Their names were Motelete and Ocleye – a student from Clare and a pot-boy from the Angel tavern.'

'Each side lost a man? Then we are even, so let us hope that marks the end of the matter.'

Michael was angry. 'The unease is Candelby's fault! He has paid a high price, though, because Ocleye was one of his own servants. But here are our colleagues, so I suppose we had better turn our minds to choosing a new Fellow. Whoever we elect cannot hope to step into Kenyngham's shoes.'

'No one can,' said Bartholomew sombrely.

Statutory Fellows' meetings had once been acrimonious events, when clever minds had clashed over petty details, and Bartholomew had resented the time they had taken. Fortunately, matters had improved since Langelee had been elected Master. Every man was permitted to have his say – although he was forbidden from repeating himself – and then a vote was taken. Because this limited opportunities to make derogatory remarks, meetings tended to finish with everyone still friends. It was a sober assembly that gathered in the conclave that morning, though, and even the rambunctious William was subdued. The Fellows took their seats, and Langelee tapped on the table with the sceptre, his symbol of authority, to declare the proceedings were under way.

'Right,' he said tiredly. 'We should try to be brief this morning, because we all have a great deal to do, especially Michael and Bartholomew. There is only one item on the agenda—'

'You forgot to say a grace, Master,' said William reproachfully. The grubby Franciscan looked even more unkempt than usual; his face was grey with sorrow, he had not shaved, and his hair stood in a greasy ring around his untidy tonsure. 'Kenyngham is scarcely cold, and our religious standards have already slipped.'

Langelee inclined his head. 'Very well. *Benedicimus Domino.*'

'*Deo gratias,*' chorused the others automatically. Wynewyk reached for his pen.

Langelee looked around at his Fellows. 'We need to appoint a Fellow who can teach grammar and rhetoric, but I do not think it matters if his speciality is law or theology.'

'John Prestone would have been my first choice,' said William. The others nodded approvingly. 'But I sounded him out informally last night, and he declines to leave Pembroke.'

'What about Robert Hamelyn, then?' suggested Wynewyk. 'He is an excellent teacher, and I happen to know he would like a College appointment.'

'I wish we could,' said Langelee. He nodded meaningfully in William's direction. 'But Hamelyn is a Dominican, and we cannot have one of *those* in Michaelhouse.'

'Of course,' said Wynewyk sheepishly. William hated Dominicans, and Dominicans were invariably not very keen on William; Michaelhouse would never know a moment's peace if a Black Friar was elected to the Fellowship. 'How foolish of me.'

'Very foolish,' agreed William venomously. 'He would bring the ways of Satan to our—'

'There are not many men in a position to drop all and join us immediately,' interrupted Michael. 'And we do need someone as quickly as possible.'

'It will have to be Honynge or Tyrington, then,' said Wynewyk unenthusiastically. 'Both have their own hostels, but, like all Principals, they are worried about the outcome of this rent war – not all hostels will survive it. Thus they are currently looking for College appointments. I suppose I would opt for Honynge over Tyrington, because Tyrington spits.'

'You mean he has an excess of phlegm?' asked Bartholomew. 'I could devise a remedy—'

'No, I mean he *sprays*,' elaborated Wynewyk with a fastidious shudder. 'If you stand too close to him when he is speaking, you come away drenched. And he leers, too.'

'I have never noticed leering – the slobbering is hard to miss,' said Langelee. 'What do you think about Honynge?'

'*He* does not leer,' acknowledged Wynewyk. 'He talks to himself, though.'

'He certainly does,' agreed William, picking at a stain on his habit. 'I asked him about it once – I thought he might be communing with the Devil, and was going to offer him a free exorcism. But he told me he was conversing with the only man in Cambridge capable of matching his intellect.'

Bartholomew was taken aback by the immodest claim. 'His scholarly reputation is formidable, but there are others who more than match it – Prestone and Hamelyn, to name but two.'

'It is not Honynge's vanity that disturbs me,' said Michael. 'It is his other gamut of unpleasant traits. I had occasion to deal with him over the death of Wenden – you will recall that Wenden was walking home from visiting Honynge when he was murdered by the tinker. I was obliged to interview Honynge, and I found him arrogant, rude and sly.'

'He is a condescending ass,' declared William. 'However, I do not like the notion of leering, either, as we shall have if we elect Tyrington. It might frighten the students.'

'We should consider Carton for the post,' said Bartholomew, thinking of the shy Franciscan who was Falmeresham's friend. 'He has been a commoner for a whole term now, and we all know him.'

'We all *like* him, too,' mused Michael. 'He is not overly argumentative, does not hold too many peculiar religious beliefs, and his keen intelligence will improve our academic standing in the University.'

'I agree,' said Langelee. 'But, unfortunately, now is not a good time to appoint him – he is too upset about Falmeresham. He might skimp his academic duties to go hunting for shadows.'

'Falmeresham is not a shadow,' said Bartholomew, more sharply than he had intended. 'He will return soon – I am sure of it.'

'Yes, but he might return dead,' said William baldly. 'It is obvious that Blankpayn has hidden the body in order

53

to avoid a charge of murder. I am sorry, Matthew, but we must be realistic.'

'We can still hope for his safe return, though,' said Wynewyk, seeing the stricken expression on the physician's face. 'I have a friend who drinks in Blankpayn's tavern. I shall visit him this morning, and see if he has noticed signs of recent digging in the garden.'

'Thank you,' said Bartholomew, aware that if Wynewyk really expected Falmeresham to come home, he would not be offering to look for shallow graves. Like William, he believed the worst.

'Unfortunately, we are not in a position to be choosy, not if we want the post filled quickly,' said Langelee, going to a window and peering into the yard below. 'The students are waiting for us to lead them to church, so we had better take a vote. Who wants Carton, a man distracted by grief?'

Bartholomew raised his hand, but was the only one who did.

'And Honynge?' asked Langelee. 'Said to be sly, with a preference for his own conversation?'

Wynewyk inclined his head, while William wagged his finger to indicate he was still thinking.

'If you vote for Honynge, you will regret it,' warned Michael. 'When he arrives, and you become more familiar with his disagreeable habits, you will be sorry.'

He should have known better than try to sway William, because the friar rarely took advice, and his grimy paw immediately shot into the air in Honynge's favour. 'Some of my students are little more than children, and I do not like the notion of electing a man who might leer at them.'

'And finally, Tyrington,' said Langelee, raising his own hand. 'Alleged to spit and leer.'

Michael lifted a plump arm to indicate his preference, although with scant enthusiasm. Langelee had made none of the candidates sound appealing.

'Tyrington and Honynge have two votes each, Master,' said William, lest Langelee could not count that high. 'That means we are tied, so *you* must make the final determination.'

Langelee rubbed his jaw as he assessed his options. 'I am not enamoured of either, to be frank, but we cannot procrastinate or our students will suffer. So, we shall appoint them both.'

'You cannot do that!' blurted William, startled. 'You must make a decision.'

'I *have* made a decision,' snapped Langelee. 'We were desperately busy last term, with Clippesby and Suttone away, and an extra Fellow will not go amiss.'

'But admitting Honynge *and* Tyrington will raise our membership to nine,' said Bartholomew, puzzled. 'I thought the College statutes stipulated one Master and *seven* fellows.'

'Actually, they do not,' said Michael, who knew the rules backwards. 'We have always had that number, but it is tradition, not law. Still, to break a time-honoured custom for Honynge—'

'But the money,' objected Wynewyk, more concerned with practical matters than legal ones. 'How will we pay an additional teacher?'

'By accepting twenty new students,' replied Langelee. His prompt reply suggested he had already given the matter some thought. 'Candelby's antics have resulted in several hostels being dissolved, and dozens of good scholars are desperate for a home. I can fit four in my quarters, and Bartholomew can take five. The rest of you can divide the remaining nine between yourselves.'

'It will be cosy,' said Bartholomew, declining to comment on the Master's dubious arithmetic.

'I should say,' muttered Michael. 'There is not space in your chamber for a bed and five mattresses, so you will have to sleep in shifts. This is sheer lunacy!'

'So, it is decided,' said Langelee, banging his sceptre to indicate the meeting was at an end. 'We elect Tyrington and Honynge, and we recruit a score of new students – hopefully very rich ones who might be inclined to make regular donations.'

The next phase of the academic year was not due to begin for another ten days, so technically the scholars who had remained in Cambridge during the break between the Lent and summer terms were free to do as they pleased. However, the University did not like groups of bored young men wandering around the town with time on their hands, so hostels and Colleges were expected to find ways to keep them occupied. Michaelhouse's method was to hold mock disputations in the hall, which were intended to hone the students' debating skills. The Fellows were obliged to supervise the proceedings, but they were not all needed at once, so they took it in turns.

Bartholomew was scheduled for 'disputation duty' that grey Monday, but as he had agreed to examine Lynton's body for Michael, he asked his colleagues whether they would stand in for him. When he went to tell the monk that they could not help – William was taking part in a vigil for Kenyngham, while Wynewyk and Langelee were due to meet a potential benefactor – he found him holding a letter. Michael's expression was one of deep concern, and the physician hoped it was not bad news about the rent war.

'Worse. It arrived a few moments ago, although the

porter does not recall how it was delivered. It offers me the sum of twenty marks for uncovering the identity of Kenyngham's killer.'

Bartholomew snatched it from him, and read it himself. The author claimed that Kenyngham's death had not been natural, and that it should be investigated immediately. The reward money would be delivered to Michaelhouse as soon as the monk had made an arrest. The parchment was the cheap kind that might have been purchased by anyone, and the style of writing was undistinguished.

'But Kenyngham was *not* murdered,' objected Bartholomew, distressed.

Michael nodded unhappily. 'I reflected on what you said yesterday, and I have decided to accept your reasoning. The business with the "antidote" was nothing – I was reading too much into a casual remark made by a man who later said odd things to you, too. So, I imagine this letter was written by someone who grieves – a way of refusing to acknowledge that death comes to us all, even to saintly men like Kenyngham.'

He put the document in his scrip, but Bartholomew wished he had tossed it in the latrine pit, where he felt it belonged.

'I told Langelee that Lynton was shot,' the monk went on. 'He can be trusted to keep quiet, and he needs to know why we may be out a lot in the coming days. He says we are excused nursemaid duties at these wretched disputations, as long as we find someone to take our places.'

Bartholomew watched the students file into the hall, full of eager anticipation. The Fellows might find the debates a chore, but the junior members loved them. 'No one is free to help us today, so you will have to start the investigation alone,' he said to Michael. 'I will join you as soon as I can.'

'But I need you to inspect Lynton *now*. And I want your help at Peterhouse, too. I am determined to solve this crime. Lynton was an impossible old traditionalist, but he was decent and kind-hearted, and I will not let his killer evade justice. To do that I require your wits, as well as my own.'

'Falmeresham would have supervised the disputations for me,' said Bartholomew dejectedly.

'Deynman can do it, then,' decided Michael. 'He is our oldest undergraduate by a considerable margin, and even *he* should be able to sit at the back of the hall and make sure no one escapes.'

Bartholomew was doubtful, but in the absence of a choice – he also wanted Lynton's killer under lock and key as soon as possible – he beckoned the lad over.

'You can trust me, sir,' Deynman declared, delighted to be put into a position of power at last. 'I shall make sure they stay in, and do not slip out later to join the lads from Clare in the Angel inn.'

Bartholomew regarded him sharply, and found himself staring into a pair of guileless eyes; it had not occurred to Deynman that he had just betrayed his classmates' plans.

'Come, Matt,' said Michael, taking his arm before the physician could have second thoughts about leaving his home in the care of such a man. 'We have a lot to do today, and there is not a moment to lose.'

'The Lilypot first,' said Bartholomew. 'I want to see if Blankpayn is back yet.'

'Brother!' Michael turned to see Langelee hurrying towards him. 'I need you to deliver these for me. They are letters of appointment for Honynge and Tyrington. Do not pull sour faces! I know you are busy, but this is important. We need to know as soon as possible if they are going to accept.'

'Honynge!' spat Michael. 'How could you all be so foolish? I wager I will be saying "I told you so" within a week of his admission.'

Langelee turned to Bartholomew. 'And I am trusting *you* to make sure he does not accidentally "lose" Honynge's letter along the way.'

They left, but Bartholomew refused to deliver the invitations until they had been to the Lilypot. He was acutely disappointed to learn that Blankpayn was still away, and no one had any idea when he might be back. While Michael continued to quiz the tavern's occupants, Bartholomew's eyes lit on a man who sat in a dark corner, bundled in a hooded cloak. He went to stand next to him.

'I am not fooled by that disguise, Carton,' he said softly to the commoner Franciscan. 'And that means neither will anyone else. Michael's beadles are looking for Falmeresham in the taverns this morning – they will catch you here, and you will be fined for breaking University rules.'

'They have already been in,' replied Carton. 'But they know I am not here to cause trouble.'

'It will cause trouble if Blankpayn catches you spying in his domain. Leave the hunt to Michael's men. They know what they are doing.'

Reluctantly, the friar followed him outside. 'A dozen witnesses – us included – saw Blankpayn stab Falmeresham. It is *vital* we talk to him as soon as possible.'

'It is vital,' agreed Bartholomew. 'And any clues he provides will be carefully investigated. But not by you. You do not have the right kind of experience, and you may do more harm than good. If you care for Falmeresham, you will leave the matter to others.'

Carton's face was grim. 'Blankpayn is Candelby's lap-dog, and may well hurt a student to please him. He is a lout – all brawn and ale-belly, and not two wits to rub together.'

'Even more reason to leave him to the beadles.'

The Franciscan glanced up at the sky. 'I shall walk to Madingley, then, to visit his mother.'

'Cynric has already been. She has not seen him in months.'

'She would say that,' said Carton. 'He is her son. Of course she is going to help him hide.'

'Yes, but we are talking about *Cynric*,' said Bartholomew, not altogether approvingly. 'A man who never allows locked doors to keep him out. He searched her home from top to bottom – hopefully with her none the wiser – and says there is no sign of Blankpayn.'

Carton closed his eyes in despair. 'Then what *can* I do? Falmeresham is my friend, and I cannot stop thinking that he might need my help.'

Bartholomew felt much the same way. 'Go to the Carmelite Friary, and ask if any of the novices saw anything. If so, come back and tell Michael – do not race off to investigate on your own.'

Carton shot him a wan smile. 'I am not the kind of fellow who rushes headlong into danger without due thought. If the truth be told, I am something of a coward.'

Bartholomew was watching him walk away when Michael emerged from the tavern, leaving behind a number of angry men. They had resented his accusing questions.

'Nothing,' he said in disgust. 'Blankpayn has disappeared into thin air, just like his victim.'

As Bartholomew walked along the High Street, he stared at the jumbled chimneys of the Angel tavern, famous for its pies and for being owned by the University's most vocal opponent. The inn was massive, with whitewashed walls and well-maintained woodwork. It stood opposite the ancient church of St Bene't, and recently Candelby had objected to the fact that blossom from the graveyard blew into the street and became slippery when wet. Because the church was used mostly by scholars, he claimed the flowers were a University plot to make him fall and break his neck. When the accusation became common knowledge, students had raided the surrounding countryside for cherry saplings to plant.

'I searched the Angel when I was hunting for Falmeresham last night,' said Michael following the direction of his gaze. 'A group of lads from Clare was there, so I offered to waive the fine if they could tell me where Falmeresham had gone. None could, so they are all a groat poorer.'

'You said a Clare student was killed in yesterday's brawl,' said Bartholomew worriedly. 'I doubt his friends were at a town alehouse for peaceful reasons.'

'That did cross my mind, Matt,' said Michael dryly. 'Especially as the other victim was a pot-boy from the Angel. We shall have to stop at Clare on our way home, to make sure no one is planning revenge. Then we must do the same with the Angel.'

'I do not suppose they killed each other, did they? That would be a neat solution for you.'

'The bodies were found near each other, so it is possible. I have certainly encouraged my beadles to tell everyone that is the case.'

'But it may not be true.'

Michael regarded him soberly. 'No, it may not. However, I do not want more deaths on either side, and if a few timely lies can ease the tension, then I shall encourage them. Neither faction can justify a killing spree if both perpetrators are dead, and I must do all I can to avert strife.'

61

'Yet you plan to investigate Lynton's murder. That might ignite the situation.'

'You said we should keep details of Lynton's demise to ourselves. *Ergo*, no one will know I am investigating his murder, because no one will know he was murdered in the first place. It will require considerable skill to maintain discretion, but we can do it. We *must* do it.'

They walked in silence, cutting down several nameless alleys, until Michael stopped outside a pair of timber-framed houses. Both were hostels, although such foundations came and went with such bewildering rapidity that it took Bartholomew a moment to recall their names. Piron was a large establishment, built on three floors with a cellar below for storage. Its smaller neighbour was Zachary, named for the nearby church. Their principals were Tyrington and Honynge, respectively.

'I know we are desperate for another teacher,' said Michael. 'But I would rather be worked off my feet than appoint the wrong person – and I am not happy with either of these two.'

'You should have made more of a fuss at the meeting, then,' said Bartholomew tartly. He also thought his colleagues were making a mistake by opting to take whoever happened to be available, and was sure Carton would have been the better choice. 'It is too late now.'

'It is Honynge who is the problem,' Michael went on. 'Supposing he cheats us?'

Bartholomew was startled. 'There has never been any suggestion of dishonesty on his part, and you malign him unjustly. Besides, I have heard him in the debating hall, and he is impressive. He will improve Michaelhouse's academic reputation, and that is what counts.'

'You may not think so when he makes off with the College silver,' warned Michael coolly.

Bartholomew thought he was overreacting. 'Do you want to visit him or Tyrington first?'

'Tyrington. I am not ready for Honynge yet. Remember to stand well back when he speaks, and do not allow him to entice you into a scholarly disputation. We must make a start on this Lynton business as soon as possible, and have no time to waste on scholastic debates. Did you know both these houses are owned by Candelby?'

Bartholomew shook his head. 'I thought they belonged to Mayor Harleston.'

'He sold them. As you know, the University compels landlords to keep any buildings rented by scholars in good repair. But Harleston said he would rather sell his properties than pay for their upkeep when the only people to benefit would be University men.'

Bartholomew studied them. 'Piron is well-maintained, and it looks as though the work has been carried out recently. Zachary is shabby, though. Why has Candelby spent money on one building, but neglected its neighbour?'

Michael shrugged. 'Who knows what a man like Candelby thinks? Still, Honynge and Tyrington will not have to worry about him in the future. They will be comfortably installed at Michaelhouse.'

Their knock on Piron Hostel's door was opened by a well-dressed youth who wore a heavy purse on his belt. Bartholomew could see a blazing fire in the room beyond, and several books lay open on a table. Books were expensive, so it was clear that Piron was occupied by wealthy students who could afford such luxuries.

'Doctor Bartholomew,' said the student with a courtly bow. 'How kind of you to call. However, I am fully recovered now, and have no further need of your services.'

Bartholomew regarded him blankly, before recalling that

the lad had consulted him about a troublesome rash. He had prescribed a decoction of chickweed, which was usually effective against such conditions.

'I was actually cured by Magister Arderne,' the lad chatted on. 'He made me an electuary. I swallowed it all, and woke up with fading spots the very next day.'

'An electuary?' asked Bartholomew, startled. It was an odd thing to prescribe. 'What was in it?'

'Arderne declined to tell me, but it cost a fortune, so it must have been full of expensive herbs.'

'Indeed it must,' murmured Bartholomew. 'We are actually here to see your Principal. Is he in?'

They were led along an airy corridor that was paved with coloured tiles, and into a large room that boasted wood panelling and a pleasant view of the garden. It was elegant compared to anything available at Michaelhouse, and it occurred to Bartholomew that Tyrington would be taking a step in the wrong direction as far as personal comfort was concerned.

Tyrington was sitting at a desk, reading. He was a large, squat man with a low forehead and thick dark hair. He stood when the visitors were shown in, and smiled. Or rather, leered, because there was something about the expression that was not very nice. An image of a lizard Bartholomew had seen in France came unbidden into his mind, and he half expected a long tongue to flick out. When one did, he took an involuntary step backwards.

'Gentlemen,' said Tyrington affably. 'All our rashes are healed, so we no longer need the services of a *medicus*. My student hired Magister Arderne to do the honours in the end.'

'Everyone calls him Magister,' said Michael, going to the window to escape the saliva that gushed in his direction. None too subtly he ran a hand down the front of his habit

64

to wipe it off. 'But does he actually hold such a degree? He did not earn it from Cambridge, and our records show he did not get it from Oxford, either.'

'Probably Montpellier, then,' sprayed Tyrington. 'May I offer you wine? A pastry? We can always find victuals for men from a fine foundation like Michaelhouse.'

Michael was about to accept when it occurred to him that anything provided was likely to arrive with a coating of spittle. 'Actually, we came to ask whether you would consider becoming one of our Fellows. Unless you have had a better offer, of course, in which case we understand.'

'But we hope you have not,' said Bartholomew quickly. Fellows often stayed in post for years, and he did not want what might be a lengthy association to start off on the wrong foot because Michael was having such obvious second thoughts. 'It would be an honour to accept you.'

Tyrington flushed red with pleasure, and the tongue shot out again. 'You are inviting *me* to take Kenyngham's place?'

'To fill the vacancy he left,' corrected Michael pedantically, handing over the letter.

'Yes!' cried Tyrington. 'Of course I accept! May I bring my students? There are three of them – all wealthy and well able to pay a College's fees.'

'Three? In this huge building?' asked Michael. 'You could have twice that number.'

Tyrington leered. 'Yes, but I was loath to supervise more when I was on my own. Education is a sacred trust, and I have always refused to accept funds from students if I cannot offer them my very best. A College will be different, of course, because teaching is shared.'

'Perhaps Michaelhouse is not the right place for you after all,' said Bartholomew uneasily. Langelee and Wynewyk accepted funds any way they could get them, and the quality of the teaching provided in exchange was invariably deemed immaterial.

'I understand this house is owned by Candelby,' said Michael, looking around appreciatively. 'It is very well maintained – unlike most of his scholar-occupied buildings.'

'Our lease expires in September,' explained Tyrington. 'So he keeps the place in good order, because he wants to rent it to a rich merchant the moment we go.'

'Does that mean Honynge's lease expires at the end of the next century, then?' asked Bartholomew. 'His building is tatty compared to yours.'

'I believe it is due to lapse at the beginning of the upcoming term,' replied Tyrington. 'Perhaps Candelby wants it vacant before beginning a major restoration. We had to endure noisy builders last month, when we were trying to study, and it was very inconvenient.'

'Honynge will be pleased when he hears our invitation, then,' said Michael. 'He and you will be appointed at the same time.'

'He is a good choice,' said Tyrington sincerely. 'One of the best teachers in the University. His students are a bright crowd, too.'

'What about your three?' asked Michael. 'I assume you are willing to vouch for their academic merit? We are Michaelhouse, after all, and do not accept just anyone. We have standards.'

'Do you?' asked Tyrington. 'I thought Deynman was one of yours, and he is barely literate.'

'He is an anomaly,' said Michael icily. 'Carton and Falmeresham have won prizes for their disputations. Are you ready, Matt? We should deliver the news to Honynge before I lose courage.'

Tyrington grabbed Bartholomew's hand, tears in his eyes as he wrung it. 'Thank you! I cannot tell you what this means to me, and I promise you will never have cause to regret your offer. I shall strive to be the best teacher in Cambridge, and will make you proud to own me as a colleague.'

Bartholomew tried not to flinch from the deluge. 'Then let us hope you feel the same about us.'

The door to Zachary Hostel was opened by a student who was eating a pie that looked as though it came from the Angel. Although the building was unprepossessing on the outside, its occupants had made it comfortable inside. It was scrupulously clean, and there were bowls of crushed mint on the windowsills to mask the smell of cabbage. Someone had polished the furniture to a rich sheen, and the walls had been given a wash of pale gold, which lent each room a warm, cosy feel. There were prettily woven rugs on the floor, and an abundance of home-made cushions on the benches.

Roger Honynge was tall, thin and aloof. He had a narrow face and a long nose; his bony fingers were covered in ink, indicating he had been hard at work that morning. He was cool when Michael presented Langelee's letter, and did not smile when he opened it and read the contents.

'Well?' demanded Michael, when Honynge did nothing but stare out of the window. The visitors had not been offered a seat, and the monk disliked being obliged to stand while Honynge ruminated.

'I shall think about it,' replied Honynge. 'I know you are desperate for someone to teach the Trivium now Kenyngham is dead, but I never leap into such breaches without due consideration.'

'Very well,' said Michael. 'You can please yourself, because there are others who—'

'There are others,' agreed Honynge. 'But the best ones

have commitments, and cannot come to you immediately. The only scholars of quality available at this instant are Tyrington and me – and I can see why you offered me the post first.'

'Actually, we spoke to *him* first,' said Michael, seizing the opportunity to wound the man's pride. 'And we are not as desperate as you seem to think, because there are several monks at my abbey who would be willing to help us out for a term or so.'

'Do not let him leave,' whispered Honynge, as the monk headed for the door. 'It will be inconvenient, because you will have to go to Michaelhouse and deliver your acceptance yourself.'

'What?' asked Bartholomew, puzzled. He glanced behind him, wondering if a student had entered without him noticing, but no one was there.

'You can tell Langelee I accept his offer,' said Honynge. He brandished the letter in a way that was vaguely threatening. 'I have it in writing, so you cannot renege. However, there are three conditions. I am a light sleeper, so I must have my own bedchamber. I do not teach on Mondays, because that is reserved for my erudite research. And I do not eat dog.'

'Dog?' blurted Bartholomew. 'What makes you think dog forms part of the Michaelhouse diet?'

'Because it is not a wealthy College,' replied Honynge superiorly. 'Why do you think I am wary about accepting your invitation? However, I shall know if you give me dog and try to pass it off as mutton, so do not even attempt it.'

'We shall bear it in mind,' said Bartholomew, not sure how else to respond.

'Good,' said Honynge, adding in a mutter, 'That told them! They will not try to trick you now.'

'God's Blood!' swore Michael, as soon as they were outside. 'What has Langelee done?'

'Foisted a lunatic on us,' replied Bartholomew worriedly. He had not taken to Honynge at all. 'He spent more time talking to himself than to you and me.'

'My poor College,' groaned Michael. 'Invaded by drooling sycophants and madmen.'

When Bartholomew and Michael passed through the Trumpington Gate – Peterhouse stood outside the town's defences – the physician had the uncomfortable feeling that they might not be allowed back in again. The soldiers sided with Candelby in the rent war, and without Sheriff Tulyet to keep them in order, they were apt to be awkward and surly with scholars. He felt the purse that hung on his belt. It was all but empty, and he hoped Michael had enough for bribery, should the need arise.

Peterhouse was the oldest of the Colleges, a handsome foundation with a beautiful hall and pleasant living accommodation. Its chapel was the ancient Church of St Peter, which had been partly rebuilt and rededicated to the Blessed Virgin Mary after the plague. Michael knocked at the gate, and they followed a student across the cobbled courtyard to a house where the Master, Richard de Wisbeche, resided. Wisbeche was a scholarly man, famous for his skill in theological debates. He was growing old – Bartholomew recalled a time when he had sported a head of thick brown curls; now he was stooped, and his hair was grey. The physician thought about Kenyngham, and was unpleasantly reminded that everyone he knew was slowly heading towards the grave.

'Yesterday was a black day,' said Wisbeche softly, when his visitors were settled on a bench in his airy solar. 'You lost Kenyngham, and we lost Lynton. The world is a poorer place without them in it. Did you find your wounded student? Carton was here last night, asking if any of us had seen him. He was distressed when no one had.'

'Unfortunately not,' replied Michael. 'Falmeresham seems to have disappeared without a trace.'

'Have you considered the possibility that he may have fallen in the river or the King's Ditch? Both are swollen from spring rains, and will carry a body some distance before depositing it. I know, because I lost a favourite cat that way two weeks ago.'

'Cynric is searching the waterways as we speak,' said Michael. He saw the stricken expression on Bartholomew's face; no one had told him what the book-bearer was doing. 'I am sorry, Matt.'

'I understand a student from Clare was killed yesterday, too,' said Wisbeche. 'In that brawl.'

'And all because of this wretched rent dispute,' said Michael bitterly. 'It is getting way out of hand. Candelby does not care about averting riots, of course – all he wants is to make himself rich.'

'He is a merchant – that is what they do,' said Wisbeche. 'He says the low rents we pay mean he and his fellow land-lords are effectively subsidising the University. I can see his point – if he could lease to laymen, he could earn three times the amount he gets from scholars.'

Michael pulled a disagreeable face. 'Do not tell me *you* take Candelby's side? I am acting for the whole University here – indeed, there will not *be* a University if the rents are raised to the level Candelby demands. A little support from my colleagues would be appreciated.'

'You have it, Brother. I am just pointing out that there is another side to the argument – I am a scholar, after all, and that is what we are trained to do. Lynton was very vocal about the unfairness of the situation, and he never offered any of *his* houses to students. Why should he, when he could make far more money from townsfolk?'

Michael gaped at him. 'Are you telling me *Lynton* was a landlord? *He* owned buildings?'

Wisbeche looked disconcerted. 'I thought you knew. It was not a secret, although it was obviously not something he advertised. However, Lynton and Bartholomew were fellow physicians, so I assumed *he* would have told you about it.'

'I did not know,' said Bartholomew, when Michael spun around to glare at him. 'We never discussed houses – just medicine and the mean speed theorem.'

'Lynton was a successful practitioner,' said Wisbeche, when the monk's glower returned to him. 'And therefore wealthy. He owned three houses on the High Street, and two on the Trumpington road, all of which he leased to laymen. Students did come and demand that he lend the properties to them, but we have good lawyers at Peterhouse, and they helped him decline these requests legally.'

Michael was outraged. 'The Statutes say scholars have a right to use *any* available house. Lynton's refusal represents an offence against the University, no matter how the law was twisted to say otherwise.'

'We knew he was sailing close to the wind,' admitted Wisbeche sheepishly. 'But he did it for years, and no one ever objected.'

'No one objected because no one knew!' exploded Michael. 'What a time for me to find this out! Can you imagine what Candelby will say if he learns our own scholars prefer to loan their houses to laymen? And besides, Fellows – of any College – are not supposed to be awash with money and property. It is against the rules to earn more than ten marks a year.'

Wisbeche raised a laconic eyebrow. 'Oh, come now,

Brother! Surely, you do not believe anyone obeys *that* anti-quated decree?'

Michael rubbed his eyes wearily. 'Who will inherit all these buildings?' he asked, declining to pursue the matter. He did not have time.

'Peterhouse, of course. However, I can probably persuade the Fellows to donate one to the University. Would that compensate for Lynton's past misdemeanours?'

'It would be a start. Do you think his decision to lease his houses to wealthy townsmen made him enemies?'

Wisbeche was aghast. 'No! I do not think it was common knowledge that he was so rich – *you* did not know, and you are aware of most of what happens in the University. Why do you ask? Do you have reason to think someone delib-erately startled the horse that killed him?'

'Of course not,' said Michael hastily. 'I imagine he was well liked in your College?'

'Oh, *very* well liked,' averred Wisbeche, nodding earnestly. 'We enjoy a harmonious Fellowship at Peterhouse, and our students loved him. We will *never* replace him – not that we intend to try.'

'You will not appoint another physician?' asked Bartholomew. It was not good news. The town population was growing, and losing a practitioner would mean more work for those remaining.

'We will not,' replied Wisbeche. 'And a public announce-ment to that effect will be made this morning. We are strapped for cash, you see, because rebuilding the church cost more than we anticipated, so we cannot afford to renew the post. We only have six medical students, anyway, and I am sure you will not mind taking two. For Lynton's sake.'

'I have too many already.' Bartholomew saw Wisbeche's reproachful face, and thought how *he* would feel if someone had refused Kenyngham's students. 'But there is always room for a couple of Lynton's boys.'

Wisbeche took his hand, rather tearfully. 'Thank you. I shall not forget your kindness.'

'Can we see Lynton's corpse?' asked Michael, watching them coolly. He was angry, and felt betrayed. The Peterhouse physician had been a quiet, doddering fellow, and the monk would never have imagined him to be knee-deep in houses – nor would he have imagined him to be the kind of man who ignored University Statutes in order to make himself rich. He sincerely hoped no one else would find out, because it would weaken the case against Candelby so seriously that the University might have no choice but to capitulate to the landlords' demands.

Wisbeche eyed him with sudden suspicion. 'Why would you want to do that?'

'Because I need to record an official cause of death,' replied Michael. 'So Matt must ascertain whether a hoof struck his head, or whether his neck was broken by the fall.'

Wisbeche did not look entirely convinced. 'Very well, although I think I shall come with you.'

'Damn,' whispered Michael, as Wisbeche led the way across the cobbled yard. 'I shall have to divert his attention while you go about your business.'

The Church of St Mary the Less, so named to avoid confusion with the bigger, grander St Mary's on the High Street, boasted windows that allowed daylight to flood inside, and its churchyard was a haven of leafy peace, full of spring flowers. There was a large mound at the eastern end, where Peterhouse's scholars had been buried during the plague, but the bare earth had been claimed by grass and primroses, and it no longer stood as such a stark reminder of grimmer times.

Lynton was in the vestry. He occupied the College coffin, and his face was covered by a richly embroidered cloth. Wisbeche removed it gently, revealing the blood-matted hair underneath.

'A woman is coming to wash him this morning,' he said, to explain the apparent lack of care. 'But she was hired to do Kenyngham first, and then the tavern boy who died yesterday – Ocleye.'

'This is the first time I have been in your chapel since it fell down and you had to rebuild it,' said Michael, beginning to move away. 'It has been very tastefully remodelled.'

Wisbeche was flattered by the praise. 'Do you like the windows? I designed them myself.'

'Did you?' asked the monk, immediately heading for the one that was farthest from the bier. 'Is that a vulture or a woodpecker on the left?'

'A dove,' explained Wisbeche, evidently seeing nothing suspicious in the monk's sudden fascination with stained glass. 'It represents peace.'

Deftly, Bartholomew began his work, suspecting he would not have much time before Michael ran out of things to say – or Wisbeche realised the monk had staged a diversion. There was a cut on Lynton's temple, but the bone underneath appeared to be sound. It confirmed the conclusion he had drawn the day before – that Lynton would probably have survived the blow to his head.

Next, he pushed aside the fine clothes and inspected the wound in the chest. It was not large, but a prod with one of his metal probes told him that the missile had gone deep. He wondered whether the woman who was coming to clean the body would notice it, and point it out to Lynton's colleagues. But Wisbeche said she was the same crone who had been hired to tend Kenyngham, and Bartholomew knew Mistress Starre was unlikely to notice anything amiss, because she only ever washed the bits that showed. Yet he was unwilling to take the risk that she might decide to be thorough for once, so he took a piece of cloth and fashioned it into a plug. He slid it quickly into the hole, packing it down as tightly as he could. Then he smothered it with a thick, glue-like salve. When he had finished, the injury looked like something Lynton might have physicked himself, and was certainly not a blemish Mistress Starre would inspect. It was not a deception of which he approved – and he did not like to imagine what Lynton would have said about it – but if it prevented another brawl, then he supposed it was worthwhile.

Wisbeche was holding forth about eschatological symbolism, and although Michael's eyes were beginning to glaze, Bartholomew saw he had a few moments yet. A graze on Lynton's cheek – but a corresponding absence of marks on his hands – suggested he had not tried to break his fall. It made the physician even more certain that Lynton had been dead before the horse had bucked out of control and he had toppled from the saddle. Whoever had murdered him had been an excellent shot. It was not easy to hit moving targets, and suggested the killer owned considerable skill with his weapon of choice.

He was just setting all to rights when he saw something in Lynton's hand. Gently, he prised open the fingers to reveal a scrap of parchment – the old physician had been holding a document when he had died, and someone had apparently snatched it from him after his death, leaving a fragment behind. The fact that it had torn suggested it had been retrieved quickly, perhaps furtively, and that it had probably not been taken by anyone who had a right to it. Puzzled, Bartholomew peered at the letters in the faint light that filtered through Wisbeche's stained-glass windows. What he read made his stomach churn in alarm.

CHAPTER 3

Bartholomew did not want to share his findings with Michael until they were well away from Peterhouse, but returning to the town proved difficult. The soldier on duty at the Trumpington Gate claimed he did not recognise them, and refused to allow them through. Michael was first bemused, then indignant, and finally furious. He begged, cajoled and threatened, but the guard remained firm – they could not enter until someone came to vouch for them. They might have been stuck outside for hours, had Bartholomew's brother-in-law not happened to ride by.

'Stop playing the fool, man,' ordered Stanmore sternly. 'Of course you know Brother Michael – he fined you for relieving yourself against King's Hall last Christmas.'

'He looks different,' mumbled the soldier, sullen now he was caught out in a lie. 'Maybe he was not so fat then. Besides, he just tried to bribe me to let him in, and I got standards.'

'He did not slip you enough?' asked Stanmore. He turned to Michael. 'Incentives are more costly in the current climate of unease, Brother. Next time, you had better offer double.'

'He can offer triple, but I still would not take it,' declared the guard. 'Damned scholars! They invade our town, and start imposing rules that see us the poorer. I hope Candelby wins the rent war, because then we can start challenging all their other unjust laws, too.'

Stanmore leaned down from his horse to speak in Bartholomew's ear. 'The whole town is behind Candelby, so watch yourself. If you assume everyone is an enemy, you will not be far wrong.'

Bartholomew watched him canter away, feeling unease grow inside him. When he turned to look at Michael, he saw he was not the only one who was troubled.

'Lord!' muttered the monk. 'I knew the rent war was serious, but I did not anticipate that its repercussions would be quite so far reaching. Guards do not often reject bribes on principle.'

'Perhaps you should arrange another meeting with Candelby and the landlords, to try to resolve the situation before it grows any worse.'

Michael sighed his exasperation. 'Do you think I have not tried? Candelby refuses even to sit in the same room with me unless I agree – in advance – to let him charge whatever he likes. And because what he likes is three times the current amount, I cannot comply.'

'So you are at an impasse?'

Michael nodded, then sighed again. 'Tell me what you learned from Lynton's corpse. I hope it was something useful, because time is running out fast, and we desperately need answers.'

Bartholomew showed him the fragment of parchment he had recovered. 'This.'

Michael angled it to catch the light. 'This is part of one of our standard tenancy agreements. They outline the responsibility of a landlord to keep the building in good repair, and to stay out except for maintenance. And they order the leasing scholar to pay his dues on pain of excommunication. You have managed to acquire the bottom quarter. Where did you find it?'

Bartholomew told him.

'Look at the names,' he prompted. 'The two signatures – tenant and landlord.'

Michael turned it this way and that as he attempted to decipher the small words. 'One is Lynton's – I would recognise that flowing hand anywhere. And the other is . . . I cannot read it.'

'Ocleye.'

Michael looked first blank, then puzzled. 'Ocleye is the murdered pot-boy from the Angel – Candelby's inn. But this makes no sense. First, a pot-boy is unlikely to be rich enough to hire a house. Secondly, if he were, surely he would have signed an agreement with Candelby, his master?'

Bartholomew regarded him soberly. 'Exactly, Brother. I imagine Candelby would feel betrayed if he knew what Ocleye had done. And now Lynton and Ocleye are dead.'

'You think Candelby had something to do with their deaths? Hah! I *knew* it!'

Bartholomew was thoughtful as he considered what the find meant. 'So, two men did something of which Candelby would disapprove, and now both are dead – one during an accident in which Candelby was the second party, and the other in a brawl arising from that accident. Of course, it *may* be coincidence. However, in that case, why was the document torn from Lynton's dead hand?'

'I do not understand the last part.'

'It was snatched with enough vigour to rip it, which must have required a remarkable sleight of hand, given that the accident had attracted so many onlookers. That healer – Arderne – was there, and he has the air of a magician about him. Perhaps *he* took it.'

'Why would he do that? I can see why he might have shot Lynton – he is now *sans* one rival *medicus* – but why would he steal writs from his victim's hand?'

'Perhaps he thought it was something else.'

Michael disagreed. 'These particular documents are distinctive, even to the illiterate, because they are headed with red ink, and they all have that book motif at the top. They cannot possibly be mistaken for something different.'

'Then whoever took that one from Lynton made a dismal blunder, because he left the important part – the bit containing the names – behind. He might just as well have left the whole thing.'

Michael nodded, eyes gleaming. 'And his mistake means we have a clue. Of course, I have no idea why a rent agreement between Lynton and Ocleye should be important, but it gives us something to think about. Perhaps Arderne wanted to live in the house Lynton was about to lease to Ocleye.'

'How would killing Lynton – the landlord – help him achieve that end?'

Michael shrugged. 'Arderne was your suggestion as a culprit, not mine. Besides, there is nothing to say that the killer and the person who grabbed the agreement are one and the same. What else did you learn from Lynton's corpse?'

'That it was definitely the crossbow that killed him. The wound would have been instantly fatal. He fell from his horse as he died, and a hoof probably caught his head on the way down.'

'Someone must be pleased. He thinks the crime has gone undetected, because everyone is assuming the mare is to blame. What happens if the body-washer notices this wound?'

'I disguised it, and Mistress Starre is not the curious type anyway. What shall we do now?'

'Visit the Angel and ask questions about Ocleye. He is

a townsman, so his death is none of my affair, but your discovery suggests the matter might bear some probing.'

'Good,' said Bartholomew, beginning to walk more briskly. 'And while we are there, we can ask if anyone has seen Blankpayn.'

The Angel was set back from the road, separated from it by a pretty courtyard with a well. It was a substantial building, and offered rooms for travellers, as well as stabling for horses. It was known for clean bedding, sweet ale and generous breakfasts, as well as its famous pies, so was popular with visitors and locals alike. The main chamber was a large, busy place that smelled of pastry and wood-smoke. The flagstone floor was always scrupulously swept, and any spillages were immediately mopped up by Candelby's army of polite, well-dressed pot-boys.

The tavern was full for a morning when there was work to be done, but Bartholomew soon saw why. Candelby was in a chair near the hearth, holding forth. Sitting across from him was another familiar figure. Arderne was looking pleased with himself. He wore his scarlet robes, and through a window Bartholomew could see his brightly painted cart parked in the yard at the back of the tavern.

'You want a pie?' asked a yellow-haired pot-boy. He spoke softly, so as not to disturb the listeners. 'But be warned: Master Candelby says we cannot sell them to scholars any more, unless they pay triple.'

Michael grimaced. 'I wondered how long it would be before he decided to use his pies against us. But I am here to see your master, not to eat. You can talk to me while we wait for him to finish his yarn. How well did you know Ocleye?'

'Not very,' admitted the lad. 'He came to work here

fairly recently, and tended to keep himself apart from the rest of us. He was decent, though, and always shared the pennies he got from our customers, so we all liked him. I am sorry he was murdered by one of your lot.'

'And *I* am sorry he stabbed a scholar,' retorted Michael. 'But, as we have lost a man apiece, I hope the matter will end there. I do not suppose you have seen Blankpayn, have you? He seems to have gone missing – as has one of our students.'

'Falmeresham,' said the boy, nodding. 'Carton came here last night, asking if we had seen him.'

'And had you?' asked Bartholomew.

The lad shook his head, starting to move away. 'I saw him make a dive for Blankpayn, but then those Carmelite novices rushed me, and my attention was taken with fending them off.'

Bartholomew watched him go, then turned his attention to the gathering by the hearth. Candelby was still speaking, and his audience was listening in rapt admiration. Arderne looked like a cat that had swallowed the cream, relishing the awed looks that were continuously thrown in his direction.

'So Magister Arderne took his feather and tapped it three times on my left hand,' said Candelby. 'At first, nothing happened. Then there was a great roaring, and my senses reeled. I heard a snap, and when I opened my eyes, there was my arm as whole and sound as it had ever been.'

'Did it hurt?' asked Isnard the bargeman. It was a tavern, so Bartholomew was not surprised to see Isnard there. The chorister–bargeman liked ale, and his missing leg meant work was not always available, so he often had time to squander in such places.

'Not one bit,' declared Candelby. 'I thought it would – bone-setting is a painful process, as many of us can attest.

But when Magister Arderne cured me with his feather, I felt nothing.'

'Does he cure anything else?' asked Agatha. Bartholomew *was* surprised to see Michaelhouse's laundress in the Angel, because taverns tended to be the domain of men – and prostitutes – and she should not have been there. However, as she was larger than most male patrons, and infamous for her touchy temper and powerful fists, no one was likely to oust her.

'I have remedies for all manner of ailments,' announced Arderne grandly. 'Why? Is there something you would like me to repair? Or does your question relate to my other skills – for example, my ability to restore beauty to those of mature years?'

'*I* have no need of beauty potions,' said Agatha, astonished by the implication that she might. There was absolute silence as men held their breaths, lest even the merest sigh be misinterpreted. No one wanted to be on the wrong side of Agatha. 'But I would not mind a love potion.'

There was another taut silence, and the man sitting next to her gulped. He glanced at the door, as if assessing his chances of making a successful dash for it.

'I can provide you with one of those,' said Arderne, quickly regaining his composure. 'Of course, it will be expensive. Good remedies always are, which is why you should distrust the low fees of men like Robin of Grantchester. You get what you pay for in the world of medicine.'

'Is Robin cheap?' asked Michael of Bartholomew. 'I always thought him rather pricey.'

'I would say he is about average. I wonder why Agatha wants this potion.'

'It is for Father William,' said Michael with a malicious snigger. His chortling stopped abruptly as another possibility occurred to him. 'God and all His saints preserve us! I hope it is not for *me*!'

'Do you see yourself as irresistible to portly matrons then, Brother?'

Michael pursed his lips. 'I am irresistible to anyone. Powerful men always attract that sort of attention – just ask the King.'

Bartholomew laughed, appreciating a brief moment of levity in what had been a bleak few hours. Unfortunately, Arderne heard him. The healer stood suddenly and began to stalk towards them.

'Damn!' muttered Michael, as the tavern's patrons started to look around, to see where he was going. 'I wanted to catch Candelby alone, and we cannot risk a confrontation with this arrogant peacock. Do not let him goad you into an indiscretion, Matt. Not here.'

'Why would he want to argue with me?'

'Because Beadle Meadowman told me last night that Arderne has engineered public quarrels with all your medical colleagues – Robin, Paxtone, Rougham and Lynton. You have only escaped his vitriol because you have been busy teaching. Of course, the others are easy targets, and you will be far more difficult to harm. That means he will probably strike you hardest of all.'

'What do you mean?'

'Rougham is arrogant and objectionable, Lynton was narrow-minded, and Robin is a repellent creature, to put it mildly. Paxtone is competent – just – but the Cambridge *medici* are, on the whole, an unprepossessing shower. You are by far the best, so Arderne will see you as his most dangerous opponent. He will want to silence you as soon as possible.'

Bartholomew regarded him in surprise. 'Silence me about what?'

84

'About his dubious claims that a feather can mend broken bones, for a start. Here he comes. Be on your guard – and remember that we have a killer to catch. We have no time to waste on spats.'

'Speak of the Devil and he will appear,' drawled Arderne, as he approached. His unblinking eyes shone oddly, and his long black hair tumbled from under his red hat. 'I was just saying how the people of Cambridge have been badly served by dirty surgeons and ignorant physicians since the plague, and here is one of them.'

'Now just a moment,' said Isnard, hobbling over to join them. 'Bartholomew is a decent man. When my leg was crushed under a cart, he cut it off and saved my life.'

'If *I* had been here, there would have been no need for amputation,' declared Arderne. 'My feather would have cured your leg, just as it did Candelby's arm. Could *you* have salvaged Candelby's limb, Bartholomew? Or would you have lopped it off?'

'There is no way to know,' replied Bartholomew calmly. 'I did not examine Candelby's injury, so I am not in a position to offer an opinion about it.'

'That is a good point,' said Agatha, elbowing her way through the listening patrons to stand next to him. 'And the same might be said for Isnard's leg. You were not there, Magister Arderne, so how can you pontificate on what was, or was not, the right thing to do?'

Arderne shot her a pained look. 'I most certainly *can* pontificate, madam. *I* am a professional man with a wealth of experience. I do not hide behind excuses, but boldly offer my views when they are sought. And I could have saved your leg, Isnard. There is no doubt about it.'

'Really?' asked Isnard. 'I do not suppose you can make it grow back again, can you? This wooden one is all very well, but it keeps falling off as I make my way home from the alehouse.'

'I could try,' replied Arderne. 'My feather has worked miracles before, and will do so again. A cure will be expensive, but if you really want your leg back, you will not begrudge me the money.'

'I *do* want it back!' cried Isnard eagerly. 'More than *anything*.'

Bartholomew fought to suppress the anger that was burning within him. It did not take a genius to see that Isnard was gullible, and it was cruel to prey on his weakness. 'It has gone, Isnard,' he said quietly. 'And it will never come back. Do not squander your money on tricks.'

'Tricks?' echoed Arderne. 'How dare you! You have never seen me work, so you have no idea what I can do. My brother is the great John Arderne. Surely you have heard of *him*?'

'Why?' asked Bartholomew tartly. 'Is he in the habit of dispensing false hope, too?'

'Are you calling me a liar?' demanded Arderne, eyes blazing. 'You are not even a surgeon, but a physician who has no right to perform amputations. You are a disgrace to your profession!'

'Hey!' snarled Agatha. 'This is one of *my* Fellows, and anyone who insults him answers to *me*.'

'My apologies, madam,' said Arderne with a bow. He was not a fool, and knew when it was wiser to retreat. 'I spoke out of turn.'

'Yes, you did,' agreed Agatha, still glaring. 'I am going to finish my ale now, but I shall be keeping an eye on you, so you had better behave yourself.'

She stamped away, and most of the patrons followed, eager to discuss Arderne's remarkable claims among themselves, so it was not long before the healer was left alone with Bartholomew, Michael and Isnard. Candelby was itching to join them, but Agatha had cornered him, and was demanding to know the whereabouts of Blankpayn. The taverner was shaking his head rather desperately, trying to convince her that he did not know.

'Where did you earn your degree, *Magister* Arderne?' asked Michael, before Bartholomew or Isnard could resume the subject of missing limbs. 'Paris? Montpellier?'

'I do not hold with book-learning,' replied Arderne loftily. 'My great body of knowledge comes through observation and experience.'

'Why use the title, then? If you despise formal training, you should not need its trappings.'

'It is a form of address that people like to bestow on me,' replied Arderne smoothly. 'I do not want to offend them by declining it.'

'Are you really John Arderne's brother?' asked Bartholomew, changing the subject when he saw the man would have glib answers to account for all his deceits. 'I met him once in Montpellier, at a lecture on bladder stones. He told me—'

'I have not seen him in years,' said Arderne, rather quickly. 'However, I am his superior in the world of medicine. I am better than anyone in Cambridge, too.'

'Like Lynton?' asked Michael innocently. 'You are better than him?'

'Of course! He was a relic from a bygone age, and that made him dangerous.'

'So, you think Cambridge is better off without him?' pressed Michael.

Arderne regarded him with an expression that was impossible to interpret. 'Without question. And now I must be about the business of healing. I have a patient who wants a leg.'

'Make it grow back, then,' challenged Bartholomew.

He knew from the desperately hopeful expression on Isnard's face that the bargeman would never listen to reason. 'But he will not pay you a penny until you have succeeded – right down to the last toe.'

Arderne shot him a black look. 'That is not how it works. Do *you* wait until every patient is fully recovered before demanding recompense?'

'He does, actually,' said Isnard. 'And sometimes he forgets to ask altogether.'

'Well, I am not so careless,' declared Arderne in a voice loud enough to ring through the tavern like a bell. People stopped their own conversations to listen to him. '*I* am a professional. Do you have enough gold to pay me, Isnard? Miracles do not come cheap.'

Bartholomew was appalled. 'Isnard will lose everything he has,' he said to Michael. 'Do something!'

'Isnard's greatest failing is his propensity to believe anything he hears, especially if it is something he wants to be true. I can no more stop him from making Arderne rich than I can make him sing a soft *Te Deum*.'

There was a babble of excited conversation as Arderne strutted from the Angel tavern with Isnard limping at his side. The miraculous saving of Candelby's arm had captured public imagination, and folk wanted to be there when Arderne did it again. They started to follow him, and Bartholomew glimpsed the healer's grin of satisfaction when he realised his self-promoting declarations had worked. It was not many moments before the tavern was deserted, except for Candelby and his pot-boys. The servants began to clean up the mess left by the abrupt exodus, and the taverner himself came to see why two scholars should dare linger in his domain.

'I have nothing to say to you, monk – unless you have

come to your senses, and are here to tell me that I may charge what rent I choose in my own properties?'

'I do not own that sort of authority, as I have explained to you before,' said Michael. 'It would involve a change in the Statutes, and *that* would require a vote by the University's Regent Masters.'

'Then leave my tavern,' said Candelby, beginning to walk away.

Michael caught his arm. 'I am here about another matter – nothing to do with rents.'

'What?' demanded Candelby. 'The fact that I charge scholars more for my pies than I charge townsmen? Your Statutes cover the price of ale and grain, but they do not mention the price of pies. I can do what I like as far as pies are concerned.'

'How do you know what our Statutes allow?' asked Michael, rather coldly.

Candelby's expression was hostile. 'Because I have made myself familiar with them. They are keeping me from charging my tenants a fair rent, after all.'

'I hear you lost a pot-boy in the brawl yesterday,' said Michael, changing the subject abruptly in the hope of disconcerting him.

Candelby glared. 'Ocleye was a good fellow. I intend to offer a reward to anyone who provides information that exposes the vicious scholar who stabbed him.'

Michael was horrified. 'Please do not! It will result in a rash of unfounded accusations, because some folk will say anything for free pennies. You are almost certain to be led astray, and arresting the wrong man will lead to trouble. Your stance over the rents has already brought us to the brink of civil war, and this will make matters worse.'

'Rubbish,' snapped Candelby. 'I am just standing up for

what is right. I should be allowed to rent my own houses to whomsoever I like.'

'I did not write the Statutes – they were composed more than a century ago, so do not blame me. If you do not like them, go and reside in some other town.'

'I shall not!' declared Candelby hotly. 'It is your scholars who will leave, because either they will pay the rent *I* decide to charge, or they can live elsewhere. It is a straightforward choice. Personally, I hope they disappear – set up their nasty hostels in some other hapless town.'

Michael changed the subject, because they had been over the same ground a dozen times, and nothing would be gained by doing it again. 'I did not come here to fight,' he said tiredly. 'All I want is to gain a clear picture of what happened yesterday.'

'I was lucky Arderne was on hand to heal me. It is good to see medical care in the hands of a man who has nothing to do with the University. Patients will flock to him, leaving your scholar–physicians with nothing.'

'Yes, yes,' said Michael with an affected sigh.

'Your colleagues are hypocrites, Brother. You order me to lease *my* buildings to scholars, but Lynton rented *his* to townsmen. Did you know that?'

'Yes,' said Michael, abruptly taking the wind out of his sails. Bartholomew was uneasy, though, wondering how Candelby was party to such information, when Michael had only just learned it himself. 'And if he were alive, I would fine him for it. But let us discuss yesterday's events. Can you tell me exactly what happened?'

'I was in my cart, taking Maud Bowyer home after church. Ocleye was riding in the back. Suddenly, I heard a snap. I looked up, and there was Lynton, riding straight at me. The next thing I knew was that my wagon was in pieces,

90

Maud and I were in the wreckage, and Ocleye was fussing over me like a hen. Then Arderne arrived, and—'

'And he healed you with his feather,' finished Michael. 'I think we have heard that part enough times. Do you mind if my colleague inspects this miraculous cure?'

Candelby proffered his arm. 'He *should* see what lay-healers are capable of. Perhaps he will learn something. Ignore the discolouration, Bartholomew – Arderne says it will fade in two weeks.'

'Did Lynton say anything when he rode at you?' asked Michael. 'Were his eyes open? Where were his hands? Clutching his chest or holding the reins of his horse?'

Candelby shrugged. 'I have no idea – it all happened too fast. Ask Maud. She may remember.'

'We shall,' said Michael. He sighed again. 'Look, Candelby, Lynton was not the kind of man to commit murder, and anyone who knew him would say the same. I doubt he intended to harm you.'

Unexpectedly, Candelby relented. 'It did seem out of character. Let me think about your questions for a moment. I do not think he was holding the reins, but good horsemen control their mounts with their knees, so that is no surprise. He did not say anything that *I* heard. And I was more concerned with that great stallion bearing down on me, so I cannot tell you about his eyes.'

'It was a mare,' said Michael. He knew a lot about horses. 'And a comparatively docile beast. She must have been startled by this snap you said you heard.'

'It is possible,' acknowledged Candelby. 'The whole incident was dreadful, made worse by the brutal murder of Ocleye. And now Maud refuses to see me. I have asked Arderne to give her a potion that will bring her to her senses.'

'She refuses to see you?' asked Bartholomew, finishing his inspection of the man's arm. 'Why?'

'I wish I knew, but there is no fathoming the female mind. It is a pity you cannot ask Ocleye about the accident, but scholars certainly murdered him – probably that rabble from Clare. At least poor Ocleye took one of them with him.'

Michael was thoughtful. 'Yes, it is a pity we cannot speak to Ocleye. Tell me, does he have any family here, or close friends?'

'No one. He arrived at Christmas, and he was lucky I offered him employment, or he would have been destitute. Still, he was a decent soul.'

'Where did he live?' asked Michael, a little carefully. He did not want to give too much away about the parchment his Corpse Examiner had recovered. 'Here, or did he have his own lodgings?'

Candelby's face was inscrutable. 'He was a pot-boy, Brother, so what do you think? Now, is there anything else, or can I go back to work?'

'Just two more questions. First, how did Ocleye die?'

'He was stabbed in the chest by a student. The poor fellow lies in St Bene't's Church, so go and inspect him, if you do not believe me. Take your Corpse Examiner – he will confirm what I say.'

'Unfortunately, it is hard to distinguish between wounds made by townsmen and wounds made by scholars,' said Michael ruefully. 'If he could do it, it would make my work very much simpler. And secondly, have you seen your friend Blankpayn? He seems to have disappeared off the face of the Earth, along with one of our students.'

Candelby retained his unreadable expression. 'I have not seen either of them, although I understand the boy was grievously wounded when he raced to attack poor Blankpayn.'

* * *

Michael left the Angel tavern aware that they had learned nothing useful. Either Candelby was unaware that his potboy had signed a rental agreement with a scholar, or he was unwilling to admit to it. Meanwhile, Bartholomew seethed with frustrated anger at the taunt in the taverner's parting comment, and it had taken all the monk's diplomatic skills – and physical strength – to make him leave the tavern without throats being grabbed.

'He knows where Blankpayn is hiding,' the physician snarled, freeing the arm Michael held with rather more force than was necessary. Michael staggered backwards. 'But he refuses to help us.'

'Perhaps. However, I suspect he just wants you to *think* he does. He is trying to aggravate you.'

'He has succeeded.'

'Throttling him will help no one, satisfying though it might be. I will set Meadowman to watch him, and if Blankpayn visits, we shall know about it. You will have to be patient. I know it is difficult, but there is nothing else we can do. If we use force, it will cause trouble for certain.'

Bartholomew supposed he was right, and took a deep breath in an attempt to calm down. Absently, he noticed that Bene't Street was not as busy as it should have been at that time of day, and he wondered whether Arderne had taken half the town with him when he went to magic Isnard's leg back into place.

'Would you mind examining Ocleye?' asked Michael. He spoke tentatively. Bartholomew did not often lose his temper, and the monk was not sure how to react to it. 'He is not a scholar, and he did not die on University property, so technically my Corpse Examiner can refuse to do it. I know Candelby said he was stabbed, but I need to be sure.'

Bartholomew nodded, but his attention was still fixed on the tavern. 'Is that Honynge, just going into the Angel?'

'It is!' Michael's green eyes gleamed with delight at the notion of catching his future colleague flouting the rules. 'The more I deal with him, the less I like him.'

Bartholomew had not taken to Honynge either, and sensed the man's arrogance would create discord among the Fellows – William would take umbrage at his manner, and Michael would begin a war of attrition that would force everyone to take sides.

'I had better follow him, to see what he is doing,' said Michael, rubbing his hands as a plan took shape in his mind. 'If he is buying ale, I shall advise Langelee to withdraw the offer we made this morning.'

'You are too conspicuous – Candelby is sure to notice you. I will go.'

Michael reached out to stop him, sure it was an excuse to resume the conversation about Blankpayn, but the physician jigged away from his hand and began to trot back towards the inn. The monk started after him, but was no match for his more fleet-footed colleague.

'Do not to go in,' he called urgently, giving up when he saw it was hopeless. 'Just poke your head around the door and then come back and tell me what he is doing.'

Bartholomew ducked behind the courtyard well when he saw Honynge had not gone very far inside the inn. The cold fury he had felt towards Candelby was already subsiding, and his natural common sense was telling him that another confrontation would do nothing to help Falmeresham – and might even do some harm. With a sigh, he realised that shaking the truth out of the taverner would not be a good idea, and that Michael's plan to set Meadowman to watch him was far more likely to yield results. Immediately, he began to wish he had not offered to spy on the man who was to be his colleague. It was hardly ethical, and he sincerely hoped Honynge would not catch him.

Honynge and Candelby were near the entrance, talking. Unfortunately, a chicken chose that moment to announce the laying of an egg, and taverner and scholar turned instinctively at the abrupt frenzy of squawks. Bartholomew did not think they had seen him, but could not be sure. The two resumed their discussion, and after a moment Honynge's voice began to rise. Words quickly became audible.

'. . . an outrage,' he snapped. 'And I will not endure such remarks.'

'I do not care,' said Candelby. 'It is true. Michaelhouse *is* full of second-rate scholars.'

'Well, your pies are rancid,' retorted Honynge childishly. 'You probably make them with dog.'

He turned and stalked away, leaving Candelby to mimic his stiff-backed gait in a flash of juvenile petulance. The pot-boys grinned, but their smiles vanished when the taverner began to bark orders at them. Bartholomew moved further behind the well as the furious Honynge stamped past him, and was disconcerted to hear the man talking quite loudly to himself.

'You do not have to put up with his insults, not even for a pie. In fact, you should tell him his ale is not up to scratch, either.' He stopped, glared back at the Angel, but then resumed walking. 'No, you have more dignity than that. Go home and prepare for your removal to Michaelhouse.'

Bartholomew waited until he had gone, then set off to find Michael. He faltered when he saw the monk talking to Honynge himself, but Honynge did not linger long. He growled something, then continued on his way, anger radiating from him like heat from the sun.

'What did he say?' asked Bartholomew curiously.

Michael was bemused. 'He suggested I use my powers

as Senior Proctor to stop the Angel from trading. It seems Candelby said something rude about Michaelhouse, and he took it as a personal affront. Well? Was he buying ale?'

'Food – although I think he squabbled with Candelby before he could get any. He is an odd man. I would not have thought him the kind of person to leap to our defence – he made disparaging comments about Michaelhouse himself this morning – yet it seems he feels some spark of loyalty.'

Michael groaned. 'Lord! Now here comes Tyrington, grinning at us like a gargoyle. Will we *never* be allowed to investigate these murders? All I want is to concentrate on finding out what happened to Lynton and Falmeresham. Is that too much to ask? Tyrington is eating, by the way. This could be dangerous.'

'Good morning, colleagues,' gushed Tyrington. Bartholomew did not step away quickly enough, and found himself liberally splattered with cake. 'I cannot wait to be installed in your – *our* – College. Oh, the debates we shall have, on all subjects from theology to alchemy!'

'What about natural philosophy?' probed Bartholomew, prepared to overlook a few missiles of oral origin if the reward was a discussion on one of his favourite subjects.

Tyrington simpered at him. 'I have a great interest in anything that necessitates complex arithmetic and geometry, especially if it can be used to define our universe.'

'Really?' asked Bartholomew. 'What do you think of the work of the Oxford *calculatores*, who use mathematics to measure the increase and decrease in intensity of qualities—'

'Not much, if he has any sense,' muttered Michael.

Tyrington's leer threatened to split his face in half. 'It fascinates me deeply, particularly as it applies to what

96

happens in the first and last instants of potentially infinite processes.'

'I hope you two will not spend all your evenings *calculating* together,' said Michael coolly. 'There are other issues to debate, besides mathematics.'

Tyrington laughed uneasily, sensing he had annoyed the monk. He hastened to be conciliatory. 'There will be plenty of time for discourses on all manner of exciting matters, and I shall grant them all equal attention, I promise.'

Bartholomew watched him walk away. 'Lynton lectured on the work of the Oxford *calculatores* last term, and Tyrington made several intelligent contributions. Honynge was not there, though – I would have remembered *him*. I hope Honynge does not transpire to be one of those scholars only interested in discussing his own speciality, because he is a theologian and therefore dull—'

He faltered when he recalled that Michael's academic expertise was also in the 'Queen of Sciences', and shot him a sheepish glance. The monk smothered a smile. 'We have wasted too much time already today. Let us see what Ocleye can tell us.'

St Bene't's thick walls immediately quelled the clamour from the street, and the scholars' footsteps echoed softly through the ancient arches as they walked up the nave. The building smelled of the fresh rushes that had been scattered in the chancel, and of the flowers that had been placed along the windowsills in celebration of Easter. Bartholomew looked around appreciatively – he had always liked St Bene't's – but Michael was more interested in his investigation. He frowned when he removed the pall that had been placed over the coffin.

'Ocleye seems rather old to be called "boy" – he must

be nearing sixty! I was expecting an apprentice. Are you sure he is the right one?'

'I thought you knew him,' said Bartholomew, surprised. 'He was standing near Candelby after the accident – obviously, given that he had been riding in the back of Candelby's cart.'

'Candelby is a demanding master and servants tend not to stay with him long. Hence I know very few of them. But my point remains: Ocleye is old for such an occupation.'

'He was a newcomer, so probably took whatever work was offered.' Bartholomew began his examination. 'It explains why he wanted his own accommodation, though – a man of his years will not want to share an attic with a dozen rowdy youths. Yet Ocleye could not have been earning much, so I wonder how he intended to pay the elevated rent Lynton would have charged.'

'That is a question to which we must find the answer. It *cannot* be coincidence that Lynton was holding the agreement signed by him and Ocleye, and both end up dead on the same day. Do you mind hurrying? I know we have Candelby's permission to be here, but I would rather we were *not* caught pawing the body of a townsman – not in this current climate of unrest. What can you tell me? Where was he stabbed?'

'He was *not* stabbed,' replied Bartholomew. Michael looked sharply at him. 'I know Candelby said he was, but he is mistaken. This wound is too small and the wrong shape to have been made by a blade. It was caused by a crossbow bolt, just like the one in Lynton.'

Michael stared at him. 'Are you sure?'

'Of course – and I can prove it.'

The monk averted his eyes when Bartholomew took a pair of pliers from his bag and began to do something to Ocleye's chest. There was an unpleasant grating sound that made him feel queasy, and when he plucked up the courage to glance back, Bartholomew was inspecting something bloody that lay in the palm of his hand. It was the sharp end of a crossbow bolt, about the length of his little finger.

'It snapped off inside him,' explained the physician. 'I suspect someone tried to retrieve the whole thing, but this part was embedded in bone, and it broke as it was tugged out.'

'Are you sure it was not *that* injury which killed him?' asked Michael, pointing to a gash across Ocleye's ribs. He took several steps backwards when Bartholomew began to examine it, then squeezed his eyes tightly closed. '*Please* do not put your fingers inside corpses when I am looking! I missed your company when you took that sabbatical leave of absence last year, but I certainly did not miss this kind of thing!'

'I cannot determine the depth of a wound simply by staring at it. However, probing tells me this one is not serious enough to have caused death. The bolt in the chest was what killed Ocleye. No one could have been shot there and survived.'

'So, whoever killed Lynton killed Ocleye, too?' asked Michael. 'The murderer used the same weapon on both?'

'It looks that way. Ocleye died later than Lynton, though. I saw him after the accident myself, and he was definitely alive. Also, Candelby said Ocleye was fussing over him when he regained his wits after being thrown from the cart, so he is another witness. And finally, crossbows take time to rewind, so there would have been a delay. The brawl provided the killer with a perfect opportunity to claim his second victim.'

'So, we were right: Lynton's death and Ocleye's *are* connected. But how did Ocleye come by that other cut? Do you think the Clare student stabbed himself a corpse?'

99

'Or the killer scored the wound in an attempt to disguise the real nature of Ocleye's demise – to make people *think* he died from a dagger attack.'

'How could anyone expect to deceive you?'

'Ocleye was not a scholar, and he did not die on University property. *Ergo*, your Corpse Examiner has no reason to inspect him – and the body-washer has obviously noticed nothing amiss. Further, Ocleye has no family or close friends – no one to demand detailed answers.'

'Lord!' breathed Michael. 'I do not like this at all – not least because of what *we* have done.'

'What is that?'

'If the killer went to all this trouble with Ocleye, then it stands to reason that he does not want anyone to know what happened to Lynton, either. And what did you do? Steal the crossbow bolt from Lynton's corpse and later disguise the wound. Meanwhile, I am encouraging his colleagues to believe he died when the horse kicked his head.'

Bartholomew stared at him. 'We have helped a killer to cover his tracks.'

Bartholomew left St Bene't's full of anxious questions. Who had shot Ocleye and Lynton? How could a pot-boy afford to enter a rent agreement with a man who charged princely prices for his houses? Bartholomew's concerns returned to Falmeresham. What had happened to him? What did Candelby know that he was not telling? Was Michael right, and the man was just pretending to possess information in order to provoke a member of the hated University?

'I do not like Candelby's role in all this,' said Michael, when the physician voiced his concerns aloud. 'I think *he* might be the killer.'

'We know he is not – he was in his cart when Lynton was shot, and we believe the murderer hid in St John Zachary's churchyard.'

'You said the weapon was small, so perhaps Candelby concealed it under his cloak. Then he whipped it out and loosed a bolt as Lynton rode towards him.'

'Without Maud and Ocleye noticing?'

Michael shot him a triumphant look. 'Perhaps Ocleye *did* notice, and either threatened to tell, or demanded payment for his silence. And do not forget that Candelby said Maud is refusing to see him. Maybe she is uncomfortable with murder committed under her nose.'

'Even if all that is true, and Candelby *did* kill Lynton, he could not have shot Ocleye, too. Arderne had taken him away by the time the brawl started. He was not there.'

'He must have come back,' countered Michael. 'It was a perfect opportunity to blame a violent death on a street disturbance. And, not content with that, he now wants the town to believe Ocleye was killed by a scholar – to make him a martyr, so people will fight over it.'

Bartholomew considered Candelby as the culprit. 'I suppose he may have hired an accomplice, which would account for him being elsewhere when Ocleye was killed.'

'This rent agreement makes no sense, though,' mused Michael. 'Even if Ocleye did have hidden riches, why elect to do business with Lynton? Why not Candelby, his master? Candelby has vacant lodgings aplenty, because our students are beginning to move out – either he has declined to make repairs so the buildings have become uninhabitable, or he has refused to renew their leases.'

Bartholomew was becoming frustrated by the questions that tumbled unanswered in his mind. '*Why* does Candelby want the streets running with blood? Surely he must know that if the dispute escalates, rioting scholars are likely to target *his* properties? He might find himself with burned-out shells in place of his handsome mansions.'

'If our scholars do destroy his houses, we will be forced to pay him compensation. He is bound to claim a higher value than their actual worth; he may even come out ahead.'

'I am not unsympathetic to his grievances,' said Bartholomew, earning himself a glare. 'The University has kept rents artificially low for decades, and it *is* hard on the town.'

'If we allowed landlords free rein, they would charge a fortune. Scholars would spend all their money on housing, and would be unable to pay their academic fees. The University would founder and die. But I see we will not agree about this, so we had better discuss something else. What did you make of Arderne's miraculous cure? Candelby's arm looked horribly bruised to me.'

'Bruising is all that is wrong with it – Arderne did not knit shattered bones. I imagine it was numb immediately after the accident, which accounts for why it could be pulled around without pain. The "discolouration" Arderne says will fade in two weeks would have done so anyway.'

Michael grimaced. 'Even I can tell Arderne is a fraud, and it is clear that he intends to have Cambridge to himself, medically speaking. I only hope people see through his tricks before he does some serious harm – and not only to his hapless patients. He clearly wants to hurt you, too.'

'He can try. Leeches have invaded the town before, but they make promises they cannot keep, and it is not long before people turn against them.'

'You are underestimating the risk,' warned Michael. 'There is something charismatic about Arderne that makes people more inclined to listen – something to do with his eyes. But I see we will not agree on this, either, so we had better return to the subject of murder.'

Bartholomew was thoughtful. 'You are right to be suspicious of Candelby. He does have a powerful motive.'

Michael nodded. 'Jealousy – because Lynton was making money hand over fist by leasing *his* houses to townsmen, while Candelby himself is forced to accept pittances from scholars.'

'Is he your only suspect?'

'No. Lynton may have accumulated some dissatisfied patients. Plus we only have Wisbeche's word that Peterhouse is a peaceful College – we must ask others if there were private disputes among the Fellowship. And then, of course, there are Lynton's rival physicians.'

Bartholomew gazed at him in horror. 'You think Paxtone or Rougham might be responsible?'

Michael nodded slowly. 'Suddenly, a lucrative post is available—'

'It is not available. Wisbeche intends to keep it vacant, to save money.'

'But that decision has only been made public today,' argued Michael. 'Until then, we all assumed Lynton would be replaced. Peterhouse Fellows have a far more luxurious existence than those of us who live in most other Colleges, and it would not surprise me to learn someone had killed him for his post. Obviously, I know *you* are innocent, but I certainly hope no one saw you whip that bolt from Lynton's body or finds out that you later disguised the wound.'

'On reflection, they were stupid things to have done – at the time, I just wanted to avert trouble.' Bartholomew turned his thoughts back to Michael's distressing contention. 'But no one will think we physicians killed Lynton, Brother! I am happy at Michaelhouse, Paxtone is extremely well looked after at King's Hall, and Rougham is one of Gonville's founding Fellows, and will never leave it for another College. Of course, Arderne might fancy himself a University man.'

'He might – and it does not take a genius to see he is a ruthless villain who will stop at nothing to get what he wants. However, my favourite suspect remains Candelby. What did you think of his claim that he saw nothing suspicious when Lynton died?'

'He might have been telling the truth. Maud was with him, and he has been courting her for months. It is possible that he had no eyes for anything but the woman he loves.'

'Piffle! A man like him has eyes everywhere, even when his lady of choice sits at his side. We shall visit Maud this afternoon, and have her version of events.'

'We are due to attend Lynton's requiem mass in an hour, so it will have to be after that.'

Michael glanced up at the sky. 'Lynton puts me in mind of Kenyngham. I know you say his death was natural – and I said I believe you – but the letter offering me that reward keeps preying on my mind. Will you look at him again before he goes in the ground, just to be sure?'

Bartholomew suppressed a sigh. 'If you like, but I will find nothing amiss. He just died, Brother. People do. You should know that by now.'

'Yes, but they do it rather too often in Cambridge. I sometimes wonder whether I would be safer back at my abbey in Ely. I could be prior in a couple of years, and then I would have myself appointed as bishop somewhere. Not London – too many people. Ely or Durham would be best.'

Bartholomew struggled not to gape at him. 'Those are lofty ambitions.'

'Do you not think me capable? I have been running

the University for years, and the Church is not so different.'

'I suppose not,' said Bartholomew, declining to comment further. 'And you are right about one thing – it will almost certainly be safer than life in Cambridge.'

CHAPTER 4

The next day was windy, and bright white clouds scudded across a pale blue sky with the sun dodging in and out between them. It was Bartholomew's turn to preside over the morning debate, which he did with help from Carton, which was appreciated, and from Deynman, which was not. Meanwhile, Michael had persuaded several landlords to talk to him about the rent impasse, and was due to meet them in the Chancellor's office at St Mary the Great. The monk intended to reiterate the fact that he did not have the authority to triple the hostels' rents, and then inform the landlords that they would be considerably worse off if the King became involved – which he would, unless they came to their senses and agreed to negotiate a settlement.

Unfortunately for Michael, Candelby had got wind of the gathering, and was among the sheepish burgesses who were waiting at the church. Candelby refused to accept that he was breaking the law by ousting scholars from their hostels, and, in a calculated effort to annoy, repeated his ultimatum over and over again, simultaneously placing his hands over his ears so he could not hear anything the monk said. The meeting went nowhere, and Michael brought it to a close with a sigh of frustration. His agitation increased further still when Beadle Meadowman reported that he had made no headway in discovering Falmeresham's fate, and Junior Proctor Bukenham described two brawls between scholars and townsmen the previous night, one of which had ended in a fatal stabbing.

He sent a message to Michaelhouse, asking his Corpse Examiner to meet him at St Edward's Church the moment the disputation was over, and then struggled to find beds for scholars from Tyled Hostel and Cousin's Place, rendered homeless when landlords had refused to renew their leases. Bartholomew was waiting at St Edward's when he arrived, although it did not require an expert to tell him that the great slash in the student's abdomen had been the cause of death, or that it had been made by a knife. Monk and physician stared unhappily at the body.

'He was just a child,' said Bartholomew softly. 'No more than fifteen.'

'Old enough to shoot arrows at your brother-in-law's apprentices, though. Thank God he missed! We arrested his killer this morning, but many are saying the fellow was right to rid the town of a student who is overly eager for a fight. I have a bad feeling I might be calling on your services more often than I would like in future. Damn Candelby and his greed!'

'We should visit Clare,' said Bartholomew, keen to resume their investigation. 'It is all taking far too long, and I feel answers slipping away from us with every passing moment. Falmeresham . . .'

'We will find him,' said Michael, when he faltered into silence. But his voice lacked conviction, and it was obvious his hopes for a happy ending were fading fast.

'I am sorry I could not come with you to see Maud Bowyer yesterday,' said Bartholomew as they left the church. 'Prior Morden was ill again, and I could not leave him until I was sure he was feeling better. What did she tell you about the accident?'

Michael rubbed a hand over his eyes, tired and

disheartened. 'Nothing. She was too ill to receive visitors, so I had a wasted journey. It seems answers are destined to elude us on this case, Matt, no matter how hard we try to find them.'

It was not far to Clare, but the journey took longer than it should have done, because people were worried about the escalating trouble, and kept stopping Michael to ask about it. It was not just scholars who were concerned. Bartholomew's brother-in-law, Oswald Stanmore, demanded to know what was being done to defuse the situation, and the physician's sister, Edith, begged him to leave Michaelhouse and stay with her in Trumpington until the matter was resolved.

'He cannot leave me to fight this alone,' objected Michael, indignant that he had not been invited, too. Edith kept a good table, and the monk disliked the notion that his friend might spend the holidays eating while he quelled riots.

'He should,' said Edith, a little curtly. She and Bartholomew had always been close, because as ten years his senior, she had cared for him after the early death of their parents. 'The dispute is largely of your making. If you agreed to parley, then we might have some peace.'

Michael gaped at her. 'I have agreed to parley! In fact, I wasted a good part of the morning trying to discuss terms, but no one would listen to me. *I* am not the problem here.'

Stanmore scratched his neat beard. 'Candelby told us burgesses that he is willing to compromise, but you refuse to raise the rents by a single penny. And his henchman Blankpayn backs him up.'

'Lies!' cried Michael, incensed.

'Did you know Magister Arderne claims to have healed Blankpayn's leprous sores, Matt?' asked Edith, while the monk furiously regaled her husband with a catalogue of

Candelby's misdeeds and shortcomings. 'You told me leprosy was incurable.'

'Blankpayn did not have leprosy,' said Bartholomew, startled. 'I would have noticed.'

'Arderne said he did – and added that no *medicus* worth his salt should have missed it. It was a dig at you, of course. I detest that man!'

'Have you seen Blankpayn recently?' Bartholomew was more interested in soliciting information than hearing about the healer's mad claims. 'He has disappeared, along with Falmeresham.'

'I am so sorry.' Edith touched his arm in a gesture of sympathy. 'I know you were fond of Falmeresham, and he was close to graduating, too. It is a great pity.'

'He is not dead,' said Bartholomew sharply, not liking her use of the past tense.

She smiled sympathetically. 'Of course not. I will light a candle for him this afternoon.'

'You will need her prayers for yourselves soon,' said Stanmore, speaking through Michael's tirade. 'I understand you have elected Honynge and Tyrington to your Fellowship. You must have been desperate, because neither are men *I* would choose for company at the dinner table. Tyrington would spit all over the food, and Honynge would rather talk to himself than the person sitting next to him.'

Edith was more willing to see the good in people. 'Honynge is patient with his students, and Tyrington is amiable company.'

'Lord!' breathed Stanmore suddenly, beginning to pull his wife away. 'Here comes Robin of Grantchester. I can smell him from here, so forgive us for not lingering to greet him.'

Robin was looking even more disreputable than usual, because he had been drinking. He held a wine flask in his hand, his eyes were bloodshot, and his hair was lank and unkempt. When he saw Bartholomew, he staggered forward and grabbed his hand. The physician struggled not to recoil from the warm, moist palm and the stink of old blood that hovered around the man.

'Arderne will ruin us unless we make a stand,' the surgeon slurred. 'So you, Paxtone, Rougham and I must present a united front. Such tactics are working for Candelby – he has enticed other landlords to his side, and now the University is squealing like a stuck pig.'

Bartholomew freed his wrist. 'Arderne is a fraud, so it is only a matter of time before he—'

'You are wrong,' snapped Robin. 'He has already destroyed my practice, and it will not be long before he starts on yours. I am all but finished – and so will you be, if you do not resist him.'

Bartholomew was bemused. 'How can you be finished? He has only been here a week.'

'*Seven* weeks,' corrected Robin. 'He did nothing but sit in taverns at first, listening to gossip. Then he went into action. He cured two people I said would die, and that was just the beginning.'

'You do tend to make overly gloomy prognoses.' Bartholomew had 'cured' people Robin had said would not survive himself. 'You should consider being a little more optimistic.'

'But most of my patients *do* die,' wailed Robin. 'I only treat them as a last resort, when I might as well earn a bit of money from a lost cause. The latest disaster was over that Clare boy – Motelete. I saw him stabbed and went to help, but I failed. Publicly.'

'Did you see who killed him?' asked Michael eagerly.

Robin shook his head. 'All I saw was Motelete drop to the ground with his hand to his neck, blood spurting everywhere. I am a surgeon, and spurting blood is my cue, so I rushed forward to see if I could stem the flow. As you know, clean wounds can often be mended, and I was hopeful of a fee.'

'The good Samaritan,' murmured Michael.

'Motelete was gurgling and gasping, and I saw there was no hope. So I moved away, lest anyone think *I* had injured him because I was desperate for work. Well, I *am* desperate for work, but I—'

'Motelete died almost instantly?' asked Bartholomew.

Robin nodded unhappily. 'He twitched a while, then lay still. But all of a sudden, Arderne was looming over me. He had taken Candelby home, and had come out to buy tallow grease – something to do with waxing his feather. He ordered me to heal Motelete.'

'I thought you said Motelete was dead.' Bartholomew was becoming confused.

'He *was* dead,' cried Robin. 'But Arderne said he *could* have been saved if I had been any good at my job.'

There was a very real possibility that Arderne was correct. Robin was not skilled at his trade, and another surgeon might well have saved the boy's life. But it was not the time to say so.

'Buy a new coat, Robin,' suggested Michael kindly. 'People like a smart *medicus*, because he inspires confidence. Invest in some shiny new implements, and see what happens to your practice then.'

The surgeon looked ready to cry, but sensed he had been dismissed and slunk away. When Bartholomew looked back a few moments later, he saw two potters pick up some mud and lob it. Robin scuttled down the nearest alley like a frightened rat, and Bartholomew suspected they were kin to someone who had suffered the surgeon's clumsy ministrations. If word was spreading that Robin

111

was incompetent, then he could expect reprisals from a good many people. Perhaps he had been right when he predicted he was finished in Cambridge.

Ralph Kardington, Master of Clare, was a sallow-faced lawyer with a huge gap between his front teeth that made him lisp. It meant he was difficult to understand unless he spoke Latin, which he tended to annunciate more carefully than English or French. As a consequence, most scholars used Latin when they were with him, and because he seldom conversed with townsmen, he was left with the impression that every Englishman employed it all of the time. He often bemoaned the loss of the vernacular, and was invariably surprised when no one agreed with him.

'*Salve*, Brother,' he said, hurrying to greet his visitors. 'I assume you are here about Motelete? His body lies in the Church of St John Zachary. You *must* find the villain who dispatched him. First Wenden, now Motelete. What is the world coming to?'

'He refers to the Clare Fellow who died on Lady Day,' explained Michael in a low voice to Bartholomew. 'Wenden was killed by that drunken tinker, if you recall.'

'It is a pity Wenden's murderer fell in the river and drowned,' Kardington went on. 'It meant the affair was quickly forgotten, because no example was made of him. And now look what has happened – Clare has lost a second scholar to a townsman's spiteful blade.'

'I believe Motelete was killed by a pot-boy named Ocleye,' said Michael hastily, alarmed by the way the Master was blaming the town. If his students felt the same – or they heard Kardington hold forth about it – there would be bloody reprisals for certain. 'But Motelete made an end of his attacker before he breathed his last, so vengeance has already been had.'

112

'I heard these rumours, too,' replied Kardington, 'but they cannot be true. Motelete was a gentle, timid lad, and would never have harmed anyone.'

'He was killed during a brawl,' Michael pointed out. 'Gentle, timid lads tend to avoid those.'

Kardington was indignant. 'Lynton died right by our gates, so of course we all rushed out to see what was happening – it is human nature to be curious. Unfortunately, the situation turned violent faster than anyone could have predicted. You were there, Brother. You know I am right.'

'Matters did spiral out of control rather quickly,' the monk acknowledged cautiously.

'Poor Motelete! He was by far the quietest of my lads. Ask his friends – they will all tell the same thing. Are you sure Ocleye was his killer?'

'No,' admitted Michael. 'Not completely.'

Kardington sighed and some of the ire went out of him. 'If you conduct a thorough investigation, and at the end of it you say you *are* satisfied that Ocleye was the culprit, then that will mark the end of the affair for us. We trust you, Brother. You did track down Wenden's killer, after all.'

Michael was touched by his faith. 'Then I promise to do all in my power to find the truth. Do you mind answering a few questions about Motelete?'

'You may ask me, my Fellows or my students anything you like.'

'Did Motelete know Ocleye, or did he ever visit the Angel tavern?'

'No – to both questions. I know our undergraduates defy the ban on alehouses and sneak out to partake of the Angel's excellent pies, but not Motelete. He was too new and too wary, and had so far resisted his friends' attempts to include him in their rule-breaking.'

'How long had he been enrolled?'

'Two months or so. He hailed from near Ely, and this was his first time away from home. He was lonely and frightened, and was lucky we happened to have a vacancy. I do not think he would have fared well in a hostel – they can be rough places. Colleges tend to be more genteel.'

'So, the only people he knew were at Clare?' asked Michael, ignoring the gross generalisation.

'Yes. However, before you start thinking that one of *us* might have dispatched him, consider this: the moment punches started to fly, I ordered all my scholars home. The only one missing when we arrived was Motelete.'

'Will your students confirm this?' asked Michael.

'Ask them – they are in the hall with their Latin grammars. We can go there now if you wish.' Kardington shook his head sadly. 'Our boys must be fluent in Latin if they are to live in England. I spoke to Tyrington in English the other day, and he did not understand a word I said.'

'How did you resolve the situation regarding Spaldynge?' asked Michael conversationally, as they walked towards the hall. 'He sold a hostel that belonged to your College, which was remiss of him.'

'Remiss is one word for it,' replied Kardington. 'Borden Hostel was Clare property, and Spaldynge should have asked our permission before he hawked it.'

'He should not have sold it at all – with your permission or without it,' said Michael coolly. 'I issued a writ, requesting that all University foundations should hold on to any property until the rent dispute is resolved. But that is not what I asked: my question was what did you *do* about it? Did you send him down? Order him to repurchase the building?'

'It was too late for the latter,' said Kardington ruefully. 'Candelby declined to give it back to us.'

'Candelby?' Michael was aghast. 'Spaldynge disposed of Borden to *Candelby*? How could he, when every scholar knows Candelby is intent on destroying us? This is outrageous!'

Kardington looked pained. 'I know, and we are very sorry. Spaldynge has been reprimanded, and we have rescinded his Fellowship – he only holds the post of commoner now.'

Michael was unappeased. 'Is that all? He should be excommunicated! I doubt he got a fair price for this hostel if Candelby was the buyer.'

'Actually, he struck an extremely good bargain. He used some money to feed his students, but the rest is in our coffers. Had we known his lads were starving, we would have helped him out, but we thought he was exaggerating when he made his reports. The disaster was partly our fault.'

'Perhaps I should fine *you*, then, because someone should bear the consequences of his actions. That sale put me in a very awkward position, and Candelby—'

'So, you are minus two teachers now – Spaldynge demoted and Wenden dead,' interrupted Bartholomew, to prevent Michael from scolding the Master of a powerful foundation like an errant schoolboy. 'How do you manage with lessons?'

'Wenden actually did very little tutoring,' explained Kardington, shooting Michael an unpleasant look. 'And this is not generally known, but he held a non-stipendiary post anyway – we did not pay him to be here. So, we cannot appoint another Fellow in his place, because we do not have the funds for a salary – not that it really matters, given that his death did not rob us of a master, anyway.'

'When he was killed,' began Michael, regarding Kardington disapprovingly, 'you admitted that he had no

115

students and did not contribute to College life. You also told me that he was tolerated because he had promised to leave Clare all his money when he died. Unfortunately for you, when his will was read, you learned he had reneged on the agreement and left it all to the Bishop of Lincoln instead. Have I recalled the situation accurately?'

Kardington grimaced. 'That will was a vile shock, I can tell you! Still, it cannot be helped. Spaldynge is a better man, though. He continues to lecture, even though we have rescinded his Fellowship.'

'How noble,' said Michael acidly. 'Most men in his position would have slunk away with their tail between their legs.'

'There he is,' said Kardington, pointing to where a man with an unfashionable, shovel-shaped beard was ushering a group of students towards the refectory. 'You can berate him yourself, Brother, because I dislike being held responsible for what he did.'

Michael did berate the disgraced scholar. Spaldynge stood with his head bowed while the monk railed, but his jaw muscles worked furiously, and Bartholomew suspected he was more angry than chagrined by the reprimand. When Michael asked what he had to say for himself, Spaldynge made the pointed remark that the monk had no idea what it was like to be hungry.

'I have made my peace with Master Kardington and our Fellows,' said Spaldynge, rather defiantly. 'The sale of Borden is *our* business, and none of yours.'

Michael glared. 'If we want a University, then we must work together – we will not survive as an ad hoc collection of foundations. Your colleagues here may be willing to overlook your actions, but what about your colleagues in Ovyng Hostel or Peterhouse? What you have done affects them, too.'

Spaldynge grimaced. 'I have said I am sorry, and the sale cannot be undone. Besides, Lynton sold *his* properties when he felt like it, and you never subjected *him* to a torrent of abuse.'

'Lynton did no such thing,' said Bartholomew, when Michael seemed too astonished to speak. 'We know he owned houses, and that he rented them to laymen, but he did not sell them.'

'Of course he sold them,' snapped Spaldynge, while Kardington nodded agreement. 'Who do you think gave me the idea in the first place? I saw what Lynton was doing and followed his example. I should have known better. Physicians are reprehensible creatures, and to copy one was stupid.'

In a sudden flash of memory, Bartholomew recalled that Spaldynge had lost his entire family to the plague, and that he had never forgiven the *medici* who had taken his money for a cure but had failed to provide one. He reviled physicians at every opportunity, and Bartholomew was glad their paths seldom crossed. It occurred to him that Spaldynge's antipathy to members of the medical profession might have led him to dispatch one with a crossbow.

'Are you saying Lynton sold houses to *Candelby*?' asked the monk, finding his voice at last.

'I do not know the details of his transactions,' said Spaldynge. 'And I doubt he would have confided them had I asked. Perhaps he sold them to Candelby; perhaps he *bought* them from Candelby; or perhaps he declined to have anything to do with Candelby – I would not have done, but he offered a price so far above that of his nearest competitor.'

'Lord!' muttered Michael in Bartholomew's ear. 'First we learn Lynton is a landlord, and now we discover that he bought and sold houses like a drover with cattle. I am amazed.'

117

'He never expressed any interest in property to me,' said Bartholomew doubtfully. 'Do you think Spaldynge is telling the truth?'

'Kardington supported his claims, and *he* is no liar. So, we have another link between my main suspect and his victim: money may have changed hands between Candelby and Lynton. And money invariably brings out the worst in people.'

The Clare refectory was a pleasant, purpose-built hall overlooking the vegetable gardens. The window shutters had been flung open, filling it with bright spring sunshine and the scent of warm earth. The students looked blank when Kardington lisped orders at them, and they only understood that they were to talk about Motelete when he repeated himself in Latin.

A tall, gangling youth stood, and introduced himself as Thomas Lexham. 'Motelete was only here for a few weeks,' he said, 'but we all liked him.'

'He cried for his mother at night, and I had to show him how to sharpen his pens,' added Spaldynge. 'He was too soft to have killed Ocleye – he would not have known how.'

'Tell me what happened yesterday,' said Michael. 'From the beginning.'

'We heard a monstrous crash,' obliged Lexham. 'We thought it was Rudd's Hostel falling down at last, so we dashed outside to look. The only one who did not go was Spaldynge. He stayed behind, lest thieves used the opportunity as a diversion to burgle us.'

'It happened once before,' explained Kardington. 'Now we never leave the College unattended.'

'Rudd's has been on the verge of collapse all term, and we have bets on which day it will go,' Lexham went on.

'However, it was Candelby's cart that had made the noise – Lynton's horse had smashed it to pieces. We watched Arderne cure Candelby. He examined Lynton, too, but said that although he *can* raise men from the dead, he does not consider physicians worth the effort.'

'He said that?' Bartholomew was shocked by the claim as much as the sentiment.

'I do not like Arderne,' confided Lexham. 'He fixes you with those bright eyes, and you find yourself believing what he says, even though logic tells you it cannot be true.'

'Just keep to the facts,' prompted Kardington gently. 'Brother Michael does not want unfounded opinions – they will not help him learn what happened to Motelete.'

Lexham nodded an apology. 'So Arderne waved his feather, and Candelby said he was feeling better, but Maud Bowyer just sat and wept. Arderne tried to help her, but she pushed him away.'

'Did you see Ocleye at all?'

'We know him from the Angel—' Lexham stopped speaking as a groan from his cronies told him that he had just let slip a detail that was best kept from the Senior Proctor.

Michael raised his eyebrows. 'Your fondness for that particular tavern is hardly a secret, and on Sunday evening, I caught you there myself, if you recall.'

'You fined us,' said Lexham resentfully. 'It is not something we are likely to forget. We wanted to talk to Ocleye's friends, to see if he had mentioned a plot to kill a scholar.'

Michael was angry. 'That might have precipitated another brawl.'

'But we had to do something!' cried another lad. 'Motelete was one of *us*! We could not sit at home and do nothing. We needed to know if his murder was planned or an accident.'

119

'And which do you think it was?' asked Bartholomew.

The student grimaced. 'We still do not know. The Angel pot-boys said Candelby would dock their pay if they gossiped to us while they were working, and we did not like the sound of meeting them behind the Carmelite Friary after dark, like they suggested.'

'Thank God for small mercies,' muttered Michael. 'At least you have some sense. But let us return to the accident. What happened after Arderne's advances were rejected by Maud?'

'A crowd had gathered, and we were worried by all the jostling that was going on,' replied Lexham. 'The Carmelites like a good squabble, and I was afraid they might bring one about. Then you arrived, and everything calmed down.'

'The next thing I recall is Falmeresham,' said Kardington, frowning. 'He darted forward in a way that made me think he was going to punch that horrible Blankpayn.'

'As soon as that happened, Master Kardington ordered us all home,' Lexham went on. 'Motelete and I were at the back. I thought he was behind me, but when I reached our gate, he was gone.'

'Did he speak to anyone before he became separated from you?' asked Bartholomew.

Lexham shook his head. 'He did not know anyone outside Clare.'

'Did he ever quarrel with any of you?' asked Michael.

As one, the students laughed. 'Never!' said Lexham. 'He was too polite. I cannot imagine how he would have managed his disputations, when he never wanted to tell anyone he was wrong.'

'He was a child,' elaborated Kardington. 'Does he sound like the kind of fellow to dash into a brawl and go a-killing?'

'No,' admitted Michael. 'So, we had better look at his body. Matt is good at finding clues invisible to the rest of us. He may discover something that points to Ocleye as the culprit.'

As they left the hall, Bartholomew spotted a scholar who had been one of his first patients in Cambridge – and Master Gedney had been old then. Gedney had been a brilliant theologian in his day, but now he spent his time eating, complaining or dozing by the fire. For the last decade, Bartholomew had been treating him for weak lungs, and was astonished the man had survived so long. Unfortunately, Gedney had grown forgetful as well as curmudgeonly, and had developed a habit of addressing his colleagues by the names of men who had died years before.

'Babington,' he said when he saw Bartholomew. 'Do you still have that book I lent you? Holcot's *Postillae*? I want it back.'

Michael and Kardington exchanged a grin – it was well-known in the University that the physician would never read a text on scripture when ones on natural philosophy were available.

'How are you feeling today, Master Gedney?' Bartholomew asked politely.

Gedney lowered his voice. 'This College is full of madmen. They told me it was Easter the other day, when I know it is Harvest. Did you hear that one of our students was killed in a fight? His name was Tyd, a loud-mouthed fellow who drank too much.'

'Was he?' asked Michael. 'Everyone else says he was quiet and gentle.'

'Well, *they* are all senile,' confided Gedney. 'So you should take what they say with a pinch of salt. Is that a herring on your shoulder, Brother? I like herring, but I have not eaten one since the Death, because Babington here says they make you bald.'

'Do herrings make you bald?' asked Michael of Bartholomew. 'I have noticed a certain thinning in front of my tonsure, so perhaps I should abstain from now on. I do not like herrings anyway.'

'I looked up Holcot's *Postillae* in our library records,' said Kardington, leading the way across the yard. 'Gedney loaned it to a man more than forty years ago, and it was never returned. It seems the matter still preys on his mind – such mind as he has left.'

The Church of St John Zachary, where Motelete's body lay, was a small building that stood on the corner of Milne Street and one of the many lanes that led down to the river. It served as chapel to Clare and Trinity Hall, but was closer to Clare. It stood in a leafy graveyard that was in desperate need of pruning, but that was unlikely ever to see a pair of shears. It was technically a parish church, and therefore the responsibility of the town, but most of its congregation had died during the plague, and the few who remained objected to spending vast sums on a place that was used mostly by the University. Meanwhile, the two Colleges saw no reason to divert their own resources to repair someone else's property.

The lack of care showed not only in the wilderness of the cemetery, but in the building itself. Its stained glass had been broken long ago, and the stone tracery in its windows had crumbled. The only way to keep weather and thieves out was to board them up, so all the south-facing windows were permanently sealed with thick wooden planks. The north side was in a better state of repair because it formed part of Clare's boundary wall, and the scholars did not want a ruin in their grounds. Here all the windows had shutters, although they were sturdy and could only be opened from the outside – the Fellows were worried about townsmen gaining access to their compound, and the shutters protected their College, not the church. The only exception was the window in the Lady Chapel, which was left open when the scholars were at their prayers, to allow light into what was otherwise a very dark place.

The roof also needed urgent attention, but the spiral stairs that gave access to it had collapsed the previous winter, meaning repairs were out of the question. The fall had resulted in a chaos of rubble in the stairwell, which no one had bothered to remove. The churchwardens had placed ropes across the entrance, to stop anyone from trying to use it, then put the mess from their minds. It was not uncommon to hear the hiss and patter of falling plaster during services, and Bartholomew often wondered how long it would be before the rest of the building gave up the ghost, too.

Kardington did not bother with the main door, which stood on Milne Street, but used the window in the Lady Chapel to enter the church. Crude wooden steps had been built to allow Clare scholars to climb up to the chest-high windowsill from their garden, but there was only a table on the other side, and some major leaps downwards were required. Michael objected vociferously, first about the height of the jump, and then about the fact that the opening was rather narrow for a man of his girth. In the end, he decided the manoeuvre could not be safely accomplished, so Spaldynge was obliged to escort him to the front door instead.

While he waited for the monk to arrive, Bartholomew looked around him. It was cold in the building – far colder than outside – and he shivered. The roof leaked so badly that there was barely a dry spot in the whole chapel, and the once-bright wall paintings were all but indistinguishable. There was a smell of rotting thatch, damp and incense, and the physician found it hard to imagine what the place had looked like in its heyday.

Motelete was in the Lady Chapel, which was in a slightly better state of repair than the rest of the building. He lay in the parish coffin, covered by thick blankets, as if some sensitive soul had not wanted him to be cold. Bartholomew stared down at the still, pale face, and felt an overwhelming sorrow that someone so young should have died. The clothes around Motelete's neck were stained with so much blood that it was clear one of the great vessels in the throat had been severed. His skin was white and waxy, too, another sign of death by exsanguination.

'I doubt we will find a crossbow bolt here,' said Michael softly in the physician's ear. 'Even I can see that he died from his throat being cut. Do you agree?'

Bartholomew nodded, and pulled back the clothes to inspect the wound. It was difficult to see much, because the chapel was gloomy and gore had dried around the boy's neck. He was about to ask for a lamp when there was a rattle of brisk footsteps, and he glanced up to see Arderne striding towards them. The healer was not alone; Candelby and several burgesses were at his heels, while Robin of Grantchester hovered tipsily at the rear.

'Magister Arderne,' said Kardington in surprise. He spoke Latin. 'What are you doing here?'

'I heard the Senior Proctor and his Corpse Examiner were going to inspect the body of the boy Robin failed to save,' boomed Arderne, once Spaldynge had translated. 'So, I came to watch.'

'I did my best,' bleated Robin. Several Clare students exchanged grim looks, and Bartholomew suspected more clods of mud were likely to be flying the surgeon's way. 'But the cut was fatal, and the situation hopeless.'

Arderne sneered. 'You could have *tried* to stem the bleeding. You did not bother, so you killed him with your ineptitude. Tell him, Bartholomew.'

'Robin may have arrived too late to make a difference,' hedged Bartholomew, unwilling to be used as a weapon to attack a colleague. 'Patients can die very quickly with these sorts of—'

'Rubbish!' snapped Arderne. 'You are siding with him because he is your friend. Robin was there the moment this lad was viciously assaulted, because he was hoping to earn a fee. He claims to be a surgeon, so he should know how to stop a wound from bleeding.'

'You see?' said Spaldynge to his colleagues, his voice thick with disgust. 'What did I tell you? There is not a medical practitioner in Cambridge who knows what he is doing.'

'There is now,' declared Arderne. '*If* you can afford me, of course. I do not come cheap.'

Disgusted with the man's self-aggrandisement, Bartholomew turned his attention to the corpse, and was about to resume his examination when Arderne elbowed him out of the way.

'Let me,' ordered the healer. He leaned down. 'Here is the gash that caused his demise – you can see the incised vessels quite clearly. However, I have rescued men from a state of death before. I may be able to bring this lad back to life.'

'Do not play games, Arderne,' said Bartholomew sharply, aware of the hopeful looks that were being exchanged between Motelete's classmates.

Arderne ignored him. He removed a feather from his bag, and passed it several times up and down the body. 'Yes, I sense life here.'

125

Bartholomew was too exasperated to contradict him.

The healer tapped Motelete sharply on the chest. 'Open your eyes,' he commanded. 'I know you can hear me, so show us you are alive. Come on, lad. Wake up!'

Bartholomew gaped in shock when the corpse's eyes flew open and Motelete sat up.

Thomas Kenyngham, founding Fellow of Michaelhouse and one of its most popular Masters, was buried that afternoon. He went into a vault in St Michael's chancel, to join several other scholars who rested there. It started to rain the moment the funeral procession began, a heavy, drenching downpour that turned the streets into rivers of mud and soaked through the mourners' clothes. The church was bursting at the seams, because many people had loved Kenyngham's quiet gentleness, and it was not only Michaelhouse scholars who wanted to pay their last respects.

Before the ceremony began, Bartholomew had slipped away to the old man's bier. Motelete's return from the dead had unsettled him so much that he performed a small, discreet examination while his colleagues greeted the many guests who had been invited to attend. Only when he was absolutely certain that Kenyngham was truly dead did he leave the coffin and return to his other duties. Michael regarded him with raised eyebrows.

'No blisters in the mouth?' he whispered. 'Or tiny wounds in the head or chest?'

Bartholomew did not like to admit that it was the possibility that he misdiagnosed death that had driven him back to the old man's body.

'Of course not,' he snapped, his distress over Kenyngham and his unease over the Motelete affair making him uncharacteristically irritable. 'No one harmed him.'

Michael frowned unhappily. 'So you said, but I cannot put that letter from my mind. Supposing it is *not* a hoax – that the writer has good reason to urge me to look into the matter?'

'Then why does he not come forward openly? As I said at the time, Brother, it is just someone trying to cause trouble. Do not let him succeed.'

Michael did not look entirely convinced, but he forced a smile. 'Then let us hope you are right. There is bitterness enough already, without one of Cambridge's most-loved residents being brutally slain.'

'Bitterness? Over what?'

'Over the fact that Motelete could be raised from the dead, but Ocleye could not. Candelby asked Arderne what could be done for his pot-boy after he had finished with Motelete. I followed them to St Bene't's, where Arderne said the only reason he could do nothing to help Ocleye was because a Corpse Examiner had laid tainted hands on him first.'

'Surely people do not believe such nonsense?'

'Townsmen do, because it is another reason to be angry with us. But regardless of what people think about *that* claim, Motelete is powerful proof that Arderne possesses talents you do not. Bringing someone to life after two nights in a coffin is a remarkable achievement.'

'Yes,' said Bartholomew unhappily. 'Spaldynge mentioned that, too, in one of his vicious diatribes against physicians. Arderne told Spaldynge that *he* could have saved the whole town from the plague, and Spaldynge believes him. He hates us more than ever now.'

Michael rested a sympathetic hand on his arm. 'We should discuss this later – the Gilbertine Friars have just arrived, and we must go and talk to them.'

The rain had stopped by the time the rite was over, and

people milled in the churchyard. They ranged from the Mayor and his burgesses, all wearing at least one garment of black to indicate not only their sense of loss but their adherence to courtly fashion, to a small army of beggars who had benefited from Kenyngham's generosity. Isnard was there, too, tears flowing down his leathery cheeks as he told people how Kenyngham had sent him money for food when he had been too ill to work. He led the Michaelhouse Choir in an impromptu *Requiem*, which came to a sudden and merciful end when Langelee whispered that free ale was waiting for them back at the College.

Bartholomew did not feel like going home, and lingered in the cemetery talking to his medical colleagues, Rougham of Gonville and Paxtone of King's Hall. Rougham was a bulky, belligerent man who had once opposed Bartholomew's methods violently, but who had since buried the hatchet. They were not friends, but they rubbed along amiably enough, and even consulted on difficult cases. Paxtone was kinder, friendlier and much more likeable, although he was firmly of the belief that no medical theory was worthwhile unless it had been written down for at least three hundred years; newer ideas were regarded with deep suspicion before being summarily disregarded. Paxtone was not as fat as Michael, but he was still a very large man, who looked even more so because his bulk was balanced atop a pair of impossibly tiny feet.

'I do not feel well,' said Paxtone, rubbing his stomach. It was the wrong thing to say to two physicians, because they immediately began to ask questions, Bartholomew about the nature of his diet, and Rougham about his horoscope. It occurred to Bartholomew that he should be concerned about one physician being unwell so soon after the murder of another, but he pushed the notion from his

128

mind. Paxtone was a glutton, and had probably overeaten again. His malady was nothing sinister.

'You need a clyster,' said Robin. His soft voice made them all jump because they had not seen him approach, and had no idea he had been listening. 'I have devised a new recipe that includes extra lard, and I rinsed my pipes in the river only last month. I will perform the operation, if you like.'

'No, thank you,' said Paxtone, unable to suppress a shudder. The notion of having an enema from the unsavoury Robin was the stuff of nightmares. 'It is kind of you to offer, but I ate a bag of raisins last night, and we all know what Galen says they do to the digestive tract.'

'Do we?' asked Robin warily. 'What?'

'I am more sorry about Kenyngham than I can say,' said Rougham to Bartholomew. 'And I am sorry about Lynton, too. He was not an innovative practitioner, but I shall miss him nonetheless.'

'So will I,' said Paxtone, grateful to be talking about something other than clysters. 'He was studying Heytesbury's writings, and was going to deliver a special lecture on them next term. It is a pity we will never hear what more he had to say on the matter.'

'What matter?' asked Bartholomew. 'The mean speed theorem?'

Paxtone nodded. 'You and he discussed it a month ago in St Mary the Great, and he enjoyed it so much, that he was going to ask you to meet him at the *Disputatio de Quodlibet*. Did he tell you?'

Bartholomew shook his head. Only the very best thinkers were invited to take part in the *Disputatio de Quodlibet*, the University's most prestigious forum for scholastic debate, and he was flattered that Lynton had chosen him as a sparring partner – or would have done, had someone not put a crossbow quarrel in his heart.

'The mean speed theorem is a popular subject these days,' Paxtone went on. 'But unfortunately, I cannot see men wanting to pursue it now Lynton is dead. It is a great pity.'

'Arderne is not here, thank God,' said Robin, looking around at the other mourners. 'I thought he might put in an appearance, given that he sees every gathering as an excuse to promote himself at the expense of the rest of us.'

'What do you mean?' asked Rougham sharply.

'He has been telling folk that none of us are any good,' elaborated Robin. 'He has even gone as far as whispering to some people that their loved ones would still be alive had I not intervened.'

'He *has* made derogatory remarks,' acknowledged Paxtone, graciously not pointing out that they were probably accurate in Robin's case, 'but I ignore them. Besides, his claims about his own skills are rash and stupid – he cannot possibly achieve some of the things he says he can do.'

'He claimed he could raise Motelete from the dead, and look what happened,' said Bartholomew.

'Are you sure the boy was really a corpse?' asked Rougham sceptically. 'I have my doubts.'

'He was dead,' said Robin firmly. 'I put a glass against his mouth to test for misting, I looked in his eyes, and I saw the wound on his neck. Arderne must have used witchcraft to raise him.'

'Do not say that!' cried Paxtone in alarm. 'Once one *medicus* is accused of being a warlock, it is only a matter of time before we all join him on the pyre. Keep such thoughts to yourself, Robin.'

'Perhaps he did manage something remarkable with Motelete,' conceded Rougham reluctantly, 'but his cure of

Candelby is bogus. The man's arm was not broken in the first place.'

'I agree,' said Bartholomew. He pointed to where Candelby was flexing the afflicted limb in front of a dozen awed burgesses. '*He* would not, though.'

'It is a pity Arderne could not help Maud Bowyer,' said Paxtone. 'Word is that the poor woman is not at all well. She refuses to let Candelby in to see her.'

'Perhaps the accident brought her to her senses,' said Rougham unpleasantly. 'She should not have allowed herself to be courted by such a worm. He is determined to destroy our University, you know.'

'I will see you later, Matthew,' said Paxtone, moving away rather suddenly. 'Here come the two men Michaelhouse has nominated as its new Fellows. I wish you every happiness of them.'

'You must have been desperate,' said Rougham, also beating a hasty retreat. 'Tyrington is decent enough – or would be, if you could cure his spitting – but Honynge's tongue is too sharp for me.'

'We came to lend our support, Bartholomew,' said Tyrington. His leer was less predatory than usual, perhaps because he knew it would be inappropriate to do too much grinning at the funeral of the man whose post he had been invited to take. 'Michaelhouse is our College now, and we felt we should be here, despite the fact that neither of us knew Kenyngham very well.'

'He was very old,' said Honynge, 'but I am sure you will miss him anyway. Is there anything we can do? No? Good. That will leave the rest of the day free for packing my belongings.'

'I am sorry,' said Tyrington, watching him walk away. 'If I had known he was going to be brusque, I would have kept him away from you.' He narrowed his eyes suddenly.

'Is he talking to himself? His lips are moving, and he is shaking his head.'

'He seems to do that rather a lot.'

'Then perhaps that is why he is so rude – he spends so much time in his own blunt company that he does not know how to moderate himself when he meets folk who are more civil.'

Michaelhouse was home to a sombre gathering that night. The students were unusually subdued, and there was none of their customary laughing and chatter. Meanwhile, the Fellows struggled to make conversation in the conclave, but soon gave up and sat in silence. Kenyngham's funeral had upset them all, and it had not been just the younger scholars who had wept.

The fireside chair usually occupied by Kenyngham – the best seat in the room – had been left empty, and Bartholomew wondered how long it would be before someone else would use it. Michael sat opposite, squinting at a Book of Hours. The light was dim, and Bartholomew knew he could not see well enough to read it; he supposed the monk's thoughts were either with Kenyngham or on the murder of Lynton. Langelee was at the table, going over the College accounts with Wynewyk. They made the occasional comment to each other, but neither sounded as though the matter had his full attention. Bartholomew was marking a logic exercise he had set his first-years, although he was aware that he was not catching as many mistakes as he should. He was bone-weary from orchestrating yet another hunt for Falmeresham, this time using all his medical students. It had proved as fruitless as all the others, and when darkness had forced him to abandon his efforts, he had been all but overwhelmed with feelings of helplessness, frustration and despair.

Finally, Father William was reading a tract by a Franciscan called Bajulus of Barcelona, who had written that Blood Relics – drops of Christ's blood – were a physical impossibility on the grounds that anything holy would have risen with Him at His Resurrection; only unholy substances would have been left behind on Earth. This contention was hotly opposed by the Dominicans, because of the implications for the Transubstantiation at masses, and the resulting schism was tearing the Church apart. Unfortunately, William had scant understanding of the complex theological issues involved, and his chief concern was just to oppose anything postulated by members of a rival Order. Every so often, he would give a small, crowing laugh, or snort his satisfaction.

It was not long before Michael became annoyed with him.

'I fail to understand why you feel compelled to produce all these cackles and hisses,' the monk snapped, after a particularly loud explosion of delight. 'Blood Relics are nothing to snigger over.'

'I am merely voicing my appreciation for Bajulus's argument,' said William. He was used to Michael venting his spleen on him, and insults and put-downs were like water off a duck's back. 'He *proves* we Franciscans are always right in theological matters. I wonder what Honynge and Tyrington think about Blood Relics. I know you all agree with me, so I hope *they* do not elect to be controversial.'

'I doubt they would dare,' muttered Langelee. His Fellows did hold opposing views – they just chose not to air them with William. The Franciscan was not a good intellectual sparring partner, because he was in the habit of stating his opinions, then declining to listen to the other side. Michaelhouse was used to his idiosyncrasies, but the new members were going to be in for a shock.

'When do they arrive?' asked Bartholomew.

'The day after tomorrow.' Langelee held up his hand when he saw the startled expressions on his colleagues' faces. 'I know it is sudden, but there are reasons for having them installed quickly. First, we need someone ready to take Kenyngham's classes as soon as possible, and secondly, we would have lost Tyrington to Clare had we not acted promptly.'

'Clare wanted him?' asked William. He looked pleased. 'And we got him first? Hah!'

'We pre-empted St Lucy's Hostel, too,' added Langelee, a little smugly. 'Honynge's lease on Zachary is due to expire at the end of this week, and when Lucy's heard about it, they raced around to ask him to be *their* Principal. Had Michael delivered our invitation a moment later, Honynge might have been lost to us.'

'Damn!' murmured Michael. 'Damn, damn!'

'We are lucky to get him,' said Langelee, shooting the monk a warning look. 'And I want you all to make him welcome when he arrives. He fulfils all our academic requirements perfectly.'

'There is that, I suppose,' conceded Michael. 'Although I cannot say I like him. Still, at least you do not need to wear an apron when you talk to him, as you do Tyrington.'

'Tyrington said kind things after Kenyngham's funeral,' said Wynewyk. 'But when I spoke to Honynge, I had the impression it was a three-way conversation – between me, Honynge and Honynge.'

'I hope he does not give us a reputation for lunacy,' said William. He turned to Langelee before anyone could point out that Michaelhouse was already famous for owning several strange Fellows, and that William was one of them. 'I wish they were not coming quite so soon, though. There will be no time for us to grow used to the fact that Kenyngham is gone.'

'I know,' said Langelee sympathetically, 'but term starts next week, and we need Tyrington and Honynge to begin teaching. We are all stretched to the limit, and cannot manage any more classes.'

'You must be pleased about Motelete, Brother,' said Wynewyk, after a short silence. 'It is one less death for you to investigate, and will give you more time to devise a solution to the rent war.'

Michael nodded. 'It was a shock, though. Robin had pronounced Motelete dead from a cut throat and Matt had begun his inspection of the corpse – which had been in its coffin since Sunday. Then Arderne waved his feather, and all of a sudden, the lad was sitting up.'

Bartholomew regarded him unhappily. 'Men do not rise from the dead – it is impossible.'

'And yet it happened,' said Langelee. 'There were dozens of witnesses to the fact, because all Clare was there, along with Candelby and several influential burgesses.'

Bartholomew rubbed his eyes, still not sure what to think. 'Motelete was cold, white and waxy, and there was a lot of blood around his throat from what looked to be a fatal wound. He was—'

'Then Arderne's claim must be accurate,' interrupted Langelee. 'A fatal wound is a fatal wound. I worked for the Archbishop of York before I became a scholar, and I know all about cut throats.'

There was an uncomfortable silence. No one was quite sure what Langelee had actually done for the Archbishop of York, and the occasional oblique remark like that one did nothing to dispel the notion that his duties had had very little to do with religion.

'What happened to the wound after Motelete started walking around?' asked Langelee, when no one said anything. 'Did it disappear completely?'

'When I wiped away the blood, all that remained was a scratch,' replied Bartholomew. 'But I must have been mistaken. People do not—'

'Corpses are always rising up when they lie at the tombs of saints,' interrupted William.

'But this did not happen at the tomb of a saint,' Bartholomew pointed out. 'It happened in a half-derelict church, and was instigated by a man with a feather. I do not trust it – and I do not trust Arderne. I have no idea how he did it, but I cannot believe a miracle was involved.'

'I have heard of cases where a person was pronounced dead, then started hammering on his coffin as it was lowered into the ground,' said Langelee. 'Perhaps Motelete was one of these – he *looked* dead, but there was life still in him.'

'Such cases are very unusual,' said Bartholomew, not entirely happy with that explanation, either. He knew, with every fibre of his being, that Arderne was a fraud, so how could *he* have detected a rare condition when a fully qualified physician had missed it? Or was Bartholomew losing his touch? He thought back to the many other corpses he had assessed, and sincerely hoped he had not misdiagnosed death before.

'How do you know they are unusual?' asked William. 'The churchyards might be full of contorted skeletons, all scratching furiously at the soil in their desperation to escape.'

'Please, Father!' cried Wynewyk with a shudder. 'That is an unnecessarily grotesque image to put in our minds before we go to sleep.'

'Well, whatever happened, it is good for Motelete,' said Langelee, bringing an end to the discussion. 'And I am delighted for him and for Clare. They may have lost Tyrington – and that horrible Wenden, who was killed last month – but they have managed to keep hold of Motelete.'

'Then let us hope he stays alive,' said William. 'I am told the town is furious that he lives, when Ocleye remains dead. It would be a pity if he was murdered a second time.'

CHAPTER 5

When the oil in the lamp ran out and the conclave was plunged into darkness, Langelee suggested his colleagues go to bed, because they could not afford to burn more fuel that night. Unusually, the students had retired before them, despite the fact that there was oil aplenty in their lantern, and Bartholomew supposed none of them had felt like talking after Kenyngham's funeral. The Fellows walked in a silent procession through the hall, down the stairs and into the yard, where they stood in a circle, reluctant to relinquish each other's company and be alone with their thoughts. The moon was out, dodging between clouds, and the buildings loomed black against the night sky. The College was strangely quiet, and there was none of the usual sniggering and arguing that could be heard most evenings as the students readied themselves for sleep.

'We should not linger here,' said Wynewyk, glancing around uneasily. 'Arderne delivered a love-potion to Agatha today, and she is refusing to say which poor devil has attracted her interest.'

'It will not be you,' said William baldly. 'You have always declared a preference for men.'

'Is it you, then?' asked Wynewyk archly. He eyed the friar in distaste, his gaze lingering on the filthy habit and unsanitary hands. 'I would think she was more discerning.'

'I would not take her anyway,' declared William. 'I am a man of God, and I have foresworn sinful relations. Besides, she is not my type – she is too opinionated.'

'If it is me she wants, she will be disappointed,' said Langelee. 'I have a strong mind, and will resist Arderne's concoctions with no trouble at all.'

'What do you think is in it, Matthew?' asked Wynewyk. 'I have read that mandrake has the ability to make men fall passionately in love.'

'It can also kill them, because it is poisonous,' replied Bartholomew tartly. 'However, it is expensive, and I do not see Arderne wasting it in potions that will not work anyway.'

Yet when the laundress appeared in the yard, hollering for the College cat to do its duty with a mouse, the Fellows bade each other a hasty goodnight and headed for their quarters at considerable speed. Langelee was the only one with a chamber to himself, although it was not much bigger than anyone else's. Wynewyk roomed with three civil lawyers, and William had two Franciscan novices. Bartholomew would normally have had Falmeresham for company, but although Cynric had unrolled the lad's mattress and set his blankets ready, the pallet remained empty and was a sharp and painful reminder that he was still missing.

The sight of it made the physician restless, so he lit a lamp, intending to work until he fell asleep. Most scholars could not afford the luxury of a private lantern, but Bartholomew's travels in France the previous year had put him at the Battle of Poitiers. He had fought, although neither well nor badly enough to have attracted attention, but the King had been grateful for his services to the injured afterwards, and had paid him well. Unfortunately, his reward was rapidly dwindling, because he was in the habit of offering free remedies to his poorer patients. Falmeresham constantly warned him against the practice but Bartholomew thought there was no point in ministering to the sick if he did not also provide them with the means to facilitate their recovery. Langelee, of course, was delighted by the goodwill Bartholomew's generosity was earning Michaelhouse, especially at a time when the town was beginning to rise up against the University.

The physician was writing a treatise on fevers. He had intended it to be a short guide for students, but it had expanded well beyond that, and was reaching mammoth proportions. He picked up a pen, but his thoughts kept returning to his absent student, and eventually he grabbed his cloak and set off across the yard.

'Where are you going?' asked his book-bearer, who was enjoying a cup of wine in the porters' lodge with the morose Walter. Cynric was a small, compact Welshman with grey streaks in hair that had once been black. He had been with the physician ever since a chance encounter during a riot in Oxford, and was more friend than servant. 'It must be almost nine o'clock – very late.'

'To look for Falmeresham.'

'Again? Then I had better come with you.' Cynric's voice told Bartholomew there was no point in saying he wanted to go alone. The Welshman excelled at sneaking around in the dark, and his eyes were already gleaming at the prospect of a nocturnal adventure.

Walter's long, gloomy face was a mask of disapproval. 'Master Langelee said not to let anyone out after dark, because the town is uneasy. He does not want trouble.'

'There will be no trouble,' said Cynric confidently. 'Not as long as I am with him.'

Reluctantly, Walter opened the gate and ushered them out. Cynric waited just long enough to satisfy himself that it had been properly secured again, then raised enquiring eyebrows.

'I was going to search the bushes in the graveyard of St John Zachary,' explained Bartholomew. 'Perhaps he crawled there, to escape the mêlée.'

'I have already looked, boy,' said Cynric gently. 'Twice. But we can do it again, if you like. We should be careful not to be seen, though. It will look odd if we are caught poking around in a cemetery at this time of night.'

Bartholomew sighed tiredly. 'True. Perhaps this is not such a good idea.'

Cynric grinned conspiratorially. 'Almost certainly, but why should we let that stop us?'

'Right,' said Bartholomew weakly, wishing Cynric was not always so eager to do things that were either shady or downright illegal.

They spent an hour rooting through the moonlit undergrowth around the Church of St John Zachary, Cynric shoving the physician into the shadows when the nightwatch passed, or when the last of the revellers emerged from the nearby taverns. Apart from them, the streets were deserted. When no sign of Falmeresham was forthcoming, Cynric suggested looking in Clare itself. The College had substantial grounds, and although Kardington claimed every inch had been scoured for the missing student, Cynric pointed out that the scholars would have been distracted by the news of Motelete's death, and might not have searched very carefully.

Bartholomew regarded him uneasily. 'Why would Falmeresham be inside Clare?'

'Why would he be here?' countered Cynric, gesturing at the cemetery. 'You think he may have crawled into these bushes to escape the brawl, so perhaps he limped to Clare for the same reason. The gate was open, because all the scholars had rushed out to gawp at the accident – I saw it ajar myself. Anyone, including Falmeresham, could have gone through it.'

'He would not have gone inside Clare,' insisted Bartholomew. 'He has no friends there.'

'It was the nearest point of refuge – *I* would have gone there, had *I* been injured and there was a riot erupting around *me*. It may be a rival house, but you are all scholars, and he knew he would have been safe. He may have staggered into a thicket and lost consciousness.'

'We could wake Kardington, and ask him to look again.'

'At this hour?' asked Cynric incredulously. 'He would think you had gone stark raving mad! Besides, he will accuse you of questioning his honesty, because he told you he had searched every nook and cranny. No, boy. It is better that we take matters into our own hands.'

Bartholomew gazed at the high walls with some trepidation. 'You expect me to scale those?'

'They were built to repel invaders,' acknowledged Cynric approvingly. 'However, I know a place where the mortar has fallen away, affording plenty of good hand- and footholds.'

'Why am I not surprised?' muttered Bartholomew ungraciously. 'Can we not find a way through St John Zachary instead? It backs on to Clare, and if we—'

'Impossible,' said Cynric with such conviction that Bartholomew was left in no doubt that he had already tried. He did not want to know why. 'It is easy to get inside the church from Milne Street, but even a mouse could not go from it to Clare. Those scholars knew what they were doing when they blocked all the windows with such heavy shutters.'

He led Bartholomew to the back of the College, where the wall was lower and older, and cupped his hands to make a stirrup. With grave reservations, Bartholomew placed his foot in the cradle, then yelped in surprise when he was propelled upwards faster than he had anticipated.

'Lower your voice,' hissed Cynric sharply. 'We do not want to be caught doing this – it would be difficult to explain. And watch yourself on the top of the wall. It has sharp metal spikes embedded in it, designed to make thieves think twice about scrambling over.'

Bartholomew smothered a curse when the warning came too late. 'Have you done this before?'

There was no reply, and suddenly Cynric's dark form was beside him. The Welshman clambered over the lethal spikes like a monkey, then swarmed down the other side. Bartholomew was slower and less agile, and by the time he reached the ground he had ripped a hole in his hose and skinned his knuckles. It was a small price to pay, he thought, if they found Falmeresham.

Clare's benefactress had been generous. Not only had she provided her scholars with a fine hall and several houses, but she had also given them a large plot of land. Herbs were being cultivated in neat squares, and beds were dug over for onions, leeks, carrots and cabbages. Bartholomew was looking around uneasily, when Cynric gripped his arm and pointed. They were not the only ones to be invading Clare – someone else was creeping slowly towards the College buildings.

Bartholomew and Cynric watched the hooded figure skirt the vegetable gardens and aim for the main hall. The man was trying to move stealthily, but all the care in the world did not stop him from being perfectly visible in the bright light of the full moon.

'Do you recognise him?' asked Cynric, his breath hot against the physician's ear.

Bartholomew shook his head. 'He knows where he is going, though, because he has not stopped once to orientate himself. It must be a student, sneaking home after an illicit evening in a tavern.'

'He has gone straight into the hall,' whispered Cynric.

'So you are probably right. But this is not helping Falmeresham, so you keep watch while I explore these fruit trees.'

While Cynric jabbed about with a stick, Bartholomew stared at the darkened College, waiting to see if the figure would reappear. It was late enough that even the most studious of scholars had given up his books for the night and had gone to sleep, although there was a lamp burning in the Master's house. Kardington was evidently entertaining, because Bartholomew could hear two distinct voices. He went to investigate, wondering what topic could keep men from their beds until such an unsociable hour. Kardington was a skilled and entertaining disputant of theology, and the physician was sure that whatever he was saying would be well worth hearing. It occurred to him that they might be discussing Blood Relics, and that he might learn something to improve his understanding of the subject if he moved close enough to listen. Or perhaps they were talking about Falmeresham, and eavesdropping would yield some clue as to his whereabouts; he knew it was unlikely in the extreme, but he was tired and desperate, and could not stop himself from hoping.

He padded across the garden until he was directly under the window, and insinuated himself into the shrubs at the base of the wall. Kardington and his guest were in the solar on the upper floor. They were speaking softly, but the shutters were open, and their words carried on the still night air.

'. . . had no right,' came a voice that Bartholomew recognised as that of the Master. He was speaking Latin, of course. 'It was not yours to sell, and the whole town knows it.'

'It is unfortunate,' said his companion apologetically. 'And your ready forgiveness of me is giving rise to speculation

144

and suspicion. I would not have harmed the College for the world, and I wish there was something I could do to remedy the situation.'

'I know that, Spaldynge. But it is a pity you traded with Candelby, of all men. He is determined to destroy the University, and you have provided him with ammunition.'

'Do you think Michael will win the fight?' asked Spaldynge. His tone was uneasy.

'I hope so, because if he loses, the University will cease to exist in a few years – or will be reduced to a few struggling Colleges. If that happens, Clare may be blamed, because you tipped the balance by selling Borden Hostel to the enemy. But what is done is done, and dwelling on the matter will help no one. How are your students settling in? Going from a small hostel to a large College must be difficult for them.'

'They will be all right. I am sorry to say it, but it is easier without Wenden. He had a cruel tongue, and would have made them feel unwelcome.'

'I would have ousted him years ago, had I known he was going to renege on our agreement and omit Clare from his will. The money you raised by selling Borden arrived just in time, or we would have been reduced to eating the kind of low-quality fare endured by Michaelhouse.'

'It serves them right,' said Spaldynge bitterly. 'They train physicians, so I hope they starve.'

'Speaking of physicians, Arderne's miraculous healing of Motelete means we have attracted attention – and attention is something we do not want at the moment, given . . . well, you know.'

In the bushes below the window, Bartholomew grimaced, wishing Kardington would be more explicit. Then he happened to glance across the yard and saw a figure slinking stealthily towards him. He could tell, from the shape of the hood on the cloak, that it was the same person who had been lurking about earlier. So, he thought, it had not been an errant student after all. He watched the man edge closer, and began to feel uncomfortable. Kardington's lamp and the full moon were throwing a fair amount of light into the garden, and he was not as invisible as he would have liked. Could the hooded intruder see him, and was coming to flush him out?

But the figure was moving furtively, and would surely have shouted for help if he intended to expose an invader. With a sudden flash of understanding, Bartholomew realised that the fellow's intention was to hide among the shrubs and eavesdrop on Kardington, too. There was certainly not enough room for both of them, and the physician saw he was going to be caught. For a moment, he could do nothing but watch in alarm as the man advanced across the yard. Then a plan snapped into his mind. He cupped his hands and blew into the hollow between them, making a noise that roughly approximated the hoot of an owl. The shadow stopped dead in its tracks.

'That was very close,' said Kardington, puzzled. Bartholomew heard footsteps tap across wooden floorboards as the Master came to look out of the window.

'It was not like any owl I have ever heard.' Spaldynge's voice suddenly became shrill as his finger stabbed the air above Bartholomew's head. 'Someone is there! We are being burgled again!'

'Ring the bell!' shouted Kardington. 'Hey, you! Stop where you are!'

The hooded figure turned abruptly, and broke into a run. He headed straight for the crumbling wall, moving even faster when Spaldynge's hollers began to wake others. Two night-porters appeared at the far end of the College and started to give chase. Bartholomew grimaced. He had intended to drive the other man off, not initiate a hunt. What should he do? Try to lay hands on the intruder, on the grounds that the fellow's business in Clare was clearly far from innocent? But then how would he explain his own presence? And what if *he* was captured and the hooded man escaped? Kardington would assume, not unreasonably, that it had been the physician he had seen tiptoeing towards his quarters.

Clamours and alarums in the middle of the night were not uncommon in Cambridge, and students had learned to respond quickly. They began to pour from their chambers, and some had had the presence of mind to bring pitch torches. Staying hidden was no longer an option, so Bartholomew abandoned the bushes and tore across the yard, also aiming for the crumbling section of wall. He almost lost his footing when Cynric suddenly appeared from behind a tree, and indicated they were to run in the opposite direction.

'I told you to keep watch,' hissed the book-bearer. 'Why did you let Kardington see you?'

'He did not see *me*,' objected Bartholomew, racing after him. 'He saw that hooded man.'

Cynric glanced around. 'But unfortunately, *he* has escaped, and everyone is in hot pursuit of *us*. You should have stayed where you were, then walked away when the coast was clear.'

'God's teeth!' muttered Bartholomew, risking a quick look behind and seeing at least a dozen yelling scholars on their heels. 'Now we are in trouble! Shall we try to explain?'

'I do not think so! They are not in the mood for listening.'

Bartholomew was unfamiliar with Clare's grounds, and his progress through them was slower than that of the

147

more fleet-footed students. They began to gain. He tried to run harder, heart pounding, chest heaving and leg muscles burning from the effort. Cynric was right: they were angry, and were going to vent their rage with fists and boots. He concentrated on running, aware that the ground was sloping downwards. They were at the back of the College, where a wall separated it from the river and the towpath.

Unerringly, Cynric aimed for a specific point, and was over in a trice. He straddled the top of the rampart, and leaned down to take Bartholomew's hand, hauling him upwards with surprising strength for so small a man. But Spaldynge had arrived, and he laid hold of the physician's leg. Bartholomew felt himself begin to slide back down again. He kicked out, and heard Spaldynge curse as he lost his grip. He clambered inelegantly over the wall, landing awkwardly on the other side. Cynric darted towards the nearest boat, and cut through the mooring rope with his dagger.

Bartholomew did not like the notion of adding theft to the charge of trespass. 'Isnard,' he gasped. 'We will take refuge—'

'Isnard has taken against you for severing his leg – Arderne said it was unnecessary, and Isnard believes him. He will give you up. *Hurry*!'

Reluctantly, Bartholomew jumped into the skiff and Cynric began to row. The Clare scholars milled about help-lessly, shrieking their frustration and rage as they arrived to see the little craft bobbing away from them. Fortunately, it did not occur to them to steal a boat and follow, and no one was stupid enough to risk swimming, not when the river was swollen with recent rains. Cynric powered towards the opposite bank and jumped out. Before disappearing into the marshy meadows that lay to the west of the town, he turned and gave the enraged scholars an impertinent wave.

'That jaunty little salute was unkind,' Bartholomew remarked critically, when they were safely hidden among the bulrushes and reeds. 'Was gloating really necessary?'

Cynric was laughing softly; he had thoroughly enjoyed the escapade. 'Yes, because it was not something either of us would have done.' He saw his master's look of total incomprehension. 'Now, if anyone accuses us of being the culprits, we can point out that we are not the gloating types.'

'Did you see that hooded figure?' Bartholomew asked, not entirely sure the book-bearer's tactic would work. How could they claim they were not the 'gloating types' without admitting guilty knowledge of the gesture in the first place? 'Did you recognise him at all?'

Cynric nodded. 'Oh, yes. It was Honynge – our new Fellow.'

The following day was wet, and the dreary weather matched Bartholomew's bleak mood. He had experienced an acute sense of loss that morning when he had glanced at the spot in the chancel where Kenyngham normally stood, and the sombre faces of his colleagues suggested he was not alone in grieving for the old man. Further, he was still in an agony of worry over Falmeresham, and the incident with Motelete had knocked his confidence more than he liked to admit. It was not that he objected to being proven wrong, but he was appalled that he should have been quite so badly mistaken. Two patients summoned him for consultations that morning, and he was so wary of making another misdiagnosis that even Deynman had commented on his excessive caution.

'You have some explaining to do,' said Michael sternly, when the physician eventually returned to Michaelhouse.

'What were you thinking of, marauding through Clare's cabbages last night?'

Bartholomew had more pressing matters on his mind. 'William has offered to preside over the disputations today, because he knows I want to look for Falmeresham. But Langelee and Wynewyk are out, and I am loath to leave him in sole charge.'

His concern intensified when the friar announced the topic of the day would be Blood Relics, specifically that Bajulus of Barcelona's arguments were so good that no evil Dominican would ever be able to refute them. His agitation increased further still when Deynman offered to help.

'Christ!' he muttered in dismay. 'There will be a riot *here*, never mind the town.'

'There is no call for blasphemy,' said Michael sharply. 'You are not on the battlefield now. Look, there is Carton. Perhaps he will supervise the proceedings.'

'I am afraid I have a prior commitment,' said Carton, overhearing. 'I heard you come home very late last night, Doctor Bartholomew. Were you with a patient or looking for Falmeresham?'

'Both,' said Michael quickly. He did not want anyone to know what the physician had really been doing, lest it led to trouble with Clare.

'But you learned nothing,' surmised Carton, seeing the defeated expression on the physician's face. 'And I do not know where else to look – I have visited every College and hostel in Cambridge, but no one has seen anything. Perhaps it is time to give up.'

Bartholomew shook his head stubbornly. 'Falmeresham knows how to look after himself. If his wound was not too serious, then he might have been able to—'

'But it *was* serious,' said Carton tearfully. 'We all saw the blade slide into his innards.'

'We are doing all we can to find him,' said Michael soothingly. 'My beadles hunted for him all last night, and they will not stop the search until I say so – which will not be as long as there is even a remote chance that he might still be alive.'

'They are more experienced in such matters than me,' said the Franciscan, with a dejected sigh. 'So, I shall go to the church, and pray to St Michael instead. Perhaps he will spare one of his angels to watch over Falmeresham.'

'Carton is an odd fellow,' said Michael, watching the commoner walk away. 'I cannot help but wonder whether he has a reason for constantly letting us know the depth of his concern – lest evidence ever comes to light that says Falmeresham was actually killed by a friend, not an enemy.'

Bartholomew gazed at him. 'That is an unpleasant thing to say.'

Michael grimaced ruefully. 'Yes, it is, so ignore me. I am overly tired, and cannot think straight. However, I have a feeling we may never find out what happened to Falmeresham – we may spend the rest of our lives pondering his fate.'

Bartholomew rubbed his eyes. He knew the chances of finding the student alive were decreasing as time went by, but he refused to give up hope. 'He will come home.'

'Is that what led you to invade Clare last night – a dogged belief that he might still be awaiting rescue? Did you know Spaldynge claims to have recognised you?'

'Does he?' Bartholomew supposed it was not surprising; the man had been close enough to grab his leg, and the moon had been very bright.

'Fortunately for you, Kardington maintains that such a notion is ludicrous – that the University's senior physician would never stoop to such behaviour. Meanwhile, the Clare students think Spaldynge is picking on you because you are a *medicus*. They have dismissed his testimony, and are so certain of your innocence that Spaldynge's own convictions have begun to waver.'

'Thank God!' breathed Bartholomew in relief.

'Of course, it will be difficult to explain why your hands are grazed,' Michael went on. 'We shall have to say you fell over in our yard. It is certainly slick enough today, with all this rain.'

'Kardington did not sound as angry with Spaldynge as he should have been,' said Bartholomew, attempting to change the subject and discuss what he had overheard instead. In the cold light of day, the previous night's adventure had been hopelessly misguided, and he did not blame Michael for being angry with him. 'Over selling Borden Hostel, I mean. I wonder why.'

'Because Kardington is a good and forgiving man,' replied Michael. 'He has advised his students to forget about the "burglary" last night – he believes the culprit was just someone who wanted to glimpse the miraculous Motelete.'

Bartholomew began to feel vaguely ashamed of himself. 'I see.'

Michael glared at him. 'How *could* you think Falmeresham might be in Clare's grounds? Kardington has already assured you that they have been thoroughly searched.'

'But he must be somewhere, Brother, whether he is dead or alive – and Cynric had a point when he said the Clare students might have been distracted when they performed the original hunt.'

'I am upset about Falmeresham, too, but it does not give me the right to invade rival foundations whenever I feel the urge.' Michael gave a sudden grin, suggesting his irritation was not as great as he would have his friend believe. 'Tell me about Honynge.'

152

'He was just a hooded shadow to me. It was Cynric who identified him.'

'Cynric says he is quite sure of what he saw, so I visited Honynge this morning, while you were with your patients. His knuckles are even more mangled than yours. Unfortunately, I could not think of a way to broach the subject without revealing your role in the debacle.'

Bartholomew was puzzled. 'Why would a senior scholar be lurking in the grounds of Clare in the depths of the night?'

Michael regarded him askance. 'And *you* ask this question?'

'Honynge was not looking for a missing student.'

'No,' acknowledged Michael. 'Did he see you during all the confusion last night?'

'Cynric says not.'

'Then you are probably safe – Cynric is usually right about such things. Do you think Honynge was trying to follow in your footsteps, and eavesdrop on the Master?'

'I was not eavesdropping,' said Bartholomew indignantly. He reconsidered. 'Well, I suppose I was, actually. I heard him talking and I admire his scholarship, so I went to see if I could hear what sort of topic kept him up so late.'

Michael regarded him with round eyes. 'You have been enrolled in universities for more than two decades, and you have some of the sharpest wits of anyone I know. You have fought deadly battles at the side of the Black Prince, and you have travelled to all manner of remote and exotic places. Yet sometimes you are so blithely naïve that you take my breath away. You went to eavesdrop on Kardington for *academic* reasons?'

Bartholomew felt defensive. 'He is a famous disputant, and William's mention of Blood Relics last night put me in the mood for a theological discussion.'

'Well, next time you experience such a compulsion, come to me and *I* will debate with you. It would be a good deal safer for everyone concerned. But let us return to Honynge.'

'Perhaps he was visiting a lover,' suggested Bartholomew. 'Wynewyk scales walls when *his* latest fancy lives in another foundation. However, Honynge did not look as though he was trysting.'

'I think he prefers women, anyway. I saw him smile at Agatha yesterday.'

'I smiled at her, too, but it does not mean I entertain a fancy for her.'

'You might,' warned Michael, 'if she doses you with this love-potion from Arderne. We shall have to watch what we eat and drink from now on. I have asked Cynric to stay in the kitchen when meals are being prepared, just in case she tries to slip this mixture into something *I* might consume.'

'Such draughts are fictions, invented by the cunning and accepted by the gullible. Agatha can slip it into whatever she likes, and it still will not see her surrounded by suitors.'

'I hope you are right, because I believe she has me in her sights.'

Bartholomew laughed, appreciating his friend's attempt to cheer him up. Michael was not smiling, however, and the physician saw he was serious. 'She does not! She would never seduce a monk in holy orders. Besides, I suspect you are too large, even for her tastes.'

Michael glared at him. 'Many women tell me I am a handsome specimen, and the fact that I am unavailable just serves to make me more appealing. And I am *not* fat. I just have big bones.'

Bartholomew had suspected for some time that Michael was unfaithful to his vows, although he had never actually caught him *in flagrante delicto*. But suspicions did not equal evidence, and Bartholomew certainly had no proof that Michael had ever availed himself of the many ladies he claimed were always clamouring for his manly attentions, so perhaps he was doing the monk an injustice.

'Honynge,' he prompted, loath to speculate on matters that were none of his concern. 'Perhaps he was going to steal some clothes from Clare. He is about to take up a new appointment, and he will not want to appear shabby in front of his future colleagues.'

'We already know he is shabby,' said Michael disapprovingly. 'However, I do not see him as a thief, despite my antipathy towards him. What other reason could he have had for being there?'

'None that I can think of – at least, nothing that does not involve burglary.'

'I shall think of a way to ask him later. However, he is not as important as discovering what happened to Lynton or asking how my beadles are faring with Falmeresham. And we should visit Maud Bowyer, too. She is still not recovered, and Candelby remains banished from her presence.'

'If she is angry with him, then perhaps she will not mind telling us what transpired in Milne Street on Sunday. However, I need to see the vicar of St Botolph's first. He has a swollen knee.'

'Robert Florthe?' asked Michael. 'I am sorry to hear that, because he is a friend. We shall visit him together, then, and you can cure his leg while he entertains me with gossip.'

As soon as Bartholomew and Michael stepped through the College gates, they were confronted by a strange sight. There was a queue of students standing outside, all waiting patiently in the rain. Those who were leaning against the walls straightened up when the two Fellows emerged, while others brushed down their tabards, hastening to make themselves look as presentable as possible. Some wore oiled cloaks against the inclement weather, but most were wet through.

'Word has spread that Langelee intends to accept twenty new scholars,' explained Michael. 'And these are the hopeful applicants. But Honynge has bagged seven places for Zachary, Tyrington wants three, and you need two for Lynton's boys, which means there are only eight places left.'

'But there must be a hundred students here,' said Bartholomew, shocked. 'Why so many?'

'Because the rent war has rendered the hostels' situation precarious, and Colleges offer reliable accommodation, regular meals and decent masters. Do you understand *now* why we cannot let Candelby win this dispute? *Eighty per cent* of our scholars live in town-owned houses, and most of them are on the brink of poverty as it is – they cannot afford what he wants to charge.'

'*All* these men are from hostels?' Bartholomew was astounded.

Michael nodded. 'I recognise most – many came to beg me to save their foundations from closure. All these – and more – will be permanently homeless if Candelby prevails.'

Bartholomew was moved to pity by the pinched, hungry expressions on the hopefuls' faces, and began to usher them to St Michael's Church, where they could wait out of the rain. The monk gave a long-suffering sigh, but then secretly slipped Cynric coins to buy them ale and bread. Carton, who was not petitioning the angels for Falmeresham's safe return, but dozing in the Stanton Chapel, agreed to watch them until Langelee and Wynewyk were ready to begin interviewing.

The clamour of voices disturbed the two men who were

kneeling at the high altar. Honynge and Tyrington turned in surprise, then came to see what was happening. When Michael explained, Honynge said the students' mettle should have been tested by leaving them where they were – 'only the keenest would have stayed the course' – and Tyrington asked what he could do to help.

'You should not have accepted this appointment,' Honynge muttered. 'Michaelhouse will prove to be a mistake, you mark my words.'

'I beg to differ,' cried Tyrington. 'I think it is the best decision I have ever made.'

'I was not talking to you,' said Honynge coldly. 'I was addressing myself, so kindly keep your nose out of my private discussions.'

'Oh,' said Tyrington, taken aback by the explanation. 'My apologies.'

'We came to say a mass for Kenyngham's soul,' said Honynge to Michael. 'It was Tyrington's idea, although I shall complete my devotions alone in future. He has a habit of spitting when he prays, which I find distracting.'

'I do not spit,' objected Tyrington indignantly. 'What a horrible thing to say!'

'You can make yourselves useful by helping Carton with these students,' said Michael. 'I doubt there will be trouble, given that they are eager to make a good impression, but there must be representatives from twenty different hostels here, and the competition is very intense.'

'Surely Carton can manage alone?' said Honynge with an irritable sigh. 'I have plans for today.'

'Carton is a commoner,' said Michael, startled by the response. 'He does not have the authority of Fellows-elect.'

'And what will you be doing while we undertake these menial duties?' asked Honynge unpleasantly. 'Eating a second breakfast?'

Michael glared at him, deeply offended. 'Looking for our missing student and trying to learn exactly what happened to Lynton.'

'"What happened to Lynton?"' echoed Honynge. 'I thought he fell off his horse.'

'He did,' replied Michael cagily, aware that he had said more than he should and that others were listening. 'But even accidents must be investigated.'

'Well, *I* shall not stay – I am a theologian, not a beadle.' Honynge began to walk away, adding under his breath, 'There! That told them you cannot be treated like a servant.'

'He is a strange fellow,' said Tyrington, watching him leave. He treated Michael to a leer that had the monk stepping away in alarm. 'But Carton and I can manage without him.'

'Distribute the bread and ale as soon as it arrives,' instructed Michael. 'And I will ask Agatha to bring pies from the Angel later. You may be here for some time, so bag one for yourself.'

'I do not eat the Angel's pies,' said Tyrington with a shudder. 'They are far too greasy.'

'Well, at least that is something he will not be gobbing at me,' said Michael, wiping the front of his habit as they left. 'But even so, I prefer his company to that of the loath-some Honynge.'

As Bartholomew and Michael walked along the High Street, they became aware of a commotion ahead. Michael groaned when he saw it comprised scholars from Clare and a number of apprentice leatherworkers from the nearby tannery.

'Motelete cheated Death,' one apprentice was yelling. 'But Death does not yield his prey so readily, and Motelete will soon be seized and dragged down to Hell, where he belongs.'

'Is that a threat?' demanded the student called Lexham.

'No, it is not,' said Michael, thrusting his way between them. Knowing he had the power to fine, the apprentices did not linger. They stalked away, muttering a litany of insults that were not quite loud enough for the monk to take action on. The Clare students understood the sentiments, though, and their expressions were cold and angry.

'They will not leave us alone,' explained Lexham sullenly, when Michael regarded him with raised eyebrows. 'Every time we go out, they try to fight us. It is not our fault.'

A small, slight figure stepped from their midst, and Bartholomew recognised the elfin features of the lad Arderne had cured. Motelete looked fit and well, and the grim pallor that had afflicted him the day before had gone. He appeared to have recovered from his ordeal, but Bartholomew looked away, not liking to imagine what would have happened had he been buried.

'I am to blame, Brother,' Motelete said shyly. 'If I had not been cured, no one would be angry. It is a pity Magister Arderne could not heal Ocleye, too.'

'He said it was because of you, Doctor Bartholomew,' elaborated Lexham guilelessly. 'He maintains that physicians who examine cadavers accumulate the taint of death on their hands; this rottenness is then passed to living patients, like a contagion.'

'Then his logic is flawed,' said Michael immediately. 'Matt touched Motelete, too.'

'Actually, I did not,' said Bartholomew tiredly. 'Only the clothes near his neck.'

Michael was never very patient with superstition. He turned to Motelete, ignoring the way the Clare students

159

gave Bartholomew a wide berth. 'Do you recall what happened the day you . . .'

'The day I died?' asked Motelete with a wry smile. 'I watched Magister Arderne heal Candelby, but the situation began to turn ugly after they left. Master Kardington ordered us all home, but I tripped over Candelby's broken cart, and by the time I had picked myself up, the others had gone. Everyone was fighting around me.'

'It must have been unpleasant,' said Michael encouragingly when the lad faltered.

Motelete nodded. 'I do not like violence. Then I saw Falmeresham, lying on the ground and bleeding. I tried to help him up, but he was too weak. Almost immediately, I felt a searing pain in my neck, and blood cascaded everywhere. The next thing I recall was waking up in the church.'

'Falmeresham was unable to stand on his own?' asked Bartholomew worriedly. It was the only account he had had of his student after the brawl had started, and it did not sound promising.

Motelete stared at the ground. 'I think he was dying,' he said in a choking whisper. 'I am so sorry.'

Michael gave him time to compose himself. 'Did you see Ocleye?' he asked eventually.

'It might have been him who attacked me,' said Motelete. He seemed close to tears, and Lexham put a comforting arm around his shoulders. 'It is all a blur, but I vaguely recall him being close by.'

'You did not attack him, though,' pressed Michael.

Motelete was horrified. 'No, of course not! I was trying to help Falmeresham.'

'How do you know Falmeresham?' asked Bartholomew. His stomach was churning, and for the first time he began to think perhaps Falmeresham had not survived the

160

incident. 'He did not fraternise with scholars from other Colleges.'

'I fell into a pothole on my first day here,' said Motelete, flushing scarlet with mortification. 'He helped me out, then carried my bag to Clare. He said I was too clumsy to be left alone.'

Michael ordered the students home, afraid that Motelete's presence on the streets might spark more trouble, then he and Bartholomew resumed their walk to St Botolph's.

'I think Motelete is telling the truth,' said the monk. 'He is gangling and inept, exactly the kind of lad Falmeresham might take pity on. I do not think he harmed Ocleye, either. He would not know what to do with a crossbow – and he did not have one with him on the day of the murders anyway, because his friends would have noticed.'

'I hope he is mistaken about Falmeresham,' said Bartholomew. 'About him being weak . . .'

Michael patted his shoulder. 'Motelete is not a physician Matt. He saw blood and assumed a fatal wound. Do not put too much store in the observations of a layman.'

'Unfortunately, they are the only observations we have been given.'

Many churches located near city gates were dedicated to St Botolph, a saint said to be sympathetic to travellers. His chapels allowed people to ask for his protection before they began their journeys, and recite prayers of deliverance when they came back. Cambridge's St Botolph's was a pleasant building, although it suffered from its proximity to the odorous King's Ditch. It was seldom empty – England's roads were dangerous, and few folk used them without petitioning the saints first. That morning, a party of wealthy nuns was going to London. They sang psalms in the chancel, while their servants inserted pennies into an oblations box, hoping to encourage Botolph to watch over them until they reached their distant destination.

Robert Florthe was in the cemetery, pulling brambles from the primrose-clad mound that contained those of his parishioners who had died during the plague. He was humming, oblivious to the fact that it was raining, and his priestly robes were stained with mud. He was pleased to see visitors, and insisted they join him in his house for a cup of warmed ale.

'You should rest,' advised Bartholomew, palpating the hot, puffy knee with his fingers. 'It will not mend if you do not keep your weight off it.'

'So you said last time,' said Florthe with a grin. 'But those brambles were annoying me and I like being outside. I was sorry about Kenyngham, by the way – and sorry about Lynton, too. He and I were neighbours, and we saw a lot of each other.'

Michael sipped his ale. 'I would hardly call Peterhouse a neighbour. It is some distance away.'

'I mean his Dispensary,' said Florthe, wincing when Bartholomew's examination reached a spot that hurt. 'Where he saw some of his patients.'

'I thought he saw his patients in his College,' said Bartholomew. 'Or visited them at home.'

Florthe pointed through the window, to the smart cottage next to his own modest dwelling. Its main door opened on to the lane that bordered the churchyard, and it looked like the kind of house that would be owned by a moderately wealthy merchant.

'People came to see him there in the evenings – perhaps his colleagues objected to townsmen and scholars from other foundations descending on them at night. He gave me a key once, to keep in case he ever locked himself out. Would you return it to Peterhouse for me? They probably do not know I have it, and poor Lynton will not be needing it now.'

Michael held out his hand. 'They will not mind if I look inside first. It might serve as a hostel, and the University needs every building it can lay its hands on at the moment, what with Candelby ousting scholars from places we have occupied for decades.'

Florthe nodded sadly. 'The students of Rudd's evacuated this morning – the building is no longer safe, and Candelby refuses to effect repairs. Ovyng has taken them in, although it will be cramped. And Garrett's lease expired today, so that returns to Candelby, too.'

Michael insisted on inspecting Lynton's Dispensary before they did anything else, so he could ask the Master and Fellows of Peterhouse – the sole beneficiaries of Lynton's will – to make it available for homeless scholars. He unlocked the door with Florthe's key, and he and Bartholomew entered.

The house comprised one room on the ground floor, and a pair of attics above. The lower chamber was substantial, with a hearth, a huge table and a number of cushion-strewn benches. It smelled sweet and clean, but there was not the slightest indication that medical consultations ever took place in it. Bartholomew wondered where Lynton had kept the items he had 'dispensed', and climbed the ladder to the upper floor to look for urine flasks, astrological tables, medicines and other equipment. All he found was a large collection of silver goblets.

'He was never one for physical intervention,' he said, more to explain to himself the lack of basic tools than to enlighten Michael. 'And he may have committed essential celestial charts to memory. I consult them when I prepare horoscopes, because they are a waste of time and I cannot be bothered to learn them, but Lynton was a firm believer and probably knew them by heart.'

'This is a pleasant chamber,' said Michael, frowning. 'But the window shutters are painted closed, and I cannot open them. Why would that be?'

Bartholomew shrugged. 'So no one could look in and watch him with his patients, I imagine. Some will have had embarrassing conditions, and would have wanted – demanded – privacy.'

'I thought he had fewer patients than you, but these benches suggest they came to him in droves.'

'He never seemed busy to me – at least, not with medicine. He did not accept just anyone as a patient, and tended to enrol folk who were not actually ill – ones who wanted preventative treatment rather than curative. He took some charity cases, but not nearly as many as Paxtone and Rougham.'

'Or you,' said Michael. 'Almost all yours are poor.'

Bartholomew looked around him, trying to equate what he saw to the practical application of healing. 'Perhaps Lynton examined his patients *en masse* – ordered everyone with ailments of the lungs, for example, to come at a specific time. Then he could purchase the appropriate remedies in bulk, and dispense them all at once. It is quite common for Arab physicians to specialise in particular ailments or specific parts of the body.'

'Lynton would never have embraced a practice favoured by foreigners. And what did you mean when you said he was busy, but not with medicine? Was he busy with something else, then?'

'He was interested in the kinetics of motion; I think he might have been writing a treatise about it. He was always asking to borrow my copy of Bradwardine's

Tractatus de continuo and he knew the subject extremely well.'

'The mean speed theorem,' mused Michael. 'You have talked about it before, and I can see it is an important advance in natural philosophy, although it is dull stuff with its "uniform velocities" and "moving bodies". I would rather talk about Blood Relics, and that should tell you something, because William has beaten the subject to death and I am bored of it. However, a complex notion like mean speed seems an odd subject to attract Lynton.'

'The mean speed theorem is *not* dull,' argued Bartholomew irritably. 'Nicole Oresme's account of the intension and remission of qualities is—'

'Another time,' interrupted Michael. He elbowed the physician outside, and locked the door behind them. 'I am too worried about Lynton, Falmeresham and the rent war to give it my full attention. Do you mind if we take a moment to visit Wisbeche, and ask if he will lend me the Dispensary to house some of these homeless scholars? It will not take a moment.'

Bartholomew followed him the short distance to Peterhouse. As they approached, a flicker of movement caught his eye. Someone was running, heading quickly towards the Gilbertine Friary. He frowned, puzzled.

'That person was watching Peterhouse, Brother. He was sheltering in the doorway opposite, but his attention was fixed on the College. When he saw us coming, he made a dash for it.'

'It is not Honynge, is it?' asked Michael, screwing up his eyes as he peered up the road. 'He lurks around Clare at odd times, so perhaps he spies on other Colleges, too. You had better give chase while I speak to Wisbeche. It will be the most efficient use of our time.'

'For you, maybe,' grumbled Bartholomew, objecting to

racing after shadows in the rain, while Michael would probably be feted with cakes and warm wine. He raised his hands when Michael started to point out that a Corpse Examiner was not authorised to make arrangements for new accommodation – and the Senior Proctor could not move fast enough to catch up with the figure that was rapidly dwindling into the distance, anyway.

'And *not* because I am fat,' said Michael, anticipating the next objection. 'My heavy bones mean that the velocity of my mean speed is lower than yours. Go, before you lose him.'

Despite a spirited effort, Bartholomew did not succeed. The man glanced behind him once, and when he saw he was being followed, ducked into the woods behind the Gilbertine Friary. He had had too great a start, and although Bartholomew explored several paths and even climbed a tree, he was forced to concede defeat. Michael was waiting for him outside Peterhouse, wiping crumbs from his face with his piece of linen.

'I had better luck,' he said. 'Wisbeche agreed to loan me the Dispensary for as long as I need it.'

'Did you ask where Lynton kept his medical equipment?' asked Bartholomew. 'And why his attics are full of silver goblets?'

'I did, but he said I should consult a physician for answers to those sorts of questions.'

Maud Bowyer occupied a handsome house on Bridge Street, near the equally fine home that was owned by the Sheriff. Michael was bitterly disappointed when servants told him that Dick Tulyet was still away, and that he was not expected home any time soon. He needed the Sheriff's calming hand to quell the growing unrest, and was not sure he could do it alone.

'I shall write to him again this evening, and tell him to come as soon as he can,' said the monk unhappily. 'I do not like the atmosphere – people keep glaring at me.'

Bartholomew was concerned. 'It is because everyone knows you – not Chancellor Tynkell – run the University. Perhaps you should take Cynric with you when you go out in future.'

'I would rather he watched where Agatha put her love-potion. A town full of angry men does not hold nearly the same terror as being caught in an amorous embrace by Agatha.' Michael sighed. 'Three days have passed, and I still have no idea who killed Lynton. Do you?'

'Arderne,' said Bartholomew, surprising himself with the speed of his reply and the conviction in his voice. 'He has the most to gain. He has virtually destroyed Robin, and with Lynton dead, there are only three others left to tell folk he is a fraud.'

'But Paxtone and Rougham also benefit from Lynton's demise, because several wealthy patients are now looking for a new physician. And I cannot help but think that Peterhouse is withholding information. Did Wisbeche really lend me the Dispensary out of charity, or did he just want me gone from his College without asking too many questions? Ouch!'

Bartholomew looked sharply at him, and saw a clod of mud had hit him in the chest. The physician turned quickly, and spotted two men who worked at the Lilypot. They were cronies of Isnard, and were racing away as if their lives depended on it. One stopped when he reached the corner. He saw the physician watching and raised his fist.

'Charlatan!' he yelled, before disappearing down the lane.

'That is certainly true,' declared a heavyset woman with a moustache. Her name was Rosalind fitz-Eustace, and she

167

and her husband had a reputation for being gossips. 'Damned scholars.'

'We should oust the lot of them,' agreed fitz-Eustace. 'When they are not bleeding us dry with demands for cheap rents, cheap ale and cheap flour, they kill and maim us with bad medicine.'

'Magister Arderne was wrong to have saved Motelete,' whispered Rosalind, although it was clear she intended people to hear. 'He should have raised Ocleye instead.'

'It was too late – the Corpse Examiner had been at him.' Fitz-Eustace cast a malicious glance in Bartholomew's direction before stalking away, his wife at his side.

'The insults were directed at us both, but the dirt was meant for you,' grumbled Michael, trying without success to remove the stain from his habit. 'Damn it! This was clean on at Christmas. And now here come two more alleged charlatans – Paxtone and Rougham, your medical colleagues. Paxtone is looking seedy today.'

Michael was right: the King's Hall physician was pale, and there were bags under his eyes. The monk started to mutter something about a guilty conscience for putting a crossbow bolt in a rival, and Bartholomew was obliged to silence him with an elbow in the ribs.

'What is wrong, Paxtone?' he asked, concerned. 'Can I help?'

'I offered my services, too, but he says it is nothing,' said Rougham.

'You have not accepted tonics from Arderne, have you?' asked Bartholomew uneasily, suddenly afraid that the healer might have started work on his next victim.

Paxtone grimaced. 'Of course not! The man is a trickster, and I would no more swallow his potions than I would let Robin perform surgery on me. Credit me with some sense, Matthew.'

'You should not be out,' said Bartholomew. 'You should be lying down, resting.'

'I told him that, too,' muttered Rougham.

Paxtone sighed. 'There is nothing wrong that a good purge will not cure. I am afraid I was something of a glutton with the roasted pigeon last night. I ate eight.'

'Did you?' asked Michael, impressed. 'Were they cooked in any kind of sauce?'

'Stones were thrown at me twice yesterday,' said Rougham, changing the subject before two fat men could begin to share the delights of the dinner table. 'It is because of Arderne. He is spreading tales about our competence as physicians. He has a convincing manner, and people believe him.'

'I have received threatening letters from the family of a man I failed to save last term,' added Paxtone miserably. 'The case was hopeless – you two saw him, and you agreed with my diagnosis – but Arderne told his kin that he would have survived, had I known what I was doing.'

'You mean Constantine Mortimer?' asked Rougham. 'The one who fell from his horse and cracked his skull so badly that he never awoke?'

Paxtone nodded. 'Arderne claims he could have been woken by inserting a hot iron in his anus.'

Bartholomew winced. 'We followed a course of treatment that was humane. Of course we could have induced a reaction by causing him pain, but that is a long way from making him better.'

Rougham glowered. 'Arderne is a menace. Today, Mayor Harleston informed me that he no longer requires my services, which makes the fifth wealthy patient to abandon me this week alone.'

'I lost Chancellor Tynkell this morning,' added Paxtone, 'and he is a very lucrative source of income, because of

169

his appalling hygiene. We should form a united front to combat this wretched leech and his slanderous accusations.'

'That is what Robin said,' said Bartholomew.

'I do not want to be associated with Robin,' said Rougham in distaste. 'However, he is a medical man – after a fashion – and he *has* been ruined by Arderne, so I feel a certain empathy with him.'

'We may be losing patients, but your situation is far more perilous, Matthew,' said Paxtone. 'Arderne told Isnard his leg need not have been amputated, and Isnard believes it. Isnard is popular in Cambridge, and people are angry with you. I fear their resentment may erupt into violence.'

'I agree,' said Rougham. 'Perhaps you should confine yourself to Michaelhouse until all this blows over. And blow over it will, because Arderne cannot possibly keep all the promises he has made, and it is only a matter of time before he is exposed.'

'I cannot stay in!' exclaimed Bartholomew. 'What about my patients?'

'You still have some?' asked Paxtone bleakly. He turned suddenly. 'I thought I could sense malevolence behind me – and there he is! Arderne himself. Look at him, strutting around the town as if he owns it.'

'He is beginning to,' said Rougham bitterly. 'That is the problem.'

'Cambridge's infamous physicians,' said Arderne amiably, when he spotted the three medical men standing with Michael. 'How is business, gentlemen? If you are doing as well as I am, you must be very pleased with yourselves.'

'Pleased enough,' replied Rougham, unwilling to let the man know the extent of the damage he was causing. 'Why do you ask?'

'Because Sir Robert Ufford – your *former* patient – wants *me* to cure his swollen veins,' said Arderne smugly. His eyes

170

held a hard gleam of spite. 'I shall eradicate his ailment with my feather and a decoction of grease.'

'What manner of decoction?' asked Bartholomew, while Rougham's jaw dropped.

'I never share professional secrets,' replied Arderne. 'Besides, only *I* can attempt these treatments – you do not have the necessary skills.'

'Try him,' challenged Michael. 'He has been to Montpellier, where they study anatomy and surgery. You may find he is better at these exotic techniques than you.'

'I do not compete with men who try to bury their patients alive,' said Arderne contemptuously. 'It is fortunate *I* was on hand to effect one of my miraculous cures, or Motelete would have suffered the most dreadful fate imaginable.'

'Very fortunate,' muttered Paxtone venomously.

'It is not just Rougham's patients who are flocking to me, either,' said Arderne, rounding on the portly physician. 'Master Powys – Warden of your own College – asked me for a remedy today.'

Paxtone gaped at him. 'I do not believe you.'

Arderne shrugged, and fixed Paxtone with his pale eyes; Paxtone gazed back mutely, as though it was beyond his strength to break the stare. 'Who cares what you believe? In a few weeks, I shall have all your wealthy customers, and you will be left with the ones who cannot pay.'

'I refuse to sit still while that fellow damages my reputation – perhaps permanently,' snarled Rougham, when the healer had gone. 'We *must* act.'

'And do what?' asked Bartholomew. He glanced at Paxtone, whose expression was rather blank. 'Launch into a slandering match, which will show us to be as petty and despicable as him?'

'It would be demeaning,' blurted Paxtone when

171

Bartholomew poked him with his finger. He shook himself and took a deep breath.

'I was thinking of employing more devious tactics,' said Rougham. 'How about tampering with his feather – putting some substance on it that will make his patients ill?'

'We cannot do that!' Bartholomew was shocked. 'It would break all the oaths we have sworn.'

'It is a case of expediency,' argued Rougham. 'Would you rather have a couple of folk with rashes, or some real deaths, when needy patients go to him for a cure and he fails them?'

CHAPTER 6

Michael knocked on Maud Bowyer's door while Bartholomew faced the road. The physician had noticed several people glaring, and someone had thrown a stone. It had missed, but he was afraid to turn his back on the street lest the culprit try it again. He had assumed people were angry with Michael over the rents, and had been shocked to learn that some of the sour glances had, in fact, been directed at him. He was not sure what he could do about it – he had explained countless times to Isnard that the removal of his leg had been unavoidable, but the bargeman had never really come to terms with the loss. Arderne had homed in on Isnard's vulnerability like a fly to dead meat, and had known exactly how to exploit it to his own advantage. But how could Bartholomew tell Isnard that? Or the men and women who sympathised with him?

Michael's rap was answered by a thickset man who wore a sword. He conducted them to a pleasant solar on the ground floor, explaining as he went that he had been hired to make sure Candelby did not try to force his way inside the house.

'Mistress Bowyer has washed her hands of him,' he said. 'He only wanted her for her money, poor soul. Wait here while I fetch her housekeeper, Isabel St Ives. She will tell you whether the mistress is well enough to receive wellwishers.'

Michael looked around appreciatively when the guard had gone. 'Fine rugs on the floor, gold goblets on the windowsills – Maud is wealthier than I thought. She is probably right to be suspicious of Candelby: I imagine he *was* courting her for her riches.'

'She owns houses, too,' said Bartholomew, remembering something his sister had told him. 'Perhaps those are what attracted him.'

It was not long before a pretty woman in her thirties came to greet them. Isabel St Ives wore a white goffered veil over her hair, and her blue surcoat – an ankle-length dress – was slightly baggy, suggesting it had been handed down from someone larger. Bartholomew recalled something else his sister had said – that Isabel had started to work for Maud after the plague, when both had lost husbands to the disease. He had seen her before, because it had been Isabel who had tried to comfort her mistress at the scene of the accident in Milne Street.

'Good morning, Brother,' said Isabel politely. 'I am afraid my mistress is still too unwell to receive guests, but thank you for coming to enquire after her health again.'

'You are welcome,' said Michael, with a gracious bow. 'However, there is another purpose to my visit. I would like to ask her about the accident. As Senior Proctor, I am obliged to make a report to the Chancellor, but it is proving difficult to trace reliable witnesses.'

'Unfortunately, it is a blur in her mind, and her fever is making it worse. *I* saw some of what happened, though – I was nearby at the time. I will answer questions, if you think it might help.'

'I need to understand exactly what happened to Lynton,' said Michael carefully. 'I would like to know who killed Ocleye, too. The other death – Motelete's – transpired to be no death at all.'

'So I heard,' said Isabel. 'A true miracle. However, the accident was odd, and I am not surprised you are having trouble establishing a clear order of events from eyewitness accounts.'

'How was it odd?' asked Bartholomew. He had taken a liking to Isabel's pretty face and pleasant manner. Unlike many University men, he had not taken major orders, and so women were not forbidden to him. He was still not supposed to fraternise with them, but there were ways around that particular prohibition, and he was not averse to female company, like some of his colleagues. He had even come close to marrying once, and still loved Matilde, despite the passing of time. He supposed he always would, and wondered whether she would ever return to Cambridge – and whether she would consent to be his wife if she did. Although common sense told him Matilde was gone forever, part of him refused to believe he would never see her again, and he had not given up hope that one day she would reappear and tell him that she loved him, too.

'It was odd because there was no reason for Lynton to have ridden his horse at Candelby,' Isabel was saying. Bartholomew's attention snapped back to the present. 'As far as I could tell, he suddenly slumped in his saddle, and the horse cavorted sideways, as though something startled it.'

'Did you notice anything else?' asked Michael.

'Only that a crowd gathered very quickly, and folk stood according to affiliation – either with townsmen or with students. Usually, they are mixed together, but that was not the case on Sunday.'

'Because they were anticipating trouble,' surmised Michael grimly. 'Were any of these townsmen armed – armed with *real* weapons, I mean, like swords or crossbows?'

'I did not see any. However, it would not surprise me to learn that Candelby did something to Lynton's mare – that Lynton is innocent of all blame for the accident.'

'Why would Candelby do that?' asked Bartholomew.

'Because Lynton owned a lot of houses, and was doing with them what Candelby yearns to do – rent them to those who can afford higher prices. It may have been simple jealousy.'

'Matt tells me Lynton was Maud's physician,' said the monk. 'We all know Lynton preferred wealthy patients to poor ones, and your mistress must be one of the richest women in the town.'

'She is. And Lynton's consultations may be another reason Candelby wished him harm.'

'Why?' asked Bartholomew, bemused. 'She probably consulted butchers, bakers and candlestick-makers, too, but that should not induce a suitor to drive carts at them.'

'Lynton was a conscientious, thorough man, and his sessions with my mistress were often lengthy. Perhaps Candelby objected to the amount of time another man spent in her presence.'

'Then Candelby's jealousy addled his wits,' said Bartholomew in disgust. 'Lynton would never have done anything untoward with a patient. He was too old for a start.'

'Quite,' said Isabel. 'Is there anything else I can tell you?'

'Did you see Arderne mend Candelby's arm?' asked Michael.

Isabel nodded. 'I rushed to my mistress's side when I saw she was hurt; Candelby was clutching his wrist. Then Magister Arderne arrived and said Candelby's bones needed to be set immediately. He waved a feather over him, and he was healed instantly. It was a miracle.'

'It was?' asked Bartholomew. He found he was disappointed in her, because she had seemed too sensible to be deceived by cheap tricks.

She was surprised by the scepticism in his voice. 'Of

course. Magister Arderne is a remarkable man, quite capable of marvellous deeds. However, I wish he had applied his talents to my mistress instead. She has not been well since the accident, and I am very worried about her.'

'You do not seem to like Candelby,' said Michael. 'And Maud has forbidden him to visit. Why?'

'I tolerated him when I thought he made her happy, but the accident opened her eyes to his true character, so I can say what I like about him now. We were both shocked and disgusted by the way he gloated over Lynton's death.'

'What is wrong with your mistress?' asked Bartholomew. 'I noticed a splinter in her shoulder. Did Arderne remove it?'

She nodded. 'Yes, but it was basic surgery, and he did not apply his magic, which is why she is not recovering. I do not mean to offend you, Doctor Bartholomew, but medicine is not very effective unless it is also accompanied by spells and incantations. I learned that during the plague, when physicians failed to save my family.'

'Right,' said Bartholomew, not sure how else to respond.

'Will you see her?' Isabel asked impulsively. 'Despite my beliefs, you were a friend of Lynton's, and my mistress may be pleased to see you. I would give anything to see her smile again.'

Isabel led Bartholomew and Michael upstairs to a pleasant chamber lit by a fire; the shutters were closed, lending the room a warm, cosy feel. However, even the herbs set in bowls on the windowsills could not disguise the stink of sickness and corruption, and Bartholomew went to the bed with a heavy heart, already knowing what he would find.

The splinter had been driven deep into Maud's shoulder,

but it had been carelessly removed, leaving slivers behind. The wood had been tainted with filth from the street, so the wound was badly infected. Had the injury been on an arm or a leg, Bartholomew would have recommended its removal, before bad humours could permeate the rest of the body, but he could not amputate a shoulder, and Maud was going to die.

'I cannot cure her,' he whispered to Isabel. 'I am sorry.'

Isabel's expressive face registered her distress, but she smiled at him anyway. 'I know you would have done, if you could. It is not your fault you cannot help her now, just as it was not your fault when you could not help her last year.'

'Maud's eyes,' explained Bartholomew to Michael. 'Lynton asked for a second opinion, because her sight was clouding and he did not know how to stop it from getting worse. And, I am sorry to say, neither did I.'

'I will summon Magister Arderne again,' said Isabel, speaking softly so as not to disturb the patient. 'If I give him six gold goblets, he may agree to work one of his miracles.'

'They will certainly encourage him to try,' muttered Bartholomew. 'I can give Maud something for the pain, though. She does not have to suffer like this.'

Isabel watched him dribble a sense-dulling potion between the sick woman's lips. 'Let us hope that will see her through until Magister Arderne arrives. Then he will cure her, and all will be well,' she said.

Bartholomew bathed Maud's face with a wet cloth, and after a few moments, she opened her eyes. She was smiling distantly. 'I thought you were Master Lynton. He had a way of wiping a hot face with a cool rag, too. Arderne uses a feather to draw out poisons and reduce fevers.'

'Yes,' said Bartholomew noncommittally. He refrained

from denigrating Arderne's methods, on the remote chance that the man might succeed where traditional medicine failed. He knew from experience that a person who believed in a cure was more likely to survive than one who did not, and he wanted Maud to have every chance of recovery, no matter how small.

'Hugh Candelby plans to marry me,' she went on. The fever was making her ramble. 'But I will not have him. He was never more than an amusing diversion, but I see now that he was only after my property – to use against the University. I will not allow that to happen.'

'It is good to know we have one friend, at least,' said Michael softly. 'Thank you.'

'I tried to talk him out of this confrontation over rents, but he would not listen. I like the University and its scholars. They are courteous, erudite and pleasant, while most burgesses are unkempt and oafish. Do not worry, Brother. I will never allow Hugh to get *my* houses.'

'Brother Michael wants to know what happened on the day you were hurt,' said Isabel quietly. 'Can you tell him what you recall?'

Maud coughed weakly. 'Hugh had just been telling me about his latest plan to thwart the University, which involves issuing an ultimatum and refusing to budge. He says he will break your laws as he pleases, because you cannot stop him – or force him to pay any fine you care to levy.'

'He has a point,' said Michael ruefully. 'Invading his home and making off with silverware in lieu of coins will not go down very well with his fellow worthies. They will riot.'

'That is what he hopes – such an outrage would force the waverers to commit to his cause. The next thing I remember is sitting among the remnants of his cart. Then Arderne took me home.'

'Did Candelby have a weapon with him that day?' asked Michael.

'Of course,' said Maud, surprised he should need to ask. 'What sane man does not?'

'Do you know what kind?'

'He always has a crossbow – not a very large one, but one that makes thieves think twice.'

Bartholomew and Michael exchanged a startled glance. 'Is he capable of using it on anyone?' asked Michael, rather eagerly.

Maud shook her head, and Bartholomew saw her eyes begin to close. The potion he had fed her was sending her to sleep at last. 'That is the ridiculous thing. It was never loaded.'

When the two scholars left Maud's house, Isabel went with them, claiming she had shopping to do in the Market Square. Bartholomew was alarmed to see that townsmen had started to gather in sullen groups, and he did not like the way their eyes followed him and Michael as they walked. Some were his patients, folk he had known for years, but not many returned his friendly greetings. Most seemed too frightened to speak, afraid of attracting attention from those who did not approve of fraternising with the University. A few were genuinely hostile.

'Go away,' said Isabel, whipping around to glare at a gaggle of potters who had begun to shadow them. 'I do not feel comfortable with you dogging my every step, so stop it. Do not stand there, gaping like cattle. Do as I say! At once!'

There was a determined jut to her chin, and it seemed to convince them that they would be wise to obey. To Bartholomew's astonishment, they turned and shuffled back the way they had come.

'Perhaps you should go ahead of us,' he suggested uneasily. 'You do not want them to take against you for keeping company with scholars.'

Isabel's expression was disdainful. 'I shall walk with whomever I please, thank you! I cannot imagine what has got into those boys. They are normally amiable lads, always willing to carry a basket or to run errands. I deplore this current disquiet and unease. Candelby has a lot to answer for – and so does his horrible henchman, Blankpayn.'

'Have you seen Blankpayn recently?' asked Bartholomew. 'I need to speak to him.'

'About your student Falmeresham?' Isabel saw his surprise, and explained. 'It is common knowledge that Blankpayn may have done him a grievous harm, and that you have been scouring the town for them both ever since. But I am afraid I cannot help, because I have no idea where the wretched man might be. I will ask the servants when I go home, and will send word if I learn anything useful.'

Michael smiled. 'I do not suppose you would like to be my Junior Proctor, would you? I have not had a decent assistant in years.'

Isabel laughed, a hearty chuckle. 'I would like it very much, Brother. When can I start?'

'You have already started. You ordered those potters away, and they obeyed without question. They would never have done that for me. Students would, but not townsfolk.'

He was being overly modest, because few men – other than Candelby – ever had the audacity to oppose Michael. He wielded too much power, and while he could not fight townsmen directly, he could certainly do so insidiously. Over a period of time, he could impose fines, restrict trade,

181

close down businesses and excommunicate serious offenders. Even the Sheriff did not have such an awesome battery of penalties at his fingertips, which was partly why the landlords' rebellion had taken the University so much by surprise.

'That was a waste of effort,' said Michael, when they reached the Market Square, and Isabel had gone to buy meat and barley to make a strengthening broth for her mistress. 'Their testimony – such as it was – confirms what we already know, but we learned nothing new.'

'We learned that Candelby totes a crossbow around with him,' said Bartholomew. 'Maud said he kept it unloaded, but perhaps that was not true on Sunday. The town was uneasy, and he may have felt the need for extra precautions.'

'If so, then perhaps he *did* kill Lynton. He has a motive.'

'Two motives, Brother – jealousy of Lynton's professional relationship with the lady he intends to marry, and anger that Lynton was able to rent his property to townsmen.' Bartholomew was thoughtful. 'But if he shot Lynton, then it stands to reason that he also killed Ocleye – there cannot be two killers using the same mode of execution. However, Ocleye was his own pot-boy.'

Michael did not see that as a flaw in the solution. 'Ocleye was in the back of Candelby's cart when Lynton was murdered – a witness to the crime. So Candelby killed him to ensure his silence.'

'Then why is Maud still alive? If Ocleye watched the murder from the back of the cart, then surely Maud, who was sitting next to Candelby, would also have noticed something untoward?'

'But she claims to remember nothing – probably because she is afraid that if she does, he will kill her, too.' Michael's expression was triumphant. 'And do not overlook the fact that she refuses to see him. It must be because she *knows* he is a killer. I am right here, Matt. Candelby hates scholars so intensely that he would think nothing of shooting one, then dispatching witnesses.'

But Bartholomew thought Candelby as the culprit left too many unanswered questions. 'I still think Arderne is a better suspect – ridding himself of a rival, because—' He stopped speaking and stared across the street. 'There is Blankpayn!'

'Wait!' Michael reached out to stop him, but it was too late. The physician was far too agile for the heavy-boned monk. 'Let my beadles . . . oh, damn it all!'

The owner of the Lilypot tavern was swaggering along the High Street. He was slightly unsteady on his feet, suggesting he had been at the ale, and his clothes were the ones he had worn on Sunday.

'Where have you been?' demanded Bartholomew. 'I have been looking for you for days.'

Blankpayn was startled to be addressed so bluntly, and tried to walk away, but the physician's arm shot out and barred his way. Michael held his breath, anticipating violence, and his unease intensified when three of the Lilypot's patrons arrived – rough, unkempt fellows with a reputation for brawling. He hurried forward, intending to pull Bartholomew away from the confrontation while he was still in one piece – they would do better to ask their questions another time, when Blankpayn did not have the security of friends massing at his back.

But Michael had reckoned without the fellowship of the University. Master Wisbeche of Peterhouse saw Bartholomew surrounded by hostile drunks, and hastened to redress the balance. He had two students with him, burly lads who carried long knives in their belts. Then Kardington of Clare came to see if he could help. Spaldynge was at his side, clenching his fists in a way that told the monk he was more than ready to use them in defence of his colleagues, even if one was a physician. Unfortunately, then a group of Oswald Stanmore's lads approached, and pointedly ranged themselves behind the townsmen. Michael supposed they were tired of being called scholar-lovers by their friends, just because Bartholomew was their master's kinsman.

'Lord, Matt!' the monk muttered angrily. 'Now look what you have done.'

'What do you want, physician?' demanded Blankpayn. 'I do not waste time talking to scholars, so say whatever is on your mind, then get out of my way and let me pass.'

'We just want to know if you have seen Falmeresham,' said Michael, before Bartholomew could phrase the question in a more aggressive – or accusatory – manner.

'No,' said Blankpayn, shoving Bartholomew hard enough to make him stagger. 'Now get lost.'

'There is no need for violence,' objected Kardington in his precise Latin, while Michael put out a hand to prevent the students from reciprocating in kind. 'Surely we can converse in a civil manner, without recourse to common brutalities?'

'If you swear at me again, I will cut your throat,' snarled Blankpayn, rounding on him. 'Do not think I cannot understand your vile tongue, because I learned French at school.'

Kardington lisped something no one understood. He looked pleased with himself, and beamed affably at the taverner; Bartholomew supposed he had made some comment about finally meeting a man who knew a language other than Latin. His friendly smile confused Blankpayn, who stood with a look of total incomprehension stamped across his pugilistic features.

'We do not want trouble,' said Michael quickly. He heard Spaldynge mutter that trouble would be fine with him, because he would welcome the opportunity to trounce the sly villain who had murdered Falmeresham. 'We are just concerned for a lad who may need medical attention.'

'You mean the fool who ran on to my dagger?' asked Blankpayn with an unpleasant sneer.

'Perhaps *you* will run on to my fist,' suggested Spaldynge, to approving nods from the students. Kardington and Wisbeche exchanged an alarmed glance. 'And then on to the toe of my boot.'

'And perhaps *you* will dance on the end of my sword,' retorted Blankpayn. He started to reach for his weapon, but thought better of it when Wisbeche's lads immediately drew their daggers. 'But I have no idea what happened to your student, because I have been with my mother in Madingley since Sunday. Why? Is he dead? I did not wound him that badly.'

'You have not been in Madingley,' said Bartholomew, determined to have the truth. 'Your mother has not seen you in days.'

Blankpayn's expression hardened. 'You have been pestering her? An old lady who lives alone, and who would have been terrified by scholars invading her home? How dare you!'

'We do not care where you have been hiding,' said Bartholomew, not pointing out that Blankpayn's mother was a fierce matron who was unlikely to be terrified by anything. 'We are only concerned with Falmeresham.'

'If he is alive, we want him home,' said Michael. 'If he is dead, we want him decently buried.'

'I have not seen him since the accident,' stated Blankpayn firmly. 'I wish I had, because then I would have bartered – your student's corpse in return for a relaxing of the rent laws. It would be a fair exchange.'

'I will give you a fair exchange,' muttered Spaldynge, stepping forward.

Michael pulled him back. 'Do not let us detain you, Blankpayn. Thank you for your time.'

'Go and wash your ale-pots like a good boy,' Spaldynge jeered as the taverner began to slouch away. 'And while you are at it, you can wash yourself, too. You stink.'

'Spaldynge!' exclaimed Kardington, shocked. '*Rude!*'

Spaldynge looked suitably sheepish. Fortunately, Blankpayn did not consider the insult to be an especially grave one, because he made an obscene gesture as he left, but that was the full extent of his retaliation. Seeing the crisis was over, and there would be no opportunity for brawling that day, the students and apprentices began to disperse. They were disappointed, clearly itching to be at each other's throats.

'Thank you for your support,' said Michael to the two masters. He pointedly ignored Bartholomew and Spaldynge, displeased with both for almost bringing about another fight.

'Surely, there is no need for all this strife?' asked Wisbeche. 'Are you sure the stance you are taking with the rents is the right one, Brother?'

'I think it is,' said Kardington, abandoning his attempts to speak English now he was alone with scholars. 'We must maintain affordable hostels, or we will have a plethora of unpaid bills at the end of every term – if students enrol at all. Candelby's demands could destroy the University.'

Wisbeche remained unconvinced. 'I think Candelby has a point – it is time to relax the Statutes. Since the Death, prices have risen for every commodity – except rents.'

'But surely, maintaining low rents in a world of spiralling costs is a good thing?' asked Michael.

'Good for us,' said Wisbeche. 'But not for those who need the income to feed themselves.'

'That does not include Candelby, though,' said Spaldynge. 'He is already disgustingly rich.'

'You should know,' said Wisbeche tartly. 'You sold him a University-owned house, despite the Senior Proctor's request that we hold off on property sales until the rent war is settled.'

'A compromise would be the best solution,' said Kardington, stepping forward to prevent Spaldynge from responding. 'Perhaps we could raise the rents by a nominal amount. Our students will complain, and so will the landlords, but it is the best we can do.'

'I have already tried that,' said Michael. 'And it has been rejected in no uncertain terms. The landlords want to *triple* the rents, and will not accept a penny less.'

'Then triple them,' said Wisbeche with a shrug. 'Students on low incomes will have to go to Oxford instead. Nothing can be bought in this world without money, so why should a university be any different?'

'Do not do it, Brother,' warned Kardington. 'If you yield on this front, we will face ultimatums from those who provide other commodities – ale, bread, meat and other essential supplies.'

Michael rubbed his eyes. 'So, as well as having to do battle with the town, I discover that my colleagues are divided in their opinions, too – two sides offering perfectly valid arguments.'

Wisbeche smiled ruefully. 'It would seem so. I would not like to be in your position, Brother.'

'Neither would I,' said Kardington fervently. 'So, we agree on that, at least. Come, Spaldynge. Let us go home before you offend any more vulgar taverners.'

'Willingly,' said Spaldynge. 'I do not want to linger here with a physician, anyway.'

When they had gone, Bartholomew noticed that three old ladies who sold vegetables near St Mary the Great were glaring at him. One summoned him frequently to cure her stomach pains, and he had never once charged for his services. He smiled at her, and was disappointed when she spat at him. He had expected her to feel some affection towards him, after all his years of charity.

'Spaldynge has a fierce temper,' remarked Michael, sketching a wry benediction at her as he passed. 'And he, alone of the Clare scholars, has no alibi for the business on Sunday – he remained in the College when everyone else rushed out to gawp, because he thought it might be a diversion for a burglary. I wonder just how far his hatred of physicians extends.'

'But the Clare men raced out of their hall *after* the accident, when Lynton was already dead. What Spaldynge did at that point is irrelevant.'

Michael was thoughtful. 'I made a few enquiries, and learned that no one from Clare actually saw Spaldynge that afternoon – the reason Kardington and Lexham say he stayed behind to guard the College is because he told them so. They did not see him – not after the accident, and not before, either. And do not forget that Falmeresham is a physician in all but name, now he is so close to finishing his degree.'

Bartholomew stared at him. 'Spaldynge has been making barbed comments to me ever since the plague, but he has never been violent.'

'Then let us hope he has not started now.'

'Perhaps Wisbeche is right about the rents,' said Bartholomew, glancing around as they crossed the Market Square. He could not recall a time when he had felt less comfortable in his own town, and realised how fickle people could be. 'Maybe you should capitulate.'

Michael sighed. 'I lay awake most of last night, fretting about the situation. I considered tendering my resignation and fleeing to Ely before I am lynched, but that would be cowardly.'

'It is not you that is the problem, Brother. It is the rents. Raise them.'

'The only way to do that is by amending the Statutes,' said Michael. 'And that requires the permission of the Regents.' The Regents were the University's Fellows and senior scholars.

'Then call a Convocation of the Regents, Brother. *They* can decide whether the Statutes should change or stay as they are, and we can *all* take responsibility for what is happening. I do not see why you should have to bear this alone.'

Michael smiled wanly. 'I imagine most Regents will feel like Wisbeche, and will prefer more expensive accommodation in a peaceful town.'

'I hope so, because the alternative is cheap rent in a town that is rife with turmoil.'

'Arderne must have a compelling tongue,' said Michael, as they walked back to Michaelhouse. 'I thought you were popular with your patients, but several have scowled at you today. Surely you cannot have killed that many?'

'Robert de Blaston just smiled, so they are not all infected with Arderne's poison. Most of them are glaring at *you*, anyway, and Burgess Ashwelle just called you a—'

'What did you learn from challenging Blankpayn?' asked the monk, not wanting to hear what Ashwelle had said. 'Were his answers worth risking another brawl?'

Bartholomew winced as a man, cloaked and hooded

189

against the rain, walked out of St Michael's Lane directly into the path of a cart. The pony reared and the driver howled abuse. The pedestrian jerked back in alarm, then fled along the High Street. Bartholomew was puzzled. Such incidents happened all the time, and those involved either yelled back or ignored them – few people ever ran away.

'Blankpayn's testimony was inconsistent. First, he said he had not wounded Falmeresham badly, and only later did he start talking about a body. I suspect he was just trying to upset us.'

'Do not read too much into it,' warned Michael, seeing hope glow in his friend's eyes. 'If Falmeresham was alive, he would have found his way home by now. *Ergo,* I suspect he is dead, and Blankpayn's parting words will prove to be prophetic – we will start to receive letters demanding a relaxing of the rent laws in exchange for his body soon.'

'Falmeresham is resourceful,' said Bartholomew stubbornly. 'I do not believe he is dead.'

They walked the rest of the way in silence, and when they reached Michaelhouse, Cynric was waiting for them in the lane. 'I do not like the way people are looking at you,' the book-bearer said uneasily. 'What have you been doing?'

'Nothing,' objected Bartholomew. 'Unless you think I was spotted burgling Clare last night.'

'No one saw you except Spaldynge, who now thinks he was mistaken,' said Cynric. 'We were lucky. But I was loitering to give you this. It was delivered anonymously a few moments ago, and I thought it might be important.'

'Oh, Lord!' groaned Michael, as the book-bearer handed him a note. 'Now what?'

The message was written on parchment that was thin and old – someone had not wanted to spend money on a better piece. The handwriting was crabbed, and Michael turned it this way and that until he was forced to admit it was too

190

small for his eyes. He gave it to Bartholomew. The physician scanned it quickly, then gazed at the monk in horror.

'It is a confession from a man who claims he murdered Kenyngham. He says he fed him a slow-acting poison at Easter, and that is why he died.'

Michael tore it from him. 'Are you sure? You have not misread it?'

'Of course I have not misread it! It is in French, which is strange – scholars would use Latin and townsfolk prefer English. Someone is making sure he leaves you no clues as to his identity.'

'How could anyone poison Kenyngham?' asked Cynric. 'He was with you at Easter.'

Bartholomew felt a stab of unease when he realised that was not true. 'There was a vigil in St Michael's Church from sunset on Saturday until dawn on Sunday. The rest of us came and went in shifts, but Kenyngham remained the whole night and sometimes he was alone.'

'I *told* you he was poisoned,' cried Michael. His face was white with shock. 'I said so on several occasions, but you kept saying that he was not.'

'I did not think he could have been.' Bartholomew's stomach felt as though it was full of liquid lead – heavy and burning at the same time. Had he really made that sort of blunder? The poison must have been a very sly one, without odour or obvious symptoms, or he would have detected something amiss. Or would he? He thought about Motelete, and how even Arderne – a fraud – had seen signs of life that he had missed. Perhaps he had made another terrible mistake, this time with a man he had considered a friend. The thought made him feel sick.

'Can a slow-acting poison kill a man in the way Kenyngham died?' demanded Michael. 'He said he was too weary to walk to the Gilbertine Friary, then he closed his eyes and you made the assumption that he was lost in prayer. Of course, he was actually breathing his last.'

Bartholomew nodded unhappily. 'Yes, but he did not complain of being ill. I thought he was just tired after all the fasting and praying of Lent.'

'You might have been able to help him,' said Michael, stricken, 'had you paid more attention.'

'No,' said Cynric, coming to his master's defence. 'Once some poisons have been swallowed, there is nothing anyone can do, no matter how diligently they watch.'

Michael relented. He rubbed a hand across his face. 'I am sorry, Matt – I did not mean to sound accusing. It is not your fault he died, but this vile killer's.'

Bartholomew did not hear him: he was thinking about Kenyngham's last words, when he had talked about crocodiles and shooting stars. Had the old man been in the grip of a deadly substance that had made him delusional? And what about the potion Michael had seen him imbibe, which he had called an antidote? Had he known his life was in danger? And if so, had Bartholomew – his own physician – missed signs and symptoms that should have told him something was wrong? Perhaps folk *were* right to distrust his skills and call him a charlatan.

The news that someone had elbowed Kenyngham into his grave had shocked Bartholomew deeply, and he kept replaying the Gilbertine's last day through in his mind. He sat in his room, staring out of the window, not seeing the rain that slanted across the courtyard and turned hard earth into a morass of mud and wet chicken droppings. The College hens and the porter's peacock huddled under a tree, balls of saturated feathers looking sorry for themselves, while Agatha's cat stretched gloatingly on the kitchen windowsill, luxuriating in the only warm room at Michaelhouse.

Michael was finishing a cake Edith had sent Bartholomew for Easter. He picked up the plate, carefully poured the crumbs into his hand, then slapped them into his mouth. While he chewed, he took the confession in his hand and stared at it.

'Why do people use such tiny writing these days? The purpose of letters is to communicate, and you cannot do that if you scribe your message too small for normal men to read.'

Bartholomew went to the chest where he kept his belongings, and rummaged for a few moments, eventually emerging with a rectangular piece of glass that had been set into a leather frame. 'This belonged to the Arab physician I studied under in Paris. He said I might want it one day, but I think your need is greater than mine.'

Michael's face broke into a grin of delight as he passed the item across the letter. 'It magnifies the words so I can see them! This is a clever notion, Matt. Your Arab master was a genius.'

Bartholomew sat and stared across the courtyard again. 'It is obvious, when you think about it. The exact science of optics asserts that a convex lens will reflect the ratio of the width of an image to the width of an object—'

'Never mind that,' said Michael, studying the text intently. 'Who penned this letter? Do you recognise the writing? Whose scrawl is so minute that a glass is required to make sense of it?'

'Virtually everyone in the University, according to you. However, an equally important question to ask is *why* did someone write it? Is it to boast, because the culprit knows you will never catch him? Is it because he feels guilty, and wants his crime unveiled?'

'And why would anyone harm Kenyngham?' Michael flicked the letter with his finger to indicate distaste. 'He was the last man to accumulate enemies.'

'I would have said the same about Lynton.'

'Not so, Matt. Kenyngham was a saint. However, we have discovered that Lynton leased houses to wealthy burgesses rather than to his fellow scholars. *And* there is an odd association between him and Ocleye – both shot with crossbows and both with their signatures on a rent agreement. Nothing like that will ever be discovered about Kenyngham.'

'No,' admitted Bartholomew. 'He and Lynton were very different men.'

'Of course, there is nothing to say they were not dispatched by the same person. One killed by an arrow and the other by insidious poison. Neither method allows for second thoughts.'

'No one disliked Kenyngham.' Bartholomew turned away from the window and met the monk's eyes. Having had time to reflect and consider, he was now sure his initial conclusions had been right after all. 'And no one poisoned him, either. I think someone is playing a prank on you – confessing to a crime that was never committed.'

Michael regarded him suspiciously. 'That is not what you said when this missive first arrived. You were as stunned and distressed as I was. Now you say you do not believe it?'

'Yes – because logic dictates that it would not have been possible to poison Kenyngham.'

'But you said yourself that he was alone for part of Saturday night and early Sunday, because he insisted on keeping the Easter vigil. Someone could have given him something then.'

'And that is *exactly* why harming him would have been

impossible. First, it *was* a vigil, and so a time of fasting – and you know how seriously Kenyngham took acts of penitence. And secondly, he would not have accepted victuals from strangers, anyway.'

Michael considered his points. 'All right, I agree that he would not have eaten anything, but what about water? He may have been thirsty or faint. The poison was fed to him, then he walked home, where it gnawed away at his innards while we all enjoyed our Easter dinner.'

'He was *happy*, Brother. He may have been tired, but I do not think he was in pain.'

'He was happy because he knew he was going to die. He was a religious man, and not afraid. Indeed, he probably welcomed death as his first step towards Paradise, which is why he said nothing to the physician at his side.'

'That would have been tantamount to suicide, and thus a sin. He would not have risked his immortal soul in such a way. He did say some odd things before he died, though. He told me to stand firm against false prophets, which he called shooting stars, and he said you were to be wary of timely men with long teeth – crocodiles.'

'Crocodiles,' mused Michael. 'What was he talking about? Who has long teeth?'

'I imagine it was a metaphor.'

Michael scratched his chin, nails rasping against the bristles. 'He was right about the false prophet – it is Arderne, making fraudulent claims. It is apt to call him a shooting star, because that is what he is: a passing phenomenon whose fame will fade the moment people see through him.'

'We are moving away from the point. I do not believe what this letter claims, because Kenyngham would not have swallowed anything during his vigil, not even water. And

195

after that, he was with us, and we all ate and drank the same things. I stand by my initial diagnosis – that he died because he was old and it was his time.'

'Well, I *do* believe it now,' said Michael, equally firm. 'And I should not have let myself be persuaded otherwise. He told me he was taking an antidote, and I shall never forgive myself for not pressing him on the matter. I might have been able to save him. However, while I might have failed him in life, I shall not fail him in death. I *will* unmask the villain that deprived Cambridge of its best inhabitant, even if it is the last thing I do. If I apply for an exhumation order from the Bishop's palace in Ely, will you inspect the body for me?'

Bartholomew stared at him. 'I have examined it twice already, and there was nothing to see. Please do not do this Michael. Investigate, if you must, but do not drag him from his final resting place. He would not approve of that at all.'

'He will approve if he was murdered. I shall write the letter today. Will you look at him or not?'

'I will not. Ask Rougham – he acted as your Corpse Examiner when I was away last year, so he will be used to such requests. And if he has been abandoned by as many patients as he claims, he may be glad of the money.'

The rain blew over during the night, and although the streets were full of puddles, the early morning sky was clear with the promise of sunshine to come. Shivering and complaining bitterly about the sheet of ankle-deep mud that comprised Michaelhouse's yard, the scholars lined up to process to the church for their dawn offices. Langelee was in front, his four Fellows were behind him, and the students and commoners brought up the rear.

When they arrived at St Michael's, a blackbird was trilling

in one of the graveyard trees and a group of sparrows twittered near the porch; their shrill chatter echoed through the ancient stones. The church smelled damp, because there was a leak somewhere, and Bartholomew noticed that the floor needed sweeping. It was a task Kenyngham often undertook, because it allowed him to spend more time in his beloved church, and the physician wondered who would do it now. He did not have to think about the matter long, because Carton grabbed a broom while William and Michael were laying out the altar, and began to push old leaves and small pieces of dried mud into the corner Kenyngham had always used.

It was William's turn to perform the mass and, as usual, he charged through the ceremonies at a furious lick, as if his very life depended on being done as soon as possible. It meant they were out in record time, and as Langelee had agreed to preside over the disputations and he had a free morning, Bartholomew decided to visit some of his patients – and look for Falmeresham at the same time. Despite everyone's gloomy predictions, he still refused to believe his student was dead.

'You will miss breakfast,' warned Michael, seeing him start to slip away.

'I am not hungry.' Bartholomew had spent another restless night with his mind full of questions. He was anxious for Falmeresham, distressed about the fact that Michael was intent on investigating a murder he was sure had not occurred, and concerned about the mischief Arderne was causing.

'Are you ill?' asked Michael, not imagining there could be another reason for passing up a meal. He frowned. '*You* have not eaten anything offered by shooting stars or crocodiles, have you?'

'No,' said Bartholomew shortly.

'We will come with you,' offered Deynman. 'Me and Carton. You should not be out alone, not with the town so angry about the number of people killed by the town's inept physicians.'

'He means there is safety in numbers,' elaborated Carton. The commoner–friar had changed since Falmeresham's disappearance. He had never been an extrovert, but the loss of his friend had rendered him sullen, irritable and withdrawn, and the students were beginning to make excuses to avoid his company. Bartholomew wondered whether the Franciscan's surliness derived from the fact that he no longer expected Falmeresham to come home alive. His own efforts to search for his friend had certainly tailed off, and he had not been out to look for him since Sunday.

Deynman gave one of his inane grins. '*I* do not believe the lies Arderne is spreading about you, sir, and I told Isnard he was an ass for listening to such rubbish. Then I asked to see his leg, to assess whether it really was growing back again, as Arderne promised it would.'

'And was it?' asked Carton, without much interest.

'Maybe a bit,' replied Deynman. 'It was difficult to tell. Did you hear Paxtone has taken to his bed? He is still digesting the flock of pigeons he scoffed a few nights ago, and Rougham suggested he remain horizontal, to allow the birds to pass more easily through his bowels.'

Tired and dispirited, Bartholomew escaped from his colleagues, although he was obliged to enlist Cynric's help in ridding himself of Deynman. He walked to the Small Bridges in the south of the town, where a glover called John Hanchach lived. Hanchach suffered from a congestion in the chest, which Bartholomew had been treating with a syrup of colt's-foot and lungwort; the physician had been heartened recently, because

Hanchach had turned a corner and started along the road to recovery.

Hanchach's house – a pink-washed cottage with a neatly thatched roof – overlooked an odorous stretch of water known as the Mill Pond, and Bartholomew was sure its dank miasma was at least partly responsible for the glover's respiratory problems. He walked along the towpath, enjoying the early morning sun and the scent of damp earth, and tapped on Hanchach's door.

Hanchach was sitting next to a fire, watching something bubble in a pot. A delicious scent of honeyed oatmeal filled the room. It was the first time the glover had left his bed in a week, but it was what Bartholomew had expected, given the good progress of the previous two or three days.

'I do not need you any more,' said Hanchach, somewhat sheepishly. 'I am better.'

Bartholomew smiled. 'You are doing well, but do not stop taking the tonic yet. You need to clear your lungs completely, and I have brought you—'

'Magister Arderne is my healer now,' interrupted Hanchach. He stared at the flames and would not meet Bartholomew's eyes. 'He touched me with his feather yesterday and gave me a potion, which is why I am up today. Your remedy was taking ages to work, but he cured me overnight.'

'I see,' said Bartholomew, supposing Arderne knew a patient on the mend when he saw one, and had pounced on the opportunity it had presented. 'How did he know you were ill?'

'Isnard,' replied Hanchach, acutely uncomfortable. 'We are neighbours, and he told me how you made a mistake with his leg. He recommended that I employ Arderne in your place, but Arderne said he would only treat me if I broke off all contact with you. He said you would try to foist more false remedies on me, but they might react dangerously with the real cure he has provided.'

'Is it because of Deynman?' asked Bartholomew, recalling how the student had almost killed Hanchach when he had misinterpreted some basic instructions and given him too much medicine.

Hanchach grimaced. 'That *was* a factor, although only a minor one. Mostly, it was Arderne himself. He has such compelling eyes, and you find yourself believing what he says, even when you do not want to.'

Bartholomew recalled others telling him the same thing. 'Your condition may worsen again if you do not continue to take the syrup,' he warned, unwilling to see a patient suffer needlessly.

'Arderne told me you would say that.' Hanchach shot him a wry grin. 'He is very expensive – I paid him five times what I pay you – but you can see his treatment is more effective.'

'You were getting better anyway,' objected Bartholomew. But he could see that any attempt to argue would look like sour grapes on his part, and he did not want trouble. 'May I see this potion?'

Hanchach pointed to a phial on the table. Bartholomew removed the stopper, then recoiled in revulsion. 'I hope you do not intend to drink this. It contains urine.'

'Arderne says a famous Greek practitioner called Galen recommends urine very highly.'

'I have never read that,' said Bartholomew, startled. 'And I know most of Galen's writings.'

'Galen did not *write* it,' said Hanchach, as if it were obvious. 'He *told* Arderne this special recipe. You see, Galen asked Arderne to help him on a particularly diffi- cult case, and when Arderne healed the patient, Galen told him several secret cures, as an expression of his gratitude.'

'But Galen has been dead for hundreds of years, and—'

'It must have been another Galen, then. I took the first draught of that tonic last night, and I shall have another this morning. Arderne says I will be walking around the town this time tomorrow, and back at work the day after that.'

'If you rush your recovery, you will relapse. I know you trust Arderne, but let your body tell you what to do. Start by sitting outside for an hour, and do not try walking until you are strong enough. If you need me, send to Michaelhouse and I will come.'

'I know you will, but I cannot afford to lose body parts to over-ready knives, like Isnard did. Good day to you, Bartholomew – and please do not tell Arderne you came. I would not like him to withdraw his assistance.'

Bartholomew left dismayed and angry. How could Arderne possibly hope to fulfil all the promises he was making? And what would be the cost of his reckless boasts? No matter what Arderne claimed, it was *not* a good idea to feed urine to a man who had been so gravely ill – or to anyone for that matter – and Bartholomew liked the glover, and wanted to see him well again. Should he go back and try to reason with him? But he knew there was no point: Arderne had fixed Hanchach with his 'compelling eyes' and that was that. Preoccupied and unhappy, Bartholomew began to retrace his steps to Michaelhouse. He was so absorbed that he did not see Isnard until the bargeman attracted his attention with a large clod of earth.

'I want a word with you,' said Isnard coldly, while the physician shook the soil from his hair.

Isnard was brandishing one of his crutches, and

Bartholomew hoped he would not swing it with sufficient vigour that he would lose his balance and fall. Isnard was always toppling over, mostly because of his fondness for ale, but he heartily resented being helped up, and onlookers were never sure what to do when he lay floundering. He was drunk that morning, and looked as if he had been imbibing all night.

'You saw the state of your leg that day,' said Bartholomew, knowing perfectly well what the 'word' was about. 'It was mangled beyond recognition. The bones would never have knitted – and you would have been dead of fever long before that happened anyway.'

'You are wrong,' slurred Isnard. 'Arderne said so. You maimed me, so you could collect a fee.'

'I never charged you, as you know perfectly well. And Kenyngham and the other Michaelhouse Fellows paid for your medicines.'

Isnard's ale-reddened face softened for a moment. 'Dear Kenyngham. However, I imagine he bought me the remedies because he knew what you had done, and he wanted to make amends.'

'You can think what you like about me,' said Bartholomew quietly. 'But do not malign him. He would never have looked the other way if he thought I had done something wrong.'

'You destroyed my life!' shouted Isnard, ignoring his point. 'I have given Arderne five marks already, but he said you did such a terrible job with the amputation that he will probably be unable to cure me. It is not *his* fault – he is doing his best. It is *yours.*'

With sudden fury, he lobbed the crutch at Bartholomew. The physician ducked, and it plopped into the river, where it was caught in the current and began to bob away.

'Now look what you have done,' howled Isnard. 'You made me lose my stick.'

Bartholomew stifled a sigh. 'Let me help you inside before you hurt yourself.'

'Stay away from me,' shrieked Isnard. 'And if you cross my path again, I shall kill you.'

CHAPTER 7

Isnard was not the only one who expressed his disapproval of the physician that morning. As Bartholomew walked from the Mill Pond to Michaelhouse, two rivermen cast unpleasant looks in his direction. He heard one tell the other that it was common practise among University physicians to hone their skills on hapless townsmen, so they would know what they were doing when a scholar needed treatment. Then he added that the operation to remove Isnard's leg had been performed by Deynman, which Bartholomew might have found amusing, had he not been so appalled by the way the town was turning so fast against him.

He did not feel safe by the river, so he abandoned the towpath and cut up one of the narrow alleys to Milne Street. When a woman called Yolande de Blaston wished him good morning, he regarded her suspiciously, and looked around to see if she had been charged to waylay him, so he could be pelted with mud – or worse.

'Do not worry about bad-tempered apprentices, Doctor,' said Yolande. She was a part-prostitute and part-laundress, and knew virtually every man in the town for one reason or another. 'If they give you any trouble, you come and tell me, and I will sort them out for you.'

'Thank you,' said Bartholomew weakly.

'I said the same to that Motelete – the student Arderne raised from the dead. The pot-boys from the Angel had him cornered, and were going to kill him in revenge for

Ocleye. I sent them off with a flea in their ear, although Motelete is a lad who knows how to look after himself, and I suspect he would have been able to fend for himself. Still, he thanked me prettily enough.'

'Motelete?' asked Bartholomew, startled. 'I doubt he would fare very well against pot-boys.'

'He had bloodied a couple of noses,' countered Yolande. 'It surprised me, too, because he is a gentle youth. Would you like me to stop Arderne spreading lies about you? I was going to do it yesterday, but Doctor Rougham said I should ask you first – he said if I knock out Arderne's teeth in your name, the fellow might make trouble for you. Did I tell you I am expecting again, by the way? Number twelve – you missed number eleven, because you were in France.'

Bartholomew was suitably impressed, and recalled that most of her offspring bore uncanny likenesses to prominent townsmen and scholars. Her husband did not object to the way she earned extra pennies to support their growing brood, and there were few households in Cambridge that were as content and happy as the Blastons. He persuaded her that punching healers was not a good idea for pregnant ladies, although it was not easy, because she had taken an intense dislike to Arderne. He took his leave of her, and had not gone more than a few steps before he met his sister.

'Have you had news about Falmeresham?' she asked, worried to see him looking so preoccupied and careworn.

He shook his head. 'But people do not just disappear. He must be somewhere.'

'They fall in the river though, and are swept away, never to be seen again. I appreciate that is not what you want to hear, but it is true.'

'I know,' he said shortly, refusing to think about it.

'Agatha threw a loaf of bread at Arderne yesterday – in

205

the Market Square – because he was braying that your amputation of Isnard's leg was unnecessary. It was a loaf she had baked herself, so he is lucky to be alive.'

Uncharitably, Bartholomew wished she had lobbed it a little harder. 'I cannot imagine what I have done to offend him.'

'He rails against Rougham and Paxtone, too, *and* he was rude about Lynton when he was alive. Lynton was so angry that he challenged him to a trial by combat.'

Bartholomew started to laugh. 'Lynton? I doubt he knew one end of a sword from another.'

'Well, you are wrong – he was quite accomplished. He was training to be a knight when he realised he had an aptitude for scholarship and decided to become a physician instead. I do not think he honed his skills very often, but he certainly knew how to wield a weapon. Surely you must have noticed the confident way he rode his horse, and how he never went out without a proper dagger?'

'He was a good horseman,' acknowledged Bartholomew. He had never given his colleague's penchant for knives much thought, assuming them to be decorative rather than functional. He considered the new information carefully, and decided it added weight to his contention that Arderne had killed Lynton – Lynton had been shot because he had not submitted passively to Arderne's torrent of abuse, and had tried to do something to stop it.

'Arderne accepted Lynton's challenge eagerly,' Edith went on. 'And why not? What danger could an elderly scholar pose? Then he found out that Lynton knew how to fight, and he began to make excuses – delaying the time they were due to meet, finding fault with the locations Lynton suggested, and so on. And now – conveniently for Arderne – Lynton is dead. Rumour is that the horse killed him, but he was too skilled a rider to have simply fallen off.'

206

'What are you saying? That you think Arderne killed Lynton?'

'It crossed my mind, although it is difficult to see how.'

Bartholomew did not enlighten her; she was safer not knowing. 'I have not heard about this duel before, and neither has Michael.'

'Then you are obviously talking to the wrong people. You should ask your questions of townsfolk, not University men. You will have a lot more honest answers.'

'I might have a dagger in my back, too. Scholars are not popular with laymen at the moment.'

'It would all blow over if the landlords were allowed to raise the rents. You must admit that the situation is unfair: once a band of students is in a house, they are free to stay as long as they like – for a pittance. Come to Trumpington for a few days, Matt. Term is not due to start for another week, and Langelee will not begrudge you a respite with your family.'

'You want me tucked away until people stop being angry about Isnard's leg?'

She smiled ruefully. 'Yes – and you must see that I am right. Look at those baker's apprentices. They are glowering at you, and if I were not here, they would attack.'

Bartholomew glanced to where she pointed, and conceded that the gang of youths was regarding him in an openly hostile manner. As he watched, one stooped and picked something up from the ground. His arm went back, and something started to fly through the air. Bartholomew tried to interpose himself between the missile and Edith, but he was too slow. The stone hit her head with a thump and she crumpled to the ground.

For a moment, the apprentices did nothing but stare, then they took to their heels and fled, their horrified faces showing it was not the outcome they had intended. Heart pounding, Bartholomew knelt next to his sister, relieved beyond measure when she opened her eyes and looked at him. Being a scalp wound, there was a good deal of blood, but her thick hair and padded head-dress had absorbed most of the impact, and she was more shocked than seriously hurt.

He gathered her up in his arms, and carried her to her husband's Milne Street property, where Oswald Stanmore fussed and fretted until she was compelled to order him away. Although theirs had been an arranged marriage – Stanmore had wanted a wife from an old and respected family, and Edith's father had been interested in the clothier's rapidly burgeoning wealth – they were a happy couple, and loved each other deeply. He stood in the doorway and watched Bartholomew stitch the wound, his face a mask of stricken horror. It was some time before he was convinced that there would be no lasting damage, and only then did he agree to let his brother-in-law leave. He followed the physician to the front door.

'I know my apprentices stood against you in the Market Square yesterday. I have berated them for it, and it will not happen again.'

Bartholomew shrugged. 'I cannot blame them. It is not an easy choice: their master's kin or their local friends. I imagine it is not pleasant for you either.'

Stanmore smiled ruefully. 'That is an understatement! My fellow burgesses say I have divided loyalties, and I find myself "accidentally omitted" from important meetings. Candelby wanted me to bribe you – to pay you for persuading Michael to yield to him over the rents.'

'What was he offering?'

Stanmore's smile was grim. 'More money than you make in a year. However, I declined on your behalf. Now all your patients have defected to Arderne, you cannot afford to lose your Fellowship to charges of corruption.'

'*All* my patients have not defected,' objected Bartholomew indignantly. 'Most have remained with me, although they are wary about admitting it. The only notable losses are Hanchach, the three crones who sell cabbages in the Market Square, and a couple of butchers.'

'And Isnard,' added Stanmore. 'He always was a bad judge of character. When he comes to his senses – as he will, in time – you should have nothing to do with him. That will teach him a lesson he needs to learn.'

'He threatened to kill me just now. He was drunk, but I think he meant it.'

'God help us! Arderne's antics are doing you serious damage, and while *I* am willing to stand at your side, I do not want Edith to do it. Will you agree to stay away from her until this is over? We both want the same thing – her safety.'

Bartholomew nodded, knowing it was the right thing to do, but he deeply resented the necessity. For the first time, he began to feel stirrings of genuine anger towards Arderne. He left Stanmore's house in a growing rage, and had Arderne been out at that precise moment, Bartholomew would have been the second Cambridge physician to challenge him to a trial by combat – his recent experiences with King Edward's army in France meant he was sure he could give the healer a run for his money. However, it was not Arderne he met, but Michael. The monk took one look at the black expression on his friend's face, and dragged him into the nearest tavern.

The Brazen George on the High Street was Michael's favourite inn. It was a clean, comfortable place that offered a choice of several rooms to its patrons. This meant scholars could drink their ale without being in company with townsfolk – and vice versa – and two rear doors meant students could escape if the Senior Proctor or his beadles happened to enter. There was a flurry of movement towards the back that day, although Michael rarely fined anyone for drinking in the Brazen George. It would have been rank hypocrisy, given the amount of time he spent there himself.

When Bartholomew told him what had happened, the monk's eyes grew round with horror. 'This is growing more deadly by the moment. You should stay in Michaelhouse until it blows over.'

'I shall not. I have done nothing wrong, and refuse to skulk like a frightened rabbit. Do you think Arderne will accept my challenge? He accepted Lynton's.'

'And then immediately withdrew when he realised Lynton was hardier than he looked. He is not a fool, and will not make the same mistake twice. Keep away from him. It is safer that way.'

'Safer for whom?'

'Him,' said Michael wryly. 'I have never seen you so angry. You say Edith will suffer no long-term effects, so put this into perspective. It was you these lads were aiming for, not her.'

'That makes me feel better.'

'Easy, Matt. Remember that Lynton fought back against Arderne, and now he is dead.'

'I thought you considered Candelby a more viable suspect for Lynton's murder.'

'I do, but that does not mean I am happy for you to take needless risks. Even if Arderne is innocent of shooting Lynton, he is still a very dangerous man.'

'Then that is even more reason for taking steps to neutralise him. He gave Hanchach urine to drink last night, and God only knows what other toxic potions he is distributing in his ignorance.' Bartholomew changed the subject

210

when he saw Michael look worried. The monk had enough to occupy him, without being burdened by the physician's concerns, too. 'Where have you been this morning?'

'Asking questions about Lynton. It is amazing how you think you know a man, but once he is dead, you learn all manner of new facts about him. I had no idea he owned houses, or that he was almost a knight. And I did not know that he was closer to Maud Bowyer than we were led to believe, either. Were you aware that she was his lover?'

Bartholomew gaped at him. 'Are you trying to make me feel better by making bad jokes? If so, it will not work. Lynton was scrupulous about observing the University's rules, and reprimanded me several times when he thought I was spending too much time with Matilde. That was two years ago, before she . . .' He trailed off. It was never easy to talk about Matilde.

'Then we shall have to add hypocrisy to the list of character traits we never knew he possessed. Isabel told me about this dalliance – I met her on the High Street a few moments ago.'

'She just came out with it?' Bartholomew was sceptical, and suspected the monk had been the subject of a practical joke, albeit one in very poor taste.

'Hardly! It slipped out as part of a misunderstanding. You see, Agatha mentioned to me this morning that Maud and Lynton often played games of chance together on Sunday afternoons. One of her many kinsmen works in Maud's kitchen, and he told her—'

'So now Lynton is a gambler and a despoiler of the Sabbath, as well as a womaniser?'

Michael raised his hand. 'Let me finish. When we ran into each other just now, I asked Isabel exactly how much time Lynton actually spent with Maud – you do not dice

211

with *your* patients, and it occurred to me that Candelby might not be her only admirer. Isabel did not realise I was asking about Sunday afternoons, and admitted that Lynton visited Maud most nights, with the notable exception of Fridays. Fridays were apparently reserved for some other activity.'

'What?' asked Bartholomew acidly. 'Robbing travellers on the King's highways? Running a brothel in The Jewry? Chanting spells to summon the Devil?'

'Do not vent your spleen on me,' said Michael sharply. 'It is not my fault your colleague transpires to have been such a dark horse. Isabel did not know what he did on Fridays – only that he never visited Maud then. Perhaps he spent the time on his knees, begging forgiveness for his sins. God knows, there are enough of them.'

'Isabel parted with this information willingly?'

'No, she was furious when she realised she had given me more than I was anticipating, and accused me of tricking her. Of course, I did nothing of the kind, and she knows it. She assumed I had been asking questions of Maud's servants, and one of them had let the cat out of the bag. She was mortified when she saw *she* was the one who had betrayed her mistress's trust.'

Bartholomew was about to tell him it was all arrant rubbish, when various facts came together in his mind. He hesitated, and began to think about it. 'Do you remember Maud at the accident on Sunday? She was weeping bitterly. I assumed it was shock.'

'But it was grief,' finished Michael. 'Her lover was dead, and *that* was the cause of her distress.'

'It must be why she refuses to see Candelby, too. He publicly maligned Lynton – accused him of causing the accident deliberately. No wonder she was upset.'

'And we must not overlook the fact that she backs the

212

University against the town,' added Michael. 'She said she would not let Candelby get his hands on her property and use it against us. It must be because she wants to support the foundation in which Lynton spent most of his adult life.'

'How long had their affair been going on?'

'Years, apparently. They started seeing each other during the Death, but were content to let their relationship stay as it was. Lynton did not want to marry and forfeit his Fellowship, and she did not want to lose her independence.'

'You mean her independence to accept Candelby's attentions?'

'She told us herself that she never took them seriously – that they were an amusing diversion.'

Bartholomew's thoughts returned to his enigmatic colleague. 'I would have thought Lynton was too old for this sort of thing. It is hard to imagine him as a rampant seducer.'

'You are never too old for an *amour*. Do you think *you* will lose interest in ladies when you are sixty? No, of course not! Still, I am surprised, because I always thought of Lynton as rather priestly.'

'He refused to take major orders, though, despite pressure from his College. Now we know why.'

'If Candelby knew about the affair, it is yet another motive for murder. You think your case against Arderne is strengthened because of what Edith told you about Lynton challenging him to fight, but Isabel's confession means my case against Candelby has also received a boost this morning.'

'*Did* Candelby know about Lynton and Maud?'

'Isabel said it was a secret, but you know how these things get out. Maud lives on Bridge Street, which is a

213

major thoroughfare. It would only take one too many visits to set tongues wagging.'

Prudently, Michael and Bartholomew left the Brazen George through one of the back doors, unwilling to be seen there by scholars or townsmen. They walked to the High Street via a narrow, filthy alley that was partly blocked by a dead pig, and was so rank with the stench of sewage that the monk complained of being light-headed. Bartholomew took his arm and helped him into the comparatively fresh air of the High Street.

'If you are unwell, Brother, you should ask *me* for a cure,' came a voice from behind them. It was Arderne, his pale blue eyes fixed on the monk like a snake with a mouse. 'I hear you are wealthy enough to afford my fees, and I promise you will not be disappointed.'

'I do not drink urine, Arderne,' retorted Michael, laying a calming hand on the physician's arm. Bartholomew's fury about what had happened to his sister had subsided, but not by much.

'Magister Arderne to you. And drinking urine comes highly recommended by the great Galen himself. Tell your physician friend to go away and read him.'

'I have read him,' said Bartholomew. 'And nowhere does he suggest drinking urine, especially someone else's. You might have killed Hanchach. You still might, if he does not—'

'Hanchach is *my* patient now, and his treatment is *my* concern.' Arderne was smiling, pleased with himself. 'You are only interested in his health because he is wealthy and you want his money.'

Bartholomew regarded him coldly. 'Unlike you, I suppose?'

Arderne's grin widened. 'I admit money is my main

214

reason for being a healer. However, there is also the satisfaction of seeing a man get well. Hanchach is already better, and it is down to me.'

'He tells me Galen is a personal friend of yours,' said Bartholomew.

'Did he?' asked Michael, startled. 'I thought Galen had been dead for the last thousand years.'

'More,' said Bartholomew. 'So it must have been a fascinating encounter.'

'I was referring to the *other* Galen,' replied Arderne with cool aplomb. 'The one who lives in Montpellier, and who is a great admirer of mine. Surely, you have heard of him? He is the best *medicus* in the world – after me, of course. But I have no time to remedy your appalling education. Unlike you, *I* have patients who want to see me.'

'Is there another Galen?' asked Michael, watching people doff their hats to the healer as he strutted away.

'No,' said Bartholomew shortly. 'If I challenged him to a trial by combat now, he would be hard-pressed to weasel his way out of it, and I am certain I would win.'

'I am sure you are right, but can you imagine what would happen if you were to kill or maim the town's most popular *medicus*? Cambridge would erupt into violence for certain.'

Late that afternoon there was a knock on the gate, and Cynric opened it to see Tyrington and Honynge. Their students were with them, and all had hired carts to ferry their belongings from their hostels to the College. Cynric stood aside wordlessly, and watched the procession stream inside.

In the hall, where Bartholomew had been presiding over a disputation entitled 'Let us enquire whether a simple diet is preferable to a varied one', the sudden rattle of hoofs caught the junior members' wavering attention. Unusually, all the Fellows were in attendance, sitting by the small collection of tomes that comprised Michaelhouse's library; most of the books were chained to the wall, because they were an expensive commodity, and the College could not afford to lose any.

'It is the new men,' announced Deynman, leaning out of the window to see what was going on, and interrupting the point he was trying to make about vegetables. 'They have arrived with their entourage – ten in total, but all with more luggage than the Devil.'

'Satan does not own luggage, Deynman,' said William with considerable authority. For a friar, William knew a lot about the denziens of Hell.

Deynman turned to face him. 'No? Then how does he transport his spare pitchforks?'

There was laughter from the other students, but Bartholomew could tell from the earnest expression on Deynman's face that the question sprang from a genuine desire to know, and was not prompted by any desire to be insolent.

'Satan is irrelevant to our debate,' the physician said quickly, seeing William gird himself up to respond. 'Come away from the window, Deynman, and continue your analysis.'

'You had just made the contention that a simple diet is better, because it requires less memory,' prompted Carton, when he saw Deynman struggling to remember what he had said.

'Oh, yes,' said Deynman, returning to the front of the hall. Usually, Bartholomew avoided using him in disputations, on the grounds that when he did, they tended to degenerate into the ridiculous, but he could not ignore the eagerly raised hand for ever. Unfortunately, William had then offered to take the opposing side, which meant the students had so far learned very little – except perhaps how *not* to go about the business of scholarly discourse. 'It is always good to be simple.'

'And you should know,' muttered Michael under his breath. He spoke more loudly. 'You need to argue your case in more detail, Deynman. Some disputants take more than an hour to outline their arguments in a logical manner, but you have only given us two sentences. The whole point of the exercise is to anticipate your opponents' objections and address them before he can give them voice. That is the skill we are trying to hone today.'

Deynman frowned as he strove to understand. 'Yes, I have been told that before.' The monk refrained from pointing out that it had been reiterated every day for the past two weeks. 'A simple diet is better, because you can use the same dishes and never bother to wash them. Your servants will be pleased, and thus you will have a contented household.'

'I see,' said Bartholomew, aware of the third-years struggling to suppress their mirth. He was almost glad Falmeresham was not there, because the whole hall would have been rocking with laughter at the witty commentaries he would have been providing. 'And how does that pertain to medicine, exactly? What does *Galen* have to say about simple and varied diets?'

'No, no, no!' cried William. 'You are giving him an unfair advantage by providing clues. It is *my* turn to speak now. A varied diet is better, because it confuses the Devil, and means it is more difficult for him to poison you. Of course, Dominicans brag about eating simply, but that is because they like to sit down and dine with Satan of an evening.'

'Oh, really, William!' called Langelee from the back. 'You should watch what you say, because some of our students might not know you are making a joke, and they will take you seriously.'

Bartholomew saw the puzzled expression on the friar's face and knew jesting had been the last thing on his mind. 'Is there anything else, Father?' he asked. Some of the students were easing towards the windows. The debate was amusing, but not as interesting as watching the new arrivals.

'No. I have stated my case perfectly, and anyone who disagrees with me is a fool.'

'Right,' said Bartholomew tiredly. 'Does anyone else have anything to add? About Galen's hypotheses relating to diet? Or Maimonides? Or even Aristotle?' he added, a little desperately.

'Galen believed that all foods should be classified according to their powers,' said Michael, taking pity on him. 'Whether they are costive or purgative, corrosive or benign, and so on. Too much of one power can lead to an imbalance in the humours, and thus Galen's contention is that a varied diet is superior to a simple one. I think that is the answer my colleague was hoping for.'

'Oh,' said Deynman, crestfallen. 'That means I am wrong.'

'No,' said Bartholomew, beginning to be exasperated. 'No one is wrong – and no one is right. That is the nature of disputation. It is about the *arguments*, not the conclusions.'

'*I* am right,' countered William immediately. 'I always am, in matters of theology. That is why no one in the University ever dares challenge me in the debating halls.'

'I thought no one challenged him because he is in the habit of stating his own case, then going home before his opponent can take issue with him,' said Langelee to Michael. The monk sniggered, and the Master raised his voice. 'So, Bartholomew, if you will do the summing up, we shall—'

'Is this the nature of disputation at Michaelhouse?' came

a voice from the door. It was Honynge, and Tyrington was behind him. Honynge stalked in, looking around disparagingly. 'A simpleton versus a narrow-minded bigot?'

Langelee gaped in astonishment. 'Did he just refer to Father William as a simpleton?'

'Actually,' whispered Wynewyk, 'I think he meant William is the narrow-minded bigot.'

Some of the students were laughing at Honynge's remark, because most shared his opinion about the friar, and applauded anyone with the honesty to stand up and say so. Others, however, felt an insult to William was a slur on their College, and there were resentful mutterings.

'He is a dangerous fanatic,' declared Honynge. 'And I, for one, will not pretend otherwise.'

'Most men wait until they have been officially admitted before launching an attack on their new colleagues,' said Michael mildly, going to lay a restraining hand on William's shoulder.

'We *are* officially admitted,' sprayed Tyrington. 'We swore our oaths yesterday, with William and Wynewyk as witnesses.'

'It is true,' said Langelee sheepishly, when Michael and Bartholomew regarded him in surprise. 'You two were out, and no one knew how long you would be. Honynge said he would accept the offer to be Principal at Lucy's if we did not admit him straight away.'

'My students and I want to be settled in before the beginning of term,' Honynge explained. 'And Candelby was eager to repossess the house we have been using as a hostel. If Michaelhouse had not opened its doors to us, we would have gone to Lucy's. There is not much to choose between you.'

'I am delighted to be here,' gushed Tyrington, attempting to make up for Honynge's brusqueness. 'It is good of you to invite me, and I shall look forward to many entertaining debates during my tenure. Also, I would like to present this book to the College library.'

'Aristotle's *Topica*,' said Langelee, taking it with an appreciative smile. 'How kind. And there is a lovely serpent embossed in gold on the cover, too.'

'A *sea* serpent,' whispered Deynman to Carton. 'Because it is swimming in spit.'

'So much for the inaugural dinner,' said Michael, disappointed that more had not been made of the occasion. 'We do not have new Fellows very often, and a feast is a good way to welcome them.'

'Feasts are an unnecessary expense,' countered Honynge. 'I shall be urging moderation in the future. Besides,' he added in an undertone, 'they may try to serve you dog, so you should veto repasts whenever you can.'

'We do not eat dog,' objected William indignantly. 'We leave that sort of thing to Dominicans.'

'And we shall have feasts whenever we feel like them,' declared Michael, objecting to the notion that his stomach might be about to fall victim to some needless abstention. 'Besides, we have just been debating diet, and the general consensus is that Galen was right when he recommended the consumption of a large variety of foods. Matt will support me in this.'

'A "large variety" is not the same as a "large amount",' began Bartholomew. 'And—'

'I do not like my new room,' said Honynge, moving to another issue. 'It smells of mice, so I think I shall take Bartholomew's instead. He can share with Wynewyk, and Tyrington can have what was the medical storeroom. That will leave Kenyngham's chamber for my students.'

'Bartholomew is not moving,' said Langelee, after a short, startled silence. 'And he needs that storeroom for his potions. They sometimes stink, and we do not want them near the kitchens.'

'Potions are the domain of apothecaries,' said Honynge icily. 'So, it would be better if he mixed no more medicines in Michaelhouse. And it would also be wise if he severed ties with his town patients, too. There is a war brewing, and we do not want the College targeted by bereaved kin.'

'I am sorry to say he has a point,' said Wynewyk to Bartholomew. 'There have been bitter mutterings against you of late, and Isnard said—'

'Isnard would have been dead by now, if Doctor Bartholomew had not removed his leg,' interrupted Deynman angrily. 'I saw the injury myself, and I know about these things, because *I* am his senior student.'

'Are you really?' asked Honynge, looking him up and down. He lowered his voice again. 'You made a mistake in coming here. Michaelhouse is full of fools, gluttons and madmen.'

'You will get used to them,' said Deynman pleasantly, assuming the muttered confidence was meant for him. 'I barely notice my colleagues are foolish, gluttonous or mad these days.'

'Tyrington brought a barrel of wine, for the Fellows to celebrate his arrival,' said Langelee, keen to avert a row in front of the students, and so cutting off Honynge's startled response. 'It is in the conclave, so shall we adjourn?'

The Fellows trooped after their barrel-chested Master, leaving the junior members to chatter excitedly among themselves. Bartholomew hesitated, because Honynge's seven scholars and Tyrington's three were loitering, and he did not want a fight if they transpired to be anything like their masters. But Deynman approached them with a friendly smile, and they responded in kind.

'Honynge is all right, once you get to know him,' said a lad from Zachary, when Deynman commented on the fact that the new Fellow was rather free with his opinions, and that most of them were not the kind of remarks generally voiced by mannerly men. 'He is an excellent teacher, and you will learn a lot if you are fortunate enough to be in his classes.'

'He talks to himself,' said Carton disparagingly. 'How will we know whether he is lecturing to us or enjoying a discussion with his favourite person?'

'It becomes obvious after a while,' replied the student. 'You should hear him on Blood Relics! I have never known a theologian make these complex issues more clear.'

'Tyrington has interesting views on that debate, too,' said one of the Piron students. 'I am looking forward to hearing him challenge Brother Michael. Michael has a formidable reputation as a scholar, although I understand Father William is a little less able in that respect.'

No one from Michaelhouse begged to differ, and Bartholomew followed his colleagues into the conclave a little easier in his mind. The newcomers were too relieved to have found a permanent home in a College to risk it by squabbling, while the Michaelhouse students were a hospitable crowd. He suspected they were going to be better friends than the Fellows.

'This is nice,' said Tyrington, looking around the conclave appreciatively as Bartholomew closed the door behind him. Now the senior members could argue all they liked, content in the knowledge that the students could not hear them. 'I am glad I chose Michaelhouse over Clare – they offered me a Fellowship, too, and I was obliged to make a decision faster than I would have liked.'

'We were delighted when we heard we had pre-empted them,' said William, rubbing his hands together as Wynewyk broached the cask of wine. 'It is always a pleasure to learn one's College has scored a victory over an inferior foundation.'

Tyrington treated William to one of his leers. 'I am gratified that you want me here, but please do not gloat over Clare. They will not like it, and I would hate to be a cause of discord.'

'That is good advice,' said Michael to William. 'And if I hear you have been aggravating Master Kardington, Spaldynge or any other Clare man over securing Tyrington, I shall not be pleased.'

'I am not a fool, Brother,' said William, hovering close to Wynewyk, to ensure he laid claim to the first available goblet of claret. 'I know we are poised at the edge of a precipice, and you need all your Regents to be friends with each other. I shall even lay aside my dispute with the Dominicans until the rent war is resolved, although it will not be easy.'

'I shall take this seat,' announced Honynge, making a beeline for the chair Kenyngham had usually occupied. 'It is a little tatty, but it will suffice. Make sure it is always free for me, if you please. I have a bad back, so must be careful where I sit.'

'In that case, I shall take this stool,' said Tyrington, attempting to distance himself from his new colleague by claiming the least desirable place in the room. 'If no one has any objection.'

William strode towards Honynge, grabbed him by the scruff of his neck and hauled him upright. Bartholomew winced, and Michael held his breath. '*That* belongs to the Master, and anyone who places his rump on it pays a non-negotiable fine of threepence.'

'Thank you, Father,' said Langelee, playing along by sitting and beaming around him. 'Now, let us have this wine. I am parched. You must serve it, Honynge, because you are the Junior Fellow, and that is a time-honoured tradition at Michaelhouse.'

Honynge gaped at him. '*I* serve no man.'

'Then you must pay another threepence,' said Langelee with a benign smile. 'These fines build up, and we are entitled to dismiss Fellows who cannot pay their debts, so do not incur too many.'

Honynge was seething. 'I am not junior to Tyrington. I am older than he.'

'It does not work like that,' said Wynewyk. 'Fellows are ranked by the order in which they are admitted, and Tyrington took his oath first, because you were late and we started the ceremony without you. If you had not been delayed by other business, you might have beaten him to the post, but I am afraid he has the edge over you now. You will remain Junior Fellow until someone else is sworn in.'

'But that might be years!' cried Honynge, aghast.

'Yes, it might,' agreed Langelee smugly. 'And you cannot leave us and go to Lucy's too soon, because you are obliged to give us a term's notice if you resign.'

'However, as Senior Proctor, I have the authority to waive that clause,' said Michael quickly. 'I can give you permission to leave today, if you find pouring wine repellent.'

Honynge thought about it. 'I shall stay,' he said stiffly. He lowered his voice. 'Do not allow yourself to be ousted by the unpleasantness of colleagues, Honynge – not on your first day.'

'We shall have to oust him on his second day, then,' murmured Wynewyk to Bartholomew. 'Lord, what have I done? Had I known he was like this, I would have voted for Tyrington instead. Tyrington leers and drools, but he is preferable to *this* sharp-tongued cockerel!'

'Perhaps these are nervous manners,' suggested Bartholomew hopefully. 'And he will become more amenable when he has settled in. Have you ever watched hens? They peck and scratch at each other until a mutually acceptable hierarchy is reached. Maybe people are not so different.'

'He had better not peck or scratch at me,' said Wynewyk pettishly. 'Or I shall peck and scratch back.'

'How well do you know Master Kardington, Honynge?' asked Michael conversationally, raising his goblet in a salute to Tyrington for his generosity. Bartholomew braced himself, seeing from the monk's predatory expression that an interrogation was about to take place. He recalled Michael saying he intended to put his questions subtly, and supposed Honynge's curt manner had goaded him into staging a frontal assault instead. 'Do you ever visit Clare? After dark?'

Honynge maintained an admirable calm as he poured the wine. 'No. Why would I?'

'I have no idea,' said Michael sweetly. 'Why does any man frequent another foundation? Perhaps he wants to pass the time of day – or night – with friends or lovers. Perhaps he likes the look of that foundation's silverware. Or perhaps it is documents that catch his eye.'

Honynge blinked. 'Are you accusing me of a felony?'

'Me?' asked Michael, placing a fat hand on his chest. 'Why would you think that? Unless your guilty conscience prompted you to ask such a question, of course?'

'I do not visit Clare, because I do not approve of fraternising between Colleges. It is safer that way. I have never been to Clare. Never. Ask Kardington if you do not believe me.'

He was so convincing that Bartholomew wondered if Cynric had been mistaken, but it seemed unlikely – if the book-bearer said he had seen the intruder's face, then he had seen it. He glanced at Honynge's hands as the man thrust a goblet of wine at him. The knuckles were grazed, and there was a deep gash on one thumb.

'What happened to you?' Bartholomew asked, indicating the wounds with a nod of his head.

'I scraped them during the process of moving,' replied Honynge. He pointed to the physician's fingers, which also bore the marks of an encounter with Clare. 'And you?' he demanded.

'I like Clare,' said Tyrington pleasantly, cutting across the stammering reply Bartholomew started to make. Honynge was sharp, and the physician had not expected him to counter-attack. 'It is a very nice College, although not as pleasant as here, of course.'

'Tyrington is a dreadful sycophant,' murmured Michael to Bartholomew, when the others were engaged in a strained discussion about the day's inclement weather. 'And I do not know whether I find his leers or his spitting more objectionable. However, he is charm personified when compared to Honynge. Do you think *he* killed Kenyngham?'

'Honynge?' asked Bartholomew startled. 'Of course not! Why would he do such a thing? And, as I have told you several times, no one killed Kenyngham.'

'Why is obvious – he wanted a Fellowship here,' Michael shot back. He stood and sauntered over to where Honynge was pouring more wine for William. 'Why did you chose us over Lucy's? I would have thought that particular hostel would have suited you very nicely – it overlooks a bog.'

Honynge regarded him warily, not sure if he was being insulted. 'Books,' he replied shortly. 'You have a library, Lucy's does not.'

'You did not choose us because you admire our tradition of academic excellence?' asked Michael, a little dangerously.

Honynge snorted. 'Hardly! You have Father William as a Fellow, and Deynman as a student. Those two alone make Michaelhouse a laughing stock in the world of scholarship. However, I shall help you to oust them, and then our reputation will improve.'

'What did you think of Kenyngham's scholarship?' asked Michael softly.

'Solid,' replied Honynge. 'Not exciting, but perfectly acceptable. Why?'

'Because I miss him. He was one of few men I respected, and if I find something untoward happened to him, I shall not rest until the culprit is hanged.'

Honynge regarded him with contempt. 'Is this what your Order teaches you? Vengeance?'

'Not vengeance – justice. And I dislike men who send me gloating letters.'

'I shall have to remember not to write you any, then. Forget Kenyngham, Brother. He was an old man who shortened his life with his religious excesses – if anyone killed him, it was Kenyngham himself. Besides, some good has come out of his death, because now you have me. I shall drag Michaelhouse from mediocrity to something other scholars will admire.'

'Shall we have a debate before dinner?' asked Langelee brightly, aware of the low-voiced confrontation between the two men and keen to put an end to it before it escalated. 'We have time.'

'Blood Relics?' suggested Tyrington. He spoke before swallowing the wine in his mouth, and Wynewyk scrambled to blot the resulting mess from the Book of Hours he had been reading. 'It is a matter with which we are all

227

familiar, and is at the heart of many important theological issues.'

'Go on, then,' said William, pleased. 'I am always ready to expound my views on religion.'

'And to listen to those of others,' added Langelee pointedly, unwilling for the friar to show them up on the newcomers' first day.

'I have changed my mind,' whispered Michael to Bartholomew a while later. 'Candelby is no longer my chief suspect for killing Lynton and Kenyngham. Honynge is.'

'Because you dislike him?'

'Because he is an arrogant pig who would think nothing of committing murder to further his own interests. And he is a liar, too. Cynric saw him up to no good in Clare, and you can see the evidence on his knuckles. He is hiding something.'

'Lying is a long way from murder.'

Michael was not interested in the physician's reservations. 'Perhaps I will steal some of Agatha's love potion and feed it to *him*. He will fall hopelessly in love with her and make advances. Then she will advance back, and he will be lucky to survive the encounter.'

It was still light when the Fellows left the conclave and went to their rooms, but when they did, there were none of the usual relaxed pleasantries that normally characterised the end of their day. Langelee was dismayed, because the harmony he had sought to achieve among his senior members had evaporated like steam, and the conclave had been full of bitterness and sniping. Bartholomew was subdued and preoccupied, worried about his sister, Falmeresham, and what Arderne might do to his patients. Michael and Honynge had quickly gone from antipathy to open hostility, and Wynewyk had taken against Tyrington because the man had salivated all over his favourite book and then denied that the resulting damage was his doing.

'I will *not* purchase him a new one,' said Tyrington resentfully, before walking to his room. 'The ink had already run. I am eager to make myself agreeable, but I will not be taken advantage of.'

'If he calls me a liar one more time, I shall . . .' Wynewyk ground his teeth in impotent rage. 'I do not know what I shall do, but he will regret ever coming to Michaelhouse. That book was in perfect condition before he slobbered all over it, and now it is ruined. For ever.'

'It is a pity,' agreed Bartholomew, who also abhorred harm to books.

William slunk down the spiral stairs, the last to leave the conclave. He was mortified, because it transpired that not only did both Honynge and Tyrington support the Dominicans' side of the argument pertaining to Blood Relics, but they were familiar with the nuances of the whole debate, and could argue them well. They had made mincemeat of his poor grasp of the subject, and he, a man supremely and blissfully oblivious to his own intellectual shortcomings, was at last forced to confront his inadequacies. Bartholomew tried to support his old colleague, but he did not give the matter his full attention, and he ended up being as savaged as the friar.

'Thank you anyway, Matthew,' said William gloomily, before heading for his chambers as a chastened man. 'It was good of you to take my side. I shall not forget it – and if that Honynge ever asks me to mind his students or take one of his classes because he is indisposed, I shall tell him to go to Hell, where he belongs.'

Bartholomew doubted Honynge would ever solicit the Franciscan's assistance on any academic matter, and suspected William would never have the satisfaction of wreaking even minor revenge for the unpleasantness he had endured that evening.

Langelee watched him go, then came to stand with Bartholomew, Wynewyk and Michael. 'I wish Kenyngham had not left us so suddenly, because then we would have had more time to consider his replacement. I think we have made a terrible mistake with this pair.'

'Do not worry,' said Michael with a wink. 'There are ways and means to deal with this sort of situation, and I am not Senior Proctor for nothing.'

'I do not want any bloodshed, though,' warned Langelee. 'At least, not bloodshed that can be traced to us. Be discreet.'

'Discretion is my middle name,' said Michael smoothly. 'And do not worry about bloodshed, either. There will be no need for that, because I was thinking of using my wits, not knives.'

'Yes, but remember they are both rather well armed in the wits department,' said Langelee. He began to walk away, but stopped briefly and called over his shoulder, 'I have a sword in my chamber.'

'What did he mean by that?' asked Michael, startled.

'Just what he said, I imagine,' replied Bartholomew. 'Do not forget where he came from. He was the Archbishop of York's spy for years, and it would not surprise me to learn that he had solved problems by resorting to weapons.'

'Just like you then,' said Michael tartly. 'Itching to challenge Arderne to a trial by combat.'

'I suspect it will be wiser to use the College statutes, and devise an administrative excuse to be rid of them,' said Wynewyk. 'I am a lawyer, so if I can help, do not hesitate to ask.'

'Thank you,' said Michael. 'I shall almost certainly take you up on it. What is that commotion?'

'Cynric!' exclaimed Bartholomew in alarm, beginning to run towards the gate.

'No,' said Michael, peering into the darkness. 'It is Falmeresham!'

A short while later, Falmeresham sat in the hall, surrounded by students, commoners and Fellows – all the Fellows except Honynge, who claimed he did not know Falmeresham, so could not be expected to celebrate his return. Tyrington stood shyly at the back at first; then he gave a leering grin when the Master hauled him to the front. It would not do for senior members to relinquish the best spots to students, and no master wanted to preside over a foundation where the hierarchical balance was in disarray.

'So, we are not going to be blackmailed by greedy landlords after all,' said Michael to Bartholomew, watching Carton fuss about his friend with wine and blankets. 'That is a relief!'

'The relief is in seeing him alive and well,' said Bartholomew. He felt better than he had done in days, and realised what a tremendous strain the student's disappearance had been.

William inveigled himself a cup of the students' claret, and came to stand next to the monk. 'You can call off the Convocation of Regents now – we do not need them to decide whether to change the University Statutes after all. We have our student back, so we can keep the rents as they are.'

'I wish it were that simple,' said Michael unhappily. 'Can I count on your vote?'

'No,' replied William. 'I do not think we should throw out ancient laws just because Candelby wants more money. I believe the rents should stay as they are.'

'But you are a member of Michaelhouse, and the Senior

Proctor has a right to expect your support, regardless of what you think about the issue,' said Tyrington quietly. 'It is the way things work.'

William scowled as he brushed spit from his revolting habit, and considered Tyrington's words carefully. He took a swig of wine, swilling it noisily around his brown teeth. 'All right,' he said eventually. 'I suppose I can ignore my conscience in the interests of solidarity – and I would not like Michaelhouse made a laughing stock because the Senior Proctor's proposal is defeated.'

'It is hardly a matter of conscience, Father,' said Langelee impatiently. He turned to the monk. 'I shall stand with you, Michael, and I shall persuade a few others to do likewise.'

'You will not use rough tactics, will you?' asked Bartholomew uneasily.

'I might,' said Langelee airily, rubbing his hands together. 'It depends how willing they are to accept my point of view. William is right: if Michael loses, his failure will reflect on our College, and I do not want to be seen as the Master of a place that cannot get its own way.'

Bartholomew was not very interested in Langelee's political manoeuvrings, and was more concerned to find out where Falmeresham had been for the last four days. The student was pale and thin, but his eyes were bright, and his old grin was plastered firmly across his face. Carton was also smiling, although not as broadly as the physician would have expected.

'We were worried about you,' said Bartholomew chidingly, as he went to sit next to his student. 'Could you not have sent word to say that you were safe?'

'You had several days to do it,' added Carton, rather coolly.

'Magister Arderne said it would be better to wait, to make sure his treatment of my fatal wound was successful,' replied Falmeresham apologetically. 'He feared for my life the first two days.'

'It was not a *fatal* wound,' said William pedantically, 'if it did not kill you.'

'But it *did* kill me,' said Falmeresham earnestly. 'I was dead, and Magister Arderne brought me back to life. It was a miracle!'

'Was it indeed?' murmured Bartholomew. 'Where were you wounded?'

Falmeresham raised his tunic to reveal a small, neat scar. 'Blankpayn's knife plunged deep into my liver. Magister Arderne pulled the whole thing out, stitched it up, and replaced it again.'

'Did he?' asked Bartholomew, astonished. In the past, he had extracted damaged organs, gently sutured them, and then put them back, but there was nearly always a fever afterwards, and it was often fatal. However, he had never attempted the procedure with anything as vital as a liver. Like most *medici*, he tended to leave livers alone.

'And it hardly hurt at all,' Falmeresham went on, clearly impressed. 'Well, the stitching-up did, I suppose, but having my liver removed did not. I *saw* it in Magister Arderne's hands.'

'What did it look like?' asked Deynman with ghoulish curiosity.

'Large, knobbly and green,' replied Falmeresham.

There was an awed gasp from his listeners. Bartholomew frowned, recalling from dissections he had attended at the universities in Salerno and Montpellier that human livers were never 'knobbly and green'. However, because anatomy was forbidden to English scholars, it was not something he could tell anyone. He wondered whether Falmeresham had been fed a potion that had made his wits reel during what must have been a serious undertaking. He knew from personal experience that it was better to have patients insensible during surgery, rather than thrashing around and fighting back.

'How did you come to be in Arderne's care?' asked Carton, pouring Falmeresham more wine. 'I asked virtually everyone in Cambridge, but no one recalls you being carried away.'

'And Arderne was busy with Candelby and Maud after the accident, anyway,' added Michael. 'He took them in his cart, because theirs was wrecked.'

'That brutish Blankpayn laid hold of me,' said Falmeresham resentfully. 'I thought at first that he was going to haul me off to a quiet place and finish me. But he believed I was dead already, and his chief concern was to hide the body before he could be accused of murder. He took me to the Angel, because it was closer than his own inn, and his plan was to drop me down the well.'

'People drink from that,' said Bartholomew in distaste. 'He might have poisoned the—'

'But I was not dead, and Candelby refused to let him do it anyway,' interrupted Falmeresham, eager to finish his tale. 'Magister Arderne happened to be in the Angel, seeing to Candelby's arm, and he ordered me taken to his own house on the High Street.'

'You mean you were held captive by townsfolk?' asked Michael. 'First Blankpayn, then Candelby, and finally Arderne?'

'Magister Arderne was *helping* me,' said Falmeresham firmly. 'Candelby was not all bad, either. He would not let Blankpayn drop me down the well, and he was angry with him for knifing me in the first place.'

'And you are completely recovered?' asked Langelee.

'Completely,' said Falmeresham with a bright, pleased grin. 'Magister Arderne gave me some medicine that he said would facilitate good healing, and it has worked. He recommended that I return to you as soon as I was able to walk – which was tonight. So, here I am.'

'I am pleased to see you safe,' said Bartholomew, wishing the healer had told him what he had done. It had been unkind to keep him – and Falmeresham's friends – in an agony of worry for four long days. 'There has been rather too much death of late.'

Falmeresham nodded. 'But Magister Arderne is fighting death wherever he can. He and I talked for hours, and he knows *so* much. He invited me to study with him, and it was a tempting offer, but I decided my place was here.'

'It is,' said William. 'You have already paid next term's fees, and they are non-refundable.'

'But it was a hard choice,' said Falmeresham wistfully. 'Magister Arderne has such exciting ideas. You once told me that it was impossible to mend a split liver, Doctor Bartholomew.'

'I thought it was. I have seen surgeons try it on three separate occasions, but the patient died in each case. What did Arderne do that was different?'

'He applied his feather,' said Falmeresham, quite seriously. 'It is very effective. Patients were coming to his house all day, and I could see him curing them through the door he left ajar. Magister Arderne is a wise and learned man.'

'Magister Arderne this, Magister Arderne that,' grumbled Michael to Bartholomew, when the others had gone. 'I am tired of hearing the name. Do you think Falmeresham is telling the truth?'

'The truth as he knows it,' replied Bartholomew. 'However, the scar on his side is too small for a liver to have been pulled through it, and it is in the wrong place. He was probably in pain from his cut, and drowsy from strong medicine – not in a position to know what was really happening.'

'He is beginning to worship the man,' said Michael. 'We are lucky he came back.'

'Why did Arderne let him?' mused Bartholomew. 'It sounded as though he wanted an apprentice. And why not? Falmeresham is intelligent, quick witted and he learns fast.'

'Perhaps he is an unwitting spy. We shall have to be careful what we say around him.'

'Why would he spy on us?'

'Spy on *you*. I am not saying Falmeresham would deliberately hurt you – he would not – but Arderne is quite capable of manipulating him. Our healer is a dangerous man, who will stop at nothing to get what he wants. And he wants you gone, so we shall have to be careful. I, for one, do not want to see him succeed.'

CHAPTER 8

Although William and Wynewyk were scheduled to preside over the mock disputations that Friday morning, Langelee decided the new Fellows should earn their keep, and had informed them at breakfast that they were free to choose any topic they pleased. Honynge sighed heavily, and muttered something about using the free days outside term to conduct his own research, although Tyrington was more amenable.

'Anything for Michaelhouse,' he said, rubbing his hands and leering at Langelee in a way that made the Master clench his fists. Langelee disliked sycophantic men, and was not overly pleased to be decorated with the remnants of Tyrington's breakfast either.

'Do not debate Blood Relics, though,' said William, standing with his hand covering the top of his breakfast ale to prevent Tyrington from adding to it. It was a defensive gesture that all the Fellows had employed the previous evening, and one Wynewyk had already dubbed 'the Michaelhouse Manoeuvre.' Bartholomew suspected it would not be long before they did it without thinking, and rival foundations would laugh at them for it. 'We had enough of that last night.'

Tyrington nodded. 'You are right – the College does not seem ready for such weighty theology, so we should stick to simpler issues. How about whether counterfactuals – natural impossibilities, as they are also known – can overthrow the fundamental principles of an Aristotelian world view?'

'I think I will stay here this morning,' said Bartholomew to Michael. A debate on theoretical physics sounded a good deal more appealing than investigating the murder of a colleague.

'Now just a moment,' said William, offended by the slur on his colleagues' collective intellect. 'I resent your implications, Tyrington. Michaelhouse owns some of the best minds in the University.'

'Actually, it does not,' countered Honynge. 'Tyrington and I will redress the balance, but it will take time. He is also correct in saying that we should debate simple topics to start with, which means the subject he has proposed is too advanced. We must select something even more basic, and build up to more complicated issues as term progresses.'

'I wonder what he has in mind,' said Michael, watching the servants dismantle the trestle tables in the hall and stack them behind the screen at the far end. William might splutter indignation at the new members' comments, but the monk knew there was truth in them. He and Bartholomew were well-regarded in academic circles, but Wynewyk was more interested in College administration than in honing his mind, and Langelee had never made any pretence at scholarship. The two absent Fellows were solid but not outstanding, and he was perfectly aware that standards had slipped below foundations like Gonville, Clare and Trinity Hall.

'Of course,' Honynge muttered under his breath, 'an inflated view of their worth is to be expected from men who put dog in their breakfast pottage.'

'We do no such thing!' said William angrily. 'It is a Friday, and we never eat meat on Fridays.'

'That means they have dog on other days,' whispered Honynge. 'You will have to watch them.' He turned and walked away, having achieved the impossible: leaving William at a loss for words.

When the servants had rearranged the benches to face the high table, the students began to take their places. The hall was rather full that morning, especially given that term had not yet started, because of the twenty new students. Honynge's seven, Tyrington's three and Lynton's two were sitting together at the back, while the eight who had been chosen from the sodden hopefuls chose the front rows, eager to prove themselves to their new teachers.

'*I* shall preside,' announced Honynge, elbowing Langelee unceremoniously from the dais. 'As I am obliged to be here, I may as well be in charge.'

Langelee's eyes narrowed. 'Watch who you push around, man – unless you want to be pushed back. At Michaelhouse, people shove the Master at their peril.'

Langelee had a way of sounding pugilistic even when he was trying to be pleasant, and when there was genuine menace in his voice, folk tended not to argue with him. Honynge nodded a prudent apology, and began to pace back and forth in front of the high table. When he spoke, his ringing voice silenced the rumble of conversation in the hall.

'The subject we shall debate is: *frequens legum mutato est periculosa.* Who will translate?'

'I will,' said Deynman, leaping to his feet with one of his guileless smiles. 'It means "frequently asking vegetables to remain mute makes them very discontented".'

'Lord!' groaned Bartholomew. 'He knows even less Latin now than when he first arrived.'

Falmeresham and his cronies were sniggering, although the new students were too unsure of themselves to join in. Langelee nodded, suggesting that he found Deynman's interpretation perfectly acceptable, while Wynewyk and

Michael were uneasy, anticipating that Honynge's inevitable scorn would bring about a quarrel. William looked puzzled and Tyrington was regarding Deynman warily, not sure what to think.

'No, Deynman,' said Honynge, surprisingly gently. 'Although you have correctly identified the verb and the noun, which is to be commended. However, the proper translation is: a too frequent alteration of the laws is dangerous.' Here he looked meaningfully at Michael.

'By laws, do you mean Statutes?' asked the monk icily.

Honynge shrugged. 'Changing the University's Statutes to suit townsmen's pockets is not a good idea, and I shall vote against it.'

'I agree with your sentiments,' said William. 'But loyalty to colleagues comes first, and you should back Michael's attempts to placate these landlords.'

'I shall not,' declared Honynge. '*I* shall vote as my conscience dictates. However, our students will not learn much today if all they do is hear us squabble. Let us begin this disputation.'

'He is a sharp-tongued cur,' whispered Langelee to Bartholomew, as the Fellows retreated to the back of the hall, leaving Honynge and Tyrington at the front. 'I cannot say I like him.'

'It was your decision to elect the man,' said Bartholomew, feeling the Master had a lot to answer for. 'If you had taken Carton, Michaelhouse would still be a haven of peace.'

'Not necessarily,' said Michael, overhearing. 'He has odd habits, too – such as going out after the curfew and declining to say where.'

'Tyrington is all right, though,' said Langelee. 'I am not keen on his leering and slobbering, but at least I do not feel the urge to plunge a blade in his gizzard every time he opens his mouth. It is a good thing Honynge does not

240

sit next to me at meals, because I would not like my appetite spoiled by an effusion of blood.'

Bartholomew regarded him uncomfortably, not sure how much was humour and how much heartfelt desire. 'Michael will find a non-violent solution to the problem. Just give him time.'

'He has too many other things to worry about – finding Lynton's killer, ending the rent war, averting trouble brought about by Arderne. He cannot manage Honynge, too.'

'Oh, yes he can,' said Michael firmly. 'Especially if it transpires that Honynge killed Lynton.'

Langelee was alarmed. 'I sincerely hope that is not the case! If it is, Peterhouse might demand compensation from us – for the murder of one of their Fellows by one of ours.'

'The crime was committed while Honynge was still at Zachary,' said Michael. 'It had nothing to do with us.'

'But Zachary no longer exists,' Langelee pointed out. 'Candelby reclaimed it yesterday, the moment Honynge and his students vacated. He grabbed Tyrington's hostel, too, and a wealthy goldsmith is already installed there. He must be delighted, because Tyrington was not due to leave Piron until September.'

'Piron was well maintained,' said Bartholomew, recalling the sumptuous building. 'It needed no repairs before it could be leased again, so I am not surprised Candelby has filled it quickly.'

'Zachary is the same,' said Langelee. 'It is a bit shabby on the outside, but the inside was always clean and neat. I imagine Honynge and Tyrington were ideal tenants from that standpoint.'

'Here we go,' said Michael, breaking into their discussion. 'The disputation begins.'

241

'I like your notion, Deynman,' said Honynge, smiling pleasantly at the student. 'The topic of a debate is irrelevant, and what is important is our ability to present coherent, logical arguments. In fact, I would suggest that debating the absurd requires greater skill than topics with which we are familiar. So, as president, I have decided that the subject will be the one Deynman has mooted: Let us enquire whether frequently asking vegetables to remain mute makes them very discontented.'

The students laughed.

'We cannot debate that,' cried William, aghast. 'I do not understand what it means!'

'That is part of the exercise,' explained Tyrington, not bothering to hide his exasperation with a man who should have known better. 'You must define your terms. And then an opponent will challenge them.'

Falmeresham stepped up to propose that vegetables disliked being asked to remain silent, and although his analysis had the hall ringing with laughter, his logic was impeccable. When he had finished, Tyrington put the opposite side of the argument. It was a lively debate, and Honynge was careful to let each student have his say, even Deynman. When someone made a mistake, it was highlighted patiently and kindly; Bartholomew wished Honynge was as considerate of his senior colleagues.

Tyrington's enthusiasm was infectious, so there was very little wandering of attention. When Carton – the only one of the assembled scholars who did not seem to be enjoying himself – began to gaze out of the window, Tyrington balled up a fragment of parchment and pitched it, hitting the commoner plumb in the centre of the forehead. Carton spun around with a start, and the other students smiled at his confusion. When Tyrington scored another direct hit a few moments later, Bartholomew suspected he had honed

242

the skill to perfection: Carton glared at Tyrington, his normally bland face dark with fury.

'Damn!' murmured Michael. 'They are both skilled teachers. I expected Honynge to be pompous and over-bearing, but the students like him. And Tyrington's obvious love of learning has even enthused my dispassionate Benedictines – I have never seen them so animated. What a nuisance! I was hoping to use incompetence as a means to be rid of Honynge, but now I cannot.'

'Damn indeed,' said William. 'We shall have to think of something else, because I do not want him in my College. He is a vile creature – probably a secret Dominican.'

'Where are you going?' Bartholomew asked, as the friar shoved past him, heading for the door.

'To buy some dog-meat,' replied William. 'And lots of it.'

I have grown confused with all we have learned,' said Michael, when he and Bartholomew had left the hall to continue their investigation into Lynton's murder. 'And I am not sure what to do next. Come to the Brazen George with me, and summarise everything.'

'We have only just had breakfast,' objected Bartholomew. 'And I am not sure it is wise to frequent taverns, given what is happening in the town. We would do better to stay here.'

'Nonsense, Matt. Candelby's antics will not prevent *me* from walking about my own streets – or from enjoying my favourite alehouse.'

Cambridge was quieter that day, and the roads held fewer people, although Bartholomew suspected this was because a troupe of travelling players was performing in the Market Square, not from any lessening of hostility. He could hear cheers, and was glad the crowd was good-humoured.

Michael pointed along the High Street. 'Candelby is heading our way. Can we reach the Brazen George before our paths converge? I am not in the mood for a spat.'

'Not unless you pick up the pace, Brother.'

'I am not running from the man. Very well, we shall bandy words, then. Perhaps he will be drunk, and I can persuade him to sign an agreement that will end our sordid squabble.'

Candelby was impeccably dressed, and the gold rings on his fingers glittered in the sunlight. He looked smug and prosperous, and Bartholomew wondered why he was making such an issue over rents, when it was clear he already had more money than he could spend; not being an acquisitive man himself, the physician failed to understand the bent in others. Blankpayn was with Candelby, although *his* clothes were dishevelled and he looked unkempt and unshaven.

'Why does Candelby keep company with a disreputable rogue like him?' asked Bartholomew, as the two taverners drew nearer. 'Blankpayn is uncouth and stupid.'

'But loyal. The other burgesses follow Candelby because he is powerful and influential; Blankpayn follows him because he thinks he can do no wrong.'

'I hear you plan to hold a Convocation of Regents, Brother,' said Candelby without preamble, as their paths converged. 'To ask whether it is right to go on defrauding honest townsfolk.'

Michael was startled. 'The Convocation is not public knowledge yet. My clerks have not finished drafting the official proclamation, so no one outside the University should know about it.'

'I have my sources. Let us hope your colleagues see sense and rescind this ridiculous Statute once and for all.'

'They may decide rents should remain as they are,'

warned Michael. 'And if they do, I will lose the authority to raise them even by a small amount. You may find yourself worse off than ever.'

Candelby smirked. 'If that happens, I shall tell my fellow landlords to evict all poor scholars from their houses, and lease them to wealthy townsmen instead. I will not be worse off, Brother.'

'There cannot be that many rich citizens wanting to hire houses,' said Bartholomew, puzzled. 'If you decline to lease your buildings to students, you will have such a small pool of customers that competition will drive prices down. You will be poorer in the long term.'

Candelby's expression was patronising. 'I have never said I will not lease my properties to the University; I have only said I will not lease them for a pittance. There will always be a demand for accommodation in Cambridge, and academics will have to pay the market price for their lodgings in future, just like anyone else.'

Michael glared at him. 'Is a heavier purse worth the trouble this dispute is causing? Men have died. Do you want more bloodshed on your conscience?'

'Any fighting is the University's fault, not mine,' declared Candelby firmly. 'Incidentally, I heard you visited Maud, Bartholomew. Do not do it again, because she is worse today. Arderne says it is because you touched her with your Corpse Examiner's hands.'

'Maud no longer cares for you,' said Michael tartly. 'So her health is none of your concern.'

Candelby eyed him with dislike. 'She is feverish and does not know what she is saying. She will welcome my courtship when she is well again, and then I shall marry her.'

'The accident exposed your real feelings towards her,' said Michael contemptuously. 'She sees now that you only want her for her money. She probably noticed your indifference towards your pot-boy, too – Ocleye is dead, and you do not seem to care.'

'Ocleye was a spy,' snapped Blankpayn, leaping to defend his friend. 'You cannot blame Candelby for not being grieved about a man like that. Ocleye was not to be trusted.'

Candelby shot him a pained look. 'Thank you, Blankpayn; your support is greatly appreciated. Now perhaps you will deliver this letter to Maud. Arderne wrote it for me, and he has a way with words, so it will not be long before she invites me to visit.'

The taverner stamped away, clutching the missive in his grubby fingers.

'You are lucky to have such a fine friend,' said Michael ambiguously.

Candelby's expression was blank. 'Yes, I am. I missed him when he was in the Fens, hiding, because you accused him of murdering Falmeresham.'

'According to Falmeresham, Blankpayn was ready to drop him down a well,' said Bartholomew quietly. 'Our accusations were not as far-fetched as you make out.'

'I imagine you were very worried,' said Candelby with a malicious grin. 'I would have been.'

'So, Ocleye was a spy, was he?' mused Michael, before Bartholomew could take issue with him for keeping Falmeresham's whereabouts secret. 'I imagine your fellow burgesses will be very interested to know you hire such men – especially if you paid him to watch *them*.'

Candelby blanched. 'I did not hire Ocleye to watch them,' he said, licking his lips uneasily. 'I employed him to watch *you*.'

Michael smiled, pleased to have nettled the man at last. 'Then he cheated you, because my beadles would have noticed anyone spying on me. Obviously, he was not doing what he was told.'

Candelby grimaced. 'It pains me to admit it, but you are right. At first, I assumed he was just not very good at his job, because he never had any intelligence worth reporting. It was only later that I came to realise he was actually in someone else's pay – the rogue was taking my money, but instead of spying on you, he was spying on *me*!'

'Yet he was riding in your cart on the day of your accident,' said Michael, unconvinced. 'If you knew he was betraying you, why did you permit such familiarity?'

'He asked in front of Maud, and I was trying to impress her,' replied Candelby sheepishly. 'Telling him to pack his bags and leave the town would have made me look unmannerly. So I let him ride with us, but was going to dismiss him as soon as we had a moment alone.'

'Who was he spying for?'

Candelby grimaced a second time. 'I assumed it was you, but I can see from your reaction that it was not. It will be another scholar, although God alone knows which one. They all hate me.'

'I wonder why,' murmured Michael, as he walked away.

When the proprietor of the Brazen George came to greet Michael and Bartholomew, he expressed none of his usual pleasure in seeing old friends. His large, plum-shaped face was a mask of worry.

'What is wrong, Master Lister?' asked Michael, watching him secure the door behind them. 'Surely you have not taken against me now?'

Lister winced. 'Of course not, Brother. However, I have had warnings.'

'Warnings?' asked Michael, bemused. 'What kind of warnings?'

'Ones that tell me I would be wise to break off my association with scholars.'

'Who has been saying such things?' demanded Michael angrily.

'The notes were anonymous, but Blankpayn is the obvious culprit. He and Candelby want to drive a wedge between the University and any townsfolk who provide it with essential services.'

Bartholomew tried not to smile at the notion that the Brazen George provided 'essential services'. Michael saw nothing amusing in the situation, though. 'Lord!' he breathed. 'What next?'

'If Candelby wins this war, he will pit himself against those of us who defied him,' said Lister miserably. 'I shall be ruined. So, you *must* defeat Candelby, Brother. My livelihood depends on it.'

'I shall do my best,' vowed Michael. 'But you have quite destroyed my appetite. Instead of roasted chickens, I shall content myself with half a dozen Lombard slices. Matt will have the same.'

'Matt does not want anything at all,' countered Bartholomew, feeling slightly queasy at the thought of eating sticky date pastries so soon after breakfast.

Michael eyed him balefully as Lister left. 'Please do not refer to yourself in the third person. It reminds me of Honynge. Do you think *he* is the scholar who hired Ocleye to spy on Candelby?'

'What would he gain from doing that?'

'He was living in one of Candelby's hostels – a place that was seized the moment he moved into Michaelhouse. Obviously, he wanted information about the man who was planning to evict him.'

'The same is true of Tyrington. However, I suspect Arderne employed Ocleye. We know he did nothing but listen and watch during his first few weeks in Cambridge, learning the lie of the land before he made his presence known. Hiring a spy is an easy way to amass knowledge.'

Michael gave a grim smile. 'We are both allowing personal dislike to colour our judgement. So, let us review what we know *without* taking Arderne and Honynge into account, and see what other suspects emerge.'

Bartholomew knew he was right. 'You start, then.'

'First we have Lynton, murdered with a crossbow in the middle of Milne Street, in broad daylight. Ocleye was killed the same way, at more or less the same time. It seems obvious that he saw the archer, and was killed to ensure his silence. Do you agree?'

Bartholomew nodded. 'It cannot have been the other way around – Lynton killed because he saw Ocleye's killer – because Ocleye was fussing about Candelby *after* Lynton had been shot.'

'Ocleye was a spy, not a pot-boy,' continued Michael. 'That explains three things: why he was older than most tavern scullions; why he made scant effort to socialise with the other lads from the Angel; and why he seems to have appeared out of nowhere.'

'Four things,' corrected Bartholomew. 'Spies are better paid than pot-boys, and he probably *could* afford to rent his own house, rather than live in the inn where he ostensibly worked.'

'And the man he chose as his landlord was Lynton. Perhaps he was Lynton's spy, then.'

'It is possible. Lynton had the rent agreement in his hand, and was probably reading it when he died. I wonder who took it from him.'

'Ocleye?' suggested Michael. 'He would not have wanted any links between him and a man who was unlawfully slain

– spies do not like that sort of attention. Then he was murdered in his turn.'

'Carton!' exclaimed Bartholomew suddenly, recalling something that had happened. 'He knelt next to Lynton's body and was straightening the cloak that covered him. Perhaps he removed it.'

'He would have given it to us, had that been the case – he has no reason to steal such a thing and keep it quiet. Perhaps I am wrong to dismiss Candelby in favour of Honynge. Candelby was present when the crime occurred, *and* he owns a crossbow. Unfortunately, Maud does not recall him pulling it out and committing murder, and no other witnesses have come forward. How can I catch him? I need real evidence, or he will claim I am just accusing him because of the rent war.'

'Meanwhile, we have learned facts about Lynton that have surprised us. He kept a long-term lover; he owned a Dispensary near the Trumpington Gate; he was a knight in all but name; and he was a landlord, raking in lucrative profits by renting his houses to wealthy townsmen.'

'Do you think a disgruntled student shot him? Scholars are losing their homes all over the town, yet Lynton still preferred to lease his properties to rich civilians.' Michael did not wait for an answer. 'And what did he do on Fridays, when he never visited Maud?'

'*There* is a motive for Candelby wanting Lynton dead: Lynton was Maud's lover – the woman Candelby still intends to marry.'

Michael was uncertain. 'Isabel said the affair was a secret, and I have never heard any gossip, so perhaps they did manage to keep it to themselves. Further, Agatha knew they played games of chance together on Sundays, but did not guess the real nature of their relationship – and *she*

250

knows just about everything in the town, given the number of folk she counts among her kin.'

'Perhaps Candelby was suspicious about Lynton and Maud, and sent Ocleye to find out what they were doing together.'

Michael nodded slowly. 'You are right – and that *is* a good motive for murder. So, we have Candelby as our chief suspect, with a resentful student second. What about Kenyngham?'

'Kenyngham was not murdered,' said Bartholomew adamantly.

'Yes, he was,' said Michael, equally firmly. 'I am not blaming you for missing clues, Matt. A mistake is understandable under the circumstances, and we were all upset by his death.'

'I did *not* make a mistake,' objected Bartholomew. 'I was concerned I might have done, which is why I examined him a second time. However, there is nothing to suggest his death was unnatural.'

'Poisons are difficult to detect – you said so yourself. You may have overlooked something, because you were not expecting to find it. We shall know after the exhumation. Rougham will—'

Bartholomew was becoming exasperated. 'I was *very* careful – *both* times. And if I could not detect anything amiss, then neither will Rougham. I concede you might learn something if you open him up, but I doubt Rougham will agree to that.'

'Open him up?' echoed Michael, round-eyed. 'You mean *dissect* him? Oh, Matt!'

'It is a discussion you started. Tearing him from his final resting place is just as distasteful as anatomising him.'

Michael's expression was flinty. 'You have become very

ghoulish since you returned from those foreign schools. They have reignited your desire to be controversial and heretical, which is a habit I thought you had grown out of.'

Bartholomew changed the subject before they could annoy each other any further. 'At least we have Falmeresham home.'

'What do you think of Arderne's claim to have cured him?'

'He cannot possibly have pulled Falmeresham's liver through that hole in his side. It would be like pulling a heart through a shoulder. Arderne was lying to him.'

'Arderne *did* cure Motelete, though. I accept your contention that the lad may not have been fully dead in the first place, but he certainly lay in a corpse-like state for two days. There are dozens of witnesses to that fact.'

Bartholomew nodded towards the Brazen George's small, but secluded garden. It was a pleasant space with a tiny pond and the kind of vegetation that benefited from a sheltered, sunny position. The tavern had the luxury of glazed windows, and although it was not easy to see through them, he recognised Clare's personal Lazarus, even so.

'Motelete is out there. Shall we ask him about his resurrection again?'

'Why not?' asked Michael with a weary sigh. 'I cannot see any other way through the ungodly maze of facts we have accumulated.'

Motelete had abandoned the academic tabard that identified him as a scholar of Clare, and was wearing a surcoat of dark green with multicoloured hose. He was in company with a fair-headed girl and a youth who looked so much like her that Bartholomew assumed they were siblings. The lad looked bored and resentful, but Motelete and the woman seemed to be enjoying themselves.

'Motelete's companion is named Will Sago,' said Michael, watching them. 'He is one of the Angel's pot-boys. Now why would Motelete be in such company?'

'It is not Sago he is interested in,' said Bartholomew dryly. 'It is Sago's sister.'

When Lister brought more Lombard slices, Michael asked why he was allowing a student and a pot-boy to drink together, when it might bring trouble. Lister pulled a resentful face.

'Candelby's lads have taken to patronising my inn of late – they come to spy, of course. How else would Candelby know the occasional academic visits my humble establishment?'

Everyone in Cambridge knew the Brazen George catered to scholars, and Bartholomew suspected Candelby had ordered his servants to frequent the place as a way to intimidate Lister into banishing them, rather than to gather intelligence.

'The lass is Siffreda Sago,' Lister went on. 'And the student is Motelete, who was raised from the dead by that remarkable Arderne. Sago is there to make sure she does not lose her virtue, although Motelete will have her soon, watchful brother or no.'

Bartholomew was thoughtful. 'Motelete courts towns-women, bloodies noses in brawls, and outwits chaperons. He does not sound like the quiet, timid student described to us at Clare – the one who would never have harmed Ocleye, who never visited taverns, and who cried for his mother.'

'He is said to have changed since his resurrection,' explained Lister. 'I am not surprised – it must have been an eerie experience.'

253

Bartholomew and Michael walked outside, where Motelete hurriedly removed his hand from down the back of Siffreda's gown.

'Wine is good for me,' he said, gesturing to the jug on the table in front of him. 'Magister Arderne said I should drink lots of it, to make sure I do not fall into death again.'

'That is the kind of physician any man would be pleased to own,' said Michael smoothly. 'Mine is always telling me to abstain, which is a wretched bore.'

Motelete smiled. 'I would rather have Arderne than any *medicus* alive. He is a genius, and I shall always be in debt to him for saving me. Would you like to see my neck? You will recall it was marred by a great gash that saw me lose all my blood, but now there is virtually no mark at all.'

It was an offer no physician could decline. Bartholomew examined the bared throat, and saw a cut that had scabbed over and was healing nicely. In a few days, it would fade to a faint pink line, and a month might see it vanish altogether.

'Do you remember being dead?' he asked.

Motelete shook his head. 'People keep asking me that – did I see Christ, was I in Purgatory, was my soul weighed? All I recall is being very cold, and when Magister Arderne commanded me to rise, it was difficult, because I was stiff. He says all corpses undergo a phase of stiffness.'

They talked a while longer, mostly about the fact that Motelete was not wearing his prescribed uniform, and that even scholars newly risen from the grave were not exempt from the University's rules. Motelete was not entirely won over by Michael's logic, but agreed to go home to Clare – without his sweetheart – when the monk mentioned that he had the authority to demand a fine of up to six pence from students who preferred taverns to their schools.

As soon as Michael was satisfied that Motelete was

heading in the right direction, Bartholomew headed for a stinking alley known as Butchery Row. It was behind the Market Square, identifiable by its rank stench and large population of bluebottles. Children sold rhubarb leaves at either end so customers could use them to keep buzzing flies from their faces as they browsed the wares on sale.

'I want to find out whether any meat-sellers have hawked livers that were knobbly and green,' he explained to Michael, 'because the organ Falmeresham saw cannot possibly have been his own.'

'This place always makes me glad I am not a woman,' said Michael, holding his sleeve over his nose with one hand, and flapping furiously with the other. 'They are obliged to come here every day, and it turns my stomach.'

'There is Agatha, buying meat for your dinner. She does not seem to mind the flies or the smell.'

'No fly would dare alight on her,' retorted Michael, flailing harder as they ventured deeper inside the shadowy alley. 'And nor would any smell.'

'Arderne delivered my love-potion yesterday,' Agatha announced as she approached. The sack hefted over her shoulder was huge, and probably contained the best part of a sheep. 'It contains real mandrake, and we all know there is nothing like mandrake for making folk fall in love.'

'It is also a powerful poison,' said Bartholomew, alarmed for the man who might drink it. 'It *can* induce wild fancies, but the dosage must be very carefully measured.'

'Who is it for?' asked Michael warily.

She grinned mischievously. 'You will know soon enough. Do not worry, Matthew. I will not give him too much of it.'

'I shall hold you to that,' said Bartholomew, hoping her idea of 'too much' was the same as his own. 'Edith told me you threw a hunk of bread at Arderne yesterday. If you dislike him enough to lob loaves, then why did you buy his remedy?'

Agatha was thoughtful. 'I hurled the bread because he insulted you, and I was going to refuse his charm when it arrived. But when he delivered it, and looked at me with those eyes of his, I could not stop myself from reaching for my purse. He *is* a clever man, though, despite his sharp tongue. He cured Motelete and Falmeresham of death, and he healed Blankpayn's leprosy.'

'I have not seen a genuine case of leprosy in England for years,' said Bartholomew doubtfully.

'Arderne said it was leprosy. I know all about it, because Blankpayn is my cousin.'

'*Blankpayn?*' asked Michael in astonishment, while Bartholomew supposed he should not be surprised. Agatha was related to at least half the county.

Agatha became defensive. 'I know he is not kin of which to be proud, but you cannot choose your relations, so I am stuck with him. He says he did not harm Falmeresham on purpose, though.'

'We know,' said Michael. 'I was witness to the fact that it was an accident myself, and there was no need for him to have run away. However, that does not justify him neglecting to mention Falmeresham's whereabouts when he knew we were worried.'

'He is a spiteful fool,' agreed Agatha venomously. 'He has no wits, not like me.'

'I do not suppose he told you anything else, did he?' asked Michael hopefully. 'Perhaps about Candelby and the crossbow he keeps to repel thieves and scholars? Blankpayn will never talk to me, but he might have confided in you.'

'He does confide,' acknowledged Agatha, liking the notion that she might possess information the monk did not. 'But Candelby did not shoot anyone on Sunday. His crossbow is never loaded, and as they take a few moments to arm, I never bother with them personally. I prefer a sword.'

'I see,' said Michael, swallowing hard at the notion of Agatha armed. 'Who is in the sack?'

'Who?' she echoed. 'You mean *what?* It is a bit of mutton for your supper. I thought I might cook something special tonight, seeing as you have two new Fellows. Tyrington praised my pottage this morning, so I want to show him what one of my roasts is like.'

'You never do that for me,' said Michael plaintively.

She winked at him. 'I might, if you were a bit more charming.'

'Do you think she intends to feed her potion to Tyrington?' asked Michael, after she had gone. 'She seems enamoured of him.'

'She is just flattered that someone has complimented her cooking at last,' replied Bartholomew. 'We take her for granted, and it must be a pleasant change to be appreciated.'

Michael gagged as they reached a particularly noxious section of Butchery Row. 'Can we go now? The stench is making me nauseous.'

Bartholomew was obliged to approach three meat-merchants before he found one willing to talk to him. The first two gave him short shrift, informing him bluntly that they had no wish to be seen talking to scholars. The third owned the smallest shop, and was not noted for the fresh-ness of his wares. As a consequence, 'Putrid Peter' tended to be patronised by those who could not afford the better stuff, and he and his family barely made ends meet.

'Pay no heed to them,' said Peter, flicking a thumb at his colleagues. 'One owns a house that is used as a hostel, and the other is his nephew. They are both with Candelby

257

against the University, and are going around telling everyone not to sell meat to scholars.'

'They sold mutton to Agatha,' Bartholomew pointed out.

Peter regarded him as though he was short of a few wits. 'They support Candelby, but that does not make them madmen. No one refuses Agatha, not if he values his vitals. If you want an end to this rift, Brother, you should send *her* after Candelby. You would have peace quicker than you can say your *pater nosters.*'

'I might do that,' said Michael. 'God knows, I am running out of other options.'

'Does Magister Arderne ever buy meat from you?' asked Bartholomew.

Peter shook his head. 'Not meat, just entrails for his dog. I sold him the innards from a sheep on Monday. They were a bit past their best, but he said Rex would not mind.'

Bartholomew made his way out of the cluttered, reeking shambles, Michael stumbling behind him. One of the butchers chose the moment they passed to upend a bucket of bloody water into the street. Bartholomew was agile enough to jump out of the way, but the back of Michael's habit ended up drenched. The physician was not quick enough to dodge the bone that was lobbed at him, however, and it caught him a painful blow on the elbow.

'Was that escapade worthwhile?' snapped the monk irritably, when they were away from the stalls and in the Market Square. 'You learned that Arderne buys cheap meat for some animal he keeps, but at what cost? I am soaked and you are bruised.'

'It was worthwhile,' said Bartholomew, rubbing his arm. 'Falmeresham was stabbed on Sunday. The next day, Arderne purchased sheep guts, and went to "operate". Falmeresham was too dosed with potions to know what was really happening, and was deceived in the most appalling manner.'

258

'How can you be sure?'

'First, if Falmeresham really had been badly wounded, he would not have survived being toted to the Angel and then to Arderne's house. Secondly, the injury was in the wrong place to have affected a liver, as I have told you – something Falmeresham does not know, because I am not allowed to teach him anatomy. Thirdly, I doubt Arderne owns a dog, so he must have had another reason for wanting cheap entrails. Fourthly, Falmeresham said his liver was "knobbly and green", which looks like no human liver that I have ever seen, but Putrid Peter sold Arderne entrails that were turning bad. And finally, you do not pull an organ from a body, suture it, and have the patient walking around in three days.'

Michael was thoughtful. 'Do you think Arderne deceived young Motelete, too?'

Bartholomew nodded slowly. 'But I cannot see how. Not yet, anyway.'

'Are you sure you have not taken against him because his claims resulted in Edith being hurt?'

'I *have* taken against him for that, yes. And for misleading Falmeresham, for making Hanchach drink urine, and for giving Isnard false hope and stealing his money. Shall I go on?'

'There is no need,' said Michael tiredly. 'I see your point.'

Because they were passing, Bartholomew stopped at King's Hall to ask after Paxtone, whose indisposition still confined him to his quarters. The large physician was lying down, but declared himself to be better. He rubbed his ample paunch ruefully.

'I am a devil for pigeon, but I shall limit myself to three of them next time we have a feast.'

259

'I like pigeon, too,' said Michael conversationally. 'Although Agatha does not always remove all the feathers. They get stuck in my throat and make me choke.'

'Our cooks are the same,' sympathised Paxtone. 'I choke, too.'

'If you took time to *look* at what you were eating, instead of gobbling, these problems would not arise.' Bartholomew became aware that Paxtone and Michael were regarding him in astonishment, unused to him giving such tart advice. He relented. 'I am sorry. It is Arderne – we have good evidence that he is defrauding people, but I do not know how to stop him. And my arm hurts.'

While Paxtone smeared Bartholomew's elbow with an ointment of elder leaves and marjoram, Michael summarised what they had deduced about Arderne's treatment of Falmeresham.

'I am not surprised,' said Paxtone. 'And Blankpayn does *not* have leprosy – his skin flakes when he eats too many eggs. He always mends in a few days, and if Arderne is claiming *that* as one of his successes, then he is deluded – and so is Blankpayn for believing him.'

'Can you think of a way to expose him?' asked Bartholomew, watching Paxtone replace his salve on a shelf. 'We must do something, because it is only a matter of time before someone dies.'

'Even if someone does perish, he will deny responsibility,' said Paxtone gloomily. 'Maud Bowyer is sinking fast, but he declines to accept the fact that he failed to clean her wound properly. He is blaming her illness on you, because you gave her something to swallow.'

'Poppy juice and henbane.'

Paxtone raised his hands in a shrug. 'A powerful elixir for a painful condition. It is what I would have prescribed myself. Wretched man! To catch him will be like laying hold of a snake – whichever end you grab will result in a bite. But you know all this, so there is no point in me harping on it. Have you come any closer to learning why Lynton rode his horse at Candelby?'

Michael shook his head. 'Although we are certainly learning a lot about Lynton himself. Did you know he trained as a knight, and that he owned buildings all along the High Street?'

Paxtone raised his eyebrows. 'I knew about the properties, but not about his military expertise, although it does not surprise me. He was elegance itself astride a horse.'

'He was murdered,' said Michael baldly. 'Shot. We have not told anyone else, except Langelee, because we fear reprisals. However, Matt believes Arderne may be responsible, so you may be in danger, too. I tell you for your own safety, although I would appreciate you keeping it to yourself.'

Paxtone was appalled. 'But this is dreadful! I had no idea!'

'Good,' said Michael. 'That is what we intended.'

Paxtone took a gulp of wine, straight from a container that looked suspiciously like a urine flask. 'You must do all you can to catch this monster – whether it is Arderne or someone else. But, of course, that is what you have been doing. Forgive me. It is the shock. Poor Lynton!'

'You must look out for Rougham, too,' said Michael. 'Do not confide in him, because he is fiery, and outrage may lead him to confront Arderne, which will help no one.'

'I shall be discreet,' vowed Paxtone. He paled suddenly. 'I have noticed someone watching me several times recently. Lord! It might have been an assassin hired by Arderne.'

'Watching you how?' asked Bartholomew.

Paxtone raised his hands. 'Sometimes he is in the street

261

opposite our gatehouse, sometimes I see him at the apothecary's shop, and he was at Kenyngham's funeral. I mentioned him to Rougham, and he said the fellow had been dogging him, too. Have you noticed anyone following you?'

Bartholomew shook his head. 'I am usually accompanied by Michael, Cynric or students. They would have noticed something amiss, even if I did not.'

'We *did* notice something amiss,' said Michael. 'You chased a hooded figure who was lurking outside Peterhouse, but lost him in the woods nearby.' He turned to Paxtone. 'Can you describe this person?'

Paxtone shook his head. 'He is always bundled up in his cloak, and I have never seen his face. Neither has Rougham.'

Michael was concerned. 'You must be on your guard.'

Paxtone's malaise seemed to have evaporated now he had something more serious to worry about. He stood and headed for the door, tottering slightly on his tiny feet. 'I shall walk to Gonville Hall now, and make sure Rougham is in one piece. Poor Lynton! Did I tell you we had a disagreement last week?'

Michael followed him down the stairs. 'What about?'

'The mean speed theorem. He made an assumption that I considered erroneous.'

'In what way?' asked Bartholomew.

'The basis of the theory is that a body will traverse a specific distance in a given amount of time. However, I see no evidence that the speed should be constant, and I disagreed with him about his mathematical assumptions.'

'I see your point,' said Bartholomew. 'However, if that same body were to move during the same interval of time with a uniform velocity equal to the instantaneous speed acquired at the *middle instant* of its uniform acceleration, it would traverse a predictable distance. Would it not?'

Paxtone paused at the bottom of the stairs to catch his breath. 'He kept varying his definition of "uniform", which meant his deductions were difficult to predict. I was right more often than not, but a man of my standing does not like to be proven wrong. All this happened in his Dispensary.'

Bartholomew was surprised Paxtone had taken the matter so much to heart. Being wrong was part of the learning process, and anyone who minded having his conclusions questioned had no right to be a scholar. 'You visited his Dispensary? I did not even know he had one until yesterday, although it is like no Dispensary I have ever seen – there is nothing in it to dispense, for a start.'

'Just wine,' said Paxtone, leading the way across the yard. He looked a little furtive. 'Lynton liked to give wine to the patients who visited him. It was a very popular habit.'

'I am sure it was,' said Bartholomew.

Michael lowered his voice when they reached King's Hall's mighty gatehouse. 'While I am in the mood for confidences, I have received a letter saying that Kenyngham was poisoned. And there was another note offering me twenty marks for bringing the culprit to justice.'

Paxtone regarded him uncertainly. 'Kenyngham was old. I imagine he died of natural causes, and the writer of these letters – I assume they are one and the same – is playing a nasty game with you.'

'That is what I have been telling him,' said Bartholomew.

'I am unwilling to take the chance,' said Michael. 'So, I shall take the matter seriously until a proper examination of Kenyngham tells me otherwise. Besides, these missives cannot have been written by the same man. He is hardly likely to offer me a reward for his own capture, is he?'

'But Kenyngham is buried,' said Paxtone. 'How can you

examine him? Unless . . . surely, you cannot mean to *exhume* him?' He rounded on Bartholomew. 'Are you party to this outrage?'

'No. Michael intends to ask Rougham to help him.'

'Rougham will have nothing to do with it – and rightly so. I strongly urge you reconsider, Brother.'

Michael watched him waddle away, a frown creasing his fat features. 'Perhaps *he* killed Kenyngham. He certainly objected very strongly to my determination to learn the truth.'

'He objected to you digging up a dead colleague,' said Bartholomew quietly. 'As do I.'

As Bartholomew and Michael walked home to Michaelhouse, they met Father William. He was talking to the Warden of the town's Franciscan Friary, an austere, unsmiling man named Pechem. Pechem was one of Bartholomew's patients, and regularly consulted him about the poor state of his digestion. He usually blamed his discomfort on a bad alignment of stars, although the physician was more inclined to think a penchant for pickled rhubarb might have something to do with it.

'The Grey Friars will stand with you at the Convocation next Monday, Brother,' said Pechem, as they approached. 'William has been telling me how it is your attempt to avert trouble, so we shall support your proposal to change the Statutes.'

'Thank you,' said Michael, pleased.

'The Dominicans are being awkward, though,' said William gloomily. 'I went to see them today, but Prior Morden said he intended to vote for whatever *I* voted against.'

'Damn!' muttered Michael. 'I shall have to visit Morden later, then.'

'Do not bother,' said Pechem. 'The Black Friars have eighteen Regents, but we have nineteen. As we cannot possibly be expected to vote for the same side, you are better accepting *our* pledge.'

Michael sighed crossly. 'Surely you can put your differences aside, just this once?'

'We have been happily opposing Dominicans on *everything* for nigh on two hundred years,' said Pechem indignantly. 'Why should we change now?'

'That stupid Honynge says the Dominicans are right about Blood Relics,' said William to Pechem, oblivious to the monk's exasperated disapproval of the Warden's stance. 'Can you credit it? The man is an ass! However, I have had my revenge.'

'What have you done?' asked Bartholomew uneasily. William was not a subtle person, and his vengeance was likely to be something crude that would cause another quarrel.

'As Junior Fellow, he is obliged to manage the Illeigh Hutch,' said William. He explained to Pechem. 'Hutches are chests containing money that can be borrowed by our students. In return for coins, they leave something of equal or greater value – a book, a piece of jewellery, and so on.'

'And?' asked Michael warily. 'What did you do? Remove all the money, so he will look foolish when a student asks for some and he finds it is empty?'

William's face fell. 'How did you guess?'

Bartholomew was disgusted. 'He will know someone is playing tricks, and may reciprocate with something vicious. I doubt he is the kind of man to take a joke.'

Michael's expression was crafty. 'I think we can salvage something from the idea, though. Go and put it all back, Father, but include the gold coronet from the Stanton Hutch, too. Honynge will conduct an inventory, and discover an addition. Then we shall see how honest he is.'

'We shall declare it stolen,' crowed William, delighted. 'And then it will be found in *his* room!'

Bartholomew was appalled. 'This is an ill-conceived plan – and dangerous, too, to risk something so valuable. He might manage to spirit the thing away. And *then* what will we say? That it was last seen by William, who hid it in the Illeigh Hutch to trap a thief?'

'That is a clever notion, Matt,' said Michael comfortably. 'We do not have to declare it was Honynge we wanted to catch out, do we?'

Grinning like a madman, William raced away to do as Michael suggested. Bartholomew gave up trying to reason with the monk, and started to think about Arderne instead. He was still deep in thought when Carton approached, Falmeresham at his side. Carton was holding his friend's arm, alarmed that he was walking about when Bartholomew had recommended rest after his ordeal.

'Isabel St Ives has just been,' said Carton. 'Maud Bowyer is worse, and wants you to visit as soon as possible. It sounded urgent, so I thought I should find you myself, but Falmeresham insisted on accompanying me, even though he should be in bed.'

'I came because Maud has no right to summon you,' said Falmeresham, freeing his arm. 'She is Magister Arderne's patient, and he will not like it if you interfere. Isabel should not have come.'

'Isabel thinks the same, actually,' said Carton to Bartholomew. 'She believes her mistress should be left to Arderne, too. But Maud wants you, and Isabel cannot ignore a direct order.'

'Arderne is a good man,' said Falmeresham, rather defiantly. 'If Maud can be healed, *he* will do it. She does not need the services of another *medicus*.'

'Arderne cannot be a good man, or he would not be

266

saying spiteful things about the town's other practitioners,' said Carton snidely.

'You mean Robin of Grantchester?' asked Falmeresham. 'It is about time someone reviled *him* – he is a menace. And Rougham is no better, with his archaic skills. They *should* be denounced.'

'What about Doctor Bartholomew?' demanded Carton archly. 'Should he be denounced, too?'

'Of course not,' snapped Falmeresham. 'But it is not Arderne who is doing that. It is Isnard.'

'Because Arderne *told* him to. He raised Isnard's hopes by saying he might be cured, but dashed them cruelly when it proved impossible. Then he blamed Doctor Bartholomew, even though it was *his* failure.'

'But Arderne might be right about amputation,' argued Falmeresham. 'We are taught certain injuries are irreparable, and specific diseases are incurable. But I *saw* Arderne healing several such complaints with my own eyes. I think he possesses skills superior to anyone in Cambridge.'

'Visit Maud, Matt,' said Michael, cutting into the debate before it could erupt into a serious quarrel. 'She trusts you, even if your students do not.'

'I trust what works,' countered Falmeresham. 'My mind is open to anything new.'

Bartholomew took Falmeresham with him when he went to tend Maud, seeing it as a chance to teach the student something about fatal fevers. Michael insisted on accompanying them, lest a lone physician and his apprentice prove too tempting a target for mud-slingers and bone-lobbers, and Carton followed without being invited, loath to let his friend out of his sight.

When they arrived at the handsome house on Bridge Street, Maud was indeed worse. The smell of decay was stronger, and Bartholomew knew she did not have long to live. Isabel was almost in tears.

'You have done enough damage already,' said Isabel accusingly, watching Bartholomew kneel by the bed and examine the patient. 'I would never have called you, had my mistress not insisted. I summoned Magister Arderne first – although she objected. He waved his feather, but said *you* had destroyed all hope of a cure, because you had laid tainted hands on her. It is your fault she is dying.'

'Arderne says tainted hands are the reason why he could not save Ocleye, either,' added Falmeresham, rather unhelpfully.

Bartholomew regarded Isabel unhappily. Her eyes were red from crying, but there was a hard, cold glint in them that he had not seen before. He had a feeling he was about to acquire yet another enemy. 'I gave her a potion to relieve her pain,' he said quietly. 'And that is all.'

'You put your hand against her cheek to feel her fever,' countered Isabel. 'And you raised the bandage to inspect the wound. Arderne said that was enough to cause the damage, because evil miasmas went from you to her.'

'Claptrap,' declared Carton angrily. Falmeresham glared at the friar, and with a shock, Bartholomew saw his student believed Arderne's wild claims.

'You can discuss this later,' said Michael softly, nudging the physician with his elbow. 'Tend Maud, Matt. You know you can do more for her than a leech with a feather.'

Bartholomew began to administer a powerful potion that would ease her pain. After a few moments, the lines of suffering around her eyes and mouth began to fade. He mixed more of the remedy, and gave it to Isabel with instructions on how to use it.

'But it will not make her live?' she asked in a small voice.

'I am sorry,' said Bartholomew. 'This often happens with

268

wounds caused by jagged splinters – small fragments remain behind, and they fester. The medicine will ease her end, but no more.'

'I can hear you,' said Maud, in a voice that was unexpectedly strong. She opened her eyes. 'Or rather, I can hear voices. Are you talking about me?'

'We are talking about Master Lynton,' said Isabel, saying something she thought might please her. 'He was a good friend of Doctor Bartholomew, who has come to see you.'

Maud smiled. 'Did you know Lynton and I were close? We grew up together – born in adjoining manors. I should have married him, but we left it too late; he became a scholar, and I took another husband. He was a fine warrior in his day – tall, strong and true of hand. Still, at least we enjoyed each other after I became a widow.'

'It is difficult to imagine him as a knight,' said Bartholomew. 'Or a lover.'

Her smile became wistful. 'He was an enigma, and one I shall love to my dying day. Arderne tells me that might come sooner than I would like. What do you say, Bartholomew?'

'I imagine that is true for most people.'

She smiled again. 'You have a clever tongue. And now tell me the truth.'

'I am sorry,' he said, taking her hand. 'I doubt you will see another Sunday.'

'Arderne said I would not see another hour, and that it is your fault that I am doomed. I do not believe him, though. You told me the truth – and did not demand five shillings for it.'

'Magister Arderne always charges for consultations,' said Falmeresham defensively. 'He says offering services free of charge suggests they are not worth paying for.'

'Hush,' said Bartholomew sharply. It was impolite to

argue with a patient, especially one who was dying, and he was surprised at Falmeresham.

'Arderne is shallow and mean,' said Maud. 'I know you summoned him because you are desperate to help me, Isabel, but I do not want him here again. Doctor Bartholomew's medicine is working, and the pain is less now. I ask for no more.'

She began to drowse, and Isabel opened the door, indicating it was time for the visitors to leave. 'Magister Arderne is coming back later, and I do not want him to find you here,' she said. 'You will quarrel, and it might upset her.'

'Maud just said she does not want him,' said Bartholomew, loath to abandon anyone to the healer's dubious ministrations.

'He is not coming to see *her*,' said Isabel with a smile that was a little wanton. 'He is coming to see *me*. But I shall make sure he does not come up here, if that is what she wants.'

'So, Isabel has a fancy for Arderne,' mused Michael, as he and Bartholomew walked home, Carton and Falmeresham trailing behind them. The two younger men were quarrelling in low voices. Falmeresham was angry because Carton was making rude comments about the healer he had come to revere, and Carton was apparently disgusted that his friend should be so easily deceived.

Bartholomew considered the predicament of Isabel St Ives. She was about to lose her mistress, her home and her employment, and was in an acutely vulnerable position. He hoped the arrogant Arderne would not take what he wanted, then abandon her. 'There is no accounting for taste.'

'I imagine most women consider him handsome, and he is very charismatic,' said Michael. 'I know from personal experience that ladies find that particular combination of traits attractive in a man. But speak of the Devil, and he will appear. Here comes the fellow himself.'

The healer was not alone. Blankpayn was announcing in a loud voice that Arderne had cured him of leprosy – although Bartholomew noticed that no one wanted to stand too close to him even so – and Candelby was still showing off his 'broken' arm. Carton asked Falmeresham in an uncharacteristically acerbic voice whether he would like to join them and flaunt his mended liver.

'Good,' said Bartholomew, as Arderne swaggered towards them. 'I want a word with him.'

'Do not tackle him here,' warned Michael in alarm, seeing the determined set of the physician's jaw. 'We are heavily outnumbered, and this is neither the time nor the place for a confrontation.'

'I do not care,' said Bartholomew. 'I have been patient, but he has gone too far.'

Falmeresham was also worried, and tugged on his arm. 'Come down this lane, so you avoid meeting him. I can see you are itching to accuse him of bringing about the death of Mistress Bowyer, and that would be unfair. It is *your* fault she is dying, not his.'

Bartholomew stared at him in astonishment, Arderne momentarily forgotten. 'What?'

'You touched her and gave her medicines, when he said it was best to leave her alone,' explained Falmeresham. 'I have *seen* him work miracles, so there is no doubt in my mind that it was your interference – albeit well-intentioned – that brought about Maud's decline.'

Bartholomew decided it was time for Falmeresham to hear a few facts. 'Arderne bought sheep entrails from Putrid Peter on Monday, and performed some sleight of hand to make you think they were your own. He could not possibly have drawn your liver through that small cut in your side.

271

It is a medical impossibility, and were I allowed to teach you anatomy, you would see I am right.'

Falmeresham took a step away. 'Magister Arderne said you would try to turn me against him, by denigrating his achievements. I did not believe him, but I see he was right.'

Bartholomew regarded him in surprise. 'You take his word over mine? After all these years?'

'He does not,' said Carton quickly. 'He is still unwell, and—'

Falmeresham pulled away from him. 'On the contrary, I have never felt better. While I was recovering, I spent hours talking to Magister Arderne, and was amazed by the depth of his knowledge. Everything he said makes sense. You say there is a lot about the body that you do not understand, but he knows *everything*. He *always* has answers and *never* says he does not know.'

'Then he is a fool, as well as a fraud,' said Michael tartly.

Falmeresham regarded him coldly. 'You are the fool, Brother, for not seeing what is staring you in the face. You have grown so used to Doctor Bartholomew's failures that you are unnerved by a man who is flushed with success.'

'Watch yourself, lad,' warned Michael. 'I appreciate you have had an unpleasant experience, but it does not give you the right to be insolent. I suggest you go home and think about what you "saw" when you were with Arderne. Consider it logically, in the light of your training, then ask yourself whether these miracles are credible. Arderne is not a saint, infused with the power of Heaven.'

'I disagree,' said Falmeresham quietly. 'And I want to learn more from him. He asked me to be his assistant, and I think I should accept his offer.'

Bartholomew was dismayed, knowing the lad was making a terrible mistake. 'At least finish this term. Then you will have your degree.'

Falmeresham edged away. 'I cannot waste another moment – it would be irresponsible to the people I can cure in the future. Will you stop me?'

Bartholomew seriously considered locking him up until he came to his senses. 'Not if you think you are doing the right thing.'

'I am,' said Falmeresham. 'My eyes have been opened, and a whole new world has unfolded. I shall always appreciate what you have taught me, though – it is not your fault the academic study of medicine falls so far short of what might be achieved.'

Bartholomew watched him walk away, recalling his own excitement after hearing a lecture by the Arab physician who would later become his teacher. He understood exactly how Falmeresham felt.

'You should stop him,' said Carton, horrified. 'I do not want him to go to Arderne. He may—'

'May what?' asked Michael, when the commoner stopped speaking abruptly.

Carton shrugged, and refused to look at him. 'May learn facts that will do him no good.'

It was an odd thing to say, but Bartholomew was too preoccupied with Falmeresham to think about it. He turned away when the student reached his hero and began talking. Arderne shot a gloating smile in the physician's direction, and put a possessive arm around the lad's shoulders.

'I think we *will* go home the back way,' said Michael, pulling Bartholomew in the opposite direction. 'I do not feel like walking down Bridge Street today.'

CHAPTER 9

The tinkle of the College bell woke Bartholomew the following morning, and he sat up to find the students who now shared his room had risen, dressed, and left. A heavy sleeper, he had not heard a thing. He appreciated having the chamber to himself as he washed in the bowl of cold water Cynric had left for him, shaving quickly with one of his surgical blades. The clothes he had worn the day before were not too crumpled from where he had left them in a heap in the corner, so he donned them again, hopping from foot to foot in an effort to keep his bare feet off the cold stone floor.

He trotted into the yard, pulling his tabard over his head. It was not a pleasant day. There was a sleety drizzle in the air, and the wind whipped in from the Fens like a knife. There was not a student, commoner or Fellow who was not shivering as he waited for Langelee to lead the procession to the church for daily prayers, and the only warm person was Agatha, who watched the assembly from the comfort of her wicker throne next to the kitchen fire.

Suddenly, there was a piercing scream that had the new students exclaiming their alarm, but it was only the porter's peacock being let out of its coop. It strutted boldly into the open, then scuttled inside again when it saw the state of the weather. The hens were made of sterner stuff, and were scratching about in the mud, scuttling diagonally every so often, as the wind caught them.

'Who is still missing?' demanded Langelee, looking round irritably. 'Someone is not here. Who?'

'Honynge and Carton,' said William, looking around irritably. 'Honynge was still in bed when I passed his door, but he said he was coming. Do you want me to hurry him up?'

'Deynman will do it,' said Langelee. 'Where is Carton? *He* is not usually late.'

'There,' said Wynewyk, pointing towards the front gate. The porter had just opened it, and Carton was slipping quickly inside. 'Where has he been?'

'Reciting masses,' replied the friar, when Langelee repeated the question to him. 'In St Michael's. I came back when I heard the bell.'

Yet he was very wet, and had clearly been out longer than the time it would have taken to walk from church to College. Bartholomew was about to demand the truth, but the Master was speaking.

'Right,' Langelee shouted. 'The rest of you gather around me. Come on, hurry up!'

Everyone formed a tight huddle, with him in the centre, waiting expectantly for what sounded as though it was going to be an important announcement. Bartholomew wondered if he had found a way to dispense with Honynge, and was going to confide it while the man was not there.

'What?' asked Michael impatiently, after several moments of silence.

'Nothing,' said Langelee. 'I just thought you could keep the rain off me while we wait.'

There was a chorus of weary groans. Bartholomew started to laugh, although William failed to see the humour in the situation, and began a litany of bitter grumbles that saw the Dominicans to blame for the Master's jest and the foul weather at the same time.

'I am glad *I* am not a Black Friar,' said Tyrington, standing close to the physician and speaking in a low voice. 'William is not entirely sane when he starts ranting about them, and I would not like that sort of venom directed at me. How can you let him spout such poison? The students will hear it, and might think it is true.'

'I suppose we should tell him to moderate himself,' said Bartholomew. He tried to edge away from the cascade of spit. 'We take no notice of him, so we assume no one else does, either.'

'You have twenty new members who do not know he should be ignored. I do not mean to be objectionable – finding fault with my new College so soon – but I am offended by these tirades and would like them to stop. Is that unreasonable?'

'No,' said Bartholomew tiredly. 'Of course not, and you are right. I will talk to Langelee about it.' He shivered. 'It is freezing out here! Where is Honynge?'

'He and I were invited to a debate in Bene't College last night. It went on longer than we expected, and we came home very late.'

Bartholomew nodded, recalling how it had not been late enough to prevent Honynge from joining him and Wynewyk in the conclave afterwards. Wynewyk had been working on the accounts and Bartholomew had been reading, enjoying the remnants of the fire in companionable silence. Then Honynge had arrived and ordered them to move so he could warm himself. Wynewyk had objected, and Bartholomew had left when the ensuing argument had degenerated into an exchange of personal insults.

'Honynge is imbued with great energy at night,' Tyrington went on. 'I was exhausted, but he was all for continuing the debate. I declined, so he tried to persuade others instead. All refused, because of the lateness of the hour, but he even approached Candelby in his desperation for a discussion.'

'Candelby?' asked Bartholomew, startled. 'I doubt he has much patience with scholarly pursuits.'

Tyrington shrugged. 'I think Honynge was so keen for a disputation that it did not occur to him that a taverner might not be the man to ask. It did not take him long to find out, though. He had caught me up by the time I reached St Mary the Great, and we walked the rest of the way home together.'

'Where is that man?' demanded Michael. Rain had plastered his thin hair to his head, which looked very small atop the vast mountain of his body. 'Does he not know he is keeping us out here in the wet?'

Tyrington pulled a phial from his scrip and handed it to Bartholomew. 'Here is something that may occupy you while we wait. I bought it from Arderne – or rather, he forced it on me, then demanded a shilling. I was too taken aback to protest.'

'What was ailing you?' asked Bartholomew, taking it cautiously. The stopper did not fit very well, and it was leaking. He would never have dispensed medicine in such a container.

Tyrington looked indignant. 'He told me I have too much saliva in my mouth, and that this potion would dry it out. What was he talking about? I do not spit!'

'You will not be doing anything at all if you swallow too much of this,' said Bartholomew, sniffing the flask warily. 'I detect bryony in it, and that can be harmful in too concentrated a dose.'

Tyrington gaped at him, shocked. 'You mean he was trying to *poison* me? Why? I have never done anything to him! In fact, I had never even spoken to him before yesterday.'

'I suspect he just saw an opportunity to earn himself a shilling,' said Bartholomew. 'And bryony is used to clear the chest of phlegm, so it is not poison exactly.'

'Just another example of Arderne's incompetence,' muttered Michael.

Eventually, Honynge arrived, and did not seem to care that he had kept his colleagues lingering in the wet while he made himself ready. He was clad in an expensive cloak, his hair was neatly brushed, and he was shaved so closely that Bartholomew imagined the procedure must have taken a very long time. Langelee was only willing to be pushed so far. He nodded to his Fellows, who stepped into formation behind him, and set off. Cynric whipped the gate open to ensure there was no delay, and Langelee stormed up St Michael's Lane at a furious lick. As a consequence, Honynge was obliged to run to catch up. He was seething when he finally took his place, and glowered at Langelee in a way that made Bartholomew uneasy.

The physician put Honynge from his mind as Michael began the mass, enjoying the monk's rich baritone as he intoned the sacred words. Although he was a Benedictine, Michael had been given special dispensation to perform priestly duties during the plague, and the shortage of ordained men since meant he had continued the practice. The psalm he had chosen was one of Kenyngham's favourites, and Bartholomew found himself wishing with all his heart that the old man had not died. Even without Honynge's malign presence, Michaelhouse was a poorer place without him.

When the monk had finished, the scholars trooped back to the College at a more sedate pace than they had left it, and waited in the yard until the bell announced that breakfast was ready. Michael was first to reach the door, thundering up the spiral stairs that led to the hall, then pacing restlessly until everyone else had arrived. Honynge was last, because he had found something else to do along the way, and Langelee said grace before he had reached his seat. Pointedly, Honynge murmured his own prayer before he sat, and then took so much of the communal egg-mess that there was none left for Bartholomew and Tyrington. When Tyrington voiced his objection, the hands of the Fellows sitting near him immediately adopted the Michaelhouse Manoeuvre.

'I am concerned about this exhumation you propose to conduct,' said Honynge, when the meal was over and the Fellows were in the conclave, deciding who should invigilate the disputations. The comment was somewhat out of the blue. 'Are you sure it is necessary?'

'I must know how Kenyngham died,' said Michael. 'Besides, I always investigate odd deaths.'

'*Is* Kenyngham's death odd?' asked Tyrington. 'I thought he died of old age.'

'He was poisoned.' Michael brandished the parchments he had been sent. 'This confession proves it, and so does the letter offering me twenty marks for finding his killer.'

'Perhaps they are pranks,' suggested Wynewyk, studying them thoughtfully. 'Or a plot devised by someone who wants to hurt you because of the rent war.'

'Why would anyone confess to a murder he did not commit?' demanded Michael.

'Why would a killer want you to know what he had done?' countered Honynge. 'If Kenyngham really was poisoned, the culprit would be grateful that his crime had gone undetected. He would not brag about it, and risk having you launch an investigation that might see him exposed. Of course these missives are hoaxes! And anyone who cannot see it is a fool.'

'The killer wants me to know how clever he is,' Michael shot back.

'Piffle,' declared Honynge. 'If you disturb a man's corpse after it has been buried, you are agents of the Devil. I strongly urge you to reconsider this distasteful course of action, Brother.'

'I cannot,' said Michael shortly. 'It would not be right to turn a blind eye to murder.'

'Then I want my objections made public,' said Honynge. 'I want it recorded in the College annals that I consider this exhumation wicked and unnecessary.'

'Honynge is right,' said Tyrington shyly. 'Although I would not have phrased my reservations quite so baldly. The whole business does not seem proper, somehow.'

Langelee sighed. 'We had better vote on it. We shall meet back here in an hour, which will give us all time to reflect. It is not something that should be decided without proper consideration.'

'You can vote,' said Michael. 'But I am Senior Proctor, and I shall do what I think is right.'

'You may be Senior Proctor, but you are also a Fellow of Michaelhouse,' said Langelee quietly. 'And I assert my authority over you to bide by the decision of your colleagues.'

Michael was furious as he stamped from the conclave.

'I cannot believe *you* are against me, Matt!' The monk was almost shouting as he and Bartholomew walked towards Peterhouse, aiming to ascertain whether there were other aspects to Lynton's character that had been kept from the general populace.

'And I cannot believe you are contemplating exhumation,' argued Bartholomew. 'It is horrible.'

'You have done it before.'

'Not to someone close to me.'

'He has only been dead six days. I do not think you will see anything too distressing.'

'That is not the point. Kenyngham was laid to *rest*. That does not mean hauled out of his tomb a few days later because you are beguiled by some lunatic letter.'

'It bragged about the murder of a colleague. How can you remain dispassionate about it?'

'For two reasons. First, the confession is false – Wynewyk is right, someone is trying to hurt you because of the rent war. And secondly, you will not learn anything by unearthing Kenyngham anyway. I examined him twice and saw nothing amiss.'

Michael looked sly. 'The fact that you went back for a second paw means there was something about the first examination that bothered you. You are not as sure about this as you claim to be.'

'Motelete,' explained Bartholomew. 'I thought he was dead, and was shocked when he sat up in his coffin. It made me question myself – especially after Arderne's claims about my competence.'

Michael's anger faded when he saw the unhappiness in his friend's face. 'I would not take *his* criticism to heart. He is a . . . oh, Lord! Here comes Isnard. He is holding a sword, so I recommend you stand behind me. He will not strike a man of God – especially one who is his choirmaster.'

'Let me at him!' shouted Isnard, hobbling faster than was safe for a man with one leg. 'I said I would kill him the next time we met. Well, we *have* met.'

His voice was loud, and people hurried to see what was happening. Before Michael could stop them, Kardington, Spaldynge and a group of students from Clare had come to stand next to him, while three pot-boys and Blankpayn hastened to show their solidarity with Isnard.

'You are out a lot these days, Master Kardington,' remarked Michael coolly. 'In fact, this is the third time since Sunday that you have been present at a confrontation.'

'There are confrontations at every turn these days, Brother,' said Kardington with a shrug. 'You cannot take two steps without town louts forming battle lines.'

Fortunately, he spoke Latin, so the 'town louts' did not understand. They knew it was nothing pleasant though, and Blankpayn scowled. Meanwhile, Isnard was more concerned with carrying out his threat against Bartholomew. He was not drunk, but he was not sober either, and there was a fierce light in his eyes. He took a step forward, gripping his sword two-handed, like an axe.

'Put that down at once,' ordered Michael sternly. 'Brawling may damage your throat, and I need you for the solo on Sunday.'

Isnard stopped dead in his tracks. 'Solo?'

'Never mind singing, Isnard,' hissed Blankpayn. 'Think about your leg – the one that was sawn off when you were too ill to prevent it. The Bible says an eye for an eye, and a leg for a leg.'

'Does it?' asked Isnard, disconcerted. The weapon wavered. 'I do not think I can bring myself to chop off a limb. It is too . . . well, too *personal.*'

'Kill him then,' whispered Blankpayn. 'He has all but killed you.'

'If you do, I shall make sure you never sing in a choir again,' said Michael, interposing himself between physician and bargeman. Bartholomew tried to stop him, not wanting the monk to bear the consequences for something he had done, but it was not easy to step around the Benedictine's bulk.

Isnard's sword drooped a little more. The Michaelhouse ensemble was one of the greatest joys in his life. Not only did it let him bellow at the top of his lungs with people he liked, but the College provided food and treats after performances, and he enjoyed those, too. 'But my leg . . .'

'It was crushed beyond repair,' said Bartholomew, finally succeeding in moving out from behind Michael. 'You saw it yourself, and I do not understand why you refuse to believe me.'

'But I cannot remember,' cried Isnard. 'You gave me wine, to dull my senses.'

'There!' muttered Blankpayn. 'He rendered you insensible before doing his evil work. Listen to what Arderne tells you. Make the physician pay for what he did.'

'I am no lover of physicians myself,' said Spaldynge, shooting Bartholomew an unpleasant look. 'But I do not recommend slaughtering them in broad daylight. They are not worth hanging for.'

'You seem very keen for someone to commit a capital crime, Blankpayn,' lisped Kardington. He spoke English, so no one understood him. 'Why is that?'

'Do not swear at us,' snarled one of Blankpayn's pot-boys, fingering his dagger meaningfully.

Isnard was confused and unhappy. 'Falmeresham – your own student – said this morning that if he knew then what he knows now, he would have stopped you from operating. How could you do this to me?'

The last part was delivered in an accusing wail that made Bartholomew wince; so did the notion that Falmeresham had turned against him. He rubbed his eyes, tired of the whole business. There was nothing he could say to make Isnard believe him, and he did not think he could bear weeks of accusing glances and angry High Street encounters until Isnard managed to do what he threatened.

'Do what?' demanded Michael, when Bartholomew made no attempt to defend himself. 'Save your life? Sometimes I ask myself the same question. But I have had enough of this unedifying spectacle. Go home and practise the *Magnificat*, or I shall ask someone else to sing instead.'

Isnard started to obey – he had never been honoured with a solo before, and dispatching physicians could wait a day – but Blankpayn was furious that a brawl was going to be averted. 'You are a coward, Isnard! A stupid cripple. He should have amputated you head, not your foot.'

There was a collective murmur of distaste at this remark, including from Blankpayn's own pot-boys. They exchanged uneasy glances and started to move away. The other townsmen were also loath to be associated with Blankpayn when he was of a mind to insult the popular Isnard, and began to follow suit. In a matter of moments, Blankpayn found himself left with only scholars for company; he did not like being outnumbered, and hastily made himself scarce.

'I shall be voting against your proposal at the Convocation on Monday,' said Spaldynge, when the taverner had gone. 'I am sorry, Brother – I know you are doing what you think is right, but the University must stand firm against these demands, because they are the thin end of the wedge.'

'Once landlords are free to charge high prices, bakers and brewers will do the same,' elaborated Kardington. 'We will be driven away by rising costs – hostels first, and eventually the Colleges.'

'Most hostels are poor,' Spaldynge went on bitterly. 'And my sale of Borden was intended to highlight that fact. But what is the University's response? To arrange a gathering of Regents, and ask them to give the Senior Proctor permission to raise the rents even higher!' He looked disgusted.

'I am sorry you will not have Clare's support, Brother,' said Kardington apologetically, 'but your letter of notification did say we should all vote as our consciences dictate.'

Bartholomew was not deceived by their so-called moral stance. '*Your* conscience tells you to vote against the amendment because Clare no longer owns any houses to lease out. Borden is sold, so you are no longer in a position to benefit from charging higher rates.'

'That is true,' said Kardington, rather coldly. 'However, my decision also happens to coincide with what I believe to be ethical.'

'Damn!' murmured Michael, as the Clare men walked away. 'I thought I phrased that letter in a way that made it clear that voting with one's conscience meant voting for my proposal.'

'You did – and it was not subtle.' Bartholomew was thoughtful. 'I have said this before, but considering Spaldynge sold a house that did not belong to him, he seems very good friends with the victims of his crime.'

Michael nodded. 'Suspiciously so. I have a feeling there is something we are not being told about that College. I wonder how well Spaldynge and Kardington knew Lynton.'

Bartholomew was silent as they walked the rest of the way to Peterhouse. An innate sense of survival made him turn sharply when he sensed something behind him, and he managed to avoid the stone that was lobbed at his head. He looked around, but could not see who had thrown it, although he heard running footsteps.

'Perhaps we should ask Wisbeche if we can borrow one of Lynton's knightly shields,' said the monk facetiously. He saw Bartholomew's unhappy expression. 'Do not worry about Isnard. He will not stay angry with you for long.'

'It is not him I am concerned about – it is the people taking up his cause. If I knew where Falmeresham had buried Isnard's leg, I would excavate it, to prove it was beyond repair.'

Michael regarded him in askance. 'You would do that, but you will not look at Kenyngham?'

Bartholomew sighed. 'Actually, I will do neither. Arderne would claim it was someone else's limb anyway, so there would be no point.'

Peterhouse's door was answered by Master Wisbeche himself. He did not look pleased to see them, and was reluctant to invite them in. Bartholomew wondered if it was because of Isnard.

'No,' said Wisbeche shortly. 'It is about Lynton. The woman who came to wash him has a habit of making off with body parts for magic charms, so I decided to watch her, to make sure she did not do it to Lynton. While she was cleaning him I noticed a wound in his chest. My colleague Estmed, who fought with the old King in Scotland, said it was made by a crossbow bolt. *Ergo*, Lynton did not die because he fell from his horse and hurt his head – he was shot.'

'I know,' said Michael quietly. He raised his hand when Wisbeche started to object. 'We were afraid of what might happen if we made the truth public. You can see for yourself how the town and the University are at each other's throats, and a rumour that a high-ranking scholar was murdered would have led to all manner of mischief. Our students would have rioted.'

'*I* would not have rioted,' said Wisbeche coldly. 'You could have confided in me. However, not only did you choose to be secretive, but you attempted to conceal the evidence – you plugged the wound with bandages. It is unconscionable, and everyone I have told agrees with me.'

'My apologies,' snapped Michael, not sounding at all contrite. 'But we did what we thought was best. I have a responsibility to the University, you know, as well as to its individuals.'

'Your actions show you do not trust me,' Wisbeche went on accusingly.

'And I am right,' snarled Michael, temper finally breaking. 'You *cannot* be trusted. The words "everyone I have told" suggest you have been gossiping to all and sundry. If you cannot see that flapping tongues are the last thing we need, then I was wise to keep you in the dark.'

Wisbeche stared at him. 'I was angry with you. I spoke in rancour.'

'And that gives you the right to bray murder?' demanded Michael. 'Now, when we stand on the brink of some major civil unrest?'

Wisbeche swallowed uncomfortably. 'I suppose my response may have been precipitous.'

Michael struggled to control himself; alienating the Master of a prestigious College would do no one any good. 'You could say that. But the damage is done, and there is no point in recriminations.'

Wisbeche regarded him coolly. 'In that case, we shall say no more about your failure to tell me my senior Fellow was murdered – or about the fact that you stuffed Lynton's wound with rags, although I still think it is a ghoulish thing to have done.'

'Yes, it was,' said Michael, looking nowhere in particular. 'So, we have a truce, then?'

'We do. And just so you know I have the University's best interests at heart, I shall vote for your proposal at the Convocation of Regents on Monday. My Fellows will do likewise. I do not want a war with the town, and your measures to raise the rents make sense to me.'

'Thank you,' said Michael. 'How many of you are there?'

'With commoners and pensioners, we number sixteen. Kardington says he will vote against you, but Clare is only fourteen, so our support puts you two men ahead.'

'Good,' said Michael. 'Of course, you have a vested interest in seeing me win. You will inherit all Lynton's houses, so my amendment will see you considerably richer.'

Wisbeche was about to argue, but he caught Michael's eye and settled for a shrug. 'You are right – higher rents will suit us. However, we have already made the decision not to follow Lynton's policy of leasing to townsmen. All our houses will be loaned to scholars.'

'While we are on the subject of Lynton, I would like to ask you a few questions about him.'

'Why?' asked Wisbeche suspiciously. 'So you can see what other University rules he flouted?'

Michael raised his eyebrows. 'From that response, I assume there is yet more to learn about the man. However, my intention is not to expose his transgressions, but to catch his killer. Will you help me? I know this is uncomfortable, but it is better – for Lynton's reputation and memory – if the information comes from you. I do not want to ask his colleagues or your servants.'

Wisbeche sighed. 'I suppose you know by now that there were two Lyntons – the fastidious physician and the secret man. Ask your questions, Brother. I shall answer them if I can.'

'So far, we have discovered that he was once a knight, he owned property, and he had a lover.'

'He and Maud Bowyer *were* friends,' conceded Wisbeche. 'But he only spent the night at her house when she was troubled by rats. He said it was preventative medicine, because she would have swooned had she seen one.'

'And you believed him?' asked Michael incredulously. Bartholomew struggled not to smile.

'Not really. But we were too polite to say anything, and the liaison was always conducted with the utmost discretion. He had been protecting her from rats for years, and the only reason you know about it now is because he is dead.'

'His talent for subterfuge is astounding,' said Michael, awed. 'When Matt had his dalliance with Matilde two years ago, he thought *he* was careful, but every man, woman and child from here to Ely knew about it. Yet Lynton managed to carry on for *years*.'

'He knew how to keep his business private. I am the executor of his will, and I am astonished by the amount of money he had accrued – and by some of the financial arrangements he had in place.'

'You mean such as renting his houses to laymen?'

Wisbeche nodded. 'He bought and sold properties at an incredible rate. He was even doing business with Candelby, although it pains me to admit it.'

Michael's expression was grim. 'Candelby has only recently come into possession of most of his houses. I do not suppose he acquired them from Lynton, did he?'

Wisbeche rubbed his eyes wearily. 'Yes, I believe he did. The last transaction was for three homes on the High Street, which Lynton let him have a month ago.'

'How did Lynton come by them in the first place?' asked Michael.

'I am not sure,' replied Wisbeche shiftily. 'His accounts are complicated, and it will take me months to sort through them. However, I suspect he won them in a bet.'

'A bet?' echoed Michael in disbelief. 'What sort of bet?'

'Agatha said Lynton enjoyed games of chance with Maud on Sunday afternoons,' Bartholomew reminded the monk. 'We already know about his fondness for dice.'

'Actually,' said Wisbeche sheepishly, 'he was rather more fond of them than his weekly sessions with his lady. He held tournaments in his Dispensary, and often returned with some very peculiar winnings. Once it was a cow, another time a boat. I suspect he may have won these houses, too. Sometimes, the stakes were very high.'

Bartholomew regarded him in open-mouthed astonishment. 'I do not believe you! Lynton would never have broken the University's rules on that sort of scale.'

'I wish you were right,' said Wisbeche fervently. 'I really do.'

'At least this explains the odd décor in his Dispensary,' said Michael, finding his voice at last. 'Why the windows were painted shut, and why you found no medical equipment.'

'Except the silver goblets in the attic,' said Wisbeche. 'For providing his guests with wine. It was all very civilised, naturally. He never used the Dispensary for medical work.'

'I suppose these games were on Fridays,' said Michael, recalling that was the night Lynton had been unavailable for Maud.

Wisbeche nodded. 'I know I should have stopped him, but he was always so generous to the College, and I did not want him to take his patronage elsewhere. I made the right decision, too, because he left us a fortune in his will.'

'All this cannot be true,' said Bartholomew, feeling as though he was in a dream. 'I mean no disrespect, Wisbeche, but Lynton was a quiet, decent man, whose interests were medicine and natural philosophy. I do not see him tossing dice with hardened gamblers.'

'Would you like to see his accounts? That might convince you.'

Michael waved a hand to indicate he would like that very much, and they followed Wisbeche across the courtyard to a set of rooms on an upper floor. Bartholomew had never been in Lynton's private quarters before, because Lynton had always entertained visitors in the College combination room. His jaw dropped when he saw the lavish opulence of his colleague's chambers. There was a bed draped with extravagant hangings, there were thick, expensive carpets from Turkey, and Wisbeche opened a chest to reveal it full of silver coins.

'Christ Almighty!' breathed Bartholomew before he could stop himself. For once, Michael did not berate him for blasphemy. 'This must be the most sumptuous accommodation in Cambridge!'

'In England,' corrected Michael, wide-eyed. 'I doubt even the King has anything this splendid.'

Bartholomew and Michael left Peterhouse in a daze. They had spent a few moments inspecting Lynton's accounts, but concurred with Wisbeche that they would take months to unravel, and a cursory glance was unlikely to tell them much. The records had indicated, however, that Lynton had gambled in some very august company, and that his winnings had come from such powerful townsmen as the Sheriff, the Mayor, Candelby, Blankpayn and Bartholomew's brother-in-law. The physician was even more shocked to learn that Paxtone had enjoyed the odd game, too, as had Honynge, Kardington, Spaldynge, Carton and even Robin of Grantchester.

Towards the end of the list was Ocleye's name, and Bartholomew saw he had won three goats. If the 'pot-boy' had been able to gamble and rent fine houses, then spying was obviously a lucrative business. Michael stabbed at the entry with his finger, and his look told Bartholomew to remember that it was another connection between two men killed by crossbow bolts. At the bottom of the register, indicating he was a fairly recent addition to the Dispensary's membership, was Arderne.

'Do you recall how furtive Paxtone became when we mentioned the Dispensary?' asked Bartholomew as they walked along the High Street. 'Now we know why.'

'You and I are about the only men in Cambridge Lynton

did *not* dice with,' said Michael, stunned by the scale of the operation. 'Why? Was our money not good enough for him?'

'He did once ask if I liked games of chance,' recalled Bartholomew. 'I thought it was an idle question, and did not imagine for a moment that it might be an invitation. I told him I did not, and he never mentioned it again. But he was hardly likely to have included *you*, Brother – you turn a blind eye to the occasional indiscretion, but this was breaking the rules on a massive scale.'

Michael began to count Lynton's crimes on fat and rather grimy fingers. 'He fraternised with townsmen – and women. He gambled. He carried arms. He owned more property than the rest of the University put together. God save us, Matt! We are lucky his antics did not cause a riot – wealthy townsmen suffering such huge financial losses to a scholar.'

'Wisbeche said Lynton acted as a kind of banker – most of the winnings went to the other players, and Lynton only took a percentage of what was gambled.'

'You can portray it how you like, but it was sordid, no matter how genteel the surroundings and the company. Of course, it is yet another motive for his murder – he might have been shot by someone who objected to losing. Candelby remains high on my list – according to Lynton's accounts, he lost a good cloak and a hunting dog last Friday.'

'Good Friday,' said Bartholomew. 'The rest of us were keeping vigil while Lynton diced. I am surprised Candelby was involved, though – and that Lynton would entertain him in the first place. Candelby hates everything to do with the University, and Lynton was a prominent scholar.'

'It is peculiar,' agreed Michael. 'And it is something we must explore. The odds are stacking up against Candelby, if you will forgive the allusion.'

Bartholomew was more interested in another name that

had been prominent in Lynton's most recent records. 'Arderne lost forty marks on Good Friday – just two days before Lynton was shot. That is four years' pay for some of us. But we had better hurry home, Brother. Langelee told us to be back in an hour.'

Michael seized his arm and jerked him to a halt. 'Look over there! Candelby is talking to Honynge. Now what can they have to say to each other? It seems Lynton is not the only scholar with a dubious private life. Honynge sneaks around the grounds of rival Colleges in the depths of the night, he gambles, and now we learn he fraternises with evil-hearted burgesses.'

'Candelby is just selling him a pie,' said Bartholomew, watching. 'It is hardly fraternising.'

'Then let us hope it chokes him,' said Michael uncharitably. 'And I will be saved the bother of finding a blood-less way of ousting him from Michaelhouse. I am none too happy with Tyrington, either. Wynewyk was right to object to his leering – it *is* sinister.'

'At least they are both good academics.'

'They are adequate,' replied Michael haughtily. He stalked towards the two men, but Candelby was already striding briskly up the High Street. The monk grimaced – he wanted to question Candelby about his dealings with Lynton, but not at the expense of an undignified sprint. He vented his spleen on his new colleague instead. 'You keep some very disreputable company, Honynge.'

Honynge took a bite of the pie. It was enormous, and looked heavy with suet. Bartholomew regarded it with disapproval, thinking that if Honynge ate it all, it would sit badly in his stomach, and bring about an excess of the yellow bile that would exacerbate his choleric temper.

'I am hungry,' replied Honynge. 'There was not enough to eat this morning.'

293

'Now there is something upon which we *can* agree,' said Michael. 'Although there might have been more had *some* Fellows not availed themselves of more than their share of egg-mess.'

'You refer to Langelee,' said Honynge, evidently deciding it could not be his own hoggishness that was in question. His voice dropped until it was barely audible. 'Michaelhouse is full of gluttons, and you were a fool to accept their offer. You should have gone to Lucy's instead.'

Commenting adversely on his colleagues' eating habits meant Honynge was skating on some very thin ice. Michael's eyes narrowed, and he went on the offensive. 'I have it on good authority that you were slinking around the grounds of Clare late the other night. Exactly why would you do that?'

'I did nothing of the kind,' replied Honynge firmly. 'Who has been telling lies about me?'

'My witness saw your face,' pressed Michael, rather taken aback by the bald untruth.

'You said it was late, which means it was dark. How could your "witness" have seen me? The fellow is either a liar or a drunkard.' Honynge glared at Bartholomew, indicating he had his own suspicions about the identity of the witness; and the physician supposed he must have heard who Spaldynge claimed to have spotted burgling his College.

Michael changed the subject before it became awkward for his friend. 'Do you like gambling?'

Honynge regarded the monk with open dislike. 'Why? Do *you* want to become a member of the Dispensary? I doubt the sessions will continue now Lynton is dead.'

Michael raised his eyebrows. 'You do not deny it?'

'Why should I deny it? I did not bet on holy days, and any winnings I earned went towards books for Zachary Hostel. What will you do? Prosecute me? If so, I will name all the others I met at these gatherings – Paxtone, Kardington, Wynewyk—'

'Wynewyk?' asked Michael incredulously. That was a name he had missed on Lynton's register.

'Yes, and he took Langelee and Carton once, although our Master is a man of brutal wits, who does not possess the necessary finesse for Lynton's games. Carton was better.'

'Finesse?' echoed Michael disdainfully. 'For betting on the outcome of the roll of a die?'

Honynge sneered at him. 'If you attempt to make an example of me, Brother, I will see you are obliged to fine half the University. I strongly advise you to let sleeping dogs lie.'

'I shall make up my own mind about that. Where are you going? To Michaelhouse? Did Langelee not tell you the meeting has been postponed for another hour?'

Honynge looked annoyed. 'No, he did not.' His voice dropped again. 'Langelee wants you to waste your time waiting for him, because you were late for his procession today. Go to the Market Square and buy yourself some vict-uals, lest they serve you dog again this evening.'

Michael sniggered as he left. 'William *did* feed him dog today, actually – Agatha put it in the egg-mess. It was just as well he took it all before you got to it, given that I forgot to warn you.'

Bartholomew was disgusted. 'Does this mean I need to inspect everything that appears on the table from now on? Honynge is not the only one who would rather not eat dog.'

'It was just the once. And as he did not notice, there was no fun in it – it will not happen again.'

'It had better not. I notice you lied about the time of the meeting. You have just ensured he will miss it, and as he is opposing you, you will probably win the vote to exhume Kenyngham.'

'Really?' asked Michael innocently. 'The thought never crossed my mind.'

Langelee was waiting when Bartholomew and Michael entered the conclave. Wynewyk was next to him, pen poised to take notes, and William was humming as he chewed something stolen from the kitchens. It was a Lombard slice, heavy with dates and honey. Michael eyed it longingly.

'You should watch yourself, Father. Agatha might put her love-potion in anything, and she knows you are in the habit of sneaking into her domain and availing yourself of whatever happens to be lying around. You do not want to develop a passion for her. Give it to me.'

Bartholomew laughed when William did as he suggested.

'And what is to stop *you* from falling under this spell, Brother?' asked Wynewyk, also amused.

Michael stuffed the cake into his mouth. 'I am immune. And this cake is free of potions anyway. If it had been otherwise, my innate sense of godliness would have told me to spit it out.'

Bartholomew laughed again.

'Where is Honynge?' demanded Langelee irritably, when Tyrington entered and there was only one empty seat remaining. 'Is he going to be late again?'

'I saw him walking towards the Market Square a few moments ago,' replied Michael guilelessly. 'He does not like College food, so has gone to lay in some personal supplies.'

William gave a triumphant cackle, and Wynewyk's small, secret smile indicated he had also been party to the egg-mess incident. Tyrington looked from one to the other in puzzlement.

'Well, we cannot wait,' said Langelee. 'I have other business to attend today – Mayor Harleston is selling a rather fine filly, and I want to put a bid on it before Candelby does. He has wanted that horse for a long time, but she will be a good breeder and I intend to build up our stables.'

'How will we pay for it?' asked Bartholomew, startled.

'Wynewyk won a—' began Langelee.

'I was named in the will of an elderly aunt,' interrupted Wynewyk, while Langelee leaned down to rub the ankle that had been kicked.

'You mean you won something at one of Lynton's gaming sessions,' said Michael. 'Honynge told me you are a regular visitor to the Dispensary.'

'That was low of him,' said Wynewyk disapprovingly. 'We all swore oaths to keep it secret.'

'Perhaps you did, but you still should have mentioned it to me after Lynton died,' said Michael reproachfully. He looked hard at Langelee, because the Master was one of few who knew the truth. 'You know I am investigating his . . . the circumstances of his death.'

Langelee was unapologetic. 'I take vows seriously, Brother – I am no Honynge, to break trust at the first hurdle. However, I knew you would find out about the Dispensary anyway, and I was right. It has taken you less than a week.'

'How long has Lynton been running these games?' asked Bartholomew, when Michael shook his head speechlessly.

'Long before I came to Cambridge,' replied Wynewyk. 'He was good at keeping them quiet, and we shall all miss the Dispensary now he has gone. He maintained discretion by inviting just nine or ten people at any one time, so the events were always quiet and comradely. Never debauched.'

'He held a session on Good Friday,' said Michael acidly.

Wynewyk nodded. 'But not for scholars or priests – only townsfolk. The likes of Candelby and Arderne attended on Good Friday; *we* were at our vigils.'

'What are you talking about?' asked William, looking from one to the other with a pained expression. He disliked being in the dark, and the discussion had piqued his interest. 'Dispensary?'

'Do not ask,' said Michael, regarding Wynewyk and Langelee coolly. 'You would be shocked.'

'It was a gaming house,' explained Tyrington. 'Lynton invited me once, saying it was a place where mathematical probabilities were discussed. I took him at his word, and was appalled when I discovered what really went on. I considered reporting him, but my students pointed out that such a course of action would make me unpopular, and damage my chances of being elected a Fellow.'

'An ethical decision, then,' muttered Michael, moving his stool away from Tyrington and wiping spit from his sleeve. 'Not one based on self-interest.'

'I only went twice,' said Langelee. 'I was bored rigid and lost three shillings, so I decided not to go again. But let us turn to the business at hand. We have waited long enough for Honynge, so you can record his absence for posterity, Wynewyk.'

Wynewyk was already scribbling. 'The motion proposed by the absent Junior Fellow is that Kenyngham should be left where he is.'

'Right,' said Langelee. 'Hands up if you agree with Honynge.'

Bartholomew shrugged an apology at Michael as he voted. So did Tyrington. 'I am sorry, Brother, but I think Honynge is right. A man's grave should not be disturbed once he is in it. It is not decent.'

'And those who want to know the truth about Kenyngham's death?' asked Langelee, raising his own hand. Michael's shot up, too, and so did William's. Everyone looked at Wynewyk.

'Damn!' he muttered. 'Can I abstain?'

'You can,' said Tyrington, 'but then Michael will win, which means you are essentially voting *with* him. If you stand with Bartholomew and me, there will be a draw, and we will have to discuss the issue again when Honynge is here.'

'But you know what Honynge thinks,' said Michael. 'So you will make me lose the fight for justice if you do *not* abstain. Besides, remember that Honynge has just betrayed your gambling to the Senior Proctor, and here is your chance to exact revenge – by thwarting his motion.'

Tyrington turned to Langelee. 'Brother Michael's commentary is manipulative. Do you usually allow such brazen coercion?'

Langelee nodded. 'My Fellows are free to say what they like in meetings, although I fine them if they say it more than once. Come on, Wynewyk, make up your mind. I have a filly waiting.'

'Very well,' said Wynewyk. 'I vote with Michael, then. I dislike the notion of exhumation, but I dislike the notion of Kenyngham's killer evading justice even more.'

Bartholomew groaned, but Michael's smile was victorious.

Tyrington offered to supervise the disputation in the hall, which left Langelee free for equine pursuits, and Michael and Bartholomew able to continue their enquiries into Lynton's murder. Bartholomew was disappointed in the outcome of the vote, not just because he hated what was going to happen to Kenyngham, but because the Fellows tended to agree on most issues, and the College was happier for it. He supposed the time for concord was over.

Honynge was strolling across the yard as the Fellows emerged from the conclave, and Michael, chortling maliciously, hastened to make himself scarce. He slipped into the kitchens, to see whether Agatha had left any more Lombard slices lying around. Bartholomew followed him, not wanting to bear the brunt of Honynge's ire when he realised he had been deceived.

'So,' said Michael, stealing a pastry when Agatha's back was turned. 'Honynge desperately wants Kenyngham left alone.'

'So does Tyrington.' Bartholomew started to reach for a cake himself, but Agatha whipped around suddenly, and he thought better of it. 'And so do I.'

'But you two are not murder suspects,' said Michael. 'Honynge is. He could have shot Lynton and Ocleye, perhaps over a dispute arising from all this gambling, and he could have poisoned Kenyngham. And because he knows I was fond of Kenyngham, he then sent me these horrible notes. One was to taunt me with the offer of a reward, and the other was to gloat.'

Bartholomew took the letters and examined them. 'They have different styles of writing. One is neat and careful, and the other is a scrawl. I do not think they were penned by the same person.'

'He wrote them under different circumstances,' said Michael, grabbing another cake when Agatha was distracted by the cat leaping on to her shoulder. She screeched and tried to dislodge it, but it merely applied claws to the situation, and clung on gamely. 'He penned one when he had plenty of time, and he scribbled the other when he was in a hurry.'

'Why would Honynge kill Kenyngham?' asked Bartholomew reasonably, going to remove the cat while it and Agatha were still relatively unscathed. 'It makes no sense.'

'We have already been through this: because he wanted to be a Fellow. And he has succeeded. Lord, I detest that man! I know it is not something a monk should admit, but I am only human, and he has pushed me too far. I *will* see him ousted from my College.'

'Good,' said Agatha, overhearing. 'I do not like him, either, and I am glad he ate all that dog this morning. I heard he was a pig for eggs, and it is true.'

'Heard where?' asked Bartholomew.

'The Angel,' replied Agatha. 'When I went in for a drink, Candelby was telling my cousin Blankpayn that the best way to hurt the University is to prevent its scholars from buying food. He was itemising what various individuals would least like to lose – Chancellor Tynkell would miss honey, Honynge would die without eggs, William would mourn fish-giblet soup. And so on.'

'These are odd details for a taverner to know,' said Bartholomew, puzzled. 'How does he come to be in possession of such personal information?'

Agatha shrugged. 'Inn-keepers listen to gossip. Incidentally, you might want to stay away from the mutton stew tomorrow. It could come with a dog sauce.'

'Will Candelby do it?' asked Michael uneasily. 'Deprive us of victuals, I mean? That would certainly bring about an abrupt end to the rent crisis.'

'It would,' agreed Agatha. 'You would sign any solution Candelby proposed if you thought the alternative might be a tightening of the belts. The food merchants are waiting to see what happens to the rents before committing themselves, though. If Candelby wins and the rents rise, then they will form a guild to force up the price of food. If Candelby loses, they will do nothing.'

'Lord!' groaned Michael. 'If the Convocation of Regents *passes* my amendment, we will have peace with the landlords, but another war with the food merchants. If the Convocation *rejects* the clause, we will remain at an impasse over rents for ever. I cannot win no matter what happens!'

'Have a Lombard slice, Brother,' said Agatha consolingly, passing him the plate when she saw the agitation her tale had occasioned. 'It will make you feel better.'

'No,' said Michael piteously. 'I am too upset for eating.'

'Have two, then,' coaxed Agatha, waving the plate.

With the air of a martyr, Michael accepted. 'Do you have that love-potion? Can we slip Honynge a few drops? He might fall for Langelee, who would break his neck. Or William, who might succeed in infecting him with some horrible disease from his festering habit.'

'Can we give some to Tyrington, too?' asked Agatha. 'His leers makes me want to punch him.'

'Do not punch him,' begged Bartholomew, having seen what one of the laundress's swipes could do. 'He cannot help it.'

'There is a commotion going on outside,' said Agatha, going to the window and throwing open the shutter. 'It concerns Honynge, of course. He is waving our gold crown about – the one from the Stanton Hutch. What is he doing with that? He is supposed to be managing the *Illeigh* Hutch.'

'Damn,' said Michael softly, watching Honynge hand the diadem to a bemused Langelee. William stood with his arms folded, looking utterly disgusted. 'He wants it returned to its rightful place. So much for our attempt to catch him out in dishonest behaviour.'

'You planted the crown?' asked Agatha. She grimaced. 'That was too crude. You should have tempted him with something more easily saleable. After all, that is how Lynton caught my cousin. Blankpayn was too sensible to steal Lynton's expensive gold goblets, but small silver rings were another matter entirely.'

'What is this?' asked Michael, turning to face her.

'Blankpayn used to help Lynton count his Dispensary profits, but Lynton suspected my cousin was cheating him, so he set a trap. Yet it was not a large prize that was my kinsman's undoing, but tiny rings.'

'How do you know?' asked Bartholomew doubtfully.

'I was there,' replied Agatha. 'I like to flirt with Lady Luck on occasion, and when my cousin told me about the Dispensary, I decided to attend a session or two.'

'I bet that pleased Lynton,' muttered Michael. 'What did Blankpayn do when he was caught?'

'Nothing – but Lynton exposed him in front of Mayor Harleston, and it has hurt his chances of being elected as a burgess. No one wants town officials who are *known* thieves.'

'I see,' mused Michael. 'That is a powerful motive for putting a crossbow bolt in a man's chest.'

Honynge was not a stupid man, and guessed exactly why the diadem had been left in the Hutch he had been instructed to manage. He was angry and offended, and berated William furiously. So did Langelee, who thought the plan might have resulted in the loss of a valuable heirloom. William was not very good at thinking on his feet, and was slow to devise an excuse that would have exonerated himself, so he had no choice but to bow his head and let them rail at him. Afterwards, the atmosphere in the conclave was acrimonious, and Bartholomew was more than happy to use Michael's investigations as an excuse to escape.

'I want to talk to Candelby,' said Michael, hurrying to leave before Langelee spotted him. 'And Blankpayn. I must learn more about their relationship with Lynton.'

'In the Angel? I do not think we should go there.'

'Candelby will not be in his tavern now; he will be in the Church of St John Zachary, lighting candles for the brother who died in the plague. And if you are wondering how I am so intimately acquainted with his habits, it is because he is not the only man who spies on his enemies. Beadle Meadowman has been shadowing him, and so has Cynric, when his other duties allow.'

As usual, the little church was damp and dark. The main door stood open to allow parishioners to see what they were doing inside, but the window shutters that bordered Clare were firmly locked. The recent rains had caused puddles to form on the flagstone floor, and Michael swore softly when he discovered one was ankle deep.

Bartholomew glanced towards the Lady Chapel, recalling that the last time he had been there, Motelete had sat up in his coffin. He thought about the student, and how he had gone from shy youth to a man with a lover who could defend himself in brawls. Bartholomew rubbed his chin. Had Motelete's brush with death really caused him to undergo a transformation? Or had defects in his character been conveniently forgotten when he had become the victim of violence? He recalled what the addled old master called Gedney had said – that the 'dead' student had been loud-mouthed and drank too much. Was Gedney's sharp-tongued portrait more accurate than that of Motelete's friends, who had been shocked by his murder and so willing to overlook his faults?

A sudden low rumble made Bartholomew turn quickly towards the spiral staircase that led to the roof. A billow of dust belched through the doorway, and he glanced up at the rafters uneasily, noting that several of the supporting beams were at very odd angles. He was not the only one to be concerned. Candelby was regarding the joists with considerable trepidation, and Blankpayn was already heading for the exit.

'If you want to talk to me, do it outside,' said Candelby

to the monk. 'It is disgusting that scholars have let this poor place decay, and I do not want to be inside when it tumbles apart.'

'We would not mind *you* being in here though, Brother,' called Blankpayn, from the comparative safety of the porch. 'That would be divine justice.'

Michael ignored him. 'I would like to talk to you about Lynton,' he said to Candelby, once they were in the churchyard. 'I understand you were one of the Dispensary's most faithful customers.'

'So?' asked Candelby, with a shrug. 'A lot of men liked Lynton's games.'

'I did not,' growled Blankpayn. 'They were too complicated, and for some reason, scholars always won more often than me. And Lynton wondered why I decided to help myself to a bauble or two! It was because those rings were mine in the first place – I lost them when I placed a bet.'

'Scholars win a lot because they have sly minds,' explained Candelby matter-of-factly. 'What do you want to know, Brother? Normally, I would object to being quizzed by you, but I have nothing to hide about my association with Lynton, so you can ask what you like.'

'Why did you not mention your gambling to me sooner?'

Candelby shrugged again. 'Because it was none of your business and, like all participants, I was sworn to secrecy. I did not want to besmirch Lynton's reputation by blabbing to you.'

Michael snorted his disbelief. 'You did not care about his reputation when you accused him of riding his horse at you last Sunday.'

'I was angry and in pain – not thinking clearly. Of course he did not ride at me deliberately. I have apologised to Wisbeche for my intemperate remarks, so let that mark the end of the matter.'

'How much did you lose at these sessions?' asked Michael.

'Actually, I won more than I lost. Why do you think I own so many houses? I was good at Lynton's games – better than many scholars.'

Something occurred to Michael. 'Is that why you are so well acquainted with the University's private affairs? You gossiped with my colleagues when you were gaming?'

Candelby's smile was enigmatic. 'I am a good listener, and scholars are naturally verbose. Thus I knew Lynton preferred to lease his properties to merchants, not students; I was told all about a debate in Peterhouse, in which the Fellows elected to charge high rents on the houses they will inherit from Lynton; and I was aware that Spaldynge was desperate to sell Borden Hostel. I made him an offer he could not refuse.'

'You must really hate scholars,' said Michael wonderingly.

Candelby shook his head. 'I am quite happy to lease my buildings to your comrades – if they pay me a competitive market price.'

'The University will not wield power for much longer,' gloated Blankpayn. 'When we win the right to charge what rent we like, it will flounder.'

'I do not care about that,' said Candelby, walking away. 'I just want to make some money.'

That evening, as lamps were beginning to gleam through the twilight, and the Michaelhouse men were preparing to retire to bed or repair to the communal rooms for company, conversation or warmed ale, Cynric slipped up to Bartholomew.

'Grab your cloak, boy,' he whispered. 'I want to show you something.'

'I am not going out now,' said Bartholomew, amazed

that the book-bearer should think he might. 'It is madness to wander the streets after dark these days.'

'Come on,' wheedled Cynric. 'Please? It will be fun, and I will not enjoy it nearly as much alone. Normally, I would invite Carton, but he is out somewhere, and I cannot find him.'

'Out?' echoed Bartholomew. 'This late? Does Michael know?'

Cynric grinned, teeth flashing white in the gloom. 'I doubt it! Hurry up, or you will miss it.'

'Miss what?' demanded Bartholomew, not liking Cynric's mysterious manner.

But the book-bearer could not be persuaded to tell, so Bartholomew followed him down the darkening lane and on to the High Street. A religious office was under way in St Michael's Church; Michael and William were singing vespers, and their chanting voices carried on the still evening air. Stars twinkled in a dark blue sky, and Bartholomew shivered – the clear weather had brought with it a snapping cold, and there would be a frost that night.

A blackbird sang its evening song, and the air was rich with the scents of the day – manure from horses and donkeys, the sulphurous reek of the river and the nearby marshes, the smell of spring flowers, and a delicious aroma from a meat stew that was someone's supper. The town was quiet, the clatter of hoofs and footsteps stilled for the night, as folk prepared for sleep.

When they reached St Mary the Great, Cynric slid into the shadows of the churchyard. Bartholomew was slow in following, because a cemetery was not somewhere he wanted to be at that time of night, and there was always the danger that a group of townsmen might be there. Since the plague, some folk had abandoned traditional religion, and haunted graveyards after dark. They performed sinister rites in the hope that the denizens of Hell would protect them against future outbreaks. After all, God and His saints had done nothing to help them, had they?

'Come on,' hissed Cynric from the bushes. 'You should see what goes on in your own town.'

Bartholomew was acutely uneasy. 'Someone will catch us, and demand to know what we are doing. And as I have absolutely no idea, how am I supposed to reply?'

Cynric beckoned him towards the back of the church. Bartholomew strained his eyes, and saw a figure lying motionless on the ground, hands folded across his chest. After a moment, a second person emerged from the trees that separated the churchyard from the Market Square, and started to move around him. It was too dark to identify faces or distinguishing features, and all the physician could see was that the second man – or woman – was swathed in a cloak. As virtually everyone in the town owned such a garment, it was impossible to say who it might be. The figure knelt, and there was a brief flicker as a candle was lit. It guttered in the evening breeze, but was too feeble to illuminate the face of either person. Bartholomew grew even more uncomfortable.

'I do not like this,' he whispered. 'Why did you drag me all the way here, when witches probably do this sort of thing every night?'

'Not in St Mary the Great,' replied Cynric confidently. 'St John Zachary and All Saints-next-the-Castle are favourites with warlocks, but they leave St Mary the Great alone. Too holy, see.'

Bartholomew tried to read his expression in the darkness. 'Do you witness these rites often?'

Cynric nodded. 'They happen more frequently than you might think, and I like to keep an eye on these Satan-lovers. You never know when they might decide to stage a rebellion, and drive out honest, God-fearing citizens like me.' He crossed himself.

'You watch with Carton?'

Cynric nodded a second time. 'He is the only one interested.'

Bartholomew supposed his colleagues had been right after all, when they had declined to elect Carton to take Kenyngham's place. He gestured to the two figures. 'What are they doing? The one lying down will catch his death. It is freezing, and the ground is wet.'

'They are casting spells,' explained Cynric darkly. 'And I brought you here because Honynge has sawn through the chains on the books in the hall, and has taken them all to his room – to protect them from Tyrington's drool, he says. The other Fellows are furious, and things are being said that will be regretted tomorrow. I thought you would be better off here.'

Bartholomew was exasperated. 'Surely the kitchen would have sufficed? Or my room? Or even the porters' lodge. You did not have to lure me out to this . . .' He waved his hand, not sure how to describe what he was witnessing.

Cynric shook his head firmly. 'You are best well out of the place. Besides, I have a feeling this is more sinister than witchcraft.'

Bartholomew did not bother to make the point that witchcraft was more than sinister enough for him. He was about to abandon his hiding place and go home, when he became aware that the cloaked figure had stood, and was looming over the one on the ground. It was not easy to see what he was doing, but the faint light from the candle certainly illuminated the fact that the person held something long and sharp. It was a dagger, and it was descending towards the man on the ground.

Bartholomew reacted instinctively, launching himself

from behind the buttress and towards the would-be killer as fast as he could. He did not stop to rationalise what he was doing – all he knew was that he was not about to stand by and do nothing while murder was committed. The cloaked figure leapt in alarm at the sound of sudden footsteps, and whipped around to face him. Then everything happened very quickly.

The cloaked figure lunged at Bartholomew, but his deadly swipe missed. Unusually slow on the uptake, Cynric took a moment to join the affray, but when he did, it was with one of his bloodcurdling battle cries. He tore towards the knifeman, but another shadow emerged from the bushes, and a well-placed foot sent the Welshman sprawling on to his face. While Cynric shook his head to clear it, the newcomer shoved Bartholomew hard enough to make him crash back against the buttress, and dragged his cloaked comrade into the undergrowth.

'After them, Cynric,' shouted Bartholomew, trying to climb to his feet, but he could see it was too late. The mysterious pair had melted away, using bushes and darkness to mask where they had gone. Cynric took a few steps after them, but knew a lost cause when he saw one, and soon abandoned the chase.

'That was rash,' he said, unimpressed. 'You flew at them without bothering to draw a weapon – or telling me what you were going to do. I thought your experiences in France had cured you of antics like that.'

'He had a knife,' said Bartholomew. He looked around uneasily, afraid the pair might return with reinforcements. Wanting to be done with the business, so he could go home to Michaelhouse, he knelt next to the prostrate figure, using the abandoned candle to see what he was doing.

'It is Motelete from Clare!' exclaimed Cynric, when light flickered across the face.

Bartholomew nodded. 'And this time, he really is dead.'

Cynric regarded him in shock. 'No! He is just part of whatever game the others were playing.'

'Obviously. But his role is that of corpse.'

Cynric continued to stare. 'You mean we have been watching a rite involving a *real* body! When I saw him lying like that, I just assumed . . . I would *never* have brought you here to watch . . .'

'He is growing stiff,' said Bartholomew, feeling Motelete's jaw. 'I know it is not a reliable indicator for a time of death, but it suggests he has been dead hours, not minutes. And, judging by the blisters around his mouth and the scent from his mouth, I would say he has been poisoned.'

CHAPTER 10

The evening went from bad to worse. Cynric fetched Michael, and they took Motelete to Clare, where Bartholomew undertook the grim task of breaking the news to the lad's friends. Kardington was shocked, the students distressed and Spaldynge suspicious that a physician should happen to discover the body. Michael tried to ask questions, but the Clare men were too overwrought for a sensible discussion, and he decided it would be better to return in the morning. By the time Bartholomew flopped exhaustedly into his bed, it was well past midnight.

The porter had forgotten to put his peacock to roost, and as a consequence it woke the entire College long before dawn the following day. The new scholars leapt from their straw mattresses in alarm, then grinned sheepishly at each other when they realised what had happened. The ungodly racket made even Bartholomew stir and open his eyes. When the students in his chamber began chatting and lighting a lamp, he saw there was no point in trying to go back to sleep, and forced himself to sit up. He rubbed his eyes, feeling sluggish and thick-headed from the lack of rest.

'It is good of Michaelhouse to take us in,' said a pleasant theologian called Simon Hemmysby, watching him step across two prone students to reach his bowl of washing water. Langelee had chosen Hemmysby from the many hopefuls because he held a post – and thus a stipend – in Waltham Abbey, and would be able to pay his fees *and* make the odd additional donation. 'However, I did not think accommodation in a wealthy College would be quite so cramped.'

'It is not a wealthy College,' said Bartholomew. Water flew as he began to wash, making one lad leap from his mattress in shock. 'King's Hall is wealthy. *We* are always looking for ways to make ends meet.'

'Wynewyk did his best,' said Hemmysby, flinching when spray flew in his direction. 'But he is a lawyer, and it would have been better if Michaelhouse had used a mathematician.'

Bartholomew regarded him blankly. 'Wynewyk did his best at what?'

'At the Dispensary,' said Hemmysby, a little impatiently. 'At winning money for his College.'

Bartholomew glanced at the other students and saw none seemed particularly surprised by the conversation. 'Are Michael and I the only ones who did not know about Lynton's little enterprise?'

Hemmysby raised his eyebrows. 'If you are saying you were ignorant of its existence, then you are certainly in a minority. Did he never invite you? I thought you and he were friends.'

Bartholomew shrugged. 'I dislike gambling. I lose interest, because of the unpredictable nature of the wins and losses. They require no skill.'

Hemmysby regarded him in surprise. 'But Lynton's contests *did* require skill. With most games of chance, everything *does* depend on luck – you can be the cleverest man in the kingdom, but your chance of success is the same as the dunce sitting next to you. Lynton, however, introduced a degree of probability to his games, which meant people were challenged to crack his system.'

'How do you know?' asked Bartholomew, bemused. 'Were you one of these gamesters?'

'I am in major orders,' said Hemmysby primly. 'Priests do not gamble.'

'They do in Cambridge,' muttered Bartholomew.

Hemmysby did not hear him. 'Before I was awarded my post at Waltham Abbey, I was always short of money. Then Lynton offered to pay me for serving wine to his guests. I no longer need the work, but I have kept it up, because I like it – the company is erudite and always entertaining.'

Bartholomew tried to understand what Lynton had done. 'He invented a game that allowed players to predict the outcome?' He could see why that would have been popular – scholars liked exercising their minds, especially when they thought they might win something for correct answers.

Hemmysby nodded. 'It did not involve dice, but imaginary horses. Participants had to guess how long a particular animal would take to travel across a certain amount of ground.'

Bartholomew stared at him as several facts snapped together. 'The mean speed theorem! That is all about the time an object – in this case a horse – needs to cover a set distance, and it is a predictive formula. Did he base his games of chance around that?'

Hemmysby nodded again. 'It was extremely complicated, and scholars loved it – Lynton would change variables and enter unknowns into the equation to make calculation more difficult – the size of the horse, the slope of the land, the weight of the rider, and so on. The sums had to be done very fast, too, which added an additional thrill to the proceedings.'

'Had I known there was intricate arithmetic involved, I might have signed up myself,' said Bartholomew, rather wistfully. 'However, I fail to see the appeal for townsfolk – they will not know the formula. Yet a number of them played.'

'They claimed they were any scholar's equal, and were just as good at predicting the outcome of these horse races. Of course, they were not, and they lost more often than they won.'

Bartholomew recalled Blankpayn saying as much. 'Why did Lynton admit laymen in the first place? He must have known it would cause trouble.'

'There were rarely problems. The Dispensary operated for years without ill feeling, and Lynton did not mind who played, as long as he – or she – paid his debts.'

'Paxtone said he disagreed with Lynton's conclusions,' said Bartholomew. '*They* argued.'

'Of course there were *arguments*. There were scholars involved, and arguing is what we do best. But Friday nights were good-natured occasions with discreet, well-behaved men who always parted friends. However, not all the merchants were as civil.'

'Candelby?' asked Bartholomew, more pieces of the puzzle falling into place.

'He has an unattractive habit of gloating when he wins. In the end, he was banned.'

'When?' asked Bartholomew, thoughts whirling. No wonder Candelby had hated Lynton.

'Good Friday. There was a fuss, and wine was spilled. Has no one told you about this?'

'No,' said Bartholomew tartly. 'Apparently, participants are bound by vows of secrecy.'

'They are. And because most are decent men, they are unlikely to break that trust. I did not swear the oath, though, because I was not a player. I only served the wine.'

'I cannot believe Lynton did this! We have been told wagers included houses, livestock, boats and money. With the stakes so high, it is not surprising that he might have attracted resentment.'

'The stakes *were* high, but Lynton refused to let anyone ruin himself. He even restored goods to losers on occasion, when he felt it was warranted. There was no resentment – not from anyone.'

Bartholomew was not sure whether to believe him. 'Was he magnanimous when Candelby lost?'

'We never had occasion to find out, because Candelby rarely came up with the wrong answer. Why do you think he was so peeved when he was debarred? All his houses came from betting on Lynton's races, you see.'

It was Father William's turn to conduct the morning mass, and, as usual, it was finished in record time. Unfortunately, it was too early to ask questions about Lynton or Motelete, so Bartholomew and Michael sat in the conclave, and the physician described to Michael – yet again – what had transpired in the churchyard of St Mary the Great the previous night.

'Are you sure Motelete was poisoned?' the monk asked. 'You told me toxins are difficult to detect, which is why you failed to notice one in Kenyngham. Yet you are able to pronounce a clear cause of death with Motelete?'

Bartholomew was too tired to argue about Kenyngham. 'The substance was caustic enough to blister his mouth – not badly, but sufficient to tell me it would have damaged his innards, too.'

'Yet someone was hovering over him with a dagger. Why would anyone want to stab a corpse?'

Bartholomew shrugged. 'Cynric thinks it had something to do with witchcraft.'

'Are you sure Motelete was dead when all this was going on? You usually tell me it is impossible to pinpoint a time of death with any degree of accuracy.'

'I can usually tell the difference between someone who

316

has been a corpse for hours and someone who has only just breathed his last.'

'And there was nothing in the two living figures that will allow you to identify them?'

'It was too dark. However, Arderne has a penchant for meddling with the dead.'

'I doubt Arderne is the killer – I imagine he would rather have Motelete alive, as a testament to his remarkable skills. However, if Motelete *had* changed from demure boy to belligerent womaniser, then perhaps he was not the kind of advertisement Arderne wanted for his handiwork.'

'Had he changed? Do you remember what Gedney said? That the dead student was loud-mouthed and drank too much?'

'Gedney is addled. However, he does have moments of clarity, and he was an astute man in his time. It is not impossible that vestiges of that brilliance still flash now and again.'

'I imagine you would like the culprit for Motelete's murder to be Candelby.'

'Actually, Matt, I would rather it was Honynge – and I happen to know he went out yesterday evening. I set Meadowman to follow him, but the sly fellow gave him the slip.'

'Unfortunately for you, Honynge was here when those two figures were with Motelete in the churchyard. He was arguing about the books he has spirited away to his room – and *you* are his alibi. He only went out later.'

Michael's expression was triumphant. 'But you said Motelete was dead *hours* before that. Honynge might have murdered him and deposited him in the churchyard, leaving Arderne to maul the corpse at a later time. That would be a convenient solution, because it would please us both.'

They left the conclave, and the monk showed Bartholomew the empty shelves in the hall, where the books had been. The severed chains dangled forlornly. Wynewyk joined them, and complained bitterly about the 'theft'. Bartholomew thought they were overreacting.

'Cynric said the tomes are in Honynge's room – he wants to protect them. They are not stolen.'

'Honynge *claims* he acted out of concern,' said Michael. 'But he has locked the door to his quarters, which means no one else can read anything unless he lets them in.'

Wynewyk snorted his disdain. 'Honynge's antics have nothing to do with caring for books. He is compiling an exemplar – a collection of readings – for third-year theologians. Its sale will make him rich.'

Michael blew out his cheeks in understanding. 'And because his exemplar will include texts from a wide variety of sources, he wants our library readily to hand. His motive is selfish.'

'Hateful man!' said Wynewyk fervently. 'I am glad William fed him dog again this morning.'

Because it was Saturday, the disputation was more light-hearted than the ones during the week, and was run by students, rather than Fellows. Falmeresham had been scheduled to take charge, but with his defection to Arderne, Langelee ordered Carton to take his place. The commoner was making for the back gate when he heard his name mentioned. He returned with a nervous grin.

'Where were you going?' demanded Langelee. 'I gave an order for everyone to stay in today.'

Carton's smile began to slip. 'I did not have enough to eat this morning, because Agatha keeps putting dog in everything. I was going to buy a pie from the Angel.'

Michael glared at him; he knew a lie when he heard

one. Nor was Langelee amused, and he had just begun to deliver a lecture about obedience, when Tyrington approached.

'God help us,' he breathed. 'I do not mean to offend, but Deynman is no scholar.'

'He is not,' agreed Honynge, overhearing. 'And if he is allowed to go and practise medicine he will kill someone. But Michaelhouse created the problem, so Michaelhouse must devise a solution.'

'I would suggest inventing some nominal post here, to keep him out of mischief,' said Tyrington. 'But we have no money to pay him, and I certainly do not want him anywhere near *my* students.'

Honynge issued a weary sigh. 'Leave it to me. *I* shall think of something. After all, it is an issue that requires intelligent thinking – something of which the current Fellowship seems incapable.'

'We did some intelligent thinking about our books,' said Langelee curtly. 'We want them back, so they can be used by everyone. If you do not return them by noon, I shall order Cynric to smash the lock on your door and remove them by force.'

Honynge glowered. 'Very well – let your precious tomes be doused in spit, then. See if I care! However, I have a far more serious issue to bring before you today, one I find deeply disturbing.'

'The breakfast dog had nothing to do with me,' began Michael immediately. 'It was a—'

'This,' said Honynge, waving a torn piece of parchment, 'was in the Illeigh Hutch. You told me to do an inventory of its contents, Master, and I happened across it.'

'It is a rent agreement,' said Michael, puzzled. 'Or the top half of one. What does it—'

'It proves *someone* is breaking the Statutes – by charging

a rent higher than that set by law,' declared Honynge. 'Since the document was found in Michaelhouse, I can only conclude that Michaelhouse men are engaged in illegal activities.'

As the monk did not have his magnifying glass, Bartholomew took the fragment from Honynge. He stared at it in confusion, then spoke in a low voice, while Honynge continued to rail at Langelee. 'I cannot be certain, Brother, but this looks like the other half of the document we found in Lynton's hand. When we compare the two, I would be surprised if the torn edges do not match.'

'What?' asked Michael, astounded. 'How does it come to be in the Illeigh Hutch?'

Honynge overheard, and levelled an accusing finger at him. '*You* brokered an illicit agreement, and tore the names from the bottom to cover your tracks. Then you hid the document in the Illeigh Hutch, but forgot to reclaim it before the chest passed to me. It proves you are dishonest.'

'It does not,' said Tyrington. 'It means *someone* is, but there is no proof that it is Michael.'

'How is it proof of dishonesty?' demanded Wynewyk. 'There are no names on the thing, so it is invalid anyway. Someone probably kept it as scrap, intending to use the back for something else. Parchment is expensive, so we all re-use what we can.'

'It proves Michael owns a High Street house, and that he rented it at an illegal rate,' Honynge raged. 'He must have won it at the Dispensary, and is intent on making his fortune from it.'

'What makes you think Michael is the culprit?' asked Langelee. 'There is nothing to say—'

'Because I saw the *bottom* half of that agreement in his room. I spotted it when I went to return a scroll I had borrowed recently. It is probably still there, on his desk.'

'In that case, it is obvious someone is trying to get him into trouble,' said Tyrington. 'Well, it will not work. Michael might be a sly old fox, but he does not break the University's rules.'

Honynge sneered. 'He spends more time in the Brazen George than at his lectures. I shall expect his resignation over this, because it is the decent thing to do. And Bartholomew's.'

'Why Bartholomew's?' asked Tyrington, puzzled. 'He has nothing to do with this document.'

'Because he concealed the fact that Lynton was murdered. Now why would he do that? There are only two reasons, and neither are pleasant. Either he killed Lynton himself, and was hoping to see him buried with no one any the wiser. Or he did it because he could not be bothered to investigate. Either way, I do not want him in my College.'

He turned on his heel and stalked away, leaving the others staring after him in astonishment.

'What *was* this rental agreement doing in the Illeigh Hutch, Brother?' asked Wynewyk. 'Is it part of your investigation, and you put it there to keep it safe?'

'It is certainly part of my investigation,' said Michael. 'Although I cannot imagine how it comes to be in a place where Honynge could find it.'

'I can,' said Tyrington quietly. '*He* put it there for the sole purpose of damaging you. Is it true that Lynton was murdered? Then perhaps you need look no further for your killer.'

Solutions and questions were coming so fast that Michael insisted on adjourning to the Brazen George to think. Bartholomew did not think it was a good idea, especially given that Honynge had commented on the monk's rule-breaking, but Michael said he was not going to let petty accusations interfere with *his* daily pleasures. So they went to the tavern, although Bartholomew did so with grave misgivings.

'Do not let him bother you, Matt,' said Michael, seeing Honynge's remarks had cut deep.

'He accused me of murder – or of concealing a crime. Of course I am bothered! He is the kind of man to share his thoughts with everyone he meets, and it is bad enough with Isnard's friends lobbing rocks at me. I do not want scholars doing it, too.'

'No one will believe him. He is objectionable and arrogant, and they would rather side with you.'

Bartholomew was not so sure. 'People are fickle, and change allegiances fast. Honynge's claims, coming so soon after Isnard's, may lead folk to wonder whether there is smoke without fire.'

'Then we must solve our mysteries as quickly as we can – either to prove Honynge is the guilty party, or to expose the real killer and prove your innocence. Let us start with the document Honynge found. Are you sure it was the upper half of the one in Lynton's hand?'

'Positive. Everything matched – the shape of the tear, the ink, the writing, and the parchment.'

'Then someone at Michaelhouse must have put it there, because no one else has access. Our College is suddenly full of men we do not know, so perhaps one of them did it. Or do you think someone left it *because* it was likely to be found – as a way to get it into my hands? It is evidence in a murder, and he may have wanted me to have it without being obliged to say how he came by it.'

'You are thinking of Falmeresham? That he found it when he was with Arderne?'

Michael nodded. 'He worships Arderne, but he is not stupid. He may well have discovered something that disturbed him, so he decided to ease his conscience by passing it to me discreetly.'

'The document was almost certainly ripped from Lynton's hand by the man who killed him. If Falmeresham found it in Arderne's possession, then it means Arderne is the killer.'

Michael touched his arm. 'Do not fear for Falmeresham. If Arderne had meant him harm, he would not have healed him in the first place. Your errant student will be safe enough.'

Bartholomew rubbed his eyes, not sure of anything. 'What are we going to do?'

'Ask questions, Matt. Just as always.'

'Then we should make a start,' said Bartholomew, standing and pulling the monk to his feet. 'We cannot waste time speculating.'

Michael snatched a piece of bread as he was hauled away from the table. 'Clare first, to ask about Motelete. And then we shall enter the lion's den and tackle Arderne.'

At Clare, they were admitted by Spaldynge, who was sombre, tired and pale. He admitted to staying up all night with some of the younger students, who had been too distraught to sleep.

'I hope you catch the monster who did this,' he said in a low voice. 'Poor Motelete. He was just learning to enjoy himself, too. He was less shy than before he died – the first time.'

'We saw him courting Siffreda Sago,' said Bartholomew. 'Is that what you mean?'

Spaldynge nodded. 'I had no idea he was a lad for the ladies, and he surprised us all when he set his eyes on Siffreda. Do not look to her brother as the killer, though. Sago was working all yesterday – including last night – in the Angel, and a dozen men can confirm it.'

'Including you?' asked Michael archly.

'I do not frequent taverns,' replied Spaldynge coolly. 'However, I did go to the Angel briefly to ask a few questions after you brought us Motelete's body. They seemed the obvious suspects, and—'

'So, you did not spend all night with weeping students,' pounced Bartholomew. 'You lied.'

Spaldynge regarded him with dislike. 'You twist my words, physician, but that is to be expected. You are as sly and devious as the rest of the men in your profession.'

Michael tapped him sharply in the chest, making him step back in surprise. 'Matt had nothing to do with what happened to your family during the plague, so do not vent your spleen on him.'

'No,' acknowledged Spaldynge bitterly. 'It was Lynton – and Kenyngham gave them last rites when his feeble efforts failed. Now physicians have killed Motelete, too. They are jealous of the fact that Arderne can heal and they cannot, so they slaughtered Motelete to "prove" Arderne's cures are only temporary. It is despicable!'

'You think Rougham or Paxtone fed Motelete poison?' asked Bartholomew, shocked. 'Or me?'

'Probably not you – you are more of a knife man.' Bartholomew saw the anguish in Spaldynge's eyes, so did not react to the insult. 'You and your colleagues were useless during the Death, but Arderne said he cured hundreds of people. If only he had been here! But I do not want to talk about it any more, especially with you. Follow me. The others are waiting in the refectory.'

Bartholomew stared after him unhappily, and was not much cheered by the situation in Clare's hall. One of the youngest students started to cry the moment he and Michael entered, and Kardington stood with his arm around the boy's shoulders. Michael was kind and patient, but no one could tell him anything useful. When the monk finally accepted that he was wasting his time, Kardington escorted them out, leaving Spaldynge to console the sobbing child.

They met old Gedney, hobbling across the yard on his stick. He glared at Bartholomew. 'Have you finished with my copy of Holcot's *Postillae* yet? I want it back.'

'I do not have it.' Bartholomew looked at the gate and longed to be through it. He was tired of accusations from members of Clare.

'That rascally Tyd must have pinched it, then,' said Gedney, grimacing in annoyance. 'Or his friend with the beard – the one who gambles at the Dispensary. What is his name?'

'Spaldynge,' said Kardington shortly, walking on before the old man could say anything else. He addressed Michael and Bartholomew in his careful Latin. 'I am sorry we have not been of more help. We are united in our hope that you will catch the person who poisoned Motelete.'

'Spaldynge thinks Matt did it,' said Michael bluntly.

'He is just upset,' said Kardington apologetically. 'And he does not like physicians. It is a shock, learning that a student is murdered, then he is alive, and now he is slain again.'

'I saw Motelete in several taverns,' said Michael. 'Yet when we first started asking questions about him, everyone said he avoided them, because he was afraid of being fined.'

Kardington sniffed. 'He liked the Angel, but who does not? Even the most rigorous adherent of the University's rules cannot resist those lovely pies.'

'He was not eating; he was drinking. Claret, no less.'

Kardington was sheepish. 'Well, perhaps he did have a fondness for it, which became more noticeable after his resurrection. And I admit he was not the scholar we thought him to be, either.'

325

'What do you mean?'

'We all wanted to get to know him better after he had that miraculous cure, but he was not the lad we remembered. He must have concealed his true character before. To be honest, I found I did not like him much, although that does not mean to say I am pleased that he is dead.'

'Did you see him with anyone who might mean him harm?' asked Michael.

'His free time was spent either with Siffreda or Arderne,' said Kardington. 'But Arderne had saved him, so it is no surprise that they struck up a friendship. Your lad Falmeresham was jealous, though – I saw him glaring enviously myself. And *he* knows about poisons—'

'No,' said Bartholomew immediately. 'Falmeresham is not a killer.'

'I hope not,' said Kardington softly. 'I really do.'

'I understand you visited the Dispensary,' said Michael coolly. 'Did you win much?'

'Not really,' said Kardington. He blushed guiltily, and could not meet Michael's eyes. 'I am not very good at calculating mean speed, although I enjoyed the exercise. Are you going to fine me?'

'I wish I could, because you are supposed to be setting an example to those in your care. But why pick on you, when virtually every member of the University took part at one time or another? Even Matt admits that he would have joined in, had he known complex arithmetic was on offer.'

Kardington smiled, more in relief than amusement. 'You would have been good, Bartholomew. I recall your performance at that debate in St Mary the Great, and it was highly entertaining. It is a pity you seem to have learned too late what was involved.'

'It is a pity for all of us,' said Michael ambiguously.

*　　*　　*

Bartholomew insisted on going to see Arderne next, so they trudged through the rain to the High Street, where the healer rented a house that had once been a hostel. Since its scholars had moved out, it had been given a new pink wash, and some of its rotting timbers had been replaced. Its thatch had been repaired, too, so it had gone from a rather seedy place to a home that any wealthy citizen would be pleased to inhabit. It raised the tone of the southern end of the High Street.

'Do you think the town resents the fact that most buildings occupied by scholars tend to be shabby?' mused Bartholomew.

'They would not be shabby if the landlords were willing to effect repairs,' retorted Michael. 'Did you hear Rudd's Hostel finally fell down yesterday, thanks to its landlord's years of neglect?'

Rain had turned the High Street into a bog, and a foetid ooze of grey-brown mud squelched around their feet as they walked. Michael lost a shoe, and had to balance on one foot until the physician had retrieved it for him. It came free with a sucking plop, and while he waited for the monk to put it back on again, Bartholomew saw Blankpayn in a similar predicament. The taverner bellowed for someone to help him, but no one seemed much inclined to oblige.

There was a line of people standing outside Arderne's door, shivering as the wind blew drizzle into their faces. Some had crutches or propelled themselves along on wheeled pallets, while others had bandages covering a variety of sores and afflictions.

'They are here in the hope that Arderne will dispense one of his miracles,' explained Michael. 'He hinted the other day that he might take one or two charity cases, and this is the result.'

'I know most of these people,' said Bartholomew sadly. 'Arderne will not be able to help them, because most are incurable.'

Several nodded to him as he passed, but more looked away and refused to meet his eyes, ashamed and uncomfortable that they were trying to defect after accepting his charity. Bartholomew did not blame them for wanting a miracle, and was only sorry that most would be disappointed. When they reached the front of the queue, they found the door open and Falmeresham standing in it. The student looked harried and unhappy.

'He will not see you,' he was saying wearily. 'He only cures paupers on Fridays. At other times, he will only tend you if you can pay.'

'We *did* come Friday,' said the sightless beggar who was first in line. 'But he only examined Will and Eudo – and he said they could not be healed because their souls were impure.'

'How convenient,' said Bartholomew to Michael. 'Blaming the patient for his own failures.'

'It is a good idea. You should do it – tell Isnard it is his own fault his leg has not grown back.'

'I do not like Falmeresham involved in this sort of thing. I thought I trained him better than that.'

'You did,' said Michael soothingly. 'He is not easy in his new role – you can see it in his eyes. It pains him to turn these people away.'

'How much does a cure for blindness cost, Falmeresham?' asked Bartholomew, approaching his student and regarding him rather accusingly.

'Forty marks.' Bartholomew gaped and Falmeresham shrugged. 'Effective treatment costs. Are you here to see Magister Arderne? He is at breakfast, but I will tell him you are here.'

Arderne had converted one of his ground-floor rooms into a dispensary, which had pots on shelves around the wall, and a wide variety of surgical and medical equipment on a bench under the window. Bartholomew looked in one or two of the containers, and was not surprised to find them empty. Nor was he surprised to note that the surgical implements either did not work or were too blunt to be effective. The man used hot air and feathers more often than proper tools and medicines.

'We heard Motelete spent a lot of time here,' said Michael, taking the opportunity to speak to Falmeresham before Arderne arrived. 'Before his sudden death last night, of course.'

'He and Magister Arderne became fast friends quite quickly,' replied Falmeresham. He stared out of the window. 'Arderne has a way of making people want to be with him.'

'Were you envious of the attention he gave Motelete?' asked Michael baldly.

'At first,' admitted Falmeresham. 'Especially because Motelete did not deserve it. He was just a common thief – I saw him shove one of Arderne's phials in his purse when he thought no one was looking. But Arderne is astute, and would have seen through him in time. I did not poison Motelete, though, if that is what you are thinking. I have not been out of Arderne's sight for a moment.'

'You do not need to be alone to poison someone,' Michael pointed out. 'If Motelete visited Arderne yesterday, he was doubtless offered refreshments, and it is easy to slip something into a cup. After all, your medical training means you do know about dangerous substances.'

'Well, I did no such thing,' said Falmeresham firmly. 'Besides, Arderne says the best way to heal is by tapping into the natural forces that lie within a person. He does

329

not have many poisons to hand – most of the pots you see here are for show, and are empty.'

'You mean magic?' asked Bartholomew in distaste.

'Yes, magic,' Falmeresham flashed back. 'Science cannot explain everything – in fact, it does not explain much at all, and raises more questions than answers. You are always saying the workings of the human body are mysteries science has not yet unravelled, but Arderne has solutions to *everything*, and it is refreshing. Do you want to see him, or are you here to debate with me?'

'What a shame,' said Michael, watching him go. 'Arderne will ruin him – fill his head with nonsense and superstition.'

'I should have anticipated this,' said Bartholomew. 'He is frustrated when he asks questions that I cannot answer, and it must be exhilarating to find someone with solutions at his fingertips.'

'And that is the real pity,' said Michael sadly. 'His new source of knowledge runs foul and dark.'

Arderne kept Bartholomew and Michael waiting longer than was polite, and when he arrived, he was wiping his lips on the back of his hand, indicating that he had finished feeding before going to see what the Senior Proctor and his Corpse Examiner wanted. Michael had been on the verge of leaving, but Bartholomew had persuaded him to stay, sensing that there were answers to be gleaned from the sinister healer. Both scholars were surprised to see Isabel St Ives behind Arderne. She was dressed, but her long hair cascaded freely down her shoulders, and looked tousled from sleep. Even Bartholomew, not the most observant of men when it came to romantic dalliances, could tell she had spent the night.

'Should you not be with your mistress?' Michael asked.

The smile faded from Isabel's face. 'She died yesterday, so I am now without a home. However, Magister Arderne has a vacancy for a good nurse, so we have been discussing terms.'

'I see,' said Michael, eyeing her disarrayed appearance pointedly. 'Well, I am sorry about Maud. She was a good woman. She made lovers of our scholars, but at least she was discreet about it.'

'What do you want, monk?' asked Arderne coldly. 'A cure for gluttony? A miracle that will melt away your fat and render you slim again?'

'I am not a glutton,' said Michael, startled. 'And I am not fat, either. I just have big bones.'

'Speaking of misdiagnoses, you gave Tyrington a remedy for spitting,' said Bartholomew, cutting across Arderne's bray of laughter. 'It contained bryony.'

'Mandrake,' corrected Arderne, while Falmeresham frowned in puzzlement. 'I would never use bryony, because it causes gripes. I used mandrake, which has secret properties, as we all know. Traditional medicine has not unlocked many of its marvels, but I know the plant well enough to be familiar with its benefits. It will cure Tyrington's unseemly slobbering.'

'You might have killed him,' said Bartholomew, disgusted. 'First you prescribe urine to Hanchach, and now some toxic potion to Tyrington.'

Falmeresham gaped at him. 'Urine? But Hanchach's health is too fragile for—'

'What I do is none of your affair, physician,' snarled Arderne. 'Leave me and my patients alone, or I shall prescribe something that will make *you* wish you had never been born.'

'Threats to cause harm?' asked Michael archly. 'That is hardly what one expects from a healer.'

331

'You can take it how you will,' grated Arderne. 'Now get out of my house.'

Falmeresham was dismayed. 'Please,' he said, stepping forward and attempting a placatory grin. His frustration at Bartholomew's inability to answer medical questions did not mean he was prepared to stand by while his former mentor was insulted. 'There is no need for hostility. We are all interested in the same thing: making people well.'

'Is that so?' said Arderne. 'Then why do University physicians lose so many patients? A dozen deaths have occurred in the few weeks since I arrived, all of which could have been prevented. Cambridge will be better off when these academics pack their bags and leave *me* in charge.'

'Where were you last night?' asked Bartholomew, not deigning to reply. He thought of Edith, and itched to punch the man. He was not often given to violent urges and was astonished by the strength of the rage he felt towards Arderne.

'Here,' said Arderne, reaching out to touch Isabel's hair. She blushed furiously at the display of public affection, and pulled away awkwardly. Then he fixed her with his pale eyes, and she gazed back, like a rabbit caught in the glare of a lantern.

'We were *all* here,' elaborated Falmeresham. 'Magister Arderne taught me a new way to cure infections of the eyes, and Isabel was listening. Why do you ask?'

'Because Motelete is dead,' said Michael.

Arderne shrugged. 'So I heard, but I am not his keeper. What does it have to do with me?'

Michael found his attitude irritating. 'Someone was pawing his corpse in the churchyard of St Mary the Great, and I wondered whether anyone here might have something to say about it.'

'Such as what?' asked Arderne, affecting a bored look.

'Such as whether you poisoned him,' Michael flashed back. 'Or whether you tried to raise him from the dead a second time, and ran away like a coward when you were almost caught.'

'It is all right, lad,' said Arderne, when Falmeresham stepped forward angrily. The ex-student might dislike Arderne insulting Bartholomew, but that did not mean he was willing to remain silent while Michael hurled accusations at his new master. 'I am used to enduring this sort of rubbish from disbelievers, and I usually treat them with the contempt they deserve by ignoring them.'

'You had better go,' said Falmeresham to the scholars. He was struggling to control his temper. 'I would not have let you in, had I known you were going to be rude.'

'What about the people outside?' asked Bartholomew of Arderne. 'Are you going to leave them there all day? It is raining, and none are dressed for standing around in the cold.'

'I have suggested they go home,' replied Arderne, 'but they remain hopeful of one of my cures. I do not mind them there, because they advertise my trade nicely, and I may deign to heal one later. I do not usually bother with the poor, but they are doing me a service, after all.'

He turned and walked away. Isabel trotted after him like an obedient dog, without so much as a nod to the scholars as she left. Bartholomew wondered whether Arderne had put her in some sort of trance; certainly her behaviour was not normal.

'I am pleased you are learning so many new things,' he said to Falmeresham, as the student escorted them to the door. He felt no resentment towards the lad, only sadness that he had proved to be so gullible. He supposed he should have trained him to be less credulous of men who

333

claimed to have all the answers. 'However, I hope Arderne's attitude to the poor is not one of them.'

'You could learn from him, too, if you would open your mind. You have no idea of the extent of his powers. I admit he has his faults, but I am willing to overlook them in the pursuit of knowledge.'

'Was Arderne telling us the truth about last night?' asked Bartholomew, declining to discuss it. 'Was he really in the whole time?'

'Yes,' said Falmeresham. 'He really was. We sat by the fire with Isabel, and he held forth about ailments of the eyes. Did you know that lost sight can be restored simply by licking the eyeball?'

'I know it is is a remedy favoured by witches, but it does not work. And neither does rubbing a gold ring across the eye's surface, if he included that particular trick in his discourse, too.'

Falmeresham sighed irritably. 'You do not know what you are missing by refusing to acknowledge his skills.' He slammed the door with considerable vigour, thus ending the discussion.

'And was *Falmeresham* telling the truth?' asked Michael, as he and Bartholomew walked back along the High Street. 'He knows his new master is not perfect, but that is a long way from seeing through him. He may well fabricate tales to ensure Arderne is not charged with Motelete's murder.'

Bartholomew shrugged, not sure what to think. 'He has never lied to me before.'

'Then what about Falmeresham as the killer? He poisoned Motelete because he resented the attention Arderne gave him – and because he stole from his hero. Despite his claim that the pots in Arderne's dispensary are empty, there are still toxic substances to hand, because you said there was bryony in the remedy he gave Tyrington. Could bryony have killed Motelete?'

'Yes – it would be in keeping with the blisters I saw. But it is not difficult to come by, and I imagine most households have a supply of it, to cure coughs, spots and wounds.'

'So the visit to Arderne did not tell us much?' asked Michael, disappointed.

'It told me I would like to make *him* try some of his remedies.'

That afternoon, when the rain stopped and the sun came out, Bartholomew went to visit patients. There were two cases of fever among the ragged folk who inhabited makeshift shacks in the north of the town, but other than Blankpayn howling abuse, his journey was mercifully uneventful. He prescribed his usual tonic for agues, and then walked to the Dominican convent, where the prior was complaining of backache. The Black Friars were a hospitable group, and plied him with wine and cakes, so by the time he left, he had overeaten and was slightly drunk. It was not a pleasant sensation, and he wondered how Michael and Paxtone could bear doing it day after day. He returned home via the Barnwell Gate, keeping his temper admirably when the soldier on duty pretended not to recognise him and demanded proof of his identity.

'You know me, John Shepherd,' he said mildly, aware that a queue was building behind him and that the delay was being perceived as his fault. 'I set your mother's broken wrist last year.'

Shepherd glanced around furtively, then spoke in a testy whisper. 'Of course I know you, but we are under orders to question everyone in a scholar's tabard or a religious habit. If I do not do as I am told, I will be reported.'

'Orders from whom? The Sheriff is away.'

'And *that* is the problem,' said Shepherd in disgust. 'Tulyet would never have issued such a stupid instruction. It comes from the burgesses, led by Candelby. They are making a point.'

'What point is that?'

'That the town has control over some matters, and will make a nuisance of itself if scholars do not yield to its demands. But I have delayed you enough to make it look good, so you are free to go.' Shepherd lowered his voice further still. 'I could lose my job for telling you this, but warn Brother Michael that there is a move afoot to set fire to the University Church.'

Bartholomew groaned. 'Not again! We have only just finished repairing it from the last time it was attacked, and a big building like that is expensive. Do you know when it will happen?'

'Monday, probably. Stop it if you can. My house backs on to its cemetery, and when it goes up in flames, soot lands on my wife's best cushions. She is getting a bit tired of it.'

Unsettled, Bartholomew went on his way. When he reached the High Street, he saw Paxtone and Rougham. Paxtone was looking unwell again, and was rubbing his stomach. Bartholomew knew how he felt, because he was suffering from the same heavy, bloated feeling himself.

'You two are in each other's company a good deal these days,' he remarked as they approached.

'They are in my company a good deal, too,' said Robin, peering out from behind Paxtone. The surgeon was small, and Bartholomew had not noticed him behind the physician's bulk. 'It is safer that way, and if you had any sense, you would join us.'

'We have formed an alliance,' explained Paxtone. 'Cambridge practitioners versus Arderne – or, to put it another way, honest *medici* against a leech.'

'Arderne attacked us without provocation or cause,' added Rougham. 'So, we have decided the best way to combat him is by standing together. Did you know he claims to have cured Hanchach of laboured breathing when you had failed?'

'He did not cure Hanchach – Hanchach was getting better anyway,' replied Bartholomew tartly. 'However, he might relapse if he declines to take his lungwort and colt's-foot. The phlegm will rebuild in his chest, and he will be back where he started.'

'I heard Arderne donated some of his own urine for Hanchach's remedy,' said Robin. 'He claims all his bodily fluids contain healing powers, so he hoards them up and charges high prices for their sale. Why did I not think of such a ruse? I could have been rich beyond my wildest dreams.'

There was a short pause, during which Paxtone and Rougham regarded the surgeon with distaste, and Bartholomew thought he might be sick.

'The fact that we are prepared to join forces with Robin should tell you how seriously we take the threat of Arderne,' said Paxtone to Bartholomew.

'Here!' said Robin, offended. 'This alliance was my idea.'

'True,' said Rougham. 'And we were none too keen when you first mooted it, but we see now that we have no choice. This is no place to talk, though. Come to the Angel, and I shall buy us all something to eat.'

'The Angel?' asked Bartholomew. 'I do not think we should go there.'

'Michael does not mind us purchasing food, just as long as we do not drink,' argued Rougham. 'Besides, you can always tell him you were investigating Ocleye's death. I can tell you something that will lend credence to the lie, if you like. It is not much, though, just a snippet.'

'What?'

'The day before he died, I saw Ocleye in conversation with a man who wore a hood to conceal his face. Ocleye was eating a pie, but his companion did not touch his, so something had robbed the fellow of his appetite. Ocleye was a spy, so he was obviously conducting some shady business.'

'He was a shady man,' agreed Paxtone. 'I also saw him meeting with an unusual array of people – Spaldynge from Clare, and Carton of Michaelhouse, to name but two.'

'Carton is not shady,' objected Bartholomew.

'He is not someone I would want as a colleague, though. He is complex – like Lynton, a man of many layers.' Paxtone turned to Rougham. 'But Matthew is right – we should be wary of breaking University rules. We shall eat these victuals in St Bene't's Churchyard. A man cannot live without a decent pie, and I would not be the man I am today, were it not for the Angel.'

Bartholomew looked him up and down, and considered telling him the Angel had a lot to answer for, but a sober voice at the back of his mind reminded him that these were friends, and he should not insult them because he was tipsy. He took a deep breath to clear his wits, and followed them through a series of back alleys to Bene't Street. They stepped into the leafy churchyard, where Paxtone sank on to a lichen-glazed tombstone. He clutched his stomach, and seemed to be in pain.

'Are you sure you should be eating?' asked Bartholomew. 'Perhaps we should take you home.'

Paxtone shook his head. 'This is more important – I will have no home if Arderne gets his way.'

'Robin can fetch the pies while we wait here,' said Rougham, handing the surgeon a coin. 'Make sure you ask for the chicken, Robin, because Honynge told me the mutton ones contain dog.'

'Get me two,' ordered Paxtone. 'I find eating helps me think, and we shall need our wits if we are to devise an effective strategy against this vile leech.'

When Robin had gone, Bartholomew and Rougham joined Paxtone on the tomb. Fortunately, trees concealed them from the folk who walked along Bene't Street, because Bartholomew was sure three physicians sitting in a row on someone's grave would be considered very peculiar behaviour. He heard two scholars discussing the Convocation of Regents as they passed, and learned that Trinity Hall planned to support Michael, but Bene't College would oppose him.

'Michael has discovered that Lynton ran gambling sessions in his Dispensary,' he said. He glanced at Paxtone, trying not to sound accusing. 'And you were one of his guests.'

'What?' exploded Rougham. 'I do not believe you!'

Paxtone sighed mournfully. 'I am afraid it is true. I enjoyed my Friday nights with Lynton – until he started to invite townsmen, at which point I withdrew my custom. So did a number of others.'

'Why?' asked Bartholomew, while Rougham sat with his mouth open.

'Because I felt I could not rely on a townsman's discretion as I might a fellow scholar's – it was in my colleagues' interests to keep quiet, but laymen have nothing to lose by blabbing. Besides, while I enjoyed the intellectual exercise – it was great fun predicting the relative speeds of these fictitious horses – the townsmen were noisy in their excitement, and they ruined the genteel atmosphere. Your brother-in-law was all right, but I disliked Candelby's company.'

'Candelby was noisy?' asked Bartholomew.

'When he won – which was often – he was a dreadful gloat. He was quick with his sums, so he acquired a small fortune, including several houses. The games have had unforeseen consequences, though, because it is these very same buildings that lie at the heart of the rent war.'

'Here we are,' said Robin, arriving with the pies. Rougham was still digesting the news that Lynton owned a gaming house as he bit into his, but the rich flavours soon pushed the matter from his mind. Bartholomew remained overloaded with the Dominicans' cakes, and declined the greasy offering, so Paxtone had it when he had eaten his own two. Then he finished Robin's as well.

'It will force out the blockage that is causing me pain,' he explained, when he became aware that all three of his colleagues were regarding him askance. 'It worked the other day.'

'Let us turn to the business at hand,' said Rougham, brushing crumbs from his hands and declining to comment. 'Robin's practice is finished – Arderne has ensured he has not a single patient left. Paxtone is now accused of seducing Mayor Harleston's wife—'

'Did you?' asked Robin with considerable interest.

Paxtone was indignant. 'Of course not! She is far too old for me.'

'Townsfolk judge us by their own corrupt standards,' said Rougham consolingly. 'Meanwhile, Arderne has been telling *my* patients that my special digestive tonics do not work. Then he set Isnard against Bartholomew, and now he has initiated that horrible rumour concerning Lynton.'

'What rumour?' asked Bartholomew, although he suspected he already knew.

'He said you shot Lynton, then concealed the wound when you examined the body for Michael. He claims he heard it from Wisbeche, although I doubt Wisbeche would have invented such a tale.'

'Actually, Lynton *was* shot, and I *did* hide the evidence,' said Bartholomew tiredly. Rougham and Robin stared at him in disbelief. 'I did not kill him, though. Obviously.'

'But I saw the wound on Lynton's head,' objected Robin. 'I went to see if I could help him, but his skull was bruised, and he was not breathing.'

Rougham was appalled. 'Why did you not mention sooner that Lynton was murdered, Bartholomew? Arderne might be responsible, and we could all be in grave danger.'

'He mentioned it to me,' said Paxtone. 'And I have been on my guard since – for you two as well as for myself. Why do you think I have spent so much time with you? Brother Michael did not want details made public, lest word leaked out, and there was trouble.'

Rougham was unappeased, and glared at Bartholomew. 'You could have trusted me. We have shared deeper and darker secrets in the past, and you know you can count on my discretion.'

'It was not his secret to tell,' argued Paxtone. 'It is Michael's.'

'We cannot let Bartholomew's reticence damage our alliance,' said Robin reasonably. 'Paxtone was watching out for us, Rougham, so no harm was done. The real question we should be considering is, who killed Lynton? Was it Arderne?'

'I am inclined to think so,' replied Bartholomew, 'but we have no evidence. Michael and I have been asking questions all week, and although we have uncovered some startling facts about Lynton, we have discovered nothing to incriminate Arderne.'

Paxtone was thoughtful. 'I was on Milne Street when Lynton died, too – as I told you before – and, like Robin, I assumed he died because the horse kicked him. But since you told me he was shot, I have recalled two odd things. They are probably nothing . . .'

'Tell him,' ordered Rougham. 'It is not for you to decide what is important and what is not. That clever monk has a way with small clues, as I saw when I worked as his Corpse Examiner last year.'

'I heard a couple of loud snaps,' said Paxtone. 'One just before Lynton's horse collided with Candelby's cart, and the other some time after, when people had started fighting.'

'The first was the bolt that killed Lynton,' surmised Bartholomew. 'Then the weapon was rewound to dispatch Ocleye. But there is a problem with that: if Ocleye saw Lynton shot – which is why I believe he was killed – then why did he not run away? Why did he wait to be picked off?'

'And *that* is the second thing I recall,' said Paxtone. 'After Lynton died and the cart was smashed, I saw Ocleye pick himself up, unharmed. Everyone was gazing in horror at the carnage, but he was looking in the opposite direction. And he was grinning.'

Bartholomew stared at him. 'He was not surprised? But that suggests he knew Lynton was going to be shot. In advance.'

'Yes,' agreed Paxtone soberly. 'I believe it does.'

The three physicians and Robin continued to discuss Lynton's death, until Rougham pointed out that they had better devise a plan to make sure the same thing did not happen to them. *He* did not want to be shot while riding down Milne Street and, as Brother Michael was having no luck in bringing the slippery Arderne to justice, then it was up to Cambridge's *medici* to think of a solution.

'We tried to get the better of Arderne yesterday, by playing him at his own game.' Rougham looked pained. 'Unfortunately, it went wrong.'

'You did not provide him with a second chance to raise Motelete from the dead, did you?' asked Bartholomew uneasily. 'By poisoning him?'

Rougham glared. 'Be serious, man! This is no time for jests. One of Paxtone's fourth-years pretended to be afflicted with leprous sores, and went – well armed with money – to buy a cure. Our plan was to force Arderne to make a diagnosis, then publicly wash off the paints to reveal him as a fraud. But Arderne got wind of it and sent him packing.'

It was not a clever idea, and Bartholomew was not surprised it had failed. He began to have second thoughts about joining ranks with men who would stoop to such transparent tricks.

Rougham sensed his reservations. 'I heard Edith was hurt the other day – she came between you and a rock. Unless you want this sort of thing to continue, you cannot refuse to stand with us.'

'Arderne probably killed Kenyngham, too,' said Robin, trying another tactic to earn the physician's support. 'I heard Michael plans to exhume him, and look for signs of poisoning, but—'

'I examined him twice,' said Bartholomew. 'No one killed him, but Michael refuses to listen.'

Rougham was thoughtful. 'Many poisons are impossible to detect. Some are obvious – like the one that killed Motelete, given your description of his blistered mouth – but most are insidious substances, invisible to mere mortals like us. I doubt you will discover anything on Kenyngham's body that will help convict Arderne, so the poor man will have been disturbed for nothing.'

'I will not be doing the disturbing,' said Bartholomew. 'You will.'

'There is not—' began Robin.

'Then Michael is going to be disappointed,' interrupted Rougham. 'I would go a long way for him – including voting for his stupid amendment to the Statutes – but I will not defile Kenyngham.'

'And do not look at me, either,' said Paxtone with a shudder. 'I dislike corpses, and never touch them if I can help it. And I certainly refuse to inspect one that should be in the ground.'

'So will I,' said Robin, although Bartholomew doubted Michael would stoop that low. 'But—'

'Kenyngham was not murdered anyway,' said Paxtone. He grimaced, wrestling with some inner conflict. 'I promised I would never tell anyone this, but I think he would not mind under the circumstances. Kenyngham had been unwell for a week or so – his pulses had begun to beat oddly.'

Bartholomew frowned. 'He was my patient, and he said nothing to me.'

'He said he did not want you distressed during his last few days on Earth,' replied Paxtone. 'That is why he sought *me* out, and not you – his normal physician.'

Bartholomew was aghast. 'He was ill, and he felt he could not tell me?'

Paxtone's expression was kindly. 'He wanted to spare you the anguish of not being able to save him. He was more fond of you than you know.'

'Perhaps he was being poisoned slowly,' suggested Robin gratuitously. 'By Arderne.'

'It was his pulses,' said Paxtone firmly. 'I felt them myself, fluttering and pounding. He said it had been happening for some time, but the condition had suddenly worsened. I told him there was nothing I could do, but he was not concerned. I think he was looking forward to seeing Heaven.'

'Well, he was a saint,' said Rougham, laying a compassionate hand on Bartholomew's shoulder.

'I prescribed a potion to alleviate his discomfort – henbane is an excellent antidote to pain. He made me write "antidote" on the pot, lest you should happen across it and quiz him. He really did not want anyone to know what was happening, and said the word was vague enough to forestall any unwanted questions.'

'Antidote,' said Bartholomew tiredly. 'Will you tell Michael all this? Before he digs him up?'

'There is no need,' said Robin, loud enough to block Paxtone's reply. 'I have been trying to tell you, but you keep interrupting. He heard from the Bishop's palace this afternoon. Permission to exhume is denied.'

'How do you know?' demanded Rougham.

'Because I saw the Episcopal messenger arrive at the town gate. Langelee asked for news, and I overheard him say that Kenyngham is to be left in peace.'

'Well, then,' prompted Rougham, after a short silence. 'We must decide what to do about Arderne.'

Bartholomew pulled his thoughts from Kenyngham. Even to the last, the elderly Gilbertine had been thinking of others, and Paxtone's description of his symptoms matched what Bartholomew himself had observed of Kenyngham's final hours – his weariness and peace.

'Arderne's eyes are the main problem,' said Paxtone. 'They bore into you, and you are powerless to resist. You find yourself believing what he says, even though you know it to be rubbish.'

'Then you must steel yourself against them,' ordered Rougham. 'He tried using them on me, but I met his gaze, and it was he who looked away first. You must be strong.'

'I know what to do,' said Robin brightly. 'Burgle his house, and hunt for his hoax potions. We shall lay hold

345

of them, then display them on the High Street for all to see.'

'He would deny they were his,' Paxtone pointed out. 'And I dislike breaking the law, anyway.'

'I suggest we fight him on his own terms,' said Rougham. 'I shall pay one of my students to play dead, and we can raise him. Then people's faith in us will be restored.'

'But Arderne would subject him to the most dreadful tests, to ensure he was really gone,' said Paxtone. 'The poor fellow would flinch or scream, and then *we* would look like the charlatans.'

'Then *you* think of something,' said Robin exasperated. 'You have pulled our ideas to pieces.'

'I could ask him for a remedy for these griping pains in my innards,' suggested Paxtone. 'Then I could swallow his cure and pretend it makes me worse.'

'He will say it is because you have an evil heart, or some such nonsense,' said Rougham. 'He will not accept responsibility for the failure himself. Bartholomew, do you have any ideas?'

'We could challenge him to a public debate,' said Bartholomew. 'We can ask an audience to present questions, and see who provides the best answers.'

'Yes!' said Rougham, eyes blazing in triumph. 'It will soon become clear that he does not know what he is talking about!'

'But they might ask questions *we* cannot answer,' said Robin uneasily. 'Like how to prevent the bloody flux.'

'Just because there is no cure does not mean there is nothing we can do,' said Bartholomew. 'There are remedies to alleviate these conditions, and we can all quote our sources.'

'Some of you might be able to,' muttered Robin.

'Bartholomew is right,' said Rougham. 'This will not be

a debate to see who can devise the wildest cures, but to assess who has the greatest knowledge of his subject. And obviously, that is going to be us. However, we must remember not to contradict each other. We can argue in private, but at this debate, we must maintain a united front. Agreed, Bartholomew?'

'You must, Matthew,' said Paxtone, seeing him hesitate. 'You are overly fond of disputation, and will start doing it with us. Arderne will take advantage of any perceived dissent.'

'We can challenge him to perform the perfect amputation, too,' said Robin, brightening. 'I wager he does not know how to cauterise blood vessels before sewing up the wound, and onlookers will see that *we* know what we are doing and he does not.'

'I think we had better to stick to the theoretical side of things to start with, Robin,' said Paxtone with a shudder. 'I am not sure *I* want to witness that sort of thing, and I am used to a little blood.'

CHAPTER 11

When Bartholomew arrived home, he found Michaelhouse in an uproar. Junior Proctor Bukenham had arrived with six beadles, and they were standing in the yard. Michael was shouting, Langelee was trying to calm him, and Honynge was looking on with gleeful malice. The other Fellows were in a huddle, lost and confused; Carton nursed a bruised nose, and Deynman was limping.

'What is happening?' demanded Bartholomew, going to help Deynman sit on a bench.

'An accusation has been levelled against Brother Michael,' explained Carton. He was pale and angry, an expression that was reflected in the face of every College member – except Honynge. 'He is said to be concealing evidence of murder, and his rooms are going to be searched.'

'An accusation made by whom?'

Carton glared in Honynge's direction. 'I tried to stop the beadles, but one punched me, and when Deynman came to my aid, he was hit with a cudgel.'

'You tried to fight beadles?' Bartholomew was horrified.

'Just one,' said Carton. 'The lout who seems to think Bukenham is right. The others did not raise a hand against us, because they are loyal to Michael.'

Bartholomew glanced at the beadles and saw none were happy about the situation. Meadowman and four friends stood apart from the remaining one, and it was obvious a division had formed. They looked from the monk to

348

Bukenham with wary eyes, waiting to see what would happen.

'The Chancellor says that because an official challenge has been issued, Michael must submit to having his quarters searched.' Tyrington was incensed on the monk's behalf. 'How *dare* he treat a Fellow of a respected College – and his own Senior Proctor – like this!'

'There are guidelines for dealing with such eventualities, and Chancellor Tynkell is right to follow them,' said Langelee, the practical voice of reason. 'I recommend we go to the hall until—'

'I certainly shall not,' declared Michael, shooting his deputy a look of pure venom.

Bukenham cringed. 'It was not my idea,' he wailed. 'Tynkell ordered me to do it.'

'Then fetch him,' challenged Michael. 'Let us hear it from his own lips.'

'I wish I could, but he has locked himself in his room, in case you storm over to St Mary the Great and shout at him. But, like me, he has no choice but to follow the proper procedures.'

'Of course he has a choice,' raged Michael. 'He could tell this malicious complainant where to shove his filthy lies!'

'But then people would be suspicious of *him* as well as you,' Bukenham pointed out. 'And they will call for his resignation. By searching your room, we can prove nothing is amiss and Hon . . . the complainant will have to retract his accusation.'

Michael was so angry, his large frame quaked like jelly. 'I will *not* give you permission to touch my belongings, and if you try, I shall sue you for trespass.'

The beadles exchanged more uncomfortable glances, and Bukenham's expression was one of agony. He did not

349

know what to do, and Bartholomew suspected he was far more frightened of Michael than the Chancellor, Honynge and the rest of the University put together.

'If the monk has nothing to hide, he would not mind obliging you,' said Honynge quickly, when he saw the force of Michael's personality and the loyalty he inspired in most of his beadles was about to win the day. 'His ire is a sign of a guilty conscience.'

Langelee eyed his new Fellow with disdain. 'It has come to this, has it? Not content with making silly accusations over documents in the Illeigh Chest, you run to the Chancellor as well?'

Honynge's expression was dangerous. 'I dislike corruption, and I will not tolerate it in my own College. When Michael is found guilty, I shall be calling for *your* resignation, too. There,' he added in a whisper, 'that told them you will not turn a blind eye to shabby morals.'

'Ignore him, Master,' said William coldly. 'He is a petty man, unfit for Michaelhouse. I knew it the moment I heard him supporting the wrong side in the Blood Relics debate.'

As Honynge and William began a nasty, sniping squabble and Langelee tried to stop them, Bartholomew turned to Michael. 'I do not understand. How has this come about?'

The monk spoke through gritted teeth. 'Obviously, Honynge has been listening to the rumours started by Wisbeche – before the man agreed to keep his mouth shut – about Lynton's wound being disguised. I told you it was a bad idea, and now look what has happened.'

'I am sorry,' said Bartholomew, shocked that his hasty action should have caused such trouble. 'I thought I was doing the right thing – I did not imagine the repercussions would be so dire.'

'Well, they are,' snapped Michael. 'Bukenham will find the bloodstained crossbow bolts you took from our two victims. They will be used to prove *I* concealed Lynton's murder, Honynge will call for my resignation, and I shall be hard-pressed to find reasons why I should not oblige him.'

'Do you mean these crossbow bolts, Brother?' whispered Cynric, sidling up to him and flashing something that was mostly hidden up his sleeve.

Michael stared at them in astonishment. 'God and all His saints preserve us! How did you get those with no one seeing? I thought you had been here the whole time.'

'Then let us hope everyone else thinks so, too,' said Cynric comfortably. 'As soon as I heard what Bukenham had come to do, I went round the back, and climbed through your bedroom window. Meanwhile, Carton and Deynman kindly staged a diversion – they tackled your beadles and kept everyone occupied for a few moments.'

'Thank God for friends,' said Michael fervently.

'I even took that flask of wine you stole from Father William,' Cynric went on, pleased with himself. 'And one or two other items I thought you might prefer to keep from prying eyes.'

Michael sighed his relief. 'Thank you, Cynric. I shall never forget this. And I shall never forget what my enemies have done, either.' He glowered in Honynge's direction.

'If Cynric has removed anything sensitive, you may as well let Bukenham do his duty,' said Bartholomew. 'Then you can demand an apology from Honynge for the trouble he has caused.'

'You can demand more than that,' said Cynric. 'You can call for *his* resignation for slandering you. I doubt Master Langelee would object.'

A grin of malicious satisfaction flashed across the monk's face. 'I am sure he will not. Perhaps Michaelhouse will be rid of its viper sooner than I anticipated.'

Bukenham swallowed hard as Michael stalked towards him. Meadowman and his four friends immediately stepped behind the monk, to show where their allegiance lay, and, after a moment of hesitation, the last beadle did likewise. The Junior Proctor was alone.

'You are in a tight corner, Brother,' sneered Honynge gloatingly. 'This search is legal, and Bukenham has no choice but to carry out his orders.'

'I will have a choice if I resign,' said Bukenham shakily. 'In fact, I do, with immediate effect.'

Honynge regarded him in disdain. 'Do your duty, man. No one likes a coward.'

'You *may* enter my chamber, Bukenham,' said Michael, with the air of an injured martyr. 'I have nothing to hide. Langelee – perhaps you and William will accompany him, to ensure it is done properly. I do not want my accuser to come back later, and say the first search was inadequate.'

'Are you sure, Brother?' asked Langelee uneasily. He lowered his voice. 'Even under that loose floorboard, where we keep the you-know-what?'

Cynric gave an almost imperceptible nod.

'Even there,' replied Michael haughtily. 'Go. I shall be here, waiting for my apology.'

'No!' cried Tyrington. 'Do not submit to this indignity. You are a senior member of the University, and Bukenham has no right to paw through your personal effects. It is not decent!'

'No, it is not,' agreed Michael gravely. 'But if spiteful villains attack me with their false charges, then this is the best way to prove my innocence.'

'Mind your own business, Tyrington,' warned Honynge. His voice dropped to a mutter. 'They are all united against you, Honynge, but you are cleverer than the lot of them put together. Hold your ground, and justice will prevail.'

He turned and led the way to Michael's room. Bukenham hesitated, but Michael nodded that he was to go, too, then ordered the beadles to do likewise. Langelee and William went to ensure Honynge did not attempt any sleights of hand that would see evidence planted, and because Wynewyk did not trust them to be sufficiently observant, he went as well. It was going to be crowded in Michael's room. The students milled about uncertainly, so Bartholomew ordered them to the hall, where he asked Carton to keep them occupied by reading from Aristotle's *Topica*.

Eventually, the yard was empty of everyone but Bartholomew, Michael, Cynric and Tyrington. Distress was making Tyrington spit more than usual, and the others tried to stand back.

'You should not have let them browbeat you,' he said, rather accusingly. 'Honynge will use anything he discovers to damage you – and he will damage Michaelhouse at the same time.'

'You seem very sure there is incriminating evidence to find,' said Michael coolly.

Tyrington regarded him uncertainly. 'You mean there is not? But you are Senior Proctor, and we all know you bend the rules in order to catch some of the cunning villains who pit themselves against you. I just drew the conclusion . . .' He trailed off and stared at his feet, mortified.

Michael smiled, amused by the fact that everyone seemed to assume he was guilty. 'Normally, you would be right, but I am above reproach in this instance. Why did you speak in my favour, if you believe Honynge's accusations might be true?'

'It is a question of loyalty,' replied Tyrington, sounding surprised by the question. 'Langelee lectured Honynge and me about College allegiances the day we were admitted, and I applaud his sentiments. I like Michaelhouse, and I am glad I came here, not Clare.'

Bartholomew raised his eyebrows. 'No wonder Honynge set out to make himself objectionable – he resented Langelee telling him how to behave. And who can blame him?'

'I can,' said Michael firmly. 'And I shall enjoy his apology in a few moments. I will ask for it in writing, too. In fact, he can read it publicly at the Convocation. What do you think?'

Tyrington leered voraciously. 'Yes! That would teach him not to take against his colleagues.'

It was not long before Bukenham emerged from Michael's room, with Honynge and the others at his heels. Honynge's face was black with fury, while Langelee and Wynewyk maintained a cool dignity. William was jabbing Honynge in the back with a dirty forefinger, crowing his delight.

'Well?' asked Michael archly. 'What did you find?'

'Well, there was this,' hissed Honynge, holding up a piece of parchment. Bartholomew's heart sank, supposing Cynric had not been as careful as he had thought. 'It is a letter from a *woman*.'

Langelee snatched it from him, then started to laugh. 'It is a note from Bartholomew's sister, thanking Michael for his prayers after she was hit by a stone. I hardly think that constitutes a crime, Honynge. Now you owe the good Brother two apologies: one for thinking he was concealing evidence of murder, and one for reading private correspondence addressed to a priest.'

'Well, come on, then,' said Michael, in the ensuing silence. 'I am waiting.'

'I am sorry, Brother,' said Bukenham immediately. 'I never believed you were guilty, and—'

'I was not talking to you,' said Michael contemptuously. 'Well, Honynge? You maligned me and you were wrong. I am purer than the driven snow, and I demand you acknowledge it.'

'Do not push it, Brother,' said Bartholomew in a low voice. 'There is a big difference between innocent and pure. Kenyngham was pure. You are not even innocent – thanks to me.'

'I will *not* apologise,' snarled Honynge. 'The Chancellor or one of the beadles must have warned you, and you removed the evidence before it could be found. They are as corrupt as you are.'

'And now you owe him even more apologies,' shouted Tyrington, as Honynge stamped away.

It was not a pleasant evening, because a wickedly cold wind was slicing down from the north, carrying with it the dank odour of the Fens. Bartholomew wanted to sit in his chamber and write his treatise on fevers, but that was impossible, because all five of his roommates were home, and there was barely space to move. Two sat on his bed. Another pair occupied the desks in the window – they offered to yield, but he was not a man to pull rank over students with upcoming examinations – and the last was sitting cross-legged on the floor.

'You cannot work – we have too much to do,' said Michael, when Bartholomew went to see if there was a spare corner in the monk's quarters. 'I have a terrible feeling that Honynge plans to make a hostile move at the Convocation on Monday – one that might divide the University even further.'

'And we need it united against the town,' said William, who had also come looking for a vacant spot. He had four students in his room, and they were chanting a tract they were obliged to learn by rote. It meant he could not concentrate on what Bajulus had to say about Blood Relics. Or so he claimed. Bartholomew suspected he had reached a difficult section, and was making excuses not to tackle it. Tyrington was there, too, drinking some wine he had brought with him.

'A divided University will be a weaker one,' agreed Michael. 'I *must* solve these murders, before rumours about them cause even more harm.'

'At least you do not have to look for Kenyngham's killer,' said Bartholomew. 'Paxtone's testimony proves his death was a natural one, and the "antidote" you saw him swallow had nothing to do with poison. The letters you received are hoaxes.'

'Two letters from two different men,' said William, taking them from the desk and studying them. 'The handwriting of the man who offered you twenty marks is not the same as that of the man who claimed he had poisoned Kenyngham.'

'Or woman,' added Tyrington. 'Some ladies can write – or hire scribes to do it for them.'

Michael acknowledged his point with a nod. 'I wonder why anyone would want to confess to such a horrid crime in the first place?'

'I expect Honynge did it,' said William, 'so you would make a fool of yourself with an unnecessary exhumation. It is exactly the kind of scheme he would concoct, because he is stupid.'

'Unfortunately, he is *not* stupid,' said Michael. 'If he were, I would have bested him by now.'

'Is Honynge the only suspect for the crimes you are

investigating?' asked Tyrington. 'I dislike speaking in his favour, but he does not seem the kind of man to break the law in so vile a manner.'

'I beg to differ,' said Michael. 'But no, he is not our only suspect. Matt still favours Arderne as the culprit, and there are several curious facts about Isabel that add her to my list. Then, of course, Candelby and Blankpayn are obvious candidates, given what we now know about Lynton.'

'What about Lynton?' asked William, using Michael's glass to examine the two documents.

'He ran this dispensary. Candelby won a lot of houses there, but was recently banned for gloating. He is said to be furious, and the abrupt loss of substantial winnings is a powerful motive for murder.'

'And Candelby *does* carry a crossbow,' said William. 'I have seen it. It is always wound, too.'

'Is it?' asked Bartholomew. 'Maud said it was not.'

'Then she is mistaken,' said William. 'I have taken to searching his cart since he started this business with the rents – I live in hope of discovering incriminating writs that will make him leave our University alone. He *always* carries a bow, and it is *always* ready to be whipped out and used.'

Michael raised his eyebrows. 'Maud seemed very certain—'

'Her eyes!' exclaimed Bartholomew suddenly, making them all jump. 'Watching William with the glass has just reminded me. She suffered from a clouding of her vision, and Lynton summoned me for a second opinion. But there was nothing we could do.'

'You mean she would not have been able to tell whether it was loaded or not?' asked Tyrington.

Bartholomew nodded. 'Candelby probably told her it was not, because I doubt she would have been impressed

357

by him toting such a deadly weapon. She must have believed him.'

William was disapproving. 'A number of lies and misunderstandings seem to be flowing from her household. Did you know there is a rumour that *you* killed her, Matthew? Apparently, you touched her face and poked about in her bandages. Then you gave her a potion that you said would ease her pain, but that actually hastened her end.'

Bartholomew nodded. 'Arderne has been spreading that tale, to prove to his new patients that anyone who puts faith in my medicine is likely to pay a high price.'

Michael's eyes narrowed. 'How did Arderne know you touched her face and looked under her bandages? He was not there. One person was, though: *Isabel* must have told him what you did.'

'Not necessarily,' said Bartholomew. 'There is Maud herself. Arderne came to see her after we left, and she might have mentioned our visit.'

Michael continued as though he had not spoken. 'Isabel must have told him about the pain-killing potion, too, giving him yet more ammunition to use against you. And do you know why? Because she is enamoured of Arderne and will do anything for him. Look at Falmeresham. I always thought him a sensible, rational fellow, but he fell for Arderne's charm like a brainless fool. Arderne attracts followers like flies swarm towards rotten meat.'

'It is his eyes,' explained William. 'They drill into you, and you find yourself going along with what he is saying whether you want to or not. It is uncanny.'

'Paxtone said the same thing,' said Bartholomew. 'And I saw Isabel go quiet and submissive when Arderne fixed her with a stare, too.'

'It must be witchcraft,' said William censoriously. 'Like this love-potion he made for Agatha.'

'Actually, I think he can just exert power over a certain kind of mind,' said Bartholomew. 'He possesses an ability to transfix people, if they let him do it.'

'You might be right,' mused Tyrington. 'I saw him with Carton earlier today, and he was gazing at our hapless commoner as though he was trying to put him in some sort of trance.'

'What was Carton doing?' asked Michael uneasily.

Tyrington shrugged. 'Nothing. He was just listening. Then he nodded and sped away.'

The monk turned his attention back to the matter of Candelby's loaded crossbow. 'Ocleye must have been in on it, because Paxtone saw him smiling and nodding in a way that suggested a plan had just come right. Doubtless Ocleye was astonished when Candelby decided a spy did not make for a very reliable accomplice, and killed him to ensure his silence.'

No matter how hard Bartholomew and Michael tried to see patterns in the evidence they had collected, they still could not reach any satisfactory conclusions regarding the identity of the killer, and both admitted that their suspicions were coloured by personal prejudices. Michael was even more keen for Honynge to be the culprit, because he wanted to avenge himself on the man who had publicly questioned his integrity, while Bartholomew wanted Arderne away from his patients.

Later that night, Bartholomew was summoned to tend Hanchach. Unfortunately, Arderne had been there first, and the 'tonic' he had prescribed had induced such violent vomiting that it had exhausted the glover's scant reserves of strength. Bartholomew watched helplessly as his patient slipped into an unnatural sleep, then stayed with him until he died quietly at dawn. Michael came to give last rites, and listened to the physician rail against Arderne until it was time for the Sunday morning mass. The peaceful ceremony did nothing to soothe Bartholomew's temper, and he was still angry when they sat in the hall for breakfast.

'Arderne is responsible for Hanchach's death for three reasons,' he said, refusing the egg-mess Langelee offered. He could not be sure what was in it, and he had no appetite anyway. Honynge, who had stationed himself at the very end of the table, away from his colleagues, ate his share.

'You are better off up here,' the scholar muttered to himself. 'The company is more civil.'

'It is a pity he does not feel that way all the time,' said Tyrington, regarding Honynge with dislike.

'First,' Bartholomew went on, 'he told Hanchach to decline medicine that would have cured him. Second, he prescribed a potion containing urine, which damaged a weakened body. And third, he dispensed a strong purgative – something even Deynman would have known not to do.'

'I know, Matt,' said Michael gently. 'But you were the one Hanchach summoned in the end.'

'When it was too late. Cynric says Isnard has a fever now, although I doubt *he* will call for me. And a beggar Arderne "cured" was found dead last night. How many more people will he kill?'

'Tell the Chancellor,' suggested William. 'He has the authority to ban anyone from his town.'

'The Senior Proctor, who is Chancellor in all but name, says he cannot oust people on the grounds that I do not like them,' said Bartholomew acidly. 'And Arderne is currently popular with everyone except his medical rivals.'

'If we expel Arderne, he will make a fuss,' elaborated Michael, 'and the town will be even more set against the University. We cannot afford that – not at the moment.'

Langelee was more concerned by the looming crisis of the Convocation and, never a man to sit still when there was action to be taken, he stood to intone a final grace. This was the sign for servants to begin clearing away dishes, despite the fact that some students had not yet started eating.

'I am off to King's Hall,' he announced, 'to see if I can persuade a few friends to vote for your amendment tomorrow, Brother. Meanwhile, *benedicimus Domino* and good morning to you all.'

'*Deo gratias*,' replied Bartholomew, the only one not desperately cramming food into his mouth.

'I hate it when he does that,' grumbled Michael, grabbing bread with one hand and smoked pork with the other.

'So do I, usually,' said William. He grinned and jerked a grimy thumb over his shoulder to where Honynge was trying to gobble as much as he could in the short moments left to him. 'But not when I am rewarded with the sight of him eating his dog-flavoured egg-mess from the pan.'

Michael chuckled, then turned to Bartholomew. 'There is a lot to do today, and I want you with me. I am afraid you might tackle Arderne if I leave you alone, and that will do no one any good.'

'I will not tackle him,' said Bartholomew gloomily. 'It would be like trying to catch an eel on the back of a shovel – far too slippery. And he will only lie and deny the allegations anyway.'

'First, we shall corner Isabel alone, to see if she can recall anything new about Lynton and her mistress. Next,

361

we shall go to Peterhouse, and ask if Wisbeche has unravelled any more of Lynton's business dealings. Then I should speak to Candelby, to see if I can learn more about Ocleye.'

Bartholomew was thoughtful. 'Their rent agreement *was* torn violently from Lynton's hand, so it looks as though the killer did not want you to know about the association between the two victims.'

'Perhaps it is the house Ocleye was to have had that is the source of the trouble. There is a desperate shortage of accommodation in Cambridge – for scholars and townsmen. Did Edmund Mildenale, one of our commoners, tell you he was planning to start a hostel of his own, but decided to stay at Michaelhouse when he saw how rapidly the rent war was escalating? Candelby's greed is not only damaging hostels already in existence, but those in the future, too.'

The High Street was busy with people going to and from their Sunday devotions, and because they were all wearing their best clothes and the sun was shining, the town was ablaze with colour. The first person Bartholomew and Michael met was Rougham, who said he had invited Arderne to take part in a public debate, but the healer had only laughed derisively. When Rougham had demanded to share the joke, Arderne had replied that he had no wish to hear academics theorise when he could be out in the real world, curing real people and making real money.

'Now what?' asked Rougham, deflated. 'The other plans we devised were not as good as that one, and left too much room for disaster, but we cannot let this continue. Not only did he kill Hanchach and that beggar, but Isnard is likely to die now, too.'

Michael was alarmed. For all the bargeman's failings, he

was still a member of the Michaelhouse Choir. 'I did not know his condition was that serious. What is wrong with him?'

'He drank one of Arderne's decoctions. Visit him, Bartholomew; he is frightened and desperate, and I doubt he will threaten to kill you now. But what shall we do about Arderne? Surely you can think of something, Brother. You are a devious sort of man.'

'Thank you,' said Michael flatly. 'I wonder if Cynric would be prepared to break into his house and have a look around. He is bound to discover something incriminating.'

'We have already thought of that,' said Rougham, 'but nothing gained from such a search could be used against him in a public trial.'

'Who said anything about public? I was thinking of acquiring the evidence, then having a quiet word while we wave it at him. The aim is to make him leave of his own volition.'

'I like the sound of this,' said Rougham, nodding eager approval.

'Well, I do not,' said Bartholomew. 'First, it is sly, and I do not want to stoop to his level. And secondly, he will just foist himself on some other hapless town, and start killing people there.'

'Our first responsibility is to our own patients,' said Rougham soberly. 'Remember that.'

'Forget Arderne, Brother,' said Bartholomew, when Rougham had gone. 'He is not your problem, and you have enough to worry about already – catching whoever killed Motelete, Lynton and Ocleye, outwitting Honynge, defeating Candelby, and preventing St Mary the Great from being set on fire.'

'If you are right, then neutralising Arderne will relieve me of at least half of these problems.'

'Oh, Lord,' groaned Bartholomew. 'There he is, and Candelby and Blankpayn are with him.'

'Say nothing, Matt,' warned Michael. 'He may try to needle you into a confrontation, but you must resist. Is that Isabel clinging to his right arm?'

Bartholomew nodded. 'And Falmeresham is clinging just as hard to the left one.'

Arderne was grinning as he approached. He looked rich, smug and confident, and had clearly been spending the money he had earned from his new patients – his clothes were so new they were stiff. Isabel had also been treated, and expensive jewellery and a fur-trimmed cloak transformed her into a woman of whom any wealthy merchant would be proud. Falmeresham looked disreputable by comparison; he had not shaved, and clothes were slovenly. Behind them were Candelby and Blankpayn, several lesser burgesses, and a lame man Arderne was said to have cured. It was not much of a miracle, because Bartholomew knew there had been nothing wrong with the fellow in the first place – the disability had been fabricated to allow him to beg.

'Easy, Matt,' warned Michael. 'You just said you do not want to stoop to his level. Remember that includes challenging him to duels and punching him, too.'

In the event, however, it was not Bartholomew who challenged Arderne, but Candelby who challenged Bartholomew. The taverner stamped up to the physician and shook a finger in his face, while Blankpayn stood behind him, hand on the hilt of his dagger.

'You killed Maud,' shouted Candelby furiously. 'You tampered with her bandages and gave her potions, one of which killed her. And why? To stop me from marrying her!'

Isabel looked uncomfortable. 'He gave her something to ease the pain, it is true, but I took a sip of it myself after he had gone. I suffered no ill effects, and—'

'I base my accusation on what Arderne says,' snapped Candelby, rounding on her. 'Not you, so mind your own business, woman. If I say Bartholomew killed Maud, then that is what happened.'

Michael stepped forward. 'Now, now,' he said softly. 'The High Street is no place for—'

'I shall do what I like, where I like,' yelled Candelby. 'You cannot stop me.'

'It is undignified,' said Michael, in the same calm voice. 'And folk expect more from a merchant of your standing. Go home, before you say something you may later regret.'

Candelby was too angry to listen to advice. 'There are slayings galore in this town, but you do not care. Indeed, it is said that you perpetrated them, and even your own Michaelhouse colleagues complain about you to the Chancellor. What have you done about Ocleye's murder? Nothing!'

'He wants to break you, because you oppose him over the rents,' whispered Blankpayn, keen to make matters worse. 'And Bartholomew killed Maud to render you helpless with grief.'

'Well, they misjudged me,' snarled Candelby, 'because I am far from being helpless. I *will* win this battle, and the whole town will be the richer for it.'

'You are right to defy them, Candelby,' said Arderne with his self-satisfied smile. 'Look at me. I challenged the Cambridge *medici*, and I am all but victorious. Robin is destroyed, Lynton is dead, and Paxtone will leave the town this morning. He is loading a cart as we speak. If you do not believe me, go to King's Hall and see for yourselves.'

'What did you do to him?' asked Bartholomew uneasily. 'Threaten to cure his blockage with one of your deadly remedies?'

Arderne's pale eyes bored into him, and Bartholomew was unsettled to find he did not like meeting the stare. He forced himself not to look away, and it was the healer who backed down first.

'Paxtone has been constipated for a week,' explained Falmeresham, looking from one to the other uncomfortably. 'So Magister Arderne offered to cure him – on condition that Paxtone leave Cambridge the moment the medicine worked. Paxtone accepted the challenge, and Magister Arderne's purge saw him racing to the latrines within the hour.'

'I pointed out that to renege on our agreement would cast a shadow of shame over the whole University,' added Arderne. 'And he did not want colleagues besmirched with his oath-breaking, so he is packing – and good riddance!'

'What was in this purge?' demanded Bartholomew, supposing that Arderne had bewitched Paxtone with one of his looks, and the poor man had been too unwell to resist.

'I have told you before – I do not share professional secrets. And Rougham will be no trouble from now on, either. He treated Mayor Harleston for stones in the bladder, but his remedies failed. *I* cured Harleston and recommended he take out a lawsuit against Rougham for incompetence.'

'Harleston was ill,' acknowledged Falmeresham, when Arderne turned to him for confirmation. 'And now he is not.'

Bartholomew glanced at his former student. He was pale, and uncomfortable with Arderne's declarations. Isabel was also uneasy, despite the transformation wrought by her new finery. She gripped Arderne's arm as if her life depended on it.

'You think this is amusing?' demanded Candelby, when Michael laughed derisively. 'You will not be sniggering tomorrow, when the town rises up against its oppressor. Of course, you can avoid unnecessary carnage by agreeing to my ultimatum with the rents.'

Michael treated him to a contemptuous sneer before turning on his heel. 'I do not discuss such matters on public highways, because *I* am a gentleman.'

'Come back here!' yelled Candelby furiously. 'I am talking to you.'

'You are *yelling* at me,' corrected Michael, pulling Bartholomew away with him.

Bartholomew risked a glance backwards. 'Candelby is making no move to follow us, although Blankpayn and Arderne are encouraging him not to let you leave. Why is Blankpayn always so eager for bloodshed? Arderne I understand – a physical fight will result in wounds, and people will pay him to have them mended. But Blankpayn?'

'He is one of those who thrives on the misfortunes of others. No one had heard of him before the rent war began. Now, as Candelby's firmest ally, his name is on everyone's lips.'

'He is losing popularity fast, though. His pot-boys did not like his attitude towards Isnard, and when he lost his shoe in the mud, no one helped him. People sense he is dangerous, and—'

Suddenly, Bartholomew felt his arm seized, and he was hauled around so fast that he almost fell. He staggered, struggling to keep his balance. It was Arderne.

'You can turn your back on merchants,' snarled Arderne in a low, menacing voice, 'but you will not do it to *me*. I am no mere townsman, and I have things I want to say to you.'

'But I do not want to hear them.' Bartholomew started to walk away, but Arderne grabbed him a second time, and jerked him hard enough to rip his tabard.

Falmeresham hurried forward, intent on pulling the two men apart, but Arderne shot him a basilisk stare that had him backing away mutely.

'Your friends are leaving,' said Michael, nodding down the High Street to where Candelby, Blankpayn and the other merchants were beginning to walk in the opposite direction. Isabel went with them, although she did so reluctantly, throwing anxious glances over her shoulder.

'They are going to the requiem for Maud Bowyer,' explained Falmeresham. He turned to Arderne. 'They do not want to be late – and neither do we.'

'I shall see you hang for Maud's murder, Bartholomew,' Arderne hissed, ignoring the student. 'So I advise you to leave Cambridge before I take my accusations to the Sheriff.'

'He did not—' began Falmeresham, shocked. Arderne's hand flicked out and struck the student in the mouth. It was not a hard blow, but it was enough to shock him into silence.

Michael regarded Arderne with dislike. 'You are distasteful company, Arderne, but perhaps we *should* take this opportunity to talk. Shall we step into the churchyard for privacy, or shall we screech at each other here, like fishwives?'

Arderne gestured that Michael was to lead the way. Bartholomew was appalled when he glimpsed a flash of steel in the healer's palm – the man kept a dagger concealed in his sleeve, and it was ready for use. He reached inside his own medical bag for one of his surgical blades.

368

Uncertain what else to do, Falmeresham trailed after them, dabbing at the blood that oozed from a split lip.

Michael led the way through the churchyard of St Mary the Great, aiming for the secluded spot where Motelete's body had been found. Bartholomew watched Arderne intently for some flicker of unease at the choice of venue, but the man's expression was bland and betrayed nothing.

'I am glad you have decided to listen to reason, Brother,' said Arderne, when the monk finally turned to face him. 'You can persuade your colleague to leave my town before he hangs for—'

'You will hang long before him,' said the monk coldly. 'It is only fair to tell you that you are currently under investigation for murder yourself.'

'Murder?' Arderne was grinning, confident in his belief that Michael had no proof of wrongdoing. 'I did nothing but try to help Maud Bowyer. And I did not harm Lynton, either, before you think to blame me for that. Bartholomew concealed the—'

'I am not talking about Maud's death or Lynton's murder,' said Michael in the same icy tones. 'I refer to Motelete. I have a witness who saw you with his body. I am going to take his sworn testimony now, and in an hour I shall have enough to send you to the gallows.'

Bartholomew tried not to show his surprise at the lie; Falmeresham's expression turned uneasy.

'I did not kill Motelete!' Arderne was aghast, smug satisfaction evaporating quickly. 'I liked him – I raised him from the dead, remember? Why would I have done that, if I intended to kill him later?'

Michael regarded him intently. 'Now there is an interesting remark. Motelete's friends say he seldom ventured outside the College before his death, yet you claim to have known him well enough to like him. That was a careless slip, Arderne, because it tells me that you – unlike virtually anyone else in the town – were acquainted with him *before* his throat was cut.'

Bartholomew smiled slowly. The monk was right. 'You and Motelete came to Cambridge at about the same time, Arderne. Were your arrivals coincidence, or was there a prior friendship?'

'Of course we did not know each other before I cured him.' Arderne's voice dripped contempt, but his fingers tightened around the blade in his hand. He was beginning to be worried. 'I do not fraternise with boys.'

'You do,' countered Bartholomew, taking a firmer grip on his own knife. 'Falmeresham proves it. You poached him from his studies. Why? So you could learn about the activities of a rival?'

'I would never spy on you,' objected Falmeresham. He glanced uncomfortably at Arderne, and Bartholomew saw the favour had been asked. And refused.

'Falmeresham hovers about me, because I saved him, too,' snapped Arderne. 'I cannot help it if the people I cure see me as a hero. And nor can I help the fact that your inadequate teaching has left him longing for better answers.'

'You did not save him. You sutured a minor cut in his side. And if you understood anything about anatomy, you would know that a liver cannot possibly have been extracted from that angle. You gave him strong medicines to befuddle him, and performed a bogus operation with entrails purchased from a butcher. Obviously, you wanted him seen as another of your triumphs.'

'Then you saw you could use him further still,' continued Michael. 'He could be your informant. You made him all manner of promises, using his passion for healing, to turn him against Matt. He ran to you eagerly – too eagerly,

370

because he was not much use once he had left Michaelhouse.'

'Take him,' said Arderne, regarding the student in disdain. 'He is a nuisance with all his stupid questions, and he is beginning to annoy me. Take him – he is all yours.'

Falmeresham did not seem overly dismayed. He shot Bartholomew a hopeful look.

'Meanwhile, Motelete was never dead – he was not even badly wounded,' Bartholomew went on. 'He just lay in St John Zachary, biding his time, waiting for his master to come. How many times have you two amazed gullible onlookers before, Arderne?'

Arderne's eyes bored into his, and the physician saw the intense rage that burned in them. 'I *did* raise him from the dead, and even you were a witness. You cannot deny what you saw.'

'What I saw was a lad who was cold and stiff – as would I be, had *I* been obliged to lie still for two days. However, Motelete was not left entirely to the mercy of the elements, because someone had covered him with blankets. When I saw them, I thought one of the Clare students had put them there for sentimental reasons, but now I see that you did it – or he did it himself.'

Arderne's eyes continued to blaze. 'His throat was cut. Even *you* could not fail to see that!'

'How *could* I see it? You appeared before I had conducted a proper examination. Your arrival was perfectly timed – doubtless you had been watching the church, making sure no one did anything to spoil your pending performance.'

Michael took up the tale. 'When you saw a Corpse Examiner about to begin his work, you knew you had to act quickly – you could fool laymen, but not a qualified physician. Doubtless you originally intended to raise Motelete at his requiem mass, when there would have been a large audience to admire your skill, but you settled for performing to Clare and a few burgesses instead.'

'You do not know what you are talking about,' snarled Arderne.

'After your miracle, I saw a superficial injury to Motelete's throat, but there was no evidence of a gaping wound,' said Bartholomew. 'There was blood aplenty, but you are a man who frequents butchers' stalls, and pigs' blood is cheap. If you and Motelete are the experienced fraudsters I believe you to be, then you both know how to scatter the stuff around to make a convincing case.'

'I was with Candelby when Motelete was killed,' said Arderne. 'I was nowhere near Motelete.'

'You did not need to be near him,' countered Bartholomew. 'He knew exactly what to do. You engineered the brawl with your confrontational statements, and he swallowed some potion to slow his heart and breathing. Before he swooned, he made the scratch, and doused himself in blood.'

'Meanwhile, there is Motelete himself,' added Michael. 'After his "cure" he let his guard down, and the shy scholar became a thing of the past. He took a lover, drank in taverns, and Falmeresham caught him stealing from you. His duties were over, and he was waiting for his next assignment.'

'Old Gedney saw through him, though,' said Bartholomew. 'He detected a wildness the others missed. What happened, Arderne? Did he demand more money? Is that why you poisoned him?'

'You have vivid imaginations,' declared Arderne coldly. 'You cannot prove any of this.'

'Actually, they can,' said Falmeresham quietly, 'because *I* will be their witness. You are a fraud, and I should never have let myself be deceived. You played on my hopes that

372

there might be more to medicine than watching patients die, but you have no more answers than anyone else.'

'Go away, boy,' said Arderne contemptuously. 'This does not concern you.'

Falmeresham addressed the monk. 'You are right in that Arderne's association with Motelete pre-dates Cambridge. They were together in Norwich and London, too. Their servants told me.'

'*There* is the killer!' Arderne jabbed an accusing finger. 'Falmeresham was jealous of Motelete.'

Falmeresham's cheeks burned, and his expression turned vengeful. 'It *was* Arderne in the graveyard with Motelete's corpse, Brother. He ordered me to lie, because—'

'Shut up!' roared Arderne. His dagger was out. 'Still your tongue or I will cut it out.'

'Fetch your beadles, Michael,' said Bartholomew, brandishing his own knife and intending to keep the healer occupied until the monk returned with reinforcements. Arderne had backed down from a physical encounter with Lynton, so was clearly no warrior. 'Go!'

'Wait!' shouted Arderne, when the monk tried to sidle past him. 'No beadles. Let me explain. I was trying to *help* Motelete. I had nothing to do with his death. Tell him, Falmeresham.'

Falmeresham hesitated, giving the impression that he would rather like to land Arderne in trouble with a lie. Michael fixed him with a glare.

'Arderne and I were home with Isabel that night,' he admitted, rather ruefully. 'Then Motelete came in, gasping and retching. Arderne waved his feather, chanted spells and even provided some of his precious urine, but nothing worked. Then he made me carry the body here, to this graveyard.'

'Cemeteries are imbued with power, because they are

haunted by the dead,' explained Arderne. 'Not that I expect you to understand such mysteries. I did all in my power to save Motelete.'

'It was your *feather* I saw!' exclaimed Bartholomew, in sudden understanding. 'I thought it was a dagger, and that murder was about to be committed. But it was a long, blade-like feather.'

'I wondered why you came at us so violently,' said Falmeresham. He turned back to Arderne, his voice accusing. 'You say you tried everything, but you did not use charcoal mixed with milk, even though it was obvious from the blisters on Motelete's mouth that the substance was caustic.'

'You know nothing,' snapped Arderne. 'Even I cannot cure everyone.'

'You said you could,' Falmeresham shot back. 'And you used all the tricks at your disposal to help Motelete, but you were useless. Doctor Bartholomew has saved people who have swallowed too much bryony. *You* could not.'

'So, I am fallible,' snarled Arderne. 'Welcome to the real world.'

'You are worse than fallible,' shouted Falmeresham. 'You are an ignoramus. And I can prove it.'

Arderne fingered his knife. 'How?' he asked dangerously.

'Because of Isnard's leg. After it was cut off, I was given the task of burying it. So I dug it up, to see for myself which one of you was right. It was hopelessly smashed, and would never have healed. Doctor Bartholomew was right to amputate, and I can show it to anyone who doubts him.'

'You damned whelp!' yelled Arderne, racing at him with his dagger. Bartholomew dived forward, but the ground was slippery and he lost his footing to fall flat on his face.

Arderne tripped over him, and gave a great shriek of pain when he landed with his full weight on one arm.

'Broken,' said Bartholomew, extracting himself and inspecting it. 'Would you like me to set it, or Robin?'

'Stay away from me,' howled Arderne. He looked for his knife, but it was lost in the grass.

'All your "cures" come from a book written by witches,' said Falmeresham accusingly. 'I saw it last night. You are a heretic, and Motelete told me you have killed people before. He said you—'

'Lies!' shrieked Arderne.

'He said you left Norwich *and* London because people died,' finished Falmeresham. 'And he said that is usually why you are obliged to move on. But you will not be going anywhere this time.'

'Damn you!' shouted Arderne furiously. 'Damn you all!'

Michael summoned his beadles, and ordered them to escort Arderne to the proctors' gaol. Once there, Arderne demanded medical attention, on the grounds that he could hardly set his own arm. Bartholomew obliged when Arderne rejected Robin, then screeched and wailed through the entire procedure. His cries echoed down the High Street, and the townsmen who heard them – word had spread fast that the healer had been arrested – exchanged glances of disapproval.

Afterwards, ears still ringing, Bartholomew visited Isnard, who was in too great a fever to know who was bathing his head and feeding him soothing tonics. Meanwhile, Michael went to Arderne's lodgings, and when he returned to Michaelhouse that evening, he had plentiful evidence of illicit practices. A dirty boy who kept house for the healer, and who was greatly relieved when informed he would no longer be working for him, told Michael that Arderne had left London because he had murdered a rival leech. A hue and cry had been raised, but the healer and his servants had escaped. Arderne, Michael decided, would wait in gaol until he could be handed to the relevant authorities.

'That is why he did nothing for the first few weeks after we arrived,' the boy explained. 'Partly to see who he needed to destroy before he started his work, but partly because he wanted to be sure he had not been followed. He only began when he was sure he was safe.'

'Tell me,' said the monk, his mind ranging along another avenue of thought, 'did any scholars visit Arderne? Michaelhouse scholars, such as Honynge?'

'Not Honynge,' said the boy. 'Arderne did not like him, because he is arrogant, but Carton came sometimes. He said it was to visit Falmeresham's sickbed, but he spent more time with—'

'Wait a moment,' interrupted Michael. 'Are you telling me Carton knew Falmeresham was alive *before* Falmeresham made his triumphant return to his College?'

'Yes. It was Carton who paid for his treatment. Arderne does not work for free.'

Isabel was disgusted to learn she was about to lose a second home within hours of the first, but packed her bags quickly when Michael said Arderne's crimes might land her in hot water, too. She packed them even faster when he asked whether she had done anything to hasten Maud's demise.

'If she did, then it would not have been by much,' said Bartholomew. It was almost dark, and he and Michael were in the orchard at the back of the College. A fallen apple tree provided a rough bench, and although it was really too cold to be outside, it was better than sitting in the hall with noisy students, or sharing the conclave with Honynge. 'Perhaps she did double the dose, but it would have been to bring a merciful release, not to escape into Arderne's arms a day sooner.'

The physician was exhausted, because after tending Arderne and Isnard, he had gone to Peterhouse, to see if any more could be learned about Lynton. He had spent hours with Wisbeche, trying in vain to unravel their colleague's complex commercial transactions. Later, he had pulled his hood over his head and gone to sit in the Angel, to see if anyone was ready to gossip about Ocleye. It had been a rash thing to do, because Blankpayn caught him, and the situation might have turned violent had Carton not caused a diversion that had allowed the physician to escape. Bartholomew was keen to ask the commoner why he had been in the Angel in the first place, but Carton claimed he had pressing business elsewhere, and left without answering questions.

'If Isabel did take matters into her own hands,' said Michael, shivering as he pulled his cloak more closely around him, 'it is murder.'

'Some would call it compassion.' Despite his weariness, Bartholomew was too agitated to sit, so paced back and forth. The killer or killers of Lynton, Ocleye and Motelete were still free, and he could not see a way through the maze of facts and information they had assembled. He was also worried about the next day's Convocation, afraid that a gathering of scholars in one place might prove too great a temptation for the many people who wished the University harm. And finally, he was concerned for Isnard, suspecting Arderne might be about to claim yet another victim.

Michael sighed. 'Well, we have dramatically rid ourselves of one suspect – two, if we count Isabel – but we are still in the dark as regards the real killer. Do you think Falmeresham poisoned Motelete, as Arderne is claiming?'

'Falmeresham would not have used bryony, because he

knows it leaves detectable traces. Arderne is trying to avenge himself, because Falmeresham's testimony saw him imprisoned.'

'Then we are left with four suspects: Candelby, Blankpayn, Spaldynge and Honynge. Five, if we count Carton, who is guilty of some very odd behaviour. Which is the culprit, do you think?'

Bartholomew shrugged, still pacing. 'Is Blankpayn sufficiently clever to fool you? Meanwhile, Spaldynge does not seem the kind of man who would want the town awash with blood, although . . .'

'Although he gambled at the Dispensary and sold his College's property without permission,' finished Michael. 'And he despises physicians – like Lynton – because they were useless in the plague. And *that* is strange, is it not? Lynton was the *medicus* who could not save Spaldynge's family from the Death, yet Spaldynge deigned to join him on Friday nights to gamble.'

'I doubt Spaldynge wants to harm the entire University,' said Bartholomew, although his tone was uncertain. 'Blankpayn would, though. If anything horrible happens tomorrow, you can be sure he will be taking part.'

'I do not know what to do for the best. Should I cancel the Convocation?'

'If you do, the landlords will be furious, and may set light to St Mary the Great anyway.'

'The culprit is Honynge,' said Michael, after another pause. 'I *know* it is. He took against me from the moment we met – when I was obliged to investigate the death of Wenden.'

'Who?' asked Bartholomew tiredly.

'The Clare Fellow who was stabbed by the tinker on Ash Wednesday. He was Honynge's friend, if you recall, and had been walking home from Zachary Hostel when he was attacked. Wenden had forgotten his hat, and Honynge ran after him, to give it back. He saw the tinker, and he heard the sound of a bow being loosed. We found the tinker drowned a few days later.'

Bartholomew stared at him. 'I had forgotten Wenden was killed by a crossbow. Are you sure it was the tinker who shot him? Crossbow deaths are not very common.'

'Wenden's purse was found among the tinker's belongings – it was clear evidence of his guilt.'

'And it was Honynge's testimony that allowed you to deduce all this?'

'I see where you are going with this. Lord! I hope I have not made a terrible mistake.'

Bartholomew flopped down next to him. 'Perhaps you should reopen the case.'

'Perhaps I should.' The monk shivered again. 'I cannot believe I am sitting out here in the cold, while Honynge enjoys the fire in *my* conclave. What am I thinking?'

'That you prefer my company to his – and I do not want to be anywhere near him. He is too argumentative. Take the fire if you will, but I am staying here.'

'We must *do* something – and soon, because I have never known the town more uneasy than when I was walking home this evening. The inevitable has happened: folk are muttering that we arrested Arderne to keep the medical business in University hands.'

Bartholomew tensed suddenly. 'Look! There is someone in the trees! Grab that branch, Brother! You may need it to defend yourself.'

'It is only Cynric,' said Michael, peering through the gloom. 'God's blood, Matt! You frightened me!'

'Come quickly,' called Cynric, hurrying towards them. 'Honynge has been poisoned.'

* * *

379

Bartholomew and Michael raced to the hall to find Honynge sitting on a bench with one hand clasped to his mouth and the other to his stomach. An upturned cup lay beside him, and virtually every member of the College stood in a silent semicircle nearby. The students looked frightened, Wynewyk concerned, William pleased, and Tyrington shocked. Carton stood slightly apart, his face oddly blank. The servants, who had been in the process of preparing a light supper of ale and oatcakes, formed a line by the screen, watching the proceedings uneasily. Agatha was among them, scowling, because she disliked her College torn by rifts and divisions. Langelee came to explain what had happened.

'Honynge was holding forth about the dog in this morning's egg-mess when he complained of a pain in his mouth. Then he said he had gripes in his belly. And then he claimed he had been poisoned.'

'He was struck down by God, for blaming the dog incident on me,' announced William, not even trying to disguise his delight with the situation. 'It is divine justice.'

'It is not!' cried Honynge. 'I have been poisoned by someone who wants me to die.'

'Doctor Bartholomew will save you,' said Deynman with touching confidence. 'Do not worry.'

'He may have been the one who tried to kill me,' wailed Honynge.

'This will not be an easy murder to solve,' whispered Wynewyk in the monk's ear. 'The students like him well enough, but the Fellows and commoners think him an ass.'

Bartholomew picked up the cup, noting that most of its contents lay splattered across the floor, so Honynge had probably ingested very little. He sniffed it gingerly, then inspected Honynge's mouth. It was covered in small blisters. He turned to the watching throng.

380

'Agatha, will you bring me some milk and eggs?'

'Are you hungry, then?' she asked, startled. 'Should you not see to Honynge first?'

'Fetch the pressed charcoal from my storeroom,' he ordered Deynman, loath to take the time to explain to her. 'And the emetic in the red flask.'

'But that is a powerful purge,' said Deynman, wide-eyed. 'It will make someone violently sick.'

'Yes,' agreed Bartholomew patiently. 'That is the intention.'

'I had better find a bucket as well, then,' said Deynman practically.

When Deynman and Agatha returned, Bartholomew fed the emetic to a protesting Honynge, then sat with the new Fellow while he emptied the contents of his stomach into a pail. Next, he prepared a mixture of charcoal, raw eggs and milk, and forced Honynge to drink as much as possible, explaining it would absorb any remaining toxins. Meanwhile, Michael cleared the hall of spectators, so the sick man would not have to perform to an audience. Eventually, only he, Honynge, Bartholomew and Langelee remained. Agatha pretended to be busy behind the serving screen, and although it was obvious that she was only doing it to eavesdrop, no one had the courage to ask her to leave.

'Thank God I was out when this happened,' whispered Michael fervently to Langelee, 'or Honynge would certainly have had me as his prime suspect for the crime. Who did it, do you think?'

'William was hanging around the wine a lot,' replied Langelee. 'But then he always does. Meanwhile, Wynewyk was pouring, because Honynge claimed he had a sore back, and Tyrington and Carton were distributing the cups. Any one of them could have poisoned him – as could I.'

'Are you feeling better?' asked Bartholomew of Honynge. 'The burning should have eased by now.'

'It has, I suppose,' said Honynge begrudgingly. 'Although I am sure there was no need to have prescribed me quite such a violent emetic. You *wanted* everyone to see me in that undignified position.'

'I wanted the poison out before it was too late,' said Bartholomew tartly. 'Motelete swallowed bryony, and no one helped him vomit, so he died. You, however, will survive to insult your colleagues another day.'

'I resign,' said Honynge. He started to stand, but was not strong enough, and sank back down again. He began to mutter to himself. 'Michaelhouse's Fellows are either sly or stupid, the meals are dismal, there is never enough wine, and the accommodation is overcrowded. Tell them to go to Hell, and accept the offer you should have taken in the first place: to be Principal of Lucy's.'

'I shall draw up the papers, then,' said Michael, reaching for a pen. 'You can be gone tomorrow.'

'Do not spend another night here to be murdered,' hissed Honynge to himself. 'Go to the Angel.'

'The Angel?' asked Michael. 'That is owned by the man determined to see our University flounder.'

'Candelby wants fair rents,' snapped Honynge. 'What is wrong with that?'

'But earlier you said you were going to vote against my amendment,' said Michael, setting down the pen and concentrating on his prey. 'Have you changed your mind, and think I am right, after all?'

'I think Honynge is better friends with Candelby than he wants us to know,' said Bartholomew, when the new Fellow did not reply. 'We have seen them together twice now. Once was in the Angel—'

'Arguing,' interrupted Honynge. 'You heard us yourself

382

– it was not as if we were enjoying a tête-à-tête. He attacked Michaelhouse and I was defending it, although I should have saved my breath.'

'You spoke loudly when you saw me listening, but I think the discussion had been rather more amiable before that. You engineered that row, to make us believe you and Candelby are hostile, but the reality is quite different. The second time we saw you with him, you were buying pies.'

Honynge sighed wearily. 'All right: I admit I am wrong to frequent his tavern. However, if you fine me, you will have to fine every other scholar in Cambridge, too. We all eat his pies.'

'Yours was a very *heavy* pie,' said Bartholomew. 'And you only took one bite before shoving the rest in your scrip. Who puts oily food in his clean leather purse? No one. So, I conclude this pie contained something other than meat – such as money for services rendered.'

'There *was* money in it,' said Langelee, startled. 'I happened to visit him in his room when he was cracking it open. He shoved it under a book when I arrived, but I saw the gleam of silver inside it first. I assumed it was his own peculiar hiding place, like you use that loose floor-board, Brother.'

'I do not have to listen to this,' said Honynge, starting to stand. 'I am a sick man, and it is despicable that you are taking advantage of the fact to browbeat me.'

'And there was a third time, too, although we did not witness it,' said Michael, resting a heavy hand on his shoulder, so he was obliged to sit again. 'Tyrington saw you. He thought you just wanted someone to debate with on your way home from the disputation at Bene't College, and you were more than happy to let him believe it.'

Honynge was glaring. 'So? You cannot prove anything untoward in my speaking to Candelby.'

'No,' sighed Michael. 'That has been the problem all along – shady activities but no proof.'

I know what you sell Candelby,' said Bartholomew, when the answer came to him, as clear as day.

'You do not,' said Honynge, his eyes glittering with triumph. 'And Candelby will never tell you, so do not think you will use him as a witness against me.'

'You spy on the University,' said Bartholomew. '*That* is why he is always so well informed. He knew about the Convocation before Michael made it public. He has intimate knowledge of the Statutes and what they do and do not cover. He has information about the food preferences of some Fellows . . .'

'These are hardly matters of life and death,' sneered Honynge. 'He could have gleaned them from listening to gossip in his tavern or the Dispensary, which is what I am sure he told you.'

'He did tell us that,' acknowledged Bartholomew. 'And the fact that you know it suggests it is an excuse *you* told him to give, should anyone question his sources. However, it was not all innocent. I suspect he used the information you provided to pressure Spaldynge into selling Borden Hostel.'

'You cannot prove anything,' said Honynge again, sitting back and folding his arms.

'We can prove you spied on Clare, because Cynric saw you,' said Bartholomew. 'You went to see what else you could learn to Candelby's advantage. I imagine it was you I saw at Peterhouse, too, doing much the same thing – you ran away and hid in the woods behind the Gilbertine Friary.'

'Meanwhile, Rougham and Paxtone have also complained that someone has been following them,' said Michael. 'And now we know who and why.'

Honynge sighed, affecting boredom. 'Prove it,' he said in a chant. His voice dropped. 'They are deeply stupid, Honynge, so do not let them intimidate you.'

'Did Candelby order you to kill Motelete, Lynton and Ocleye?' asked Michael. 'He had hired Ocleye to spy for him, but Ocleye promptly turned traitor. Meanwhile, Lynton had just banned him from the Dispensary, and Motelete may have caught him doing something untoward—'

'I have not killed anyone, and if you make any more accusations, I shall take the matter to my lawyers. I feel well enough to walk now, so I am leaving while I still can.'

'You are not going anywhere until you have signed this,' said Michael, pushing the letter of resignation towards him.

Honynge wrote his name with a flourish. 'With pleasure.'

'The man is right,' said Michael wearily, after Honynge had gone. 'We cannot prove any of this. He is a killer and a traitor to his University, and he is going to walk away. Worse, he might kill again.'

'You should not have cured him, Matthew,' said Agatha, stepping out from behind the screen. The three scholars jumped, because they had forgotten she was there.

'Probably not,' said Bartholomew. 'However, it was that or seeing *you* hanged for murdering him.'

Langelee and Michael gaped at him. '*Agatha* is this deadly killer?' asked Langelee in disbelief.

'Now, just a moment—' started Agatha dangerously.

'No, but she did poison Honynge,' replied Bartholomew. 'She used the love-potion Arderne gave her. He told her it contains mandrake, but it is actually white bryony, with which mandrake is often confused. Arderne does not know what he is doing, so he made a basic mistake.'

'You mean I really did poison Honynge?' asked Agatha. She looked rather pleased with herself.

'Yes, you really did. Perhaps Motelete swallowed one of these love-charms, too, because I am sure it was bryony that killed him.'

'Of course!' exclaimed Michael. 'Falmeresham saw him stealing one of Arderne's remedies, and we know he was enamoured of Siffreda. He took the draught in order to make her love him, but it killed him instead. He should have known better than to swallow anything Arderne had concocted.'

'He was desperate,' explained Agatha. The scholars regarded her in surprise. She shrugged. 'He once confided to me in the Angel that Siffreda was taking too long to fall for him. Young men are impatient in love, and he was eager to speed matters up.'

'If Arderne's potion is supposed to render its taker irresistible,' said Bartholomew to Agatha, 'then why did you give yours to Honynge? Surely, you cannot have wanted to be in love with *him*?'

Agatha glared at him. 'I most certainly did not! My intention was for Wynewyk to fall for him. Then Honynge would have been so disturbed that he would have packed his bags and left my College.'

'I see,' said Michael, amused. 'However, you purchased this remarkable concoction before Honynge came to Michaelhouse, so he was not your original victim. Who—'

'That is none of your business.' Agatha raised her chin defiantly. 'Everything you said earlier was right, by the way. Candelby *has* been paying Honynge for information about our University – my cousin Blankpayn mentioned it when he was in his cups last night. I was going to tell you this morning, but you disappeared and I did not know where you had gone.'

Michael sighed. 'So where does all this leave us?'

'With Motelete's death solved,' replied Bartholomew. 'It

was an accident – or a case of malpractice, depending on whether you think Arderne was right to leave dangerous substances in a place where light-fingered, love-sick accomplices might get hold of them.'

'I think we shall opt for the latter,' said Michael. 'It will go in my report to the sheriff in London. But we still do not have the real culprit, and time is running out.'

CHAPTER 12

It was late before Bartholomew, Michael and Langelee left the conclave. They went over the evidence again and again, and Michael was frustrated when answers remained elusive. A crisis was looming, and he hated the fact that he was powerless to prevent it. It was difficult to accept that whatever decision he made – to cancel the Convocation or let it go ahead – would bring trouble, and he was full of bitter resentment that he had been placed in a position where he could not determine the lesser of two evils.

When dawn broke, and the bell rang to wake scholars for church the next day, Bartholomew felt as though he had only just gone to bed. A sense of foreboding led him to don a military jerkin of boiled leather under his academic tabard, although he sincerely hoped such a precaution would prove unnecessary. He hurried into the yard, and found Michael already there. The monk was unshaven and rumpled, and there was a wild look in his eye.

'The Convocation starts in an hour,' he said. 'I should go to St Mary the Great as soon as possible, to brief my beadles before the Regents begin to gather.'

'You are relieved of College obligations, then,' said Langelee promptly. 'William can take mass, then we shall all come back here and lock ourselves in. Cynric and his sword will escort the other Fellows to the Convocation, but my duty is here, protecting Michaelhouse.'

'Why should our College be a target?' asked Bartholomew, alarmed by the Master's precautions.

388

'Because of you,' replied Langelee bluntly. 'I know you have made your peace with Isnard, but the legacy of his discontent runs on, and there are rumours about you concealing murders. Furthermore, people are saying that you encouraged the proctors to arrest Arderne.'

'He is right, Matt,' said Michael, when Bartholomew began to object. 'Your precipitous action with crossbow bolts in Milne Street last Sunday has had repercussions none of us could have predicted.'

The streets of Cambridge were growing light, but there were more people on them than was normal for such an early hour. They gathered in small groups, or raced here and there with quick, scurrying movements. Scholars were out, too, and Bartholomew noticed that some carried sticks and knives.

'I cannot fine them for toting weapons,' said Michael. 'If they feel as uneasy as I do, then I do not blame them for wanting to defend themselves. Let us hope tensions ease after the Convocation.'

'They may get worse,' warned Bartholomew. He walked faster, making a concerted effort not to look at anyone, lest it be seen as a challenge. When one of his patients wished him a good morning, he was so unsettled that he failed to reply. 'I had forgotten what Cambridge can be like when its collective hackles are raised. Perhaps you *should* cancel the Convocation. It will prevent scholars from assembling in large numbers, and you can order them to stay inside their hostels and Colleges instead.'

'It is too late,' said Michael, looking around. 'Most are already on their way.'

The University's senior members were indeed streaming towards St Mary the Great. A few were in twos or threes, but more were in bigger groups, and some had brought armed students to protect them; these strutted along in a

389

way that was distinctly provocative. Only Regents were permitted in the church for the Convocation, so the escorts waited outside in ever-increasing numbers. The door stood open, and Bartholomew walked through it to find the place already half full. He was alarmed to note that they had organised themselves into opposing sides – or rather, someone had done it for them, and it soon became apparent who that someone was.

'All those who think Michael's amendment should pass, stand to the south,' Honynge was shouting. 'And those who should think it should not, go to the north. In other words, those who believe the town should win must slink to the south, while right-minded men should come to the north.'

'What are you doing?' hissed Michael furiously. 'I wanted them all mixed up together. Now they are gathered according to faction, they will be more inclined to quarrel.'

'Then any bloodshed will be your fault, for calling this stupid Convocation in the first place,' retorted Honynge viciously. 'People will see you for the fool you are, and will call for your resignation.'

'It is none of your damned business,' snarled Michael. 'You resigned your Fellowship last night, so you have no official standing in the University until you are installed in your new post.'

Honynge was seething. 'So *that* is why you forced me to sign that deed in such haste. You sly old snake! I should have known you had an ulterior motive for acting so quickly.' He lowered his voice. 'I told you they were untrustworthy. Do not let them—'

'Leave,' ordered Michael contemptuously. 'You have no place here.'

But Honynge knew the University rules. 'That is untrue – anyone who has held a senior position owns the right to observe the proceedings. I shall remain and watch what happens.'

'Beadle Meadowman will eject you if you make a sound.' Michael decided not to make a scene. The altercation had already attracted attention, and he did not want a fight between Regents who supported their Senior Proctor, and those who thought Honynge was right. Meadowman heard his name mentioned and came to oblige.

'Chancellor Tynkell has asked me to tell you that he is indisposed this morning,' Meadowman whispered in the monk's ear. 'He says you should proceed without him.'

'You mean he is too frightened to show his face,' said Michael in disgust. 'And he has left me to bear the brunt of this alone.'

'Actually, he swallowed a remedy Arderne gave him for indigestion, and has been in the latrines all night. He says he dare not come here, lest he is obliged to race out at an awkward moment.'

'Lord!' muttered Michael, turning away and eyeing the assembling scholars. They were pouring into the church, and Bartholomew could see the two sides were fairly evenly matched. The nave and aisles were alive with the blues, browns and greens of academic uniforms, mixed with the more sober greys, creams, browns and blacks of the religious Orders. Some of the Colleges had wheeled out elderly members who were either too infirm or too addled to teach, but who were still entitled to vote.

'No, no, Master Gedney,' called Kardington patiently. 'You want to be over here, not over there.'

'Let him choose for himself,' shouted Wisbeche. 'Do not tell him what to do.'

'Very well,' said Gedney. 'I shall have the middle, then. Where is my stool?'

Reluctantly, Spaldynge stepped forward and handed it

over. Gedney placed it in the exact centre of the nave, and sat, his toothless jaw jutting out defiantly.

'Some of these men do not have voting rights,' said Michael, looking around in dismay. 'Such as Spaldynge, who lost his Fellowship when he sold Borden Hostel. They are here to make sure a particular side receives a sly boost in numbers. What shall I do? If my beadles attempt to oust them, there will be a skirmish. Or they will leave in a resentful frame of mind, and pick a fight with the first apprentice who makes an obscene gesture at them.'

'What is Honynge doing *now*?' asked Bartholomew in alarm. The ex-Fellow had climbed on to the dais normally occupied by the Chancellor, and was clearing his throat. 'You should stop him, Brother.'

But it was too late. Honynge had grabbed Gedney's walking stick, and he banged it on the floor until he had everyone's attention. 'We have half an hour before the Convocation is officially scheduled to begin,' he announced. 'So, I propose we use that time constructively, in scholarly disputation.'

'That is actually a good idea,' said Michael to Bartholomew, startled. 'It will stop everyone from throwing taunts at each other in the interim.'

'We shall talk about Blood Relics,' announced Honynge. Michael closed his eyes in despair as half the scholars groaned, while the remainder cheered. 'It is a subject worthy of clever minds.'

'Boring!' called Gedney. 'Christmas is almost upon us, so we should discuss the virtues of nice plum puddings, as opposed to these new-fangled fig things we were given last year.'

'Prior Morden of the Dominicans will argue the case *for* Blood Relics,' said Honynge, ignoring him. 'And Father

William, Franciscan of Michaelhouse, will argue the case against.'

'Stop him, Brother,' urged Bartholomew. 'Pitting a Grey Friar against a Black will cause trouble for certain – as well he knows.'

'I cannot – not now,' whispered Michael, appalled. 'Those Regents who think this is a good idea will lynch me, and the rest will race to my defence. Then Honynge will have what he wants anyway.'

'You want *me* to take a leading role?' asked Morden, aghast. He was not the University's most skilled debater, and did not like the notion of propounding a case publicly, not even against William. Honynge knew it, and Bartholomew marvelled at the depth of his malice.

'I would rather talk about puddings,' said William. The Franciscan rarely acknowledged his own shortcomings, but even he was wary of tackling such a contentious issue in front of some of the best minds in the country. 'Fig ones are superior to plum, because figs come from the Holy Land. *Ergo*, fig puddings are holy, and thus better.' He folded his arms and looked triumphantly at Morden.

'I do not like the taste of figs,' began the Dominican nervously. 'And their seeds get trapped between the teeth. Then they come out at awkward moments. The seeds, I mean, not the teeth.'

There was a smattering of laughter, from both sides of the church.

'Wasps like plums,' continued William. 'So there is always a danger that you might find one baked in your pudding. I do not eat wasps as a rule, so it is better to opt for fig pies whenever possible.'

When he could make himself heard above the guffaws, Morden replied to this contention, and the debate began in earnest. The Regents began to enjoy themselves, and called out theories to help the disputants, many of them extremely witty. Honynge's face was a mask of rage when he saw his ploy to cause dissent was failing. He tried to change the subject, but was shouted down as a killjoy.

'Where did he go?' asked Bartholomew after a while, tearing his attention from the dais. 'He has vanished, and I do not think he has finished causing harm. Meadowman is nowhere to be seen, either.'

It was impossible to locate Honynge among the seething masses, and it was some time before they were able to deduce that he was not in the nave, the aisles or the Lady Chapel. They moved cautiously, aware that jostling the wrong person might undo all the goodwill that Morden and William had created.

'Meadowman was obliged to help Gedney,' reported Michael after talking to the beadle. 'Apparently, the old man fell off his stool laughing. When Meadowman looked round, Honynge had gone. He must have decided to go home.'

'Your other beadles told me that no one has left, so he is still in here. But where? The tower is locked.'

'My office!' exclaimed Michael in alarm. 'Lord! There are sensitive documents in there.'

He broke into a waddle, hurrying to the chamber off the south aisle from which he conducted University affairs. He flung open the door and raced inside, Bartholomew at his heels. Honynge stood there, but he was not alone. The door slammed behind them, and Bartholomew whipped around to see Candelby and Blankpayn. Blankpayn waved a heavy sword and his grin was malevolent.

'How timely,' said Honynge coldly. 'Here are the pair who found out about our arrangement, Candelby. They think I killed Lynton and Ocleye, but I assure you I did not.'

'Honynge is certainly innocent of Lynton's death,' said Candelby to Michael. 'He was going to attend the Dispensary on my behalf – to use his wits to predict winners, while I provided money for bets. We were going share the proceeds, and Lynton's demise ruined a perfectly good plan.'

'You have not mentioned this before,' said Michael suspiciously.

'Why would we? It is none of your business. However, we were both furious when Lynton died.' Candelby went to Michael's desk and began to make a pile of the scrolls that were lying out on it. Outraged, the monk stepped forward to stop him, but Blankpayn brandished his weapon menacingly.

'We do not have time for this.' Bartholomew started towards the door, but Blankpayn took a firmer grip on his sword, and the physician was left in no doubt that he would very much like to use it. He stopped dead in his tracks. 'Please! Michael needs to supervise the Regents, or there may be trouble.'

'Good,' said Honynge. 'I hope there *is* trouble, and that you two will be blamed. His voice dropped to a whisper. 'With luck, some of those arrogant Fellows will die, and you can accept one of the resulting vacancies – if there is a foundation that meets your exacting standards, of course.'

'No one is going to die,' said Candelby, going to a shelf for more of the University's records.

'What are you doing with those?' asked Michael uneasily. 'Be careful. Some are very valuable.'

'We are going to have a fire,' said Honynge, waving an unlit taper at him.

'A fire?' Michael was appalled. 'But these deeds are

irreplaceable! What are you thinking of? Put them down and get out of my office. And tell your ape to stop pointing his sword at me.'

'Easy, Blankpayn,' crooned Candelby soothingly, when his henchman lurched forward. Bartholomew quickly interposed himself between taverner and monk; his leather jerkin would afford greater protection than Michael's woollen habit. Candelby glared at the monk. 'And you should settle down, too, Brother, because you are not going anywhere until I say so.'

Michael glared. 'But Matt does not need to be—'

'If I let him go, he will summon your beadles,' snapped Candelby. 'Stand against the wall, where we can see you. Hurry up! We do not have all day.'

'Blankpayn has been itching to dispatch a few academics, so I advise you against calling out or trying to escape,' said Honynge. He lowered his voice. 'Why did you warn them? You should have kept quiet and let Blankpayn cut them down. That would have showed them who is in charge.'

Candelby seemed used to Honynge's oddities, and did not react to the muttered comments, although Blankpayn regarded the ex-Fellow askance. Honynge did not keep Blankpayn's attention for long, however, because when Bartholomew hesitated to obey the instructions, he was rewarded with a poke from the blade. It was a vigorous jab, and would have drawn blood, had it not been for the armour he wore. For the first time, he began to appreciate the danger they were in.

Michael regarded Honynge coldly. 'I have no idea what is happening here, but I strongly urge you to reconsider. Candelby intends to see the University collapse. Surely you want no part of that?'

'He is trying to pretend you and he are on the same

side,' whispered Honynge. 'Do not listen, Honynge. You know how he hates you.'

Michael was disgusted. 'You are betraying your colleagues – and for what? Candelby does not pay you very generously, because *your* hostel was shabby, unlike the fine building he leased to Tyrington.'

'On the contrary,' said Honynge, putting out his hand to prevent Candelby from responding. 'He let me occupy Zachary Hostel free of charge for months. That was *extremely* generous.'

'Is that why it took you so long to decide whether you were going to accept the Michaelhouse Fellowship?' asked Bartholomew, recalling how Honynge had gazed thoughtfully out of the window for some time after reading Langelee's invitation.

Honynge nodded. 'I was reviewing whether it would be worth my while. But I need not have worried, Candelby immediately offered to recompense me in silver instead.'

'Tyrington was a good tenant,' said Candelby conversationally, rummaging in a chest to emerge with a handful of parchment. 'He always paid me on time, and he kept the place scrupulously clean. If all scholars were like him, I would not mind renting to them. But most are pigs.'

Michael was more interested in Honynge. 'How *could* you form an alliance with a man who is determined to destroy the University – *your* University?'

'Because I owed him years of back-rent,' snapped Honynge. He produced a tinderbox and began the process of lighting his taper. 'Had he chosen to file a complaint, I would have been expelled – perhaps even excommunicated – but instead he offered me a solution to my problems.'

'That should be enough for a pretty blaze,' said Candelby, stepping back to admire his handiwork. 'The smoke will put the wind up those arrogant Regents, and you will have to watch all these priceless parchments destroyed, Brother. It will take you years to sort out the resulting confusion.'

'It will not,' said Honynge, most of his attention on his tinderbox. 'Because he will be dead – him and his Corpse Examiner.'

Candelby regarded him warily. 'You said we were going to make a fire, not kill—'

'We are about to incinerate a church containing hundreds of scholars,' said Honynge impatiently. 'Of course there will be casualties. Among them will be this pair.'

'Now, just a moment,' said Candelby, alarmed. 'You suggested we should create a bit of chaos, to destabilise the University so it cannot stop me when I raise my rents, but murder is—'

'Do not be a fool,' snapped Blankpayn, speaking for the first time. 'Do you think the monk and his friend will say nothing about what they have heard here? They will tell the King, and we will hang.'

'We will not hang,' said Candelby irritably. 'The King will review the evidence, and see we were driven to desperate measures. He will never condemn us.'

Honynge addressed Blankpayn. 'Candelby and I will be able to buy our freedom, because we are important. But *you* are just a poor taverner. You are right to want to silence these scholars before they can harm you, so go ahead and do it. Go on. You know it is the sensible thing to do.'

'Ignore him, Blankpayn,' ordered Candelby. 'You are no killer, so do not be stupid about—'

'Kill them,' hissed Honynge fiercely. The taper was burning, ready to ignite Candelby's little bonfire. 'Follow what your instincts tell you to do. Do not obey a man who calls you stupid.'

'Stop it, Honynge,' snapped Candelby, when Blankpayn gripped his sword and prepared to follow the scholar's suggestion. 'We have worked well together this far, so do not spoil everything now. No one needs to die. Put up your blade, Blankpayn. I should have known better than to ask *you* to help with a matter that requires subtlety and discretion.'

It was the wrong thing to say, because Blankpayn's expression darkened. With a sigh of annoyance that his normally submissive henchman should dare defy him, Candelby tried to snatch Blankpayn's weapon. At the same time, the blazing taper singed Honynge's fingers. He howled in pain and dropped it, so it fell on the documents, which immediately began to smoulder. Blankpayn ripped his sword away from Candelby with a bellow of fury, and suddenly the two men were engaged in a desperate grappling match. Michael darted towards the flames and began to flail at them with his cloak.

'Michael, stop!' yelled Bartholomew, trying to squeeze past the furious mêlée of arms, legs and sword that was Candelby and Blankpayn. The desk was in the way, and he was trapped. 'Smother them – do not *fan* them!'

Honynge was laughing wildly. He drew a knife and prepared to plunge it into the monk's back.

Determined that Honynge should not succeed, Bartholomew flung himself across the table, scattering burning parchments as he went. He crashed into the ex-Fellow, bowling him from his feet. Honynge scrambled away when the physician was still off balance, and swiped at him with the dagger, a vicious blow that might have killed him had he not been wearing the jerkin. Bartholomew fell back among the smouldering documents, and Honynge leapt on top of him, pummelling him with his fists. The physician tried to push him off, but Honynge was stronger than he looked, and the smoke from the burning deeds was making it difficult to breathe. Bartholomew tried to shout for Michael, but Honynge landed a punch that drove all the breath from his body. Then Honynge's hands were around his throat, squeezing as hard as they could.

Just when his senses were beginning to reel, Honynge went limp. Michael hauled the physician to his feet, and threw open a window, allowing fresh, clean air to waft inside. The smoke swirled, then began to clear. Bartholomew's throat hurt, his eyes stung and he could not stop coughing. Michael went to the centre of the room, and began to swing a cloak around his head, in an attempt to dissipate the fumes. Blankpayn lay near the door, blood seeping from under him; he was dead.

'Are you all right, Matt?' asked the monk, not stopping his exertions. 'Damn these silly men! The whole place almost went up – my office is full of old wood and dry parchment.'

'What happened?' asked Bartholomew hoarsely. He coughed again. 'Blankpayn?'

'Fell on his own dagger,' replied Michael, still swinging vigorously. 'Help me get rid of this smoke, before the Regents smell it and there is a stampede. We do not want anyone crushed.'

'And Honynge?' asked Bartholomew, too shaken to comply.

Candelby was leaning against a wall, looking as though he might be sick. 'I knocked him senseless with a doorstop after Blankpayn had his mishap – he would have killed you otherwise. They were *both* deranged! I knew Blankpayn was growing dangerous, but I did not think he would actually *harm* anyone, especially me. That business with Falmeresham turned his wits.'

Michael regarded him with dislike. 'Blankpayn *was* a dangerous man, while Honynge was going to ignite the University Church with all our Regents inside it. However, *you* recruited them, so *you* are complicit in their crimes.'

'No!' cried Candelby, appalled. 'I admit I wanted to create confusion, so the Regents would not object when I tripled the rents, but no one was going to be hurt. I was planning to offer money for repairs to the church, too, just to show you that I bear no hard feelings.'

'I do not believe you.'

'But it is true,' wailed Candelby. 'Ask Honynge when he wakes up. He will tell you we discussed it, and that a box of coins is in my house, ready to be offered as reparation.'

'I am afraid Honynge will not be giving evidence in your favour,' said Bartholomew wearily. 'You hit him far too hard, and he is no longer breathing.'

'Well, save him then,' ordered Candelby, shocked. 'Flick feathers at him, like Arderne does. I need him alive, so he can tell you I am speaking the truth.'

Michael was unmoved. 'You have just murdered a member of my University – not one I liked, it is true, but Honynge was a colleague nonetheless.'

'I did it to save your friend,' cried Candelby, becoming frightened. 'You know I did.'

'Do I? It is still unlawful homicide, and thus a hanging offence.' Candelby's jaw dropped, and Michael went on. 'However, I might be prepared to broker an agreement, if certain conditions are met. One is that you use this box of coins to repair the mess you have made of my office. And the other is that you agree to new terms about the rent.'

'What new terms?' squeaked Candelby, thoroughly rattled. 'You mean to let them stay as they are?'

'I could say that,' replied Michael. 'And you are hardly

in a position to quibble. But it would be ungracious, and I would like this dispute resolved amicably. So, we shall offer a rise of five per cent for this year, with the promise of a review next winter. I think that is fair – to both sides.'

'It is not . . .' began Candelby. His face was grey, although Bartholomew was not sure whether it was the notion of being charged with murder or the prospect of losing money that dismayed him more.

'The alternative is standing trial for Honynge's death, arson, destroying University property, and whatever other charges I care to bring against you,' said Michael coldly. 'You may win, of course, and so save your life. Would you take *that* gamble, Candelby?'

'No,' said Candelby weakly. 'I do not like these odds. You University men are all the same. Honynge claimed he was keeping me informed of University business, but his information was often inaccurate. He told me Borden Hostel was an excellent business opportunity, but it was not. The roof is unstable, and there are huge cracks in the walls. It will cost me a fortune to repair.'

Michael shot him a look that said it served him right. 'The rent settlement?' he prompted.

Candelby sighed. 'Very well. I accept your offer, but you had better not mention this unhappy business with Honynge again – not ever.'

'Agreed,' said Michael. 'Now, I suggest we go into the church and announce that we no longer need the Regents to vote. We shall both smile and claim to be delighted.'

'I am pleased you have won your war, Brother,' said Bartholomew, before Michael could follow the dejected landlord through the door. 'But if Honynge and Candelby did not kill Lynton, then who did?'

'Spaldynge,' replied Michael. 'He is our killer.'

*   *   *

The announcement that the rent conflict was over was something of an anticlimax, and Gedney was not the only one to grumble that he had missed breakfast for a debate about puddings. Unhappily, Michael watched the Regents file out of the church. Some were laughing at the stupid things William and Morden had said, but others were deeply disappointed that the disagreement had ended peacefully.

'Many of our scholars cannot believe the dispute is finished, and nor will the town,' he said worriedly. 'Wheels have been set in motion, and there is nothing we can do to slow them down.'

Bartholomew rubbed his sore eyes. 'There must be something.'

'We can catch the man who killed Lynton and Ocleye,' said Michael grimly. 'It may be too late, but we must try.'

Bartholomew followed him out through the great west door and on to the High Street, where they headed towards Clare. 'You really think Spaldynge is responsible?'

Michael nodded. 'It is obvious now. He was a regular guest at the Dispensary, but he dislikes physicians – and he told us himself that it was *Lynton* who failed to save his family during the plague. Further, he probably sold Borden to Candelby because he knew it was about to become very expensive to repair, which goes to show he is sly.'

'All scholars are sly,' said Bartholomew, not sure Michael's logic was as sound as it might have been. The physician was not the only one who was exhausted and not thinking clearly.

When they reached Clare and knocked on the gate, Bartholomew stood with his back to it, aware that a group of potters was loitering nearby. One shouted something about the multilation of Isnard, and another offered to amputate the physician's head.

'We had better arrest Spaldynge now,' said Michael. 'Then, when everyone sees we have solved the murders at last, they will all calm down.'

Bartholomew regarded him in alarm. 'Arrest him how, exactly? Storm inside and grab him, while all Clare looks on? Are you insane?'

'We cannot use my beadles, because marching around with an army would not be wise this morning. We cannot afford to be seen behaving in a provocative manner.'

'Then we should leave this until later. Arresting him now is more likely to inflame than soothe.'

'He might claim another victim if we do not act at once. Do you want that on your conscience?'

But Bartholomew was growing increasingly uneasy. 'Spaldynge – *if* he is our man – is an experienced killer. He is not going to let you escort him away without a fuss. This is madness!'

It was Spaldynge who answered the door, and he carried a small crossbow in his hand. Michael glanced meaning-fully at Bartholomew, but the physician was more concerned with how the potters were reacting to the sight of such a deadly weapon. They made themselves scarce before it could be used on them, but he had the feeling they had not gone far.

Spaldynge smirked his satisfaction. 'Did you see that rabble slink away? That showed them we are not all help-less priests without the wherewithal to defend ourselves.'

'That is a handsome implement,' said Michael, flinching when it started to come around to point at him. 'How long have you had it?'

'About a week,' replied Spaldynge. 'It was a gift.'

'Very nice,' said Bartholomew, backing away and trying to drag Michael with him. 'You are clearly busy, so we will come back later.'

'A gift from whom?' demanded Michael, pulling himself free.

'From someone who said I might need to defend myself,' replied Spaldynge. 'Because of Borden.'

He gestured that they were to enter his College. Bartholomew baulked, but Michael strode confidently across the threshold. Loath to leave his friend alone, the physician followed, fumbling for one of his surgical knives as he did so. Spaldynge barred the door behind them, and Bartholomew swallowed hard, aware that it would make escape that much more difficult. He glanced at Michael, who did not seem to care that his rash determination to seize his culprit was putting them both in danger.

'What about Borden?' demanded Bartholomew, nervousness making him speak more curtly than he had intended. He braced himself, half-expecting to be shot there and then.

'I sold it to Candelby,' said Spaldynge impatiently. 'You know that. My benefactor said I might need to defend myself against colleagues who may accuse me of wrongdoing.'

'Your colleagues will applaud your actions,' countered Michael. 'You hawked Candelby a house that is structurally unsound, and that will cost him a fortune to renovate.'

Spaldynge regarded him coolly. 'Kardington asked me not to tell anyone that, because he said it would make us look deceitful. We do not want anyone assuming we rid ourselves of a burden . . .'

'I see,' said Michael, when he faltered. 'Borden was sold because it was about to become a millstone around Clare's neck, and the transaction was made with the full support of the Master and Fellows. No wonder you have remained on such good terms with them! Far from doing something

405

to damage your College, you have acted in their best interests, and nobly shouldered the blame.'

'You cannot prove it, and we will deny everything.'

'I am sure you will,' said Michael. He sighed, tiring of games. 'Who gave you the bow?'

'I decline to say. It is none of your business, and you should be out quelling riots or hunting Motelete's killer, not strutting around in company with a physician.' He almost spat the last word.

'Brother Michael,' said Kardington, striding across the yard towards them. Master Wisbeche of Peterhouse was at his side. 'I do not like the feel of the town today.'

'Neither do I,' agreed Wisbeche. 'So Kardington offered my students and me refuge until it is safe to go home. It was clever of you to reach that last-minute agreement with Candelby, and thus avoid a vote that would have split the University, but it has done little to ease the tension with the town.'

Bartholomew saw the scholars of Peterhouse talking to the members of Clare, and hoped none would remember that they had been going to stand against each other at the Convocation. Wisbeche and Kardington were civilised, but that did not mean their flocks would be equally well behaved.

'Well, you know Cambridge,' said Spaldynge, toting his bow. 'Any excuse for a riot.'

'Put that down,' ordered Kardington crossly. 'It is against the rules for scholars to carry weapons, and if you do it in front of the Senior Proctor, he will hit you where it hurts – in the purse.'

'It is not illegal inside my own College,' objected Spaldynge. 'And I do not . . . Oh, Christ! I am sorry, Master Wisbeche. Are you hurt?'

'You have ruined my tabard!' exclaimed Wisbeche. He

was angry, but aware that he was a guest in someone else's College, and so not in a position to say what he really thought. 'There is a hole in it!'

'You are a menace, Spaldynge,' snapped Kardington, mortified. 'Either take that thing to the orchard and learn how to shoot properly, or I shall confiscate it. I do not feel safe as long as you are unfamiliar with its workings.'

'Whoever killed Lynton and Ocleye was an excellent shot,' said Bartholomew to Michael, when Spaldynge had gone to do as he was told. 'He hid in a place where he could not be seen – which means he was probably some distance away – and his bolts went through their hearts. Once may have been luck, but twice suggests he knew what he was doing.'

Wisbeche looked from one to the other. 'If you suspect Spaldynge of Lynton's murder, you must think again. *He* could not hit a bull if it was standing on his own toes. He brandishes the wretched thing as if he means business, but he barely knows one end from the other, and I had to show him how to wind it.' He inspected his damaged tabard, and gave the impression that he wished he had not bothered.

'Spaldynge did not kill Lynton,' lisped Kardington, bemused. 'He was Lynton's patient, and appreciated the tactful way he treated a rather embarrassing condition. Now Lynton is dead, he will have to explain everything to another *medicus*, something he is dreading.'

'But he hated Lynton,' said Michael, not sure whether to believe him. 'Because of the plague.'

'He does despise physicians,' agreed Kardington. 'But he is still obliged to avail himself of their services on occasion.'

'The relationship between Spaldynge and Lynton could be described as coolly civil,' added Wisbeche. 'Spaldynge came to Peterhouse for consultations, but although they did not like each other, there was never any hint of hostility. Lynton would not have kept him as a patient, if there had been.'

'Spaldynge was our last suspect,' said Michael, defeated. 'I do not know where to go from here.'

'Go home, Brother,' said Kardington kindly. 'The Colleges are the only safe places to be today, and at least you are relieved of Honynge's objectionable presence. If you could be rid of Tyrington, too, Michaelhouse would be a delightful foundation.'

The monk agreed, frustration and disappointment making him bitter. 'If Tyrington spits at me one more time, I am going to empty my wine goblet over him. I wish we had not been so efficient at offering him a place. He would have been *your* problem, had we dallied.'

Kardington was startled. 'Mine?'

'He was invited to take a Fellowship here, at Clare. You had a narrow escape. However, we will willingly part with him, if you find yourselves in need of a slobbering theologian.'

'He was never offered a post,' said Kardington, astonished. 'We do not need any theologians at the moment, and we would not have chosen him if we had. We do not want *our* books soaked in saliva.'

'He said you were keen to have him,' said Michael.

'He offered us his services when Wenden died, but we declined. He applied to Peterhouse, King's Hall and Gonville, too, but they also rejected him. I imagine he was delighted when poor Kenyngham's demise opened a position at Michaelhouse.'

'He might just as easily have gone to Peterhouse,' said Michael, turning to Wisbeche. 'Lynton's death meant an opening in your Fellowship, too.'

'We had decided the next vacancy would remain unfilled long before Lynton died,' replied Wisbeche. 'I told you – we need to conserve funds, and a senior member's salary is a lot of money.'

Bartholomew frowned. 'But you did not tell anyone that until *after* Lynton was dead.'

'True,' acknowledged Wisbeche. 'Of course, Tyrington was desperate. The lease on Piron Hostel expired this week, and he had nowhere else to go.'

'No, it was due to run out in September,' corrected Michael. 'He told us so the day Langelee wrote inviting him to join us at Michaelhouse.'

'It expired this week,' repeated Wisbeche firmly. 'Why do you think Candelby spent so much money on making it nice? Because a goldsmith was ready to occupy it the moment Tyrington left. It is a lovely house, in a pleasant part of town, and Candelby was eager to charge a princely rent as soon as possible.'

'Wisbeche is right,' said Kardington, seeing Michael look sceptical. 'I overheard the goldsmith and Candelby talking myself. Tyrington is a meek, amiable fellow, who let Candelby enter the house and effect inconvenient renovations whenever he wanted, even when he was teaching.'

Bartholomew was appalled. How could he and Michael have been so wrong? 'Who gave Spaldynge the crossbow, Master Kardington?' he demanded. 'This is important.'

'It is funny you should ask,' replied Kardington. 'Because we have just been talking about him. It was Tyrington. He said he no longer had need of it.'

Bartholomew ran all the way back to Michaelhouse, Michael trotting behind him. The monk was panting like a cow in labour, and Bartholomew itched to go behind him and give him a push, to make him move faster. They did not have time for such stately progress.

'How could we have been so blind?' he groaned, disgusted with himself.

'It is only obvious now we have all the facts,' gasped Michael. 'Tyrington shot Lynton because he wanted a place at a College, not knowing that Peterhouse was going to freeze the post to save money. And he killed Ocleye because he was a witness to the murder.'

'No, that does not work. Ocleye knew what was going to happen, because Paxtone said he was smiling in a way that suggested the shooting was no surprise. However, do you recall what Rougham told me? He saw Ocleye conducting shady business with a hooded man who drank his ale, but did not eat his pie. Rougham assumed it was the nature of their business that made the man lose his appetite, but he was wrong.'

'Tyrington, alone of everyone we know, dislikes the Angel's pies,' finished Michael. 'Do you recall how easily he hit Carton with his balls of parchment in the hall the other day? Lobbing missiles does not equate to accuracy with a crossbow, but it goes to show a reasonable dexterity.'

'So, *he* must have written the letters about Kenyngham,' added Bartholomew. 'He decided to distract you away from Lynton – *his* victim – by claiming Kenyngham was murdered. And when you wanted to exhume Kenyngham, he argued violently against it.'

'Because he knew the death was natural,' completed Michael. 'And he did not want us to find out, because it would mean I would stop wasting time on a murder that never happened.'

'So, when you were refused permission to exhume, he put the top half of the rent agreement – the one *he* had taken from Lynton's body – in the Illeigh Hutch. He

410

intended you to think Honynge was the killer, another ruse to draw attention away from himself. We suspected the culprit was a Michaelhouse man, because only we have access to the College's money chests.'

'Why did he part with the deed at all, when he must have taken a considerable risk to acquire it in the first place?'

'Because he had inadvertently left the most important part – the section with the signatures – behind anyway. The top half was essentially useless, which must have alarmed him when he reached home and inspected it.'

'Why did he want it at all? It was not *his* name on the thing.'

'I imagine because Ocleye was *his* spy, and he did not want anyone learning that Ocleye could afford houses on the High Street – it would have led to questions. Tyrington dislikes attention, which is why he was always punctilious at paying his rent. He did not want trouble. *Hurry*, Brother!'

They finally reached the College, only to have Langelee report that Tyrington had not returned after the Convocation.

'Where is he?' demanded Michael, grabbing the master's arm for support. 'Is anyone else missing?'

'Just him,' replied Langelee. 'Why? Is this about the fact that the Angel pot-boys have just delivered a scroll they found among Ocleye's possessions? It is inscribed with Tyrington's name. I think they brought it as an excuse to get inside Michaelhouse, and I do not believe their tale about finding it in Ocleye's bags. But Tyrington's name is on it nonetheless. Ocleye must have stolen it from him.'

'Ocleye and Tyrington knew each other well,' said Wynewyk, overhearing. 'I saw them together at the Dispensary several times. They were on good terms, although they pretended otherwise in company. I watched Tyrington lend Ocleye money once, when he wanted to place a bet.'

'Come quickly,' shouted Cynric suddenly. He was standing on top of the main gate. 'I thought I could smell burning, so I came up here to look. Something is on fire.'

'Well?' called Michael, when Bartholomew and Langelee had scrambled up to stand at Cynric's side. The monk was far too large for that sort of caper. 'It is not Gonville, because the flames are too far away. Is it Trinity Hall? One of the hostels?'

'It is impossible to say,' said Langelee. 'You and Bartholomew check; I will stay here.'

Michael regarded him with round eyes. 'We take the risks while you have dinner?'

'You are the Senior Proctor,' said Langelee impatiently. 'As you never cease to remind us. It is your duty to investigate trouble – and people may have need of a physician. Meanwhile, I shall improve our defences. If there is a fracas today, *we* will not go up in flames.'

Bartholomew and Michael hurried along Milne Street. Bartholomew closed his eyes in relief when he saw Trinity Hall safe, and was pleased the smoke was not coming from Clare, either. They ran on, past the Church of St John Zachary, and towards the Carmelite Friary.

The smell of burning had encouraged others out, too, and because fire was feared in any town where buildings were made of wood and thatch, there was a good deal of panic. There was a good deal of menace, too, and the situation suddenly took a turn for the worse when the group of potters they had seen outside Clare earlier appeared on the road ahead of them. Bartholomew staggered when one collided with him, although the lad who tried the same with Michael bounced off the rotund figure and fell in a ditch.

'Not my fault,' wheezed Michael. 'A man my size takes a while to stop once he is on the move.'

'You have no right to arrest Arderne,' the apprentice yelled. He picked up a stone and hurled it. The physician ducked and it cracked into the wall above his head.

'We should turn back,' whispered Michael. 'It is not safe out here. Tyrington can wait.'

More missiles flew, and Bartholomew covered his head with his hands. When he glanced up, the potters were racing towards them *en masse*. 'Run, Michael! Now!'

Michael did not need to be told a second time. He set off at a furious waddle. 'Run where?'

'St John Zachary,' yelled Bartholomew. The monk would never make it to Michaelhouse, and the church was the closest available building. 'It should be open, and they will not attack us if we claim sanctuary.'

The potters were gaining. Bartholomew grabbed Michael's arm and hauled him along at a speed that threatened to have them both over, but the monk made no complaint. He did his best to move at the pace Bartholomew was dictating, but he was too fat and too slow. Bartholomew saw they were going to be caught. He increased his efforts, muscles burning with the strain.

When they reached the chapel, he took his childbirth forceps and brandished them, to give Michael time to stumble through the graveyard. The monk flung open the door, and Bartholomew turned and dashed inside. He had only just slammed it closed when the potters crashed against it, trying to shove it open with the weight of their bodies. Michael snatched up a heavy wooden bar and rammed it into two slots on either side of the doorframe. Then he collapsed in a breathless heap on the floor.

'So much for sanctuary,' muttered Bartholomew, as the

413

church echoed with the sound of angrily pounding fists and kicking feet.

'Check the windows,' gasped Michael. 'Hurry! Make sure they are all barred, or these louts will be inside in a trice. God help us, Matt, but they mean business!'

'. . . Senior Proctor and his physician,' Bartholomew heard someone holler. 'We have them trapped.'

'Storm the gaol!' cried someone else. 'Let Arderne out.'

Bartholomew dashed down the south aisle, but the windows in the dilapidated little church had long-since rotted away and had been replaced by solid boards. All seemed secure, so he ran to the north aisle, which was in a better state of repair, because it formed part of Clare's boundary wall. None of the shutters could be opened from the inside, and the single opening in the Lady Chapel was locked shut.

'Damn,' muttered Bartholomew, although he was not surprised. Cynric had once told him it was impossible to go from church to Clare once the windows were closed. 'I was hoping we could take refuge with Kardington.'

Michael's chest heaved as he tried to catch his breath. His face was scarlet, and Bartholomew hoped he would not have a seizure. 'Can you see anything? What are the potters doing?' he gasped.

Bartholomew peered through a crack in the wood. 'There must be a dozen of them. They seem intent on—' He jerked back as something heavy was hurled at the window through which he had been looking. Fragments of plaster showered down from the wall.

'The two most hated men in Cambridge,' said Michael ruefully. 'The physician who helped arrest Arderne, and the University proctor who crushed the alliance of the land-lords. We are not good company for each other today – too tempting a target.'

414

There was a colossal thump on the door.

'Kardington used the window in the Lady Chapel as a door into Clare,' said Bartholomew, darting towards it. 'We must open it somehow – we cannot stay here, because those potters mean to break in. They are using a cart as a battering ram.'

There was a sudden crack on the window in question. Bartholomew peered through a gap at the bottom of it, and saw a score of students milling outside. They were piling old wood against the shutter, and one was standing by with a lighted torch. The physician turned to Michael in bewilderment.

'It looks as though we shall all die together,' came a soft voice from the chancel.

'Tyrington!' exclaimed Michael. 'What are you doing here?'

A distant part of Bartholomew's mind registered how odd it was that the little church should be so still inside, when there was such a commotion outside. To the south, the potters were pounding the door with their cart, screaming their fury at the men trapped within. To the north, the students of Clare and their Peterhouse guests were busily piling firewood against the Lady Chapel window with the clear intent of setting it alight. They, too, were yelling.

'One of two things is going to happen,' said Tyrington in a low whisper. 'Either the townsmen will break in and we shall be torn to pieces – there will be no reasoning with them. Or the Clare boys will set the church alight and we shall die of smoke and flames.'

'Why would they destroy their own chapel?' demanded Michael, not believing him.

'Because *he* is in here,' said Bartholomew, pointing at Tyrington. 'And the Peterhouse students know he killed

Lynton, because *we* told their Master – their Clare friends are just enjoying a spot of mischief. Besides, who will miss this old building? It is on the verge of collapse anyway.'

'It was rash to blab about me to anyone who happened to be listening,' said Tyrington. He wiped his mouth with his sleeve. 'The Peterhouse lads saw me walking along Milne Street after they left Clare, and I only just managed to reach this church before they caught me. I was about to bar the door when the potters arrived, and the students fled back to Clare. I decided to wait it out – to stay here until the streets became calm. But then you two came along, and now we are all trapped, like fish in a barrel.'

'I am not going to die,' declared Michael firmly. 'Not after surviving that run.'

'The students nailed the Lady Chapel window closed, to make sure I cannot escape, and they know that if I leave any other way the townsmen will have me. I am doomed, and you will share my fate. It serves you right – you are my colleagues, but you betrayed me by telling Peterhouse what I had done.'

Michael hammered on the window until his hands hurt, but no amount of shouting distracted the students from their bonfire. They assumed it was Tyrington making the racket, and ignored it. Then came the smell of burning. The lad with the torch had touched it to the wood, and it was already alight.

'You see?' asked Tyrington. 'Is it hopeless.'

'I should have known you were not the kind of man we wanted in Michaelhouse,' shouted the monk furiously, while Bartholomew prowled the church in search of another exit. It was not looking promising, and the bar keeping the door closed was beginning to buckle under the potters' battering.

'And why is that?' asked Tyrington, maddeningly calm.

'Because of something Kenyngham said before he died,' replied Bartholomew, looking at the ruins of the spiral stairway that led to the roof. There had been another fall since his last visit, and it was now almost completely blocked with large stones. 'He must have guessed you would apply for his post, because he told me to beware of crocodiles who made timely appearances. We needed a theologian, and there you were. Crocodiles and shooting stars. You and Arderne. Dear, wise old Kenyngham.'

'He was a fool,' said Tyrington in disgust. 'And he should have died years ago, so better, more able men could take his place. I wish he *had* been poisoned, because it might have encouraged other useless ancients to resign and make way for new blood.'

'Lynton was not the first man you killed in the hope of earning yourself a Fellowship, was he?' asked Bartholomew. 'You shot Wenden, too.'

Tyrington shrugged. 'It was easy to convince everyone that a drowned and drunken tinker was responsible – all it took was Wenden's purse planted among his belongings. After all, I did not want anyone turning suspicious eyes on the man who stepped into the dead man's shoes. My plan worked perfectly – or would have done, had Clare bothered to appoint Wenden's successor.'

'His post was non-stipendiary,' said Michael. 'So Clare *could* not appoint a successor – there was no money to fund one. You should have been more careful with your selection of victims.'

Tyrington shook his head wonderingly. 'I chose Wenden because he was mean and did virtually no teaching. He hurt Clare in other ways, too, such as by leaving his money to the Bishop of Lincoln—'

'Which precipitated *another* unhappy chain of events,' said Michael accusingly. 'The realisation that there would be no money from Wenden forced Clare to sell Borden Hostel before it needed expensive repairs. That served to strengthen Candelby's hand against the University. You are a low, sly villain, Tyrington. You caused all manner of harm for your own selfish ends. You offered me twenty marks to find Kenyngham's killer, then you wrote confessing to his murder. You penned them in different hands to confuse me.'

Tyrington shrugged. 'You were paying too much attention to Lynton, so I decided to sidetrack you – to encourage you look into the death of a man you liked.'

'We saw you,' said Michael, watching Bartholomew scramble into the stairwell and wrestle with the fallen stones. 'You delivered the so-called confession to Michaelhouse, and we saw you leave. You almost collided with a cart, but instead of yelling at the driver, like a normal man, you slunk away.'

'I dislike drawing attention to myself.'

Bartholomew gave up on the stones, and dashed back to the Lady Chapel. The window was hot, and he knew it would not be long before it burst into flames. Then the students would push the smouldering wood inside the church, and the building would fill with smoke. Meanwhile, the door was beginning to yield, and it would not be long before the potters streamed in. He wondered whether they or the fire would get him first. He heard furious voices coming from Clare, loud and shrill with indignation, and strained to hear what was being said. It was not difficult. The speaker was almost howling in his rage.

'Spaldynge has just found a letter in his room, bearing his forged signature,' he said to Michael. 'He says it was a suicide note, and there was a flask of wine with it.'

'Poison,' explained Tyrington. 'My University would be better off without the likes of Spaldynge. He sold property

418

belonging to his College *and* he argued against my admission to Clare. He said I spit, which is untrue. It is a pity he found the note before the wine. If it had been the other way around, he would have swallowed my anonymous gift without question.'

'Now I see why you gave him the crossbow,' said Michael in disgust. 'I suppose this note contains a confession for killing Lynton, too – Spaldynge is in possession of the murder weapon, after all.'

A huge crash summoned Bartholomew back to the door. It bowed dramatically and, sensing they were almost in, the townsmen were redoubling their efforts. Meanwhile, smoke was billowing from the Lady Chapel. For the second time that day, Bartholomew began to cough.

'You snatched the tenancy agreement from Lynton's body,' said Michael to Tyrington, while Bartholomew darted back to the staircase again. 'You must have done it during the confusion of the ensuing skirmish, because no one has reported seeing you there.'

Tyrington smiled mirthlessly. 'A lot of people had gathered that day, and I pride myself on blending in with a crowd. No one saw me – not watching the aftermath of Lynton's shooting, and not taking the rent agreement, either.'

'But why did you grab it?' asked Michael, bemused.

'Because there was no need to besmirch my new College – Peterhouse – by having Lynton's sordid dealings exposed. But in the end I went to Michaelhouse. It is a strange world.'

'And Ocleye?' asked Michael. 'We know he was spying for you.'

'He provided me with information, but guessed what I was going to do. I predicted he would try to blackmail me, so I reloaded and killed him during the confusion of the

419

brawl. I gashed his stomach, too, so you would think a knife, not a crossbow, was responsible.'

'You seem remarkably calm for a man who is about to die,' said Michael, narrowing his eyes.

The door gave a tearing groan that had the potters roaring encouragement to the fellows with the cart. Almost simultaneously, the Lady Chapel window collapsed inwards, and flames shot across the floor. They ignited a pile of leaves that had been swept into a corner, and something in the faint remains of the wall paintings began to smoulder.

'I have wanted to be a Fellow all my adult life – to live in a College, and enjoy the companionship of like minds. Now I have lost it, I do not care what happens. But I shall die in good company, at least.'

Bartholomew was not interested in Tyrington's confessions. When the door screamed on its failing hinges, panic gave him the strength he needed to move the stone that was blocking his way into the stairwell. It tumbled into the chancel with a resounding crash.

'Michael!' he shouted, squeezing through the resulting gap. 'This way.'

The monk, keeping a wary eye on Tyrington, hurried over. He stared in dismay at the small space the physician had cleared. 'I cannot cram myself through that!'

The door gave another monstrous groan. 'Come *on*!' yelled Bartholomew, holding out his hand. 'You, too, Tyrington. You will not hang under canon law, and you may find your like-minded community in some remote convent in the Fens.'

The door was being held by splinters, and one more blow from the cart would see it collapse. Michael inserted his bulk into the opening. He blotted out all light, so it was pitch dark. Bartholomew grabbed his flailing arm and hauled. Michael yelped as masonry tore his habit. There was a resounding crack as the door flew open. Then the church was full of yells and screams. Bartholomew heaved with all his might, and the monk shot upwards. They were past the worst of the rubble.

Bartholomew groped his way up the stairs, trying not to inhale the smoke that wafted around him. Below, Michael was hacking furiously. Then the steps ended, and with a shock, the physician realised what had caused the debris: the upper stairs no longer existed. Appalled, he scrabbled around in the dark, and ascertained that small parts of the steps had survived, jutting from the central pillar like rungs on a one-sided ladder. Michael wailed his horror when his outstretched fingers encountered the void.

'What is left is too narrow for me,' he screeched. 'I will fall!'

'They are wider up here,' called Bartholomew encouragingly. He coughed. 'Hurry, Michael! Someone is coming after us.'

'Tyrington,' gasped the monk. 'He has had second thoughts about dying in the nave.'

Suddenly, Michael lost his footing, his downward progress arrested only because Tyrington was in the way. He shrieked his alarm, and Tyrington made no sound at all. Bartholomew leaned down and pulled with all his might, trying to lift Michael into a position where he would be able to climb on his own. The sinews in his shoulder cracked as they took the monk's full weight.

Then the pressure eased, and Michael was ascending again. The stairs were in better condition nearer the top, although they were littered with fallen masonry, and perilously dark. Bartholomew slipped and fell, colliding with Michael behind him. Michael gave him a hard shove that propelled him upwards, faster than he had anticipated, and he slipped again.

'Hurry, Matt! I cannot breathe!'

Bartholomew reached the door that led to the roof, only to find it locked. His arms were heavy, and he knew he was making no impact as he pounded ineffectually on it. Michael shoved him out of the way, and his bulk made short work of the rotten wood. The door flew into pieces, and clean air and daylight flooded into the stairwell.

'They have lit a fire at the bottom,' Tyrington croaked. 'I can hear it crackling. Help me!'

Michael scrambled out on to the roof, while Bartholomew retraced his steps to rescue his terrified colleague. Tyrington gripped his outstretched hand, but then started to pull, dragging the physician back down towards the nave. Bartholomew tried to free himself, but his shoulder burned from where he had lifted Michael, and he found he did not have the strength to resist. The smoke was thick, and he could not breathe. Through the haze, he could see Tyrington grinning wildly.

'Come with me,' he crooned. 'The two of us will die side by side. Fellows together in adversity.'

Bartholomew fell another three steps. He was dizzy from a lack of air, and his eyes smarted so much that Tyrington's smile began to blur. Suddenly, there was an immense pressure around his middle, and his hand shot out of Tyrington's grasp.

'No!' wailed Tyrington. 'Come back! Michaelhouse men should—'

'—not try to incinerate each other,' finished Michael, grunting as he heaved the physician upwards by his belt. 'I shall make sure I add it to the Statutes.'

Then they were at the door and out into the cool, fresh air. Bartholomew coughed, trying to catch his breath, and it occurred to him that their situation was not much improved. A rank stench of singed flesh wafted upwards, and he could hear victorious yells from the church. Meanwhile, the students of Clare and Peterhouse were peering upwards. Spaldynge was among them, and he held his crossbow. He took aim, but something was wrong with the mechanism, and he lowered it in puzzlement.

'Look,' shouted Michael suddenly, grabbing Bartholomew's shoulder and pointing. 'You can see the Trumpington Gate from here. Guess who has just ridden through it.'

'I cannot think,' Bartholomew croaked. 'And I can barely see you, let alone the Trumpington Gate,'

'It is Sheriff Tulyet. And not a moment too soon.'

EPILOGUE

The sun was shining brightly and there was no wind, so it was pleasant in Michaelhouse's orchard. A week had passed since the events that had left two apprentices and a student dead. Sheriff Tulyet had arrived just in time to quash what might have erupted into a serious disturbance, and once he had been rescued from the church roof, Michael had rallied his beadles and set about clearing the streets of scholars. Calm had reigned by nightfall, and the town had been quiet ever since. The Chancellor had decreed that term would begin early, and the undergraduates had been too busy with their books to think about brawling. The town had been restless at first, but the Mayor and his burgesses had been appeased by a gift of two houses from Peterhouse. Because the gift would last only as long as Cambridge was peaceful, any unruly factions had been told in no uncertain terms that they must behave themselves.

'So,' said Michael, luxuriating in the warmth of the sun. 'We have succeeded in outwitting wicked villains yet again. Our killer was the spitting Tyrington, and although he left a trail of clues to lead us in the wrong direction, we cornered him in the end. No one can defeat the alliance of the Senior Proctor and his trusty Corpse Examiner.'

'I suppose not,' said Bartholomew, less ready to gloat. The entire episode had left an unpleasant flavour in his mouth, and he still grieved for Kenyngham. He was uncomfortable with the knowledge that Michaelhouse had been invaded by two such devious characters, and was concerned

424

by the fact that Arderne had escaped during the commotion surrounding the attack on St John Zachary and the inferno at the Angel tavern. It had been Candelby's inn that Cynric had seen in flames – the blaze had been set by his fellow landlords, who felt he had betrayed them. Afraid he might be the next victim of their ire, Candelby had packed up a cart and left the town while he was still in one piece. No one seemed to miss him.

'And I even defeated Honynge,' Michael continued, pleased with himself. 'He thought he could best me with his sly tricks, but he failed. Did I tell you Deynman caught him poking about in my room? That is how he knew about the crossbow bolts you pulled from Lynton and Ocleye, and why he was astonished when the later search failed to locate them.'

'What did Cynric take from under your loose floorboard?' asked Bartholomew curiously. 'Langelee was worried about it.'

'The alternative statutes,' replied Michael breezily. 'The ones Langelee and I use when we want to pass certain measures, and we anticipate trouble from you other Fellows – although you did not hear that from me. The game would have been up, had they been found.'

'And you call Honynge sly,' said Bartholomew, rather shocked. 'I thought you were above that sort of thing.'

'Why ever would you think that?' Michael sighed. 'I am happy, Matt. My College is a haven of peace again, and Carton will be a decent addition to our ranks. We should have listened to you in the first place, and then none of this would have happened.'

'But Tyrington would have killed another Fellow to secure himself a post. Besides, Carton is not all he seems either, and there were a number of incidents that had us wondering whether *he* might have been the killer.'

425

'But most of those have been explained. Falmeresham knew his friend would be beside himself with worry when he "disappeared", so he asked Isabel to pass word that he was safe. Unkindly, Arderne then demanded recompense for Falmeresham's care, which forced Carton to raise the money by various devious means. Carton was hurt when Falmeresham failed to show proper gratitude, but they have settled their differences now.'

Bartholomew was not entirely convinced, and there was a nagging doubt about Carton that would not go away. He hoped they had not repeated the mistake they had made with Tyrington and Honynge – rushing a decision because they were desperate for someone to teach before term began.

'Do you mind the fact that Langelee has reinstated Falmeresham?' asked Michael when he did not reply. 'We should have sent him packing after what he did.'

'England needs qualified physicians, regardless of what men like Spaldynge believe, so it is important that Falmeresham completes his degree. Besides, we misjudged Tyrington and Honynge, and it would be hypocritical of us to denounce Falmeresham for doing the same with Arderne.'

'One good thing came from Honynge, though. He resolved the Deynman problem for us.'

'Yes,' said Bartholomew, smiling at last. Honynge's solution, suggested to Langelee before the events in St Mary the Great, was that Deynman should be 'promoted' to College librarian. The post was eagerly funded by the boy's proud father, so would cost the College nothing, and it represented an effective end to the student's studies in medicine. 'I thought he would object, but he is delighted.'

'Relieved,' corrected Michael. 'Deep down, he knew he

would never pass his disputations. It is a perfect solution, and one we should have devised ourselves. It will not be too intellectually taxing for him, because we do not own many books.'

Bartholomew changed the subject. 'Paxtone's blockage returned, by the way. Arderne's cure was only temporary, so now Paxtone feels he won the wager and is no longer compelled to leave.'

'He is a fool for accepting the challenge in the first place.'

'He says he was bewitched by the man's eyes – Arderne offered the cure, and he found himself powerless to resist it. Arderne is a dangerous villain, and I wish he had not escaped.'

'Can you cure Paxtone? I do not like seeing the poor man waddling about town with his hand clasped to his stomach.'

Bartholomew smiled again, thinking that Michael was far more of a waddler than Paxtone would ever be. 'The cause of his discomfort is his taste for greasy pies. Still, now the Angel is no longer there to sell them, perhaps the problem will rectify itself. Did I tell you I visited Isnard today? All he talks about is whether you will let him back in the Michaelhouse Choir. Will you?'

'No. I do not take kindly to men who believe the worst of us at the drop of a hat.'

'Let him be, Brother. You will break his heart if you stop him singing.'

'So, all is well,' said Michael, after a few more moments of silence. 'Tyrington shot Wenden and Lynton because he expected to occupy their Fellowships – and he left Wenden's purse with a drowned tinker to ensure someone else was blamed for that crime. Ocleye was Tyrington's spy, but Tyrington thought he might try to blackmail him – and given that Paxtone saw him grinning after Lynton's murder, I suspect he was right – so he was dispatched, too.'

'Meanwhile, Honynge had forged a dubious alliance with Candelby, and was providing him with information in return for free accommodation. It was a pity his dislike of you sent him off on a wild spree of revenge in St Mary the Great. He did not care that he might kill half our Regents – he just wanted you discredited.'

'I suppose I had better make myself more amenable in the future,' said Michael. 'Enduring that sort of hatred was unpleasant. And you will have your work cut out for you, as you try to regain the trust of your patients. They are trickling back now the Sheriff's independent investigation has proved Arderne responsible for several deaths. Some of the damage caused by that leech will never heal, though. Spaldynge's dislike of physicians has intensified, for example.'

'Have you managed to learn whom Agatha intended to dose with her love-potion?' asked Bartholomew. He did not want to think about the legacy Arderne had left the Cambridge *medici*, knowing it would be a long time before the situation returned to normal – if it ever did. 'You made a bet that you would have it out of her in a week, and your time is almost up. If you do not have the answer by tomorrow, you will owe William a groat.'

'I prised it from her this morning,' said Michael. 'She bought it for Blankpayn, her cousin.'

Bartholomew raised his eyebrows. 'Why?'

'She thought being in love would keep him away from Candelby, whom she considered a bad influence. It is a good thing she did not give it to him, or we might never have solved this case. We would have assumed Blankpayn's demise from the potion was related to Lynton's death, when it would have been nothing of the kind.'

Bartholomew stood. 'It is getting cold out here. Carton is going to play his lute, and William has offered to set the Blood Relic dispute to song. He says it is something that should not be missed.'

'I am sure he does,' laughed Michael, following him across the orchard towards the comfortable warmth of their home. 'And it certainly promises to be entertaining, although I doubt we will learn much in the way of theology.'

'Crocodiles and shooting stars,' said Bartholomew suddenly. 'Kenyngham was right, but I wish his last words had been more readily understandable. He would have saved us a lot of trouble.'

Michael clapped a hand on his shoulder. 'But solving the mystery would not have been nearly as much fun.'

A few miles away, in the Fens, a man sat at the side of a mere, staring across the sunset-stained water. Arderne was angry at the way matters had ended at Cambridge. He missed his faithful Motelete, he had been forced to abandon all his belongings – including the star-spangled cart of which he had been so proud – and he had grown tired of Isabel. He looked dispassionately at the spread of her hair just below the wind-ruffled surface. She had willingly – eagerly – imbibed the potion he said would give her eternal youth, and then he had slid her into the icy pond when the poison had rendered her immobile. It had been a relatively painless death, and he knew her body would not be found easily, if ever. And by then, Arderne would be long gone, safely plying his trade in another city. Perhaps Bristol this time. Or Oxford.

He smiled when he thought about his revenge on the men who had foiled his plans. He had sent a barrel of fine wine to the scholars of Michaelhouse, thanking them for their part in solving Lynton's murder. They would assume it came from a grateful colleague, and would never question it. Of course, when they came to drink they would be in for a shock. Arderne's famous love-potions were good for a lot more than making the fanciful swoon. The Fellows would toast each other's health, and by the following morning, they would all be dead. Rougham and Paxtone would never work out what had happened, because they were too stupid.

The thought of his enemies choking on blistered throats made him grin, and he felt the need to make yet another toast of his own. He took his flask and upended it, draining what was left. But was there a bitter taste that should not have been present? He frowned and sniffed it. The claret seemed all right. He looked in the jar where he kept his 'mandrake root' – white bryony looked similar and did much the same thing, but was a fraction of the price. He did not see why should he waste money on people who could not tell the difference anyway. He regarded the pot in puzzlement. Had he really used that much on Isabel?

He was still pondering the question when he became aware of a numbness in his mouth, followed by a burning pain. He shot to his feet. That woman! She must have detected his growing coldness towards her and tampered with his powders, trying to prepare her own love-potion that would see him fall at her feet. How could she? He tried to recall what Bartholomew had done when Honynge had swallowed the poison. People had talked about it afterwards, but he had paid scant attention. He wracked his brains.

Charcoal! He staggered to his campfire and began to gnaw on singed twigs. It was not helping. He was feeling worse – dizzier, and the burning was almost unbearable. He dropped to his hands and knees and crawled towards the pool. Water would soothe him. He leaned forward but lost his balance. An icy coldness enveloped him, and Isabel's white face loomed close. Flailing in fright, he grabbed the grass at the edge of the pond. He would feel better soon, and then he would pull himself out. He did not notice the weeds sliding through his fingers, but he did see the brown Fenland waters closing over his head.

Back at Michaelhouse, the scholars were pleased when Cynric announced the unexpected delivery of a cask of French wine. Deynman went to collect it. He broached it himself, but earned Cynric's dismayed disapproval when he declined to let the book-bearer taste it, to make sure it was good.

'Servants *always* taste gifts of wine, boy,' said Cynric indignantly. 'It is tradition.'

Deynman wavered. As College Librarian, tradition was something he felt obliged to uphold. 'Are you sure?'

'Oh, yes,' said Cynric. 'Kenyngham said it was one of Michaelhouse's most sacred customs.'

'I miss him,' said Deynman sadly. 'And Doctor Bartholomew should have asked *me* what he meant by crocodiles and shooting stars – I could have told him straight away. There is a crocodile carved on the cover of the book Tyrington gave the library – although Master Langelee called it a serpent. It is very distinctive and Kenyngham must have seen it when he visited him once. Meanwhile, Arderne's personal carriage has shooting stars painted on the side.'

Cynric regarded him askance. 'You are right! Why did I not notice them?'

Deynman shrugged nonchalantly. 'It takes a *Librarian*, I suppose.'

'Hurry up, Deynman,' called William. 'I am ready to start singing, and it would be good to loosen my throat with a mouthful of good claret first.'

With an apologetic grin at Cynric, Deynman grabbed the barrel and set off across the yard, but the peacock chose that moment to launch itself at the College cat. Librarian and bird became hopelessly entangled, and the barrel flew from Deynman's hands to smash on the cobbles.

'Oh, Deynman!' cried William. He crouched down, and might have considered lapping some of it up – it was not every day Michaelhouse was sent extravagant gifts from grateful colleagues – but the peacock had been there and so had the chickens. He thought better of it.

'It was sour, Father,' said Cynric soothingly. 'I tasted it, see. Peterhouse presented us with spoiled wine.'

'Then we shall not send them our thanks,' declared William, offended and indignant. 'We shall pretend it never arrived.'

HISTORICAL NOTE

In 1327, a College named University Hall was founded in Cambridge. It was never endowed with very much money, and its scholars were almost immediately strapped for cash. Fortunately, help was to hand in the form of the wealthy Elizabeth de Burgh, the Countess of Clare and a granddaughter of Edward I. She stepped in with a hefty benefaction in 1336, and during the next two decades, when she maintained an active interest in the place, University Hall became Clare Hall. Today, it is known as Clare College, or simply Clare, while Clare Hall is a separate foundation established in the 1960s. To avoid confusion, I have referred to the medieval foundation as just Clare, even though it would have been known as Clare Hall.

Names were the least of Clare's problems in the fourteenth century. Robert Spaldynge, who had been made a Fellow there in the 1320s, had been put in charge of a house that was being used as a hostel (the building later became known as Borden Hostel). Although it was not his to dispose of, he decided to sell it, an action that saw him deprived of his Fellowship by his peeved colleagues. The story does not end there. For some inexplicable reason, he was later awarded a substantial pension from Clare, and liked his old College well enough that he bequeathed it several valuable books. It has been suggested that Elizabeth de Burgh intervened on Spaldynge's behalf, and ordered the Master and Fellows to look after him, but we shall probably never know why he was given money after so brazenly breaking his College's trust.

Most of the scholars in this book actually existed, although there is no evidence to suggest any of them were criminals, malicious or deranged. Richard Wisbeche was Master of Peterhouse from 1351 until about 1374. Thomas Paxtone was a Fellow of King's Hall in the 1340s, and later went on to hold lucrative clerical posts all over the country, and William Rougham was a founding Fellow of Gonville Hall.

The Master of Clare in the 1350s was Ralph Kardington (or Kerdyngton), who remained in post until 1359. His contemporaries included Walter de Wenden, who was probably elected in 1327, John Gedney, who was a Fellow in 1342, and Thomas Lexham, who obtained his master's degree in 1355 and later became a powerful churchman. Henry Motelete is recorded as giving Clare the sum of five marks in 1355, but then he fades from the records, and there is no evidence that he was ever a proper member of the College.

Michaelhouse was founded in 1324. Its Master in 1357 was probably Ralph de Langelee, and his Fellows included Michael de Causton and William de Gotham, both of whom later became influential members of the academic community. Thomas Kenyngham (or Kyngingham) was a founding Fellow of the College, and was later its Master. Wynewyk occurs in Michaelhouse records as an early benefactor. John de Falmeresham (or Felmersham) took his master's degree in the 1340s, and eventually became Warden of St John's Hospital in Farley, Bedfordshire. Roger de Carton was elected a Fellow in 1359, and earned the title of Magister. Roger Honynge was another early Fellow, who gave money as a benefaction, while Roger Tyrington was recorded as a Fellow in 1349 and 1353.

Proctors wielded considerable power in the medieval Universities, although the arduous nature of their duties probably meant few scholars were very keen on holding the office. Thomas Bukenham is recorded as a proctor in the 1330s.

The town's records are less easy to research, but four-teenth-century bailiffs or citizens included Hugh Candelby, John Blankpayn, John Hanchach, Maud Bowyer and Isabel St Ives. Roger Harleston was Mayor from 1356 until 1358. Meanwhile, John Arderne was a famous fourteenth-century surgeon, who is often regarded as the 'Father of Proctology'.

The Blood Relics dispute was a bitter one, and spanned several centuries. It reached a crisis in the 1350s, when the Spanish Franciscan Bajulus of Barcelona wrote a tract about it. The issue of whether bits of Christ's body were left behind after the Resurrection seems trivial today, but in the Middle Ages it was a matter for fierce debate, and had repercussions for the Transubstantiation, as well as other theological niceties. And, of course, there were the hand-some revenues from Blood Relic shrines to be taken into account – no religious foundation that owned Blood Relics wanted to be deprived of those. The rift was deep and trau-matic, and it sent tremors of shock throughout the entire medieval Church. The scholars at Cambridge would certainly have argued about it. Likewise, the mean speed theorem proposed by the scholars of Merton College, Oxford, would also have been regarded as exciting, heady stuff in the 1350s.

Rents were a serious business, too, and statutes were drafted in the thirteenth century to make sure certain rules were followed. These seem manifestly weighted in favour of the University – for example, once a house had been rented to a scholar as a hostel, it could only stop being a hostel if the owner wanted to live in it himself. He could not demand it back to lease to someone else. Further, the University was responsible for brokering agreement on what constituted 'fair' rents. It is not unreasonable to assume that these statutes led to a good deal of ill feeling between town and University, and confrontations must have occurred on a regular basis.

THE TARNISHED CHALICE
The Twelfth Chronicle of Matthew Bartholomew

Susanna Gregory

On a bitter winter evening in 1356, Matthew Bartholomew
and Brother Michael arrive in Lincoln – Michael to accept an
honour from the cathedral, and Bartholomew to look for the
woman he wants to marry.

It is not long before they learn that the friary in which they
are staying is not the safe haven they imagine – one guest has
already been murdered. It soon emerges that the dead man
was holding the Hugh Chalice, a Lincoln relic with a
curiously bloody history.

Bartholomew and Michael are soon drawn into a web of
murder, lies and suspicion in a city where neither knows who
can be trusted.

'A good, serious and satisfying read' *Irish Times*

978-0-7515-3545-7

A CONSPIRACY OF VIOLENCE
Chaloner's First Exploit in Restoration London

Susanna Gregory

The dour days of Cromwell are over. Charles II is well established at White Hall Palace, his mistress at hand in rooms over the Holbein bridge, the heads of some of the regicides on public display. London seethes with new energy, freed from the strictures of the Protectorate, but many of its inhabitants have lost their livelihoods.

One is Thomas Chaloner, a reluctant spy for the feared Secretary of State, John Thurloe, and now returned from Holland in desperate need of employment. His erstwhile boss, knowing he has many enemies at court, recommends Chaloner to Lord Clarendon, but in return demands that Chaloner keep him informed of any plot against him.

But what Chaloner discovers is that Thurloe had sent another ex-employee to White Hall and he is dead, supposedly murdered by footpads near the Thames. Chaloner volunteers to investigate his killing: instead he is despatched to the Tower to unearth the gold buried by the last Governor. He discovers not treasure, but evidence that greed and self-interest are uppermost in men's minds whoever is in power, and that his life has no value to either side.

'Immaculate research, a well thought-out plot, and a sense of drama' *Choice*

978-0-7515-3758-1

Other bestselling titles available by mail: